POWER CITY

By
John Galt Robinson

KCM PUBLISHING
A DIVISION OF KCM DIGITAL MEDIA, LLC

KCM Publishing
a division of KCM Digital Media, LLC

To Susan Chadwick Robinson. You touched and influenced many lives, mine chief among them. We all are forever grateful. Fair winds and following seas, Mom.

Photo by Colleen Murphy Glor

Acknowledgements

Jesus – the way, the truth, and the life.

Pam – the love of my life, my sharpening stone, and my inspiration. You are Proverbs 31.

Jenna, Luke, and Jordan for the encouragement and inspiration.

James Blake, David Smith, Mac Ogburn, my Beta readers, and brothers in Christ.

Special thanks to my good friend, MJ. With over twenty years of service to our country, your experience was invaluable in assisting with the creation of this novel.

Dorothy Haynes for editing and always being there for your little brother.

My literary agent and publisher Michael Fabiano of KCM Publishing for the support and mentoring me through this adventure. Many more to come.

To all of the unnamed people working behind the scenes at KCM publishing. Everything from the editing, to the design, and cover art are top notch. Thank you one and all.

Joseph Travers, executive director of Saved In America, for the background information and for rescuing victims of human trafficking.

CEO Gary Blackard and all of the amazing staff at Adult and Teen Challenge for permission to share your vital mission.

My lifelong friend, David Taylor. One little pearl of information turned into an intriguing part of this story.

My father in-law, Richard Krysztof, for the encouragement and background information.

The Irmo and Chapin Band of brothers; Skipper Don Jenkins, XO Jeff Douglas, the Rhodesian warrior and fellow author James R. Peters, James Blake, David Smith, Wes Dorton, Stuart Morgan, Dr. Barnaby Dedmond, Sergeant First Class Jonathan Clarke, Jered Nisky, Mike Horning, Ron Vogel, Campbell McInness, Pastor Don Brock, and too many more to name. Thank you for the support and encouragement. Brother to brother, life to death.

Contents

POWER CITY

"Greater love has no one than this, that he lay down his life for his friends."   John 15:13

Chapter 1

Upper Niagara River
Grand Island, New York

A deep, vibrating hum emanated from the small sailboat as it skimmed across the waves. The Laser, a sleek single person racing sailboat made popular in the Olympics, was designed to go fast and she certainly was, currently at her peak designed speed as she shot across the Niagara River. A brisk wind charged straight up the river churning the pale blue water into a white capped chop. The white hull of the Laser kicked up a fine spray as it sped over the waves on plane. Without warning, a rogue wave crested just ahead and the Laser crashed into it sending a wall of cold water up into the face of the man at the helm.

"Hooyah!" Joe O'Shanick proclaimed, as he shook the cold water off. It was early June, and the Niagara River had finished emptying the last of the ice from the Great Lakes less than two months ago. So far, the river's water temperature had only reached the upper fifties. As a Navy SEAL, Joe had trained in cold water his entire career. It didn't faze him. Conversely, the shock of the cold water made him feel even more alive as he flew across the river on this unseasonably warm, sunny day. Joe's green eyes lit up the classic Irish face he inherited from his father that belied the darker hair and facial features he and his siblings inherited from their Filipino mother. His tall muscular frame was all his father.

Joe was home on a scheduled leave. He had grown up on Grand Island and his parents' home was just a couple of miles up the river. His parents ran a home construction company for which his older brother and sister worked. Joe was the middle of five kids, his younger sister a nurse and younger brother a local restaurant owner. Being a Wednesday, they were all busy working. Joe had spent the early part of the morning with a two-mile swim and a six-mile run and then, taking notice of the wind, came down to the yacht club for a sail on his old boat. His parents' home was actually on the water and they could have kept their sailboats up there, but they had been members of this sailing club since before Joe was even born and preferred to sail and race with the other club members. Joe's dad, Jack, used the Laser to teach the next generation how to sail and allowed some of the junior sailors to race it on weekends. She (Joe's Laser) had taken some wear and tear over the years, but Joe was glad she was still being put to good use and enjoyed by others.

The club was just a few miles upstream from the majestic Niagara Falls. Joe glanced over his left shoulder and could clearly see the telltale mist as it rose above the Falls. Being ever respectful of the strong current and the danger presented by the Falls, Joe usually sailed a heading taking him upstream upon leaving the club. Laser sailboats were too small to have an engine. If the wind ever died, Joe preferred to have more time and distance with which to work his way back to shore and safety.

Today was different. Lasers tended to become unsteady and roll when sailing away from a strong wind. Capsizing was a normal occurrence with Lasers, but righting one in this heavy air and chop would be difficult; therefore, sailing upstream today would be a challenge, whereas sailing a reach back and forth across the river, with the wind coming over the side of the boat, would be fast and exhilarating. This was actually one of the most fun ways to sail.

Joe saw the shore of Cayuga Island rapidly approaching. He deftly turned the boat through the wind and quickly brought her back up on plane heading back across the river toward Grand Island. The boat thumped its way across the chop and Joe reveled in the moment as the cold spray whipped into his face. He got to sail a fair amount down in Virginia Beach where he lived when his team wasn't off on deployment or on training rotations. The sailing was great and his platoon Chief Petty Officer recently bought a boat which he and Joe planned to race this summer now that their latest deployment had just ended. Nevertheless, this was the river and the boat Joe had cut his teeth on and the nostalgia wasn't lost on him. It was good to be home.

A few minutes later, Joe was rapidly approaching the larger of two main docks at their sailing club. Once again, he quickly turned through the wind and headed back across the River, seemingly faster than the first time. A low, methodical rumble reached his ears carried by the wind from downriver. *Probably a Scarab or a Baja,* Joe thought to himself. Not many other boats would be out in this chop today. The river and Lake Erie were full of these and Joe didn't mind them. He knew plenty of people who owned them and had been on them enough times. They were fun, but not good for much other than going fast; however, if you wanted to head up to Buffalo and spend a day at Canalside, a thirty-seven-foot cigarette boat with a deep-v hull and twin 454's was the way to get there. Their other purpose was, ostensibly, to serve as a chick magnet. The problem was, any schmuck could buy a boat and operate it on the water. Sadly, some had no clue what they were doing. There was no training or licensing course required.

It is what it is, Joe sighed.

Joe had his feet hooked into the hiking strap and leaned way out to keep his Laser level as he planed across the water. Holding this position for several minutes took great ab endurance, but was actually quite easy compared to what his training required. He heard the engines getting louder as the boat approached but, due to the position he was in, he couldn't turn his head in a manner that would allow him to see the boat rapidly approaching from downstream. By necessity, a sailboat under sail has the right of way, but far too many boaters didn't bother to learn the rules of boating safety. Knowing this and having had several close calls in the past, Joe tended to keep vigilant to what other boaters were doing.

The sound of the approaching boat grew louder. Out of concern, Joe eased out his main sail and sat up to take a quick look. Glancing behind him, he saw the sharp bow of a black hulled boat rapidly approaching his position.

Surely he sees my sail! Joe thought to himself. *Probably some young punk trying to swamp me by passing right across my bow.*

Out of growing concern, Joe secured the main sheet in its cam cleat and frantically waved hoping the boater would notice. The boat continued on and was nearly on top of Joe at a very high speed.

"Veer off, you jack wagon!"

This is going to be close! Joe thought, as he rapidly considered his options. He was on a sure collision course with this boat and was running out of time to take evasive actions. Turning downwind wasn't an option. Joe did the only thing he could do; he quickly pushed the tiller to the leeward side, turning the sailboat into the wind as he tried to rapidly turn out of the path of the oncoming behemoth. The noise of the twin engines was deafening as the boat was nearly upon him overwhelming his visual field. He needed to bail out, but that would place him between his boat and the bigger boat. Not an option. Joe desperately tried to trim in his sail, hoping to gain any speed with which to escape the now seemingly inevitable collision. Joe watched in horror as the towering hull launched off the crest of a wave and towered overhead. The world seemed to move in slow motion as the sleek black hull crashed down on the sailboat's stern violently flipping Joe and his boat into the side of the passing cigarette boat. The blackness of the boat's hull enveloped Joe as everything around him went black.

Chapter 2

The cold water washed over Joe's face with each wave. He lay shivering in the surf, breathing between the waves and desperately trying to fight off hypothermia. He wouldn't drown. They had all passed drown-proofing or they wouldn't have gotten to Hell Week. No, the objective now was not to quit. However, the cold was getting to him; weakening him mentally more than physically. He was already beyond physically exhausted. They all were. It was Day 5 of Hell Week at BUDs and they were just trying to make it through to the end. Through the near dream-like state of mental and physical exhaustion, he could hear the instructors bellowing at them...taunting them to quit.

"You're done, Ensign O'Shanick!" Instructor Stephens yelled, looking down into his face. "I can see the defeat in your eyes! Stop wasting our time and go ring the bell! There's a warm bed and a hot meal waiting for you. You haven't got it!"

No! Joe thought to himself. Just make it through this evolution. One evolution at a time. Don't look ahead.

Joe was clad in a water-logged red life vest, locked arm in arm on each side with his boat mates. He pulled them closer, hoping for any extra warmth they could provide and hoping he offered the same. Instructor Stephens turned his attention to the man on his right, Farnsworth. Joe pulled him in even tighter, the only form of encouragement he could offer under the cold surf of Coronado. They would only make it through together. The SEAL Teams were no place for lone rangers. BUDs was designed to forge a team mentality. Cold water immersion was one of many proving evolutions. Another wave washed over them. He exhaled as it passed by making him ready to take his next breath.

One more wave closer to being called out of the water. One more wave closer to completing the evolution. The surf cleared and Joe took his next breath but something went wrong and he inhaled nothing but water...

Joe came to as he choked on the cold water. He remained in the near trance-like state, but he was aware enough to realize something was off.

Where is Farnsworth? Where's my boat crew? Sand? Why is there no sand? What happened to the beach? Have I been washed out to sea?

Another wave of cold water jolted Joe to a more wakeful state. He bobbed in the water, his life vest keeping him afloat, as he quickly floated past a small island.

What the...? Where the heck am I?

As he floated past the island, he saw a familiar flat bridge-like structure stretching from the small island back to the shore a few hundred yards away. There were many concrete bases evenly spaced underneath it.

I've seen that before! What is it?

A dark feeling crept over Joe as he slowly realized where he was. That was the International Water Control Dam just above Niagara Falls. As if in confirmation, he sensed, before he actually heard, the roar of the Falls as he turned and saw he was about to enter the rapids. Fully awake now, Joe quickly assessed his situation.

Hosed! I am totally hosed! Joe quickly assessed as the raging current sucked him towards the rapids. From his receding dream while unconscious, Joe heard that demonic voice of Instructor Stephens screaming at him.

"Now? You're going to ring out on me now?" His voice admonished in Joe's head. *"You survived twenty-seven weeks of BUDs, including MY Hell Week! Ain't no way you're ringing that bell and quitting on me, O'Shanick! Work the problem, MISTER O'Shanick!"*

Joe had mere seconds before he entered the rapids. Several miles upstream in front of his parents' house, he could just barely keep against the current, but it was way too strong this close to the Falls. His only chance was to try to get to shore. The Canadian shore was too far away. Goat Island, the New York State park which separates the American Falls from the Canadian or "Horseshoe" Falls, was the better option. Joe spotted Three Sisters Island, a collection of small islands extending out into the rapids that were connected to the larger Goat Island by a pedestrian bridge. He and his buddies used to wade through the shallower waters that flowed through the tiny islands when they were teenagers. If he could just get there...

Joe set out in a rapid breast stroke. The life vest slowed him down, but he didn't dare remove it now. Out of nowhere, a huge boulder appeared as Joe slammed sideways into it. The force of the impact knocked the wind out of him, but the vest cushioned the blow somewhat and he kept on as the current washed him around the side. He was in the rapids now.

Work the problem, O'Shanick!

Joe stroked harder in the now raging rapids. His muscles burned. He had probably floated unconscious for twenty to thirty minutes after that boat ran him over. More than enough time for hypothermia to set in. His dexterity and sensation, let alone his mental capacities, were surely lacking. He slammed into and then tumbled over a smaller rock. It now hurt to breathe. Probably some broken ribs.

Ignore it, O'Shanick! Complete the evolution!

That's what it was now. One final evolution. Joe could see Three Sisters Island rapidly approaching as he continued to work his way to shore. Joe kicked harder. He slammed into another rock. This time it was his left shoulder taking the blow. Joe thought he may have dislocated it, but he continued to stroke with his arms and it seemed to work. Painful, but it worked.

Just ahead, Joe could see calmer water closer to shore where it flowed easier through the cluster of small islands. That's where he needed to get to. Joe buried his head and stroked like it was the last length of an Olympic event. *BAM!* Another rock flipped him onto his back and he struck his head as he rolled by. Joe righted himself and corrected his bearings only to realize the rapids had swept him past the entrance to Three Sisters Island.

Desperate, Joe made for the shore. He remembered that the water was shallower closer to the shore. As the young thrill seekers he and his friends once were, they used to hold contests seeing who would dare to wade out the farthest. One day there was a news report of a young girl from Niagara Falls who waded out too far, slipped on the slick rocky bottom and was swept to her death over the Falls. That put a swift to end to that contest for Joe and his daredevil friends.

Joe kept working. There were fewer rocks to contend with as he got closer to shore, but the current was just as fast. He was nearly past Three Sisters Island when he felt his foot brush the rocky bottom.

Oh, Thank God! He thought to himself, as he put both feet down to stand. The water was still too deep and the current pushed against his life vest, knocking him back over. The water was deeper and faster during the summer days as both the U.S and Canadian Power Authorities kept the water levels higher to provide the tourists a more spectacular view of the falls.

Get up, O'Shanick! Work the problem!

Joe desperately stroked closer to shore. He was now at the downstream tip of Three Sisters Island. A little further and the rapids opened up more just before flowing over the Falls. Joe touched down again, but this time crouched and lunged out of the water, diving as close to shore as he could hoping to reach shallower water. He landed, quickly got his feet under him and stood up leaning into the current to prevent another knock down. It worked! His left foot was downstream, planted on a sharp rock edge but holding his weight. The water was about waist deep allowing his life vest to remain clear of the water. Braced against the current, he could now see a group of Asian tourists pointing and staring in shock as he planned his next step. The current was tugging at him, threatening to knock him back over as it swirled around his legs.

"Anybody have a rope?" He shouted to the people on the nearby shore. The confused looks on their faces revealed to Joe that they likely did not speak English. He asked again in Tagalog, the native language of the Philippines he had learned from his mother, but they still didn't seem to understand him. As a Navy SEAL, Joe had learned several languages, but the only Asian language he knew was Tagalog and they weren't connecting. To add insult to injury, one of the women began to film him with her phone.

"GET SOME HELP!" Joe yelled frantically, hoping the urgency in his voice would transcend the language barrier and spur them to action. In response, two of the men waved, shouted something in what sounded like Japanese, and ran off.

Suddenly, Joe felt his left foot begin to slip. He desperately tried to ease it back into a firmer spot on the rock when it gave way completely. Joe slipped under the water where the raging current grabbed ahold, rapidly propelling him to the brink of Niagara Falls.

Chapter 3

Grand Island, New York

$\mathcal{M}$aria O'Shanick rapidly entered numbers into the spreadsheet on her laptop. She exuded a professional calm, dressed in a solid black skirt and sleeveless turquoise blouse exposing toned arms on her petite frame, as her hands deftly flew across the keyboard. Her long, dark hair was pulled back revealing her striking Asian face that looked decades younger than her real age. The mail had recently arrived and she wanted to have all the checks entered into their accounting system before running them through the scanner. She kept meticulous records and always backed up the finances on a separate spreadsheet. She had learned her business skills as a child helping her parents run a small restaurant by the naval base in Subic Bay, Philippines.

During the Cold War, the U.S. Navy operated a large base at Subic Bay and the throngs of sailors provided a steady cash flow for many locals, including her parents. At a young age, Maria began sweeping floors and washing dishes in their restaurant. She soon learned to cook and spent a few years in the kitchen before she began to wait tables. Having a strong aptitude for numbers and organization, she had taken over the accounting and purchasing by the time she was fourteen. She would wait tables after school and balance the books at night. By the time she finished secondary school at sixteen, Maria was managing the restaurant while her parents ran the kitchen.

By eighteen, she possessed a worldliness and work ethic that magnified her natural beauty. This was readily noticed by a young machinist's mate in the Navy by the name of Jack O'Shanick. Jack's ship was undergoing a minor refit, remaining in Subic Bay for several weeks. He immediately noticed Maria while having dinner with some shipmates and he pursued her over the next few weeks, even to the point of helping her family in their little restaurant in the evenings after completing his duties onboard ship. Maria's family were enamored by Jack's charm, work ethic, and their shared Catholic faith. Within a month, he and Maria married with the approval of both her parents. Less than a year later, Jack was honorably discharged from the Navy. He returned for Maria and they moved to Jack's hometown where they began their construction company with a used pickup truck and some secondhand tools. Nearly forty years later, their business had blossomed into a large residential development and home building company. They had over thirty employees and Maria had managed the office throughout it all. Jack and their oldest son, Jacob, oversaw the operations side of the business while their older daughter, Marina, a delightful blend of Jack and Maria, was director of sales and marketing. Business had never been better or more enjoyable.

As Maria entered the last of the accounts receivable, she smiled thinking ahead to tonight. Joe was home on leave from the Navy. She was certainly proud of the man their middle son had become but, being a mother, never stopped worrying about the work he did as a SEAL platoon leader. He served the past year in Central America rooting out the cartels as part of President Galan's initiative to destroy the drug and human trafficking trades. Joe had actually been captured and held hostage during a blown operation. He narrowly escaped with his life and the life of the charming female emergency medicine doctor he was sent to rescue. He returned to duty with what was left of his team and they had only recently returned from their deployment. Nevertheless, Joe was home safe and all was well in Maria's world. Marina would look after the office and Maria would be heading home early to begin preparing tonight's feast for the entire family, one of her favorite things to do.

JOE!

A dark sensation suddenly overtook Maria's serenity. *Joe is in danger!* Maria couldn't tell if it was her keen mother's intuition or if

God was trying to tell her something, but she was sure it was Joe and that she needed to pray for his safety. *Now!*

Maria stood to her feet and rushed over to Marina's office. Marina was on the phone but, noticing the distressed look on her mother's face, apologized to the caller and hung up.

"Mom! What's wrong?"

"I'm not sure, Marina, but I think Joey is in danger. I feel it here," Maria said earnestly with her hand on her chest.

Marina abruptly stood and came out from behind her desk. Dressed in a similar fashion, Marina and Maria could have passed for sisters with their near identical looks.

"Where is he?"

"I don't know, Marina, he said he might go for a sail, but that was early this morning as I was leaving for work."

"I'll call him," Marina said as she picked her phone up from her desk, opened it up and dialed.

"Voice mail. I'll try him again."

Thirty seconds later, Marina clicked off her phone and looked into her mother's tear-filled eyes. Marina knew her mother to be reserved, if not stoic; however, her mother also had amazing insight and intuition. If she was close to tears, something was definitely wrong. She took her mother's hands in hers.

"Let's pray for his safety, and then I'll try him again."

Chapter 4

Niagara Falls, New York

Sergeant Jon Tonelli was enjoying the warm sunny day as he patrolled Terrapin Point on foot. He had been a New York State Park Police officer for nearly ten years and never grew tired of the majestic site before him. The massive waterfall thundered as the water plunged down into the gorge 188 feet below. The frightful water was mesmerizing to watch as it rushed over the edge a mere dozen yards away. He could stand in this spot all day, but he had to continue, so he turned and strode up the walkway that paralleled the shoreline.

His radio crackled to life. It sounded like Corporal Pavis from further up near Three Sisters Island.

"Go ahead, two-five." Tonelli spoke into his shoulder mike.

"Sir, be advised, there's a swimmer in the water! White male heading your way! I don't think he's a jumper! Requesting full assist!" The distress in Pavis' voice could be felt through his earpiece.

Tonelli began to scan the rapids as he keyed his mike.

"All units respond immediately to Terrapin Point! Swimmer in distress! Repeat, swimmer in distress!"

Tonelli shielded his eyes from the sun and squinted as he looked upstream. There was a small point between his position and where Pavis was up at Three Sisters Island. His best chance to spot the man would be when he came around the point which, with the speed of the current, should be any second now. *There!*

Sergeant Tonelli saw the man's head bobbing as he rounded the corner. He appeared to be desperately trying to breaststroke his way toward shore, but he had a way to go.

"What do we have, boss?" Corporal Carr yelled, as he pulled alongside in a golf cart.

"Swimmer! Just rounded the point!" Tonelli yelled, as he grabbed a rope with a life ring out of the cart. "Grab the launcher and let's go!"

Tonelli hurried down the slope to the water with Carr at his side. They worked their way through a small clearing to the shore. He quickly reacquired visual of the man and keyed his mike.

"All units, I have eyes on a white male, about seventy yards off-shore, actively swimming toward shore, just came around the point. Carr and I will attempt retrieval but be ready downstream!"

"Mike, hand me the line launcher and loop the other line through my belt!"

Corporal Carr passed the line launcher, an air rifle that uses compressed CO2 to launch a floating pod attached to a nylon lifeline distances of up to eighty yards. The swimmer was right at the limit of this range. Knowing this, Tonelli decided he would have to risk wading into the rapids as far as possible to cut the distance.

"Go!" Carr yelled, after looping the other lifeline through Tonelli's belt.

Tonelli cautiously stepped into the water. The sheer cold felt like knives on his body as he waded in up to his knees. He dared go no farther. He raised the launcher to the optimum angle of distance and took aim.

BOOM!

Tonelli and Carr watched the bright orange float as it arced through the air toward the swimmer. They reacted with horror when the float landed far short of the swimmer.

"C'mon, man! SWIM! Grab the float!" They yelled, willing the man to close the distance to the float as the current quickly pulled him by.

He nearly closed the distance, and desperately reached out, but the line, being fixed to Tonelli, began to move away from the swimmer as it followed its arc toward the shore.

"Terrapin Point, stand by! We missed the swimmer! You're up!" Tonelli yelled into his mike in desperation. He collapsed back onto the shore in defeat. The man had one last, and very slim, chance before plunging to his death.

Chapter 5

Terrapin Point
Niagara Falls, New York

The raging rapids thundered as they whipped Joe around the point at nearly forty miles per hour. He was past the point of exhaustion, but he stroked on in frenzied fashion, desperately trying to reach shore or even a shallow that he could gain purchase. His SEAL training was what kept him going. The rigorous training of the twenty-seven-week BUDs course weeded out all but those who would die before they quit. Joe had seen many combat tours and always knew death was a bullet strike or explosion away but, even when the bullets flew past his head, he had never felt like death was imminent. It was now. He could see it just a few hundred yards away. Joe could do the math. The safety of the shore was too far away. He would not close the distance before he was swept over the edge. That sudden realization caused an adrenaline surge that seemingly put everything into slow motion.

Is this the end or is there really something beyond this life? Joe was raised Catholic. His mother particularly, but the rest of his family, except maybe for his younger brother, Sean, were all religious to some degree. Joe just didn't buy into it. It seemed so superficial and far-fetched in many ways. Years of combat and exposure to the harsh realities of life had hardened the skeptic in Joe to the point where he just didn't give religion or God a thought. Nor did he want to. He made his life as a SEAL platoon leader on his own. He never felt a need for a crutch such as religion. He just figured he would work things out himself as he always had and, if there was an afterlife, that would be worked out as well.

That changed, somewhat, this past fall when he was captured along with Christy, the ER physician, during the blown rescue operation in Honduras. While together, Christy somehow managed to penetrate his hardened exterior and open his mind to some perspectives on faith and life, in general, that had spurred Joe to further exploration. Joe still didn't know what he actually believed, but he was honest enough to admit there likely is a God and he may well be meeting him within the next minute.

Well, God, if you're real, I'm not asking for a miracle but, if you really offer forgiveness, I'm sure I could use some. It wasn't the "Our Father," but it was the best he could come up with.

Not going down without a fight, Joe summoned what strength he had left to continue vigorously stroking towards shore. Through the roar of the rapids, Joe heard what sounded like the "pop" of a bottle of champagne being uncorked. A small orange object, about the size of a baseball, caught his eye as it splashed down twenty yards before him.

A float! Lifeline!

It was so close! Joe desperately tried to summon any remaining speed he had but there was no reserve. His shoulders and arms felt like he was carrying cinder blocks. His lungs burned. Yet still he continued on trying to reach the float. A glimmer of hope appeared as he somehow closed the distance to ten yards. The float stayed parallel with him as they were quickly pulled toward the brink. Joe had closed the distance a couple of more yards when the float suddenly began to arc away from him back toward the shore. His heart sank in unison with the two Park Police officers when he saw them collapse onto the shore in defeat.

Joe nearly gave up, himself, but his training had his body on autopilot as he continued to press through the water toward shore. The bushes lining the shore gave way to a concrete wall lining the last hundred yards of shore before the brink. Many onlookers stared in horror as Joe rapidly passed by. The thunderous roar of Horseshoe Falls was overwhelming. Through the roar, Joe sensed, more than heard, two additional pops signaling the discharge of more line launchers. He slowed slightly to allow his eyes to stay above water while anticipating the floats hitting the water.

There!

Two more orange floats landed just a few feet in front of Joe. Joe stroked with everything he had.

Get it, O'Shanick!

Joe charged. The rapids were so tumultuous he could not keep track of both floats, forcing him to choose the closer one. Joe kicked and stroked. It was right there. He reached out as he kicked once again closing the final two feet. As he closed his hands on the float, the rapids caused it to lurch up away from his hands. It landed a foot beyond. He sensed the brink rapidly approaching just a few yards away. One last chance. Joe mightily pulled his arms through the water while giving a strong butterfly kick. Miraculously, he closed the distance. Joe reached out with both hands to grab the float. Just as his hands began to close down on the float, they were yanked away as Joe hurled over the edge, plunging to the tumultuous water 190 feet below.

Chapter 6

This is it. An eerie calm replaced the violent rapids that had catapulted Joe over the edge. The cold water wrapped him in a weightless cocoon of green silence as he plunged down.

Down to what? The adrenaline surge of this experience continued to create a slow motion effect in Joe's brain. He fully expected to die. Only three people had ever survived this plunge. Three who somehow were beyond lucky enough to avoid the large boulders below, the deep plunge into raging waters and the impact it brought. Miracles. Thousands more had met their fate, some never to be seen again. Joe's only hope was to be killed instantly by smashing into a boulder.

It's OK, he reasoned. *I've had a good ride. Belay that, I've had a GREAT ride.*

The immortalized words of another Navy SEAL, Adam Brown, a Tier 1 DEVGRU operator of amazing accomplishments who was killed in action in Afghanistan, came to mind:

"Life is not a journey to the grave with the intention of arriving safely in a pretty and preserved body, but rather to skid in broadside, thoroughly used up, totally worn out, and loudly proclaiming, 'Wow … what a ride!'"

Yep, it's been a great ride. Joe closed his eyes and prepared for the end.

Joe was suddenly pulled out of his surreal state of acceptance when he impacted the turbulent water at the base of the falls. He was slammed into a state of chaos as the harsh impact was instantly followed by a thunderous roar as he rolled over and over. His SEAL training had caused him to subconsciously take a deep breath when he tumbled over the edge seconds ago. The rigorous swimming above had created a state of high oxygen demand but Joe, instinctively, fought off the burning urge in his lungs to breathe. He was completely disoriented. Flashes of green and white circled around him as he continued to roll and flounder about. The massive waterfall threatened to push him further down the 170 foot deep plunge pool. The mounting pressure of the depth caused his eardrums to feel like they would burst. Water had gushed into his nose and his sinuses were on fire. The pressure in his lungs was overwhelming and Joe's body took over forcing some air to escape. Joe overrode this impulse and held on to what remained. Severely deprived of oxygen, Joe's brain began to shut down. The swirling green and white amidst the thundering chaos began to fade to black as the remaining air in his lungs began to escape.

Chapter 7

Tonawanda, New York

The loud thrum emanating from the twin 454 horsepower engines of the black hulled Scarab 377 was reduced to a deep rumble as the driver approached the boat landing at Niawanda Park. The driver finessed the throttles to gently bring the slick craft into the docking area. Terry Wood had spent years working for a fishing captain running charters down on Lake Ontario and was competent with nearly any power boat. His competence was disguised by his stocky frame, beer gut, and scruffy beard allowing him to blend in with the many other beer guzzling rabid sports fans well known to the Buffalo area.

"Ange, get ready with the dock lines."

His partner and friend, Angelo Catalano, climbed up onto the long bow and fastened a line to the bow cleat and stood ready. Slightly shorter than Terry, but just as stocky, Angelo resembled any other guy one would see seated in a bar enjoying a plate full of wings and a Labatt's while the Bills played.

Terry coaxed the throttles to allow just a touch of headway against the current as he eased the boat in alongside the dock. Angelo hopped stepped down to the dock and secured the bowline as Terry cut the throttles and secured the stern line to a nearby dock cleat.

"You don't want to put out a couple of fenders, Terry?" Angelo asked.

"No, screw that. It ain't our boat. What do we care?"

"Yeah, true dat, man."

"What we need to do, is get the flip out of here," Terry stated as he stepped up onto the dock. "Just make like we own the boat and we're heading up to Mississippi Mudds for a couple of hot dogs," Terry added as he and Angelo stepped off the dock and onto the parks jogging/bike path. A rather fit female jogger headed towards them. They parted to let her by, but both turned to ogle her as she continued on down the shoreline path. Turning back, they cut across the park and headed up the hill and across Niagara Street towards the landmark restaurant known for its char-grilled Sahlen's dogs and other fine Buffalo fare. They wore sunscreen shirts, floppy hats, and sunglasses and were indistinguishable from many of the guys in the area. Reaching the restaurant, they continued onto the side street it cornered on. Terry fished his cellphone out of his pocket and hit a number on speed dial.

"Yeah, Paulie, it's me...Yeah, I know...Look, I need you to pick us up...What do you mean, "When?" Now, you mutt...Yeah, we're right by Mississippi Mudds on Kohler Street. We're walking towards Fletcher, but we ain't stoppin'...Yeah, we'll just keep walking up Kohler until you find us...Yeah, that's good. Bye."

"Paulie P comin' to get us?" Ange asked.

"Yeah, he's over at his bar in North Tonawanda. Be here in five."

"Man, Terry, I can still smell those hot dogs from here. I've got half a mind to turn around and grab a couple."

"You've got half a mind is all you got, you friggin' moron! We don't need anyone connecting us with that boat. We can swing by Ted's in North Tonawanda before we get to the Falls and get some there."

"You really think that guy's dead?"

"What do you think, Ange? You think you could survive being run over by a big boat doin' close to seventy on the water? He's done."

Chapter 8

Niagara Falls, New York

Captain Katherine Kessler's hand deftly moved over the helm and twin throttles of Maid of the Mist VII. The eighty-foot boat sported 350 horsepower diesels to work the swirling currents at the base of the falls. She expertly maneuvered the boat to keep it idle in the currents allowing her passengers breathtaking views as they looked up at the towering cataracts. Tourist season was ramping up and the VII was filled to capacity with passengers.

The was her second season as Captain. She began working for Maid of the Mist as a deckhand while in college at nearby Niagara University. Over the years she worked her way up, obtained a captain's license from the U.S. Coast Guard and, now, was one of three female captains for the tour company.

It was a beautiful early summer day, although she could do without the strong winds, which tended to swirl down in the gorge and teamed up with the treacherous currents making it difficult to keep Seven steady for her passengers. It was a regular occurrence and she was used to it. Her passengers were seemingly captivated by their view and unaware of the maneuvering be made by their captain. Mission accomplished.

"MM Base to MM Seven," her VHF radio crackled. Katherine glanced over as her first mate picked up the mike in response.

"MM Seven, go ahead base."

"MM Seven, be advised a white male in a yellow life vest just went over the Horseshoe Falls near Terrapin Point. You are authorized to remain in the area and render assistance if necessary."

"Roger that, Base. Seven out," her first mate, Mike Reilly, said shaking his head as he replaced the handheld microphone.

"Every month there's at least one or two of them, KK."

"Yes, but they said this guy was wearing a life jacket, Mike. It sounds more like an accident than a suicide."

"Good point. All the more tragic. That's a terrible way to go," First Mate Reilly said, as he grabbed the binoculars and stood to scan the water around them.

"I don't see anything. I'm gonna go alert the crew and take a look from the bow. I'll take the handheld," he said, as he donned a poncho and grabbed the handheld radio used for docking and stepped out onto the deck. Spotting one of the deckhands, he alerted her to the situation and instructed her to inform the rest of the crew.

Reilly politely worked his way through a throng of Asian tourists gathered at the bow. Standing at the bow, he had the best viewing position, but focused on Terrapin Point on the port side. From this vantage point, Reilly could see what many couldn't see up from up above. Boulders. Lots of them. Odds were the poor soul was crushed to death on one of these rocks when he went over. Reilly hoped that whatever was left of the man would not come floating by. Nobody should have to see that.

Chapter 9

Niagara Falls, New York

*J*oe swam slowly with nervous anticipation across the bottom of the training pool. His BUDs instructors looked like sharks as they circled a few feet above. This was Joe's second attempt to pass this critical Phase Two evaluation. If he failed this, he had one last chance before failing out of the course. *That's not going to happen,* he thought as he slowly took deep breaths through his diving gear and prepared himself for what was to come.

Bam!

One of the instructors attacked from his right. Joe took a breath as his mask was ripped off instantly blurring his vision. He was knocked to his side as his regulator was pulled from his mouth. Joe willed himself to relax and go with the flow as his instructor roughed him up while tying Joe's goggles into a knot with the air hoses. His world was a swirl of green and white as the sadistic instructor forced Joe into another spin before swimming away.

Game on! Joe regained his bearings and kneeled on the bottom of the pool. He released his straps and pulled his SCUBA tanks overhead and in front of him where he could focus on the task before him. He went to work trying to loosen the knot in his air hoses. They didn't want to cooperate. Joe felt his lungs begin to burn as he willed himself to work the problem. He would either clear the knot, allowing him to use his regulator to breathe, or he would be forced to give up and head to the surface for air. Instant failure.

Screw it. I'm not going up. They'll have to come get me. Joe continued to work the stubborn knot. *Precious seconds ticked by as he struggled to fight the instinct to breathe. The knot wouldn't budge. He let a little air escape his burning lungs. His movements became slower and clumsier as his oxygen starved brain began to check out. The water around him began to turn black as he desperately tried to free the knot. He was barely coherent when he felt something grasp his arms and begin to pull him toward the surface. The light grew brighter as did the realization of his failure. Joe broke the surface and, in compliance with his training, extended his right arm overhead with his hand revealing the OK signal.*

"I'm OK!" Joe yelled weakly as he let out the last remnants of air and took a deep breath.

A few more breaths and awareness slowly came back to him. The instructors who just a minute ago were trying to drown him, were nowhere to be found. He was no longer in the Naval Special Warfare training pool in Coronado. Joe looked around until the realization hit him.

Chapter 10

" **g** ot him! Swimmer in the water! He's alive!

Mike Reilly couldn't believe what he was seeing. The man had just surfaced fifteen yards off their bow. Alive and functional!

"KK, swimmer off the port bow! Fifteen yards. Ease us alongside," Reilly requested as he pulled a life ring off the bulkhead. He quickly worked his way through the shocked crowd until he reached the ladder and headed down to the lower deck. He spotted one of the deckhands.

"Steve, find Jeff and meet me along the port beam. There's a man in the water!"

Steve hurriedly moved off in search of the other deckhand. Reilly, announced his presence and parted the crowd until he reached the port beam. They would have an easier time pulling the man out of the water here. *Lucky son of a gun!*

The man was closer now and looking directly at the boat. *Good, maybe he will be able to help us get him out,* Reilly hoped as Maid of the Mist VII closed the distance. Jeff and Steve appeared beside Reilly on the rail.

"What do ya got, First Mate? Holy..." Jeff's voice trailed off before uttering the expected exploitive when he spotted the man gently swimming toward them. "How did he get there?"

"He took the big ride down, numbskull! Now help me get him aboard."

"Sir? Can you hear me?"

Joe nodded and waved in affirmation.

"Stay right there! I'm going to toss you a line!" Reilly yelled, as he heaved the life ring in Joe's direction. It landed right in front of Joe and he easily grabbed ahold. Reilly and Jeff hauled Joe to the side. They hauled up on the line, straining as they went, but Joe was able to help out by using the rub rails for a foot hold. A few seconds later, they helped Joe over the rail to the thunderous applause of the onlooking tourists.

"Request permission to come aboard?" Joe gasped out between breaths, with a weary smile.

"Granted," Reilly replied dumbfounded. "What's your name? Are you alright?"

"Joe, Joe O'Shanick. I think I broke a couple of ribs, but other than that...I guess I'm OK, all things considered," Joe responded, still breathing heavily.

"I think we need to get you to the hospital, sir."

"KK, we've got him aboard. Have an ambulance meet us at the dock!" Reilly spoke into his radio.

"Ok, sir, let's get you out of your life jacket...Steve!"

"Sir?"

"Grab this man a blanket out of the hanging locker."

"Aye, sir!" Steve responded as he hurried off.

Helping Joe out of his life jacket, Reilly marveled at his build.

"Well, no wonder you survived the Falls, you're built like Superman!"

Joe just shrugged and gave an embarrassed half grin. The deckhand returned with a wool blanket and Reilly helped wrap it around Joe. He then led him to a nearby bench and had Joe take a seat. By the time they pulled up to the dock, Joe was in a full shiver.

The deckhands quickly tied up and then helped keep the crowd out of the way as the paramedics came on board with a stretcher. One of the paramedics placed a cervical collar around Joe's neck while the other obtained some basic information regarding pain and injuries. They quickly transferred Joe off the boat and into the elevator waiting for them at the base of the Observation Tower. Once up top, they quickly loaded Joe into the ambulance and drove off. The ride to the main hospital was only a few minutes. During that time, the paramedic obtained Joe's vital signs, obtained Joe's vital statistics, started a large bore IV and began a liter of Normal Saline. Following that, he called report into the hospital emergency department.

"Niagara County Medical Center, this is Medic Three."

"Go ahead, Medic Three."

"Falls, we are en route to your facility with a thirty-one year old male who survived a trip over the Falls in a life jacket. His vitals are as follows; BP 110/68, heart rate 90, respirations 24 and shallow with a pulse ox of 92. We have a 16 gauge IV in his right AC with a liter of Normal Saline going. Our ETA is...we're pulling in now."

"Medic Three! Say again..."

The paramedic had already replaced his radio and was prepping to move Joe out of the ambulance. His partner opened the rear doors and helped pull Joe's stretched out. They quickly wheeled him into the busy ER and were directed to one of the trauma bays. They gave a quick report to the doctor and nursing staff while preparing to slide Joe over to the ER stretcher. Not wanting to seem helpless, Joe decided to make the transfer himself to the admonishment of a petite, but rather pretty, ER nurse.

"Sir, you need to just lay still and let us handle everything."

Joe recalled all of the medical training he had received in the Teams and realized she was right. He looked at her sheepishly and muttered a simple, "You're right. I'm sorry."

The staff slid him over and the paramedics began to pack up their stretcher.

"Hey, guys? What are your names?" Joe asked the medics through chattering teeth.

"I'm Jesse and he's Todd."

"Thanks," Joe said, extending his hand.

"You're welcome. Good luck, man," Jesse responded, as they both shook Joe's hand and took their leave.

"Hello, I'm Tony Alendretti, one of the ER doctors; did you really go over the Falls?"

Joe instantly recognized the doctor who stood over him. Dr. Alendretti was unmistakably Italian with a tan complexion, dark curly hair showing a touch of gray, a classic Roman nose and friendly eyes that revealed his gentle demeanor. He was built like a trained distance runner.

"Y-y-yess, but I s-swear it was only my first time, Doc."

Joe's response caused a good laugh amongst the nurses, but left Alendretti momentarily stunned.

"Joe!"

"What up, T-t-tone?"

"Holy sheep dip, Joe!" Alendretti exclaimed. Turning to his staff he asked, "Can we please get him a warm blanket?"

"Joe! What are you doing here? I didn't even know you were in town."

"Yeah, well, I th-thought I'd d-d-drop in and s-s-see you," the two nurses smiled at Joe's double entendre.

"Wait, you two know each other?" Judy, the seasoned charge nurse, asked.

"Yeah, Joe and I go way back, Judy. We grew up on Grand Island together, we were on the swim team and graduated in the same class."

"Among other things," Joe said with a malicious smile.

"So, Joe, what the heck happened? You know the river better than anyone. You're the last person I would ever think would go over the Falls!"

"I was out s-sailing my Laser and s-s-some guy r-r-ran me over with a b-black hulled boat. Looked like a Scarab or a Checkmate, b-but I'm not sure. Anyway, I was knocked out and didn't come to until just before the rapids. I tried t-to make it to shore but the current was just too fast."

"Were you on the East River?"

"Yeah, out in front of the sailing club near your brother's house."

"Geez, Joe! How did you not go over the American Falls? You'd have never been seen again!"

"No clue, Tone," Joe answered, somberly realizing he was only alive due to several miracles.

"Alright, we can catch up later; let me check you over and see what we need to do. Where all do you hurt?"

Dr. Alendretti began asking Joe a series of questions as he performed his primary survey which assesses the ABC's of Airway, Breathing and Circulation. The staff were well trained to handle trauma patients and their actions resembled the movements of a well-choreographed performance. One of the nurses called out Joe's vital signs, which were all stable, while a tech cut off Joe's remaining clothing which happened to be his favorite pair of board shorts. Doctor Alendretti noted that Joe had decreased breath sounds on his left side, but that was the only abnormal finding on the primary survey.

A portable chest X-ray was obtained and Doctor Alendretti proceeded with the secondary survey. At the same time, the petite nurse, Amanda, as it read on her ID badge, prepped Joe's left arm for a second IV. She noted Joe's lean, muscular build with large bulging veins mapping his arms.

"Oh, I've died and gone to nurse heaven!" she quietly muttered to the other nurse who looked on with admiration.

"Hematoma of the left frontal head, tenderness left chest wall, contusions of the left hip and knee, skin cold to the touch," Dr. Alendretti called out to the nurse after finishing the bulk of the secondary survey.

"Oral temp is ninety-three,"

"Let's get ready to roll him and check the spine, check a rectal temp while we're at it," he instructed.

"Excuse me?" Joe asked.

"Sorry, Joe, you're hypothermic and I need a more accurate temp. Fold your arms across your chest and don't move while we roll you."

The staff log rolled Joe onto his left side. Dr. Alendretti methodically checked Joe's spine while the tech inserted the thermometer.

"So you say, Tone. This wouldn't have anything to do with that time I slicked up your car seats and steering wheel with Armor All, would it?"

"Ha! I forgot all about that!"

"Yeah, sure you did."

"That was funny, though. Any of this hurt along your spine?"

"N-no, it's all good, Tone."

"Ninety-one point eight," the nurse tech announced.

"Alright, roll him back. Let's get a Bair Hugger on him and start warm IV fluids in both IV's."

"Joe," Dr. Alendretti said, as he rolled the ultrasound machine up and began inspecting different parts of Joe's abdomen, "You're hypothermic, and you've suffered a head injury and probably some rib fractures. I'm going to get some CT scans while we start to warm you up. All things considered, I'm surprised you're talking, let alone alert and oriented. Shoot, I'm just glad you're still among the living, brother."

"Thanks, Tone."

Dr. Alendretti lingered over Joe's chest with the ultrasound probe. His thick dark eyebrows furled into a frown.

"What is it, Tone?"

"You might have a pneumothorax. I'm sorry, a collapsed lung."

"I know what it is. D-do I need a chest tube?"

"It depends on how big it is. The rest of your ultrasound looks fine. I'm gonna go look at your chest X-ray and see. I'll be right back."

While he was gone, the younger nurse removed a couple of warm blankets from the warmer and placed them over Joe.

"Oh, man! You're an angel. Th-th-thank you!"

Tony returned.

"Okay, Joe, you do have a pneumothorax and a couple of rib fractures. I'll need to put a chest tube in you after all. It involves cutting a small incision on the side of your chest and inserting a small tube between the ribs into your chest so we can re-inflate your lung. I'm sorry, man. I'll use the smallest tube possible to minimize the pain."

"That's alright. Do what you gotta do, Tone."

"Judy?" Tony turned to the charge nurse, "I'll need a chest tube tray and a twenty-eight French chest tube, please."

"Hey, Tone?" Joe asked.

"Yeah?"

"Remember that time I tied your shoelaces to your chair in fourth grade?"

"Yeah, I had to get stitches when my forehead hit my desk!"

"I'm sorry."

"Judy, what's the biggest chest tube that we have?" Tony smiled looking down at Joe.

Chapter 11

Grand Island, New York

Jack O'Shanick leaned over the hood of his Ford F-450 Superduty work truck, pointing at a survey plot. He was in a heated discussion with the man he had subcontracted to pave this new development.

"I'm telling you, Gene, the table slopes northeast. If you grade it north, we're gonna have water problems right here," Jack said, pointing to a spot on the survey map.

"Jack, it's not a big deal, you're gonna have a retention pond on that side."

"It is a big deal, Gene. With spring thaw and a heavy rain there's going to be a lake out there and I'm gonna have to come back in and install a drainage system, which I won't have to do if you go back and grade it out the way that it needs to be! The way I'm paying you to do it!"

Jack felt his phone begin to vibrate causing him to look at the screen.

"Jack, if you would just..."

Jack held up his hand when he saw the caller ID on the screen. "Hold on a second, Gene."

"Hello?"

"Yes, may I speak with Jack O'Shanick, please?"

"Speaking."

"Mr. O'Shanick, this is Mary Henning. I'm a patient liaison at Niagara County Medical Center. Your son Joe is here and asked me to call you..."

Jack listened intently; a concerned look etched on his face. He asked a few simple questions and hung up a minute later.

"Gene, I'm sorry, but I've got a situation and I'm gonna have to bolt," Jack said while rolling up the survey. "I want this grade fixed by next week or I'll find another paver."

Jack jumped into his truck and drove off. Gene turned around and gave a heavy sigh. Deep down, he knew Jack was right. Jack didn't have the reputation as the best quality builder for nothing. Gene would have to push his schedule back a week to fix this mess, but he wasn't going to risk losing Jack's business.

Jack dialed his oldest son's phone over his truck's Bluetooth system.

"Yeah, Dad?"

"Jacob, are you still down at the Saddlerock development?"

"Yes, sir."

"Is everything where you can get out of there?"

"Yeah, Dad, the roofers will be finishing lots three and five today and the framers are on schedule at lots six and eight. Why? What's up?"

"Meet me at the office ASAP. Joe went over the Falls."

"WHAT!?"

"I know, I'm having a tough time believing it myself, but apparently he went over the Falls and survived. He's at NCMC right now. We need to grab your mom and sister and head over there."

"I'm on my way, Dad. What about Sean and Anna? Want me to call them?"

"You get Sean and I'll call Anna. See you in a few," Jack said, as he punched the disconnect button on his steering wheel. The next call would be tougher. Anna practically worshipped her older brother.

Jack had Maria's Acura MDX pushing eighty on I-190 as they approached the North Grand Island Bridge.

"Dad, slow down," Marina reasoned from the back seat. "The minute we'll save getting there isn't worth the risk."

Maria gently placed her small hand on Jack's thigh coaxing him to listen to their daughter. Jack dutifully slowed to sixty-five. His stubborn Irish ways had long been tamed by his wife and daughters.

"So tell me again how you knew Joe was in trouble?"

"I didn't *know*, I just felt like God was telling me to pray for him. It just hit me out of nowhere. I felt like he was in danger and that we needed to pray for him right then."

"That's right, Dad. She rushed into my office and I could just see it all over her and then I sensed it too."

"And then we prayed and, ten minutes later, we felt a total sense of peace as if the danger had passed. Joe is going to be fine."

FINE? How can you possibly know that? Our son just went over Niagara Falls! There! Right there! Jack thought to himself, as he looked out the window and spotted the Falls' mist which was clearly seen as they drove over the bridge. *People don't survive that!*

As if she knew what her husband was thinking, Maria patted Jack's thigh affectionately. He looked at his wife and then her look-alike daughter in the back seat and saw total calm. *Amazing.*

Jack knew his wife was the prayer warrior of the family. She had been quite the religious Catholic when they met whereas Joe had been more of the "observant" Catholic. Maria changed over the years. She shed a lot of the superficialities of the faith and began to study the Bible in depth. A few years ago, Maria and Marina began attending a women's Bible study at a big non-denominational church in Getzville with her workout partner, Anita. In turn, Maria started a woman's Bible study of her own at their church on the Island. Her faith had become real to their family and even Jack had begun to shed his "religious" exterior for something more real. Joe was really the only hold out. Admittedly, Jack was still growing in this area and didn't understand things near to the level his wife did, but he trusted her. More to the point, he trusted Him whom she served. At least he hoped he did. That trust was currently being put to the test.

Chapter 12

Barnstable, Massachusetts

A gentle refreshing breeze drifted in off the harbor under the warm sun. The salty aroma carried the playful sounds of seagulls over the lower tone of the harbor's boating traffic. A pair of young women strolled by the water in front of Bismore Park. From a distance, they could have been mistaken as sisters. Both had long, silky dark hair that blew gently in the breeze. Their skin tones a golden tan. They were both slender; although, the taller one stood just under six feet and had an athletic tone in her arms and legs revealing years of fitness, while the other stood several inches shorter and was just showing signs of filling out. The two wore dark printed skirts with sleeveless blouses and stylish sunglasses. They strolled casually until they found a vacant bench and sat down.

The younger one slowly inhaled the ocean breeze, eyes closed and contented.

"It feels good, doesn't it, Daniella?"

"Yes, Miss Christy," Daniella responded her eyes still closed but smiling. "I can't believe it's been almost a year since you rescued me."

"I was just talking about the beautiful day by the water," Christy laughed, "but, yes, it is hard to believe how much has changed in your life. You have grown and look so much healthier!"

"Yes, Miss Sherri keeps us busy with chores and exercise when we are not in class. Nobody stays fat with Miss Sherri!"

"You were anything but heavy when I first met you. You looked malnourished."

"We had little food for our family in Honduras and then the gang...they fed us only drugs. They controlled us that way," Daniella stated factually.

Christy, Dr. Christine Tabrizi, was an emergency medicine physician in Duluth, Georgia a suburb northeast of Atlanta. Two years ago, Daniella had been lured into a cartel human trafficking ring in Honduras. She was prostituted extensively throughout various cities until she presented in Christy's emergency department with an infected miscarriage. The astute nursing staff suspected something was amiss and they quickly realized Daniella was being prostituted by a local gang. Christy and her friend Stacy, an OB/GYN treated Daniella and then worked out a way to rescue Daniella from her handlers. They eventually got her into the Adult and Teen Challenge facility here in Cape Cod where she had been receiving treatment for her drug addiction, along with schooling and vocational training.

Christy had dropped Daniella off here a year ago, scared, lonely, in the waning stages of narcotic withdrawal, and possessing minimal English skills. Today, Daniella sat before her thriving and content. The waifish girl was transforming into a poised young woman. Christy so wished Stacy could have made the trip with her.

It had been a delightful day. Christy had picked up Daniella from the center earlier this morning. They drove up to Provincetown and embarked on a whale watching tour. Much to their delight, they had seen several of the magnificent creatures, one even graced them with a nearby jump out of the water. They arrived back in Barnstable a few hours ago and Christy took Daniella clothes shopping. Daniella was wearing one of the purchases while the rest were stashed in the SUV Christy rented. They came down to the waterfront to relax and catch an early dinner before Daniella had to return to the facility.

As if on cue, Christy's phone vibrated signaling an incoming text. Their table was ready.

"That's our table. Are you ready?"

"Yes!" Daniella exclaimed, as she quickly rose.

Christy stood and walked with her into their favorite local eatery, The Black Cat Cafe. This was Christy's third trip back to visit Daniella since she first brought her up here. They had stumbled on the Black

Cat by chance one warm day last fall. Daniella had never tasted lobster before and became an instant fan of their lobster roll. The hostess seated them at a table with a decent view of the harbor. There was a flat screen television behind the bar tuned to a news station. The Red Sox wouldn't be on for another two hours.

"Miss Christy? Is that the Niagara Falls?" Daniella asked pointing toward the television.

Christy turned to look and saw the news broadcast with Niagara Falls in the background.

"Why, yes, Daniella, it is."

"We just learned about the Niagara Falls. They are one of the seven natural wonders of the world. Carved by glaciers during the Ice Age. I hope to visit them one day."

"I'll tell you what. Why don't we make plans to visit them next summer?"

"Really?" Daniella asked, her eyes lighting up.

"Sure! You'll have graduated Teen Challenge by then and we will be able to go anywhere we want. We can visit Niagara Falls, Toronto, New York City, and many other places. I want you to show you so many things. What do you say?"

"I say yes! Thank you, Miss Christy!"

"Sure sounds like fun! Can I come along?" Asked the waitress who had just approached their table.

"Sure! The more the merrier," Christy said with a laugh.

The server set down a couple of menus and took their drink orders.

"So can you believe that?" The server pointed to the television screen.

"Believe what?" Christine asked.

"You haven't heard? Some guy went over Niagara Falls and survived! It's been on the news all day!"

"What?" Christy asked, as she whirled to face the television screen just as the news cut to a different story.

"Yeah, some guy went over earlier today. Some kind of boating accident. He somehow survived. It's big news. I'll be right back with your iced teas," the server said as she walked off.

"So where were we?" Christy asked as she turned back to face Daniella. "Oh, yes, next summer. We will have to extend your visa and start working on your citizenship so we may have to stay on the American side, but we'll still go. What we need to do is start planning what you're going to do after your graduate Teen Challenge. Any thoughts?"

"I don't know. I don't like to think about it."

"What would you like to do?"

"I think about helping people in the hospital like you did for me."

"That's great. Like a nurse or a doctor?"

"A nurse perhaps, I don't know if I could be a doctor."

"Well, Miss Sherri says you show a lot of promise and that you are very close to completing your GED. Maybe we could get you certified as a Nurse Assistant and then you could work in our ER while you attend nursing school. Many of our nurses earned their RN working as CNA's while attending nearby Gwinnett Tech. You can live with me."

"Miss Christy, you have done so much for me already. I could never ask this of you."

"You're not asking. I'm offering."

"I don't know what to say. This is too kind."

"Say yes. I've always wanted a little sister," Christy said with a reassuring smile.

"But what if you get boyfriend or get married? Won't I be a…how do you say…a pain?"

"First of all, there is currently no man in my life. Second, even if there was, he would have to be the kind of man that would appreciate and accept you and support what I am doing for you or he would not be in my life for long."

"Then, I say yes. And thank you," Daniella was barely able to finish the sentence as her eyes teared up.

Christy's phone began to vibrate again as it lay on the table. Christy looked at the caller ID and saw the call was from Maria O'Shanick.

"Excuse me for a second, Daniella. This might be important," Christy said apologetically as she took the call. "Well, hello, Mrs. O'Shanick!"

Chapter 13

Niagara Falls, New York

"That's why Coach Matthews wouldn't let you be the punter," Jacob O'Shanick teased his younger brother after Joe told them how he missed the lifeline ball before going over the Falls.

"Yeah, O'Shanick," Jacob went on doing his best Coach Matthews impression, "you might punt the ball a mile, but you couldn't catch a cold!"

Joe's hospital room broke out in laughter as his family laughed at his expense. The O'Shanicks were a tight-knit family but, a good amount of the glue consisted of friendly teasing and sarcasm. Joe laughed as well, grimacing as he did so.

A knock came at the door. A tall, stately black man stood in the doorway. He wore blue surgical scrubs and had a New York Yankees surgical cap covering closely cropped hair.

"Mind if I interrupt?" He asked.

"Not at all, Doctor Bynum, come on in," Joe answered. "These are my parents, Jack and Maria O'Shanick," Joe said gesturing, "and over here are my brothers Jacob and Sean, my sister-in-law Barb, and my sisters Marina and Anna. Anna is an ER nurse over at ECMC."

"Oh, really?" he said, making eye contact with Anna. "That's where I did my residency once upon a time. Well, it's nice to meet you all," Dr. Ron Bynum said smiling, as he took the time to shake everyone's hand.

"Joe, here, is a genuine miracle!" He boomed in his baritone voice. "I've been working trauma in the Falls for nearly ten years and I've never met someone who survived the drop."

"I went over all your scans myself, like I said I would, and, other than the rib fractures and the collapsed lung, I don't see any other injuries. You're not even showing any lung inflammation like we often see in near drowning victims. It's really quite remarkable."

"I think you said it right when you said 'miracle,'" Joe's mother stated.

"You're quite right, ma'am," Dr. Bynum smiled in her direction. Turning to Joe, "May I take a quick listen and then I'll get out of your hair?"

"Yes, sir," Joe answered, obediently sitting forward and taking deep breaths as the doctor listened to several spots on his back.

Finishing, he removed the stethoscope from his ears and looked at Joe.

"Any pain when you breathe?"

"Not really," Joe replied, which was met with stern looks from his mother and Anna.

"I'm serious!" Joe emphasized, which was then met by an equally stern look from Dr. Bynum.

"Alright, just a little, but I don't need any pain meds."

"SEALs," Dr. Bynum said, shaking his head with mock disapproval.

"I'll be back in the morning, sailor. If your chest X-ray looks good, we'll turn off the suction here," Bynum gestured to the suction hose leading to the Pleurovac, which provided a water seal to prevent air from re-entering the pleural space between Joe's lung and chest wall, "and, if your lung stays re-inflated, I'll remove the chest tube tomorrow afternoon."

"And then I can go home?" Joe asked smiling.

"No. We'll watch you one more night and if your lung is still good, I'll let you out of here Friday morning."

"Fair enough. Thank you, Dr. Bynum."

"Is there anything you need, sailor?"

"If you could have the nurse bring me one of those jugs, my eyeballs are floating!" Joe said unashamedly.

"Oh, Joe!" His mother exclaimed embarrassed.

As Dr. Bynum walked out, he laughed along with rest of the family. Jacob, laughing, reached for the water pitcher and held it a foot above Joe's Styrofoam cup as he dramatically poured into it, deliberately taunting Joe. Anna, Joe's doting little sister, had mercy on Joe and quietly slipped out and returned with a bedside urinal, to Joe's relief.

"You always did like him better," said Jacob, shaking his head as he kept pouring water in front of Joe. Anna, true to her spunky self, flicked some of the water into Jacob's face as she gave him a mirthful stare to the family's amusement.

"Serves you right, you big meanie!" Jacob's wife, Barbara, scolded playfully as she and Anna shared a high five.

"How did that doctor know you're a SEAL, son?" Jack O'Shanick asked. "You never tell anyone what you do."

"He guessed."

"He guessed?" Marina asked.

"Truth be told, he was Army Special Forces before he went to medical school." Joe replied. "Us spec ops guys can kind of sense it in each other. Don't ask me how. It's above my pay grade."

"Did you sense it in him?" Sean asked.

"No, he was wearing a white coat earlier and it threw off the scent," Joe said, smiling at his younger brother.

Another knock came at the door. Joe's nurse, a young Italian woman named Gina stepped in.

"Hey, a couple of things. There are several news reporters downstairs requesting an interview..."

"I'll pass, thank you," Joe replied, cutting her off.

"Really? Your story is all over the national news! You don't want to talk to them?"

"Not really. Please tell me they don't have my name."

"Not that I know of and the hospital won't give your name without permission."

"Good. I'd prefer to stay out of the spotlight."

"That's fine, I'm just checking. The other thing was, are you sure you don't want dinner tonight?"

"No thanks, ma'am. I'm only in town for a short stay. I'm loading up on all the finest Buffalo has to offer."

"I get it. My brother lives in Vegas and he's the same way when he comes home. Marino's is just a couple of blocks up Pine and they have good everything. We order from there all the time."

Joe looked over at Sean. "You up for it?" Sean was Joe's junk food partner whenever Joe was back visiting.

"Yeah, man, or I could make a Mighty Taco run."

"Oh, Mighty!" Joe exclaimed. "I vote Mighty. Two Super Mightys."

"You got it. Anyone else?"

"Not us," Jack said apologetically, "we've got to get back and close down the shop. You gonna be alright, son?"

"I'm fine, Dad." Joe said as his mother moved in closer and kissed him.

"God worked a miracle today, Joe. He kept you alive because He has a plan for you," Maria said softly with tears in her eyes as she held her son's face in both hands. "I love you."

"I love you too, Mom."

Maria held his face a little longer as her almond-shaped eyes communicated an unspoken message.

"I know, Mom."

Maria gently smiled as she let go of Joe's face and turned for the door.

Chapter 14

"An unidentified man is in stable condition tonight after a frightening brush with death when he went over Niagara Falls. Witnesses state that the man was first spotted in the rapids near Three Sisters Island and appeared to be struggling to reach shore. Park Police state..."

Angelo and Terry stared in silence at the newscast playing on the TV behind the bar at The Power City Club. Angelo looked around nervously.

"That can't be our guy, Terry!" He said in a hushed voice. "No way would he have lived after we ran over him. No way!"

"Can it, Ange! I don't know if that's our guy or not, but there's big ears in here. You want this getting back to your uncle?"

"No! Are you kidding me? He'd throw us over the Falls next!"

"Alright then. Let's get out of here and we'll go figure this out," Terry stood and looked around.

The club was about half full. The Power City Club was a privately owned, members only club for friends and associates of the Catalano family. It occupied a building where a once popular landmark restaurant had operated for decades. There was a bar up front with a large lounge beyond that consisted of a dozen round tables, many of which currently were covered with playing cards, cash, and a variety of cocktail glasses, while surrounded by mostly middle age or older members. A few members were eating bowls of tripe, an Italian delicacy that one of the members had worked up in the kitchen that afternoon. The members took turns each day whipping up favorite recipes for each other. Outside, the club had several well-manicured Bocce courts and several games were underway.

"C'mon, let's head over to the shop," Terry said, as he decided there were no suspicious eyes upon them.

They walked a few blocks up Pine Avenue until they arrived at the auto collision shop that both Terry and Angelo worked out of. Although Terry was the official manager, auto repair and collision operations were actually run by his head mechanic. Terry used the shop as a base of operations for several less than legal activities, drug distribution, prostitution, extortion, and gambling chief among them. In addition to the legitimate auto repair and collision, the auto shop was also used as a chop shop for stolen cars.

The entire operation fell under the purview of the Catalano Family, with this area overseen by Frank Pandolfino, the Capo or crew leader, for whom Terry and Angelo worked. Terry had been extremely productive for Frank in many ongoing operations. He held Frank's favor, as well as that of Bruno Catalano, the current head of the Catalano Family.

Angelo was Bruno's nephew. The illegitimate son of Bruno's wayward brother, Carlo. Carlo had been a thorn in Bruno's side for years. His indiscretions and predisposition to brag had led to several incidents affecting the Family that should never have happened. Carlo's weakness for drugs and women was forgivable to Bruno. Having a loose mouth was not. Bruno had shut his younger brother up for good several years ago. The authorities had correctly ruled Carlo's death a heroin overdose. The error in the conclusion was that it was accidental. At gunpoint, Bruno had given Carlo a choice to either shoot an extremely large amount of heroin and exit peacefully or be fed feet first into a woodchipper.

Angelo's formative and teenage years had been spent in his mother's house and on the streets. Having more important things to keep him occupied, Bruno had paid little attention to his dead brother's offspring until Bruno's mother asked him to get involved. Bruno had little love for the kid, but he brought him into the family to keep him under his thumb. He assigned Angelo to Frank's crew. Frank wasn't happy, but he knew better than to argue with Bruno, so he assigned the kid to his chief leg breaker, Terry Wood.

Frank liked Terry and he really liked the income Terry brought in for the crew. He figured a guy like Terry might just be able to make a guy like Angelo useful. He also knew Terry wouldn't put up a fuss. Being half Irish, Terry could never be a full made member of the Family. He would always have only one foot in and one foot out. That made him expendable. So long as he did what he was told and produced for the Family, Terry would be fine. The day that changed, Terry would find himself weighted down with cinder blocks and sinking into the depths of Lake Ontario.

Terry was smart and he understood his place in Frank's crew; however, he also knew that neither Frank nor Bruno cared much for Angelo. Terry used this to his advantage and leveraged Angelo's desire to fit in to develop a loyalty to Terry. Angelo wasn't the sharpest tool in the shed, but his loyalty meant that Terry could count on him to do his job and keep his mouth shut. As long as they produced and Angelo spoke well of Terry to Frank and Bruno, Terry was good to keep his part of the family operating.

Angelo kept silent the entire walk up from the Power City Club. Once they reached the safe confines of Terry's office, the words erupted out of him.

"Terry, I don't get it. That's got to be somebody else, man! It can't be our guy!"

"I know, Ange, now shut up and let me think a minute!"

"I mean it just can't be!" Angelo continued nervously. "Look, I've still got the video I shot of us running him over. It's right here," he said, thrusting his cell phone in front of Terry.

"Would you shut up and calm down!" Terry yelled in anger. "Let's think this through," he said more calmly. "We ran right over him at close to seventy miles an hour in a big boat. That alone should have killed him. He was on the East River which means he should have gone over the American Falls and his body is likely stuck behind a rock. I don't see how that can be our guy, but we can't afford to be wrong. We mess a hit like this up and your uncle will be tossing us over the Falls, just like you said. We gotta make sure."

"What was the deal with that guy anyway? Why did Uncle Bruno want him whacked?"

"I don't know, but I also know not to ask. All I know is the Panda..." Terry used Frank Pandolfino's nickname, "...told me that the guy was some kind of special forces commando and to be extra careful. He also said to make it look like an accident. That's why we stole that boat and ran him over when Paulie P told us the guy was going sailing."

"So how do we make sure the guy in the hospital ain't him?"

"I know a chick who works in the hospital. I'll ask her."

Chapter 15

$\mathcal{T}$rina Sylvestri walked into the bar and looked around. She spotted several nurses she knew gathered around the far end and made her way down towards them. The bar was a local hangout, popular among the hospital workers due to its proximity making it a convenient place to stop and decompress after a hectic shift. Trina was off today, but Terry's call a half hour ago led her to walk down here. The day nurses had just finished their 7am to 7pm shift and many were gathered in their various department "cliques."

Trina ambled over to her fellow ER nurses to begin her fact-finding mission.

"Hey, guys!" She smiled.

"Trina!" Several answered, and hugs were exchanged.

"What brings you down here on your day off?" Matt, a tall male nurse with a goatee, closely cropped hair and a biker's look, asked.

"Well, truth be told, I wanted to hear first-hand about the guy that went over the Falls."

The bartender caught her eye, "White Zinfandel, please," she said, dropping a five-dollar bill on the bar.

"You'll have to hear it from Amanda," Matt answered, as he gestured toward the petite nurse propped up on one of the barstools. "She and Judy had that one."

"So what really happened?" Trina asked as the entire group turned their attention to Amanda.

"He wasn't exactly sure. He said he was out sailing and some speed boat ran right over him knocking him out. He woke up just before he hit the rapids. He tried to make it to Goat Island, but didn't make it. He remembers tumbling in the water and the next thing he remembered was being hauled up onto the Maid of the Mist."

"That's amazing! How bad is he injured?"

"Not as bad as you'd think," Amanda smiled, shaking her head in appreciation. "A mild concussion, two broken ribs, and a pneumothorax. That's it."

"No way! After going over the Falls?" Another nurse asked.

"Yeah, I'm serious. That was it. I couldn't believe it either. If he hadn't gotten a chest tube, he might have gone home."

"Lucky mother trucker!" Matt added.

"Oh, but you should see this guy!" Amanda added slyly. "Talk about tall, dark, and handsome, and this guy was ripped! There wasn't an ounce of fat on him. I could have started a 14 gauge IV on those bulging veins without using a tourniquet!"

"Don't get much of that around here," another nurse commented.

"No kidding," Trina nodded in agreement. "So what does he do?" She asked, turning her attention back to Amanda. "Is he from around here?"

"Actually, he went to high school on Grand Island with Doctor Alendretti. They're good friends. Doctor Alendretti said this guy is a Navy SEAL. He was the one that was given a medal by President Galan last year after rescuing a female ER doctor from the cartels."

"I remember that!" Trina exclaimed. "That was in the Rose Garden at the White House last fall! Oh, he IS a good-looking guy! Lucky you, Amanda!"

Amanda smiled and raised her eyebrows in response.

"So did he go to the floor or the ICU," Trina asked.

"Just the floor. Med-surge. In fact..." Amanda said looking behind Trina, "...I handed him off to Gina Scriviano up on the floor. She's standing over there," Amanda indicated, with a nod behind Trina. The entire group looked in unison over to where Gina and some of the med-surge nurses were gathered. Gina sensed the attention and looked back. Amanda waved her over.

"Gina, you know everybody here, right?"

"Sure. Hey, Trina! Hey, Matt."

"I was just telling everyone about the patient I handed off to you today," Amanda explained. "No one can believe it."

"I know! And he's such a nice guy too; his entire family is. He's got a cute younger brother. I almost invited him over here when I left."

"You should have!" Trina said, as she playfully backhanded Gina. "Are you working tomorrow? Maybe you'll get another chance."

"Hmm...true and, yes, I am working through Friday. He'll likely get the chest tube out tomorrow and go home Friday."

Trina casually took her phone out of her purse and fired off a quick text. She signaled the bartender with another five-dollar bill.

"Another White Zinfandel, Rob?" Mission accomplished.

Terry's phone vibrated in his pocket. He tried to reach into his pocket to retrieve it but was inhibited by the girl seated on his lap. The girl was wearing a tight miniskirt and a tube top that left little to the imagination. She was hunched over Terry's desk snorting a line of coke up her nose. Hoping this was Trina with some good news, Terry shoved the prostitute off his lap as he slid his chair back.

"Hey!" She protested.

"Shut up and do your lines. I gotta take this."

Terry pulled his phone out and looked down at the screen. He shouted a string of expletives and stood up. Grabbing the young girl by the arm, Terry roughly shoved her towards the door.

"Terry! I still have another line to do!"

"Them's the breaks, sweetheart. Maybe tomorrow," Terry said, as he pushed her into the hallway. "You know where the door is. Get your friend and go check back in with Marco. Tell him your back on duty tonight."

"Angelo!" Terry yelled down the hall. "Get down here, now!"

Angelo darted out of the head mechanic's office pulling his tank top back on. "What is it?"

"Tell the girl to check back in with Marco. You and I got work to do.

"But, Terry, can't it wait?"

"Now, numbskull!"

"Alright, alright!"
A minute later, Angelo nervously hurried into Terry's office.
"What's wrong, Terry?"
"We got a problem."

51

Chapter 16

Joe lay quietly in his room. He hadn't slept well. That was unusual. Having a chest tube protruding from his left chest limited his sleeping options to laying on his back or on his right side. He could usually sleep regardless of the circumstances or position, a necessary skill learned from years in special forces. He knew it was more than just positional.

Looking back, there were numerous times during combat when he had felt a bullet fly past him in very close proximity. Too many to count, really. Each occurrence could have been considered a near brush with death, but they never truly registered as such. The reality of dying during a combat operation was always there, but Joe simply acknowledged it, compartmentalized it, and mounted up without giving it another thought. Yesterday's experience was different. When Joe hit the rapids, he knew he was going to die. While he was tumbling over the Falls, he knew that his ticket had been punched. The fact that he was laying safe in a hospital bed defied all logic.

He could accept that. Stranger things had happened. What kept him awake was the thought of where he would be had he actually died. Despite his family's religious background, Joe went down a different path. He had seen too much evil in the world to believe that an omnipotent all-knowing god, who refused to intervene, could possibly exist. To Joe, religion seemed to be more of a crutch for most people. In his opinion, there was nothing substantial to base the belief on, but it sure was something many clung to during trying times. Joe had never felt the need. He excelled in sports and academics, earned his way into the Naval Academy, and started all four years on the Lacrosse team before passing the ultimate test and becoming a Navy SEAL. Not once did he call on any magical man in the sky to help him. Joe earned it all through developed skill, hard work, and sheer determination. He didn't begrudge other people for being religious and he certainly respected his family and how they lived out their faith. Joe simply hadn't seen any need for it in his life and rationalized it by convincing himself that there likely wasn't a god. His mother and his sisters had tried to convince him otherwise, but he wouldn't budge.

That was beginning to change. It began last fall when he had been captured along with Christy Tabrizi, the ER physician his platoon had been sent to rescue. Joe and Christy eventually escaped, but spent a couple of days in close proximity aboard a sailboat evading the cartel members who pursued them. As a situation close aboard during perilous times can do, Joe and Christy engaged in many deep conversations. Christy's strong Christian faith was readily apparent and several of the conversations had centered around matters of faith. To Joe's surprise, Christy showed herself to have a commanding knowledge of the Christian faith and also had many intelligent, thought provoking answers to Joe's challenges.

They kept in touch over the past eight months and engaged in several similar conversations. Christy never forced her beliefs on Joe. Rather, she simply asked questions that forced Joe to examine his own beliefs. He occasionally realized that some of his beliefs didn't have as firm of a foundation as he had thought. Conversely, he would challenge Christy on some fundamental issues and, to his surprise, she didn't respond with the "just have faith" answers many other people used. Her answers were rooted in sound intellectual, philosophical and, most notably, scientific reasoning. Her faith was not blind, but was actually based on evidence and reason. That left an impression on Joe. He wasn't a "believer." Far from it, but he was honest enough to acknowledge there likely is a God and, very possibly, the God Christy and his family served.

Joe was content with that. At least he had kept an open mind. Having been an agnostic, admittedly more likely an atheist, he knew many other atheists who were downright hostile towards people of faith. He didn't get that at all. If other people wanted to be religious, it didn't affect him. Several of his fellow SEALs were devout in their faith and Joe never doubted their bonafides or dependability. Live and let live.

That wasn't what had kept Joe from sleeping. *What if all that is true? I should have died. Where would I be? Man, I wish Christy was here!*

Try as he might, Joe had not been able to stop thinking about Christy since their experience last fall. He found himself irresistibly attracted to her, but he knew it was hopeless. They were from two different worlds. Christy was a beautiful, intelligent physician, refined, purposeful and compassionate. Above all, she was a dedicated Christian. Joe was merely a warrior. Yes, a highly trained elite operator, but still a warrior. A rough around the edges door kicker with bloody hands and a jaded, skeptical worldview. Christy actually did more to maintain their friendship over the past eight months but, Joe suspected, it was her commitment to leading lost souls like him to Christ. He knew she genuinely cared, but he was resigned to the fact that she was forbidden fruit. Although they talked many times on the phone, texted often, and kept in touch by email, Joe had not seen her in person since the ceremony at The White House last fall. At the time, he had not even considered anything beyond a friendship forged in fire. As beautiful and intellectually appealing as she was, he couldn't get past her spirituality, and was not interested in pursuing any such relationship. As they were going their separate ways, Christy hugged Joe goodbye and thanked him one last time. Unbeknownst to her, that hug sparked a small flame in Joe that had been growing ever since. She was still out of his league but, right now, he could sure use her voice of reason to help him sort out the conflicting thoughts his brush with death created.

Joe's thoughts were interrupted by a knock at his door. In walked another petite brunette nurse.

"Good morning," Joe said, in greeting, which seemed to startle the nurse. "Are you the day shift nurse?"

"No, I'm part of the night shift. Your day nurse will be in shortly. I'm just hanging some antibiotics that were written for you."

"Gotcha, thanks." Joe said, as he looked to see her name. The room was still dark, and he couldn't see her ID badge.

The nurse quietly placed a small IV packet on the pole, ran the line through an available pump and connected it to a port on Joe's IV. She programmed the pump and then quietly stepped out.

Almost immediately, another knock, this one quiet and tentative, came at the door.

"Come in," Joe answered.

Yet another petite brunette stepped in. *Man, they grow on trees up here!*

"Joe?" It was his little sister Anna. Definitely petite and brunette, and, like Joe and Marina, a perfect blend of their Filipino mother and dark Irish father.

"Hey, Squirt! C'mon in," Joe said, waving her in.

"How was your night?"

"Not bad. I'll sleep better once this chest tube is out."

"How are you feeling?"

"Better, now that my favorite nurse is here." Joe said, holding his arms open.

"I love you, Brother Bear," Anna said, as she leaned over for a hug. "I was hoping to catch your overnight nurse before her shift ended and get a report. Has she been in recently?"

"You just missed one of them. She literally walked out thirty seconds before you got here. She came in to hang some antibiotics."

"Why are you getting antibiotics?" Anna asked, sounding confused as she walked over to the IV tree and looked at the IV bag.

"I'm not sure, actually. She didn't tell me. I didn't even think to question her."

"You don't have any wounds, do you? I didn't think you did. Do you?" Anna asked as she turned on the low-level fluorescent light on the wall.

"No. Maybe it's for the chest tube?"

"No, that's not usually done for chest tubes..." Anna's voice trailed off as she read the label on the antibiotic bag. "What the...?"

"What is it, Anna?"

"Holy...!" Anna nearly completed the sentence as she pivoted to Joe's IV and engaged the roller clamp, instantly stopping the flow of the medication.

"Anna!" Joe said, sensing the alarm in her voice. "What is it?"

Anna punched a command into the IV pump and stormed out of the room. A short time later she came back in with Joe's day nurse, Gina, in tow.

"Who hung this?" Anna asked angrily.

"I don't know, I just got here. I haven't even been in here yet. What is it?"

"Look for yourself!" Anna said, thrusting the bag out in front.

"The label says Ceftriaxone. I wasn't aware he was getting an antibiotic. It must have been ordered this morning and just hung. It still looks full. You must have stopped it shortly after it was started."

"And you didn't hang this?" Anna asked.

"No, I wasn't even aware of it. His overnight nurse didn't mention it in report."

"Joe, did you see who brought this in?"

"Yes, but it wasn't Heather, the night nurse and it certainly wasn't Gina here. She told me she was someone else from the floor."

"What was her name?" Gina asked.

"I don't know, I couldn't see her badge. It was dark."

"What did she look like?"

"Like half the other nurses around here; young, petite, dark hair, Italian."

"I'm not sure who it was, but I'll find out. She must have walked into the wrong room with someone else's antibiotics. What's the patient's name? That might help us figure out which nurse did it."

"We're going to need to do more than that," Anna stated. "We're gonna need the police."

"What? Why?" Gina asked.

Joe felt like he was watching a tennis match with his head swiveling between the two nurses.

"Look closer at the bag," Anna instructed.

"It's Ceftriaxone, two grams," Gina said, leaning in to read the label. "An antibiotic."

"Yes, that's what the printed label says, but look at what the bag says."

Gina studied the bag closer. Her eyes went wide in sudden realization.

"Potassium Chloride!" she exclaimed in surprise. "That's a huge screw up. How fast was it going?"

"It was wide open," Anna stated emotionally.

"WHAT?!" Gina gasped.

"That's right," Anna replied. "Someone almost killed my brother."

Chapter 17

*J*oe reflected on the beehive of activity that ensued after the police arrived. They immediately declared his room a crime scene. The IV bag, line, and pump were collected for evidence. Gina was interviewed, along with every floor nurse and Certified Nurse Assistant, CNA for short, from both shifts. Nobody could figure out who the mysterious nurse was. All medications were physician-ordered through the electronic chart and no such order had been found. Once Joe was determined to have been unharmed, his name had been replaced with a trauma number and he was moved to a new floor with security only allowing pre-approved visitors.

Anna had stayed with him the entire time. Joe was fully aware that, had it not been for her nursing knowledge and sharp instincts, he very well could have been killed, again. Outwardly, Anna had assumed the role of mother grizzly bear for her big brother but, inside, she was close to tears thinking that she had nearly stopped for coffee on her way in and, had she done so, her brother would now be in the morgue. After talking it over with Joe and their mother, Anna made a list of pre-approved visitors who would be required to show ID in order to be allowed up to Joe's room.

"Joe? What is going on? Why would somebody try to kill you?"

"No clue, Anna. Are we sure that wasn't a medical mistake?"

"No, but there is no record of that order, the medication was mislabeled, no record of pharmacy error or missing medication, and nobody knows who it is that came into your room and hung the potassium chloride. You're the Navy SEAL. You tell me."

"I guess it's possible," Joe said contemplating.

"Any enemies?" She asked.

"Plenty, but most of them are dead. That was combat and special ops. Very few would know who I am or have such a vendetta. At least as far as I know and, certainly, nobody up here."

"Are you sure? As far as I can be, yes. I left for the Naval Academy right after high school and I have only been back for short visits."

"Anyone from high school?"

"Not that I can think of," Joe said, looking up at the ceiling in thought. "I never even got into so much as a fistfight."

"Well, you were made famous last year when President Galan awarded you a medal at the White House. Do you think that could have anything to do with it?"

"I suppose it's possible that some nutcase may have a self-perceived mission to fulfill for some reason, but I think that would be a bit of a stretch."

A soft knock came from the door.

"HEY!" Anna exclaimed joyfully as she leapt up, ran to the door and embraced the tall, slender, dark-haired figure in the doorway.

Joe's jaw dropped in disbelief as he instantly recognized the high cheek bones, strong chin, and emerald green eyes. She smiled as she stepped over to Joe's bed and leaned down for a hug. She squeezed hard. Joe felt his ribs protest, but they were overruled by his emotions.

"Hey, Joe," she spoke softly.

"Hey, Christy," Joe said, squeezing harder, "I can't believe it's really you!"

Chapter 18

Lewiston, New York

Frank Pandolfino anxiously weaved in and out of traffic as he sped north on the Robert Moses Parkway. He crested the Niagara Escarpment and began the descent into Lewiston. The Escarpment is essentially a cliff that runs many miles east and west, forming a division between the upper and lower tables of the Niagara Frontier. It was formed over eons by glacial and natural erosion. Niagara Falls began at the Escarpment but eroded several miles southward over many millennia. The downhill drive afforded a commanding view of the lower Niagara Region and Lake Ontario further north. It also created excess speed in less than vigilant drivers. Frank looked at the speedometer of his black Lincoln Town Car and saw that he was approaching ninety. He eased off the gas but wasn't too worried about being pulled over. Not around here.

Frank exited at the bottom of the hill, looped around, and turned left onto Ridge Road. A mile later he turned left onto a private drive cut through a thick stand of woods and drove a quarter of a mile past grazing cattle to a sprawling ranch house. He parked in the ample well-paved parking area and got out. Two well-dressed men, with large handguns exposed in shoulder holsters, met him in front of the house. They patted Frank down and ran a metal detecting wand over him. Satisfied, they nodded to the man waiting at the front door. The man opened the door, allowing Frank entrance and then led him through to the back of the house onto a well-appointed grilling patio.

Off to the right, standing over one of two large built-in stainless steel grills, was a muscular male wearing khaki pants and a golf shirt. Big band Sinatra music played from the outdoor speakers and he sang along with a gruff voice as he gently worked a grill full of Italian sausage, onions and peppers. Spotting Frank, the man turned.

"Hey! Frankie The Panda! C'mere, paisano!"

Frank stepped forward and Bruno accepted the traditional Italian greeting from Bruno Catalano. There was no kissing the Don's hand with Bruno like on TV. Bruno decided who he would greet and how he would greet them. Frank breathed a sigh of relief. Being summoned to Bruno's private estate was no small thing and one never knew what it meant. Rumor had it that some of Frank's predecessors had driven up the long drive and were never seen or heard from again.

"Fix yourself a drink, Frankie," Bruno said, pointing to the outdoor bars, "the sausage is almost ready."

"Thank you, Mr. Catalano,"

"Please, Frankie, call me Papa Bruno, my friend!"

"Thank you, Papa Bruno," Frank said, as he walked behind the bar. It was all top shelf liquor and there were two draft beer taps. Frank dropped two ice cubes into a crystal old fashioned glass and poured in a generous measure of The MacAllan scotch.

"Can I get you anything, Papa Bruno?"

"No, Frankie, I'm good. Come, have a seat," he said, as he carried a serving plate of sausage with peppers and onions to a pre-set table.

"You're in for a treat, my friend! This was fresh-made this morning at Stefano's."

Bruno selected a long roll, placed a sausage link into it, and added an ample amount of cooked onions and peppers.

"Eat up, my friend, the rolls are fresh from DiCamillo's." Bruno smiled, before taking a large bite.

He chewed with a satisfied look as Frank prepared his own plate. They ate in silence for a few minutes while Sinatra's "This Town" played all around them. Frank looked out over the expansive land surrounding Bruno's estate. Bruno raised his own cattle. He sold most of it, but he was a steak fanatic and learned how to raise the best cattle.

He took great pride in his steaks and opened two steak restaurants. That wasn't the primary reason he selected this place. The main reason was that it was surrounded by woods with a large expanse of open ground between the woods and his house. This made for easier defense. Bruno didn't have much opposition but, with the ever expanding Russian mafia and the growing street gangs, he wasn't about to let his guard down. It wasn't that long ago that the mafia had all but disappeared in Western New York. It had been considered obsolete by the FBI until Bruno began to build a new family. New York State had essentially taken over the gambling industry a few decades ago when it established the lottery and off-track betting. When the manufacturing industry left, taking the labor unions with them, followed by various Iroquois nations receiving the green light to build casinos, the FBI thought the lights were out for the mafia. Knowing the casinos would bring in a demand for drugs and prostitutes, Bruno left the concrete industry in the hands of his son and focused on the expanding opportunities. He quickly built the family's presence up to where he regained control of the drug trade, prostitution, racketeering, and, thanks again to the casinos, loan sharking, from southern Ontario through Rochester, with the main focus being Buffalo and Niagara Falls.

Bruno finished his first Italian sausage and began to prepare a second. He gestured for Frank to do the same. He looked over to his bodyguard.

"Richard, take some out to the boys. Mangia!"

Richard, taking his cue, placed the basket of rolls and the serving bowl of sausage onto a tray and carried it into the house, leaving Frank alone with his boss. Bruno took a bite of Italian sausage and chewed, looking at Frank. Frank could feel sweat begin to break out on the back of his neck.

"The sailor. Do you have a good report for me?" Bruno took another bite.

The sweat began to build. Frank didn't like not having the best answer.

"I haven't heard yet, Papa Bruno," he answered truthfully.

"That disappoints me, Frank. I thought you would have had that issue resolved for me."

"I put Terry on it with your nephew. I told him the man was to be respected and to make it look like an accident. Terry is very good, but he is also very cautious. An assignment as delicate as this takes time to plan and execute, as you well know, Papa Bruno."

"What you say is true, Frankie, but are you aware that Terry has now tried not once but twice to kill this man and has failed both times?"

"No, Papa Bruno, I was not aware." Frank knew better than to lie and he certainly knew better than to ask how Bruno had learned of this. Bruno had eyes and ears everywhere. Bruno took another bite and chewed slowly, allowing Frank to dwell on this revelation.

"The second attempt has been brought to the authorities' attention and is now being investigated as attempted murder. They have connected it to the first attempt, perhaps you have heard of that one? The man who survived a trip over Niagara Falls?"

"Papa Bruno, I honestly did not know."

"Oh, you didn't know? I'm sorry. But then, how do I know? Now this mick O'Shanick knows. The police know. In fact, the entire world knows! But you don't know? Is that a fact?"

"Papa Bruno," Frank chose his words very carefully. "Terry is a mutt, but he's a good soldier. He always gets the results we want. I give him his space to get the job done and he reports to me when it is done. Not before. Yes, I could play mother hen and stay on top of what he is doing, but he has never given me reason to do so. That is how I have run my crew. My men have always produced and they have always been loyal. I, therefore, have no excuse nor do I seek one. I stand by my actions and I will accept whatever action you choose to take."

Bruno shoved the last of his lunch into his mouth and chewed thoughtfully as he looked at Frank. The sweat was now running down Frank's back. He wiped his mouth with a cloth napkin and set it back down.

"Your boy screwed up. I want you to handle this. The authorities know there was a murder attempt so it no longer has to look like an accident. I want a good report when I see you in church on Sunday. Now go," he finished with a dismissive wave.

"Thank you, Papa Bruno," Frank said, as he stood.

"That's Mr. Catalano to you, Frank."

Chapter 19

Niagara Falls, New York

"*H*ow did you know?" Joe asked, as Christy took the seat next to a smiling Anna.

"Oh, a little bird told me."

Joe immediately looked over at Anna.

"It wasn't me; I swear!"

"Oh, Mom then. Now why doesn't that surprise me? Don't you have to work?"

"I'm off until Monday. I was actually in Cape Cod visiting Daniella yesterday when your mother called me."

"How is Daniella?" Joe asked.

"She's absolutely thriving," Christy beamed. "She and I are making plans for her to move in with me when she finishes in December. And..." Christy grabbed Anna's forearm and smiled at her, "she is going to start nursing school!"

"Christy! That's great!" Anna exclaimed. "I can't wait to meet her."

"Well, when she gets settled in and starts school, maybe you'd like to come stay with us and help her get started?"

"Yes! I would love that!"

Joe watched in amazed silence at the exchange between his sister and Christy. Had he missed something? Anna had briefly met Christy at the White House ceremony and now they were carrying on like old friends. And since when did his mother know Christy well enough to be comfortable calling her about all of this? Thinking back, he recalled his mother exchanging contact information with Christy's mother. Like Christy, they were both strong women of faith and his mother was instantly charmed by Christy. He should have known friendship would grow out of that. Thinking about it, he realized he shouldn't have been surprised that his self-appointed match-maker, career manager, and now guardian, Anna, had struck up a friendship with Christy as well.

"So I see the chest tube. What is the extent of your injuries?"

"Just a couple of broken ribs and a collapsed lung," Joe replied nonchalantly.

"He also has a mild concussion with no cognitive deficits," Anna began, as she presented the official medical report to Christy. "Mild displaced fractures of ribs six and seven on the left, the lung has re-inflated and the Pleura-vac is now on water seal so, hopefully, the chest tube will be able to come out this afternoon. He's a walking miracle, Christy."

"I'll say."

"But we had an incident here this morning," Anna continued.

"What was that?"

"Somebody tried to kill Joe by bolusing in forty of potassium chloride."

"What?!" Christy gasped.

"We don't know that for sure," Joe said trying to downplay the incident. "It might have just been a medical error."

"I disagree, Christy," Anna said shaking her head.

Anna spent the next several minutes explaining what they knew. When she finished Christy looked over at Joe.

"I don't know, Joe. Medical mistakes *do* happen but that was pretty bad. What if yesterday wasn't an accident and these events are connected?"

"I don't know," Joe said doubtfully. "You know I'm trained to be vigilant, Christy, but nobody knew I was going sailing yesterday. I have a hard time believing that someone knew and had access to a boat and ran me over. If someone were really after me, there would be many easier ways than that."

"Like staging a medical error," Anna interjected.

"Yes," Joe answered. "That would be much more likely, but I'm still having a tough time believing that's what happened."

"Well, what if the cartels were after you?" Anna asked. "President Galan did honor you on national TV last year. What if they decided to make you a target?"

"Joe? Do you think this could have anything to do with our little run in with the cartel last fall?" Christy asked.

"I have no way of knowing," Joe answered. "It makes as much sense as anything else but I don't know why they would go to such extent to kill me up here or how they would even know I was here or how to get to me. Is it possible? Theoretically, yes. Likely? No," Joe finished with a shake of his head.."

"Their reach is beyond extensive, Joe," Christy answered. "You know that. They have enormous financial resources and they wield incredible influence over all of the criminal gangs and organized crime in every major city. The cartels are the suppliers of drug and human trafficking, and they have built up a huge network of influence around the country."

"Wow! Somebody's been doing their homework!" Joe exclaimed.

"Well, rescuing Daniella from a human trafficking ring and then being personally captured and nearly killed by a cartel will do that." Christy acknowledged. "They really are the face of evil."

"Joe, if that's the case, then you're not safe here," Anna said, with concern in her voice.

"If that's the case, Squirt, then I'm not safe anywhere. The cartels have a presence everywhere. Even in our government," Joe said, thinking of the blown rescue mission that led to Christy and him being captured, as well as half his platoon being killed last year. "That's one of the reasons we don't advertise that we're SEALs. There are enough radical jihadists in the States who would love to prove their worth by mounting a SEAL head on their trophy wall. I take precautions wherever I go but I'm not going to let fear rule over me and stop living, either."

"Well, could it be a jihadist then?" Anna asked.

"Possibly, but I doubt it. There is even less of a chance that they know who I am or that they would come after me in this way. They prefer to do things on a grand scale with mass casualties. If this was an actual attempt on me, it was more precise in its nature. More personal. Not what I would normally expect from a warring faction out for revenge." Joe said, trying to lighten the mood.

"I hope it *was* just a medical error." Anna replied. "But, I think we need to keep someone in here at all times to monitor your medical care, so we don't have another incident like we did this morning."

"That's a good idea, Anna," Christy replied. "I'm not flying back to Atlanta until Sunday afternoon so I can stay with Joe."

"We will share duties then," Anna answered, smiling as she squeezed Christy's hand.

Joe felt odd listening to his sister and Christy talk about keeping watch over him. He was the warrior, the one who stood watch for others, not the other way around. On the other hand, he desperately wanted some time with Christy in person. He would prefer better circumstances but, it is what it is, and he wasn't about to complain.

"Is this thing portable?" Joe asked, looking down at the Pleura-vac his chest tube was connected to.

"Yes, now that it's on water seal, it's not connected to the wall. Why?" Anna inquired.

"I'm sick of being cooped up in this bed. I need to walk."

"Good!" Anna said, as she hopped to her feet. "You've been slacking off. I've been meaning to talk to you about that," she said, removing the tape holding the Pleura-vac to the floor so it wouldn't tip.

"Joe? Not working out?" Christy asked in mock disbelief.

"Yep. Slacker. When was your last workout, Joe?" Anna asked, as she stood up holding the Pleura-vac like a briefcase.

"Yesterday," he said, wincing slightly as he swung his legs off the bed and stood up.

"Do you need a hand?" Christy asked.

"No, thanks, I'm good. Just a little stiff is all," Joe said, trying not to breathe deeply, feeling his ribs more now that he was up.

"Just breathe through it. It will loosen up," Anna coached, sensing what her brother was feeling.

Joe's legs loosened up, along with his breathing, as he reached the hall with Anna to his left and Christy to his right.

"Hey! Look who's up and about!" Joe's nurse, Gina, remarked, as they passed in front of the nurses' station.

"Just getting a few laps in before lunch," Joe said, smiling over at his nurse.

Anna and Christy noticed several other nurses and CNA's emerge from around the other side of the station. They passed the station and Anna looked back with a cross look at the onlookers, who all reacted by averting their gaze.. She knew Joe was tall, muscular, and ruggedly handsome, but it still creeped her out to know the entire floor was ogling her brother. She and Christy shared a brief knowing glance at each other and rolled their eyes.

"Speaking of lunch," Joe began, "did you bring my wallet?"

"Yes, it's in the room with your cell phone," Anne answered.

"Oh, good. Thanks. Oh, man, that reminds me. I need to call in and let my team know what's going on. Shoot! I hope this doesn't sideline me."

"Sideline you from what?" Christy asked.

"Green Team, the selection process for DEVGRU."

"Oh! You got in!" Christy exclaimed. "That's great, Joe!"

"All I did was clear the first hurdle. Green Team is an intense six-month selection process that is far more demanding and selective than BUDs. Most guys won't be selected for DEVGRU and these are elite, combat-hardened operators. I haven't made anything yet."

"When do you start?" Christy asked.

"September."

"You should be fine. Your ribs will be healed by then."

"Maybe, but I need to ramp up my training over the summer if I want to stand a chance."

"Your ribs will need a few weeks to heal before you will be able to do any intense workouts."

"That's going to be an issue. I already started getting ready. I really don't want to back off."

"You'll be fine, Joe. You've been deployed to a combat zone for the better part of a year. Your body could use a couple of weeks to recover. Trust me."

"Can I still do *some* things?"

"Yes, so long as you listen to your body and don't overdo it."

"Well right now, my body is saying it's lunchtime." Joe looked at Anna. "I'll spring if you fetch."

"Deal. What should we get?"

"Well, since Christy went to all the trouble to grace us with her presence, I think we owe it to her to introduce her to some real Buffalo fare."

"Riiiight!" Anna agreed, as she smiled slyly at Christy. "So...what should we start her off with?"

"Well," Joe said, whispering into Anna's ear, "I'll be home tomorrow so we'll hit Sean's place for wings then. Let's go with chicken finger subs, but we better keep hers to medium hot."

"I know just the place! It's just up the street," Anna smiled.

"What am I in for?" Christy asked.

"It's a surprise, but you'll love it. Trust me!" Anna beamed.

"There should be plenty of cash in my wallet," Joe said, nodding toward the door to his room as they completed the first lap around the nurses' station.

Anna dashed into the room, emerging seconds later and took off down the hall. Joe and Christy settled into the next trip around the floor.

"Joe, I hope you don't mind that I popped in on you unannounced."

"Are you kidding me? I've been wanting to see you for months! Seeing you walk in made my day!"

"Really?"

"Yes! I've really missed you, and there is so much I want to talk to you about."

"Like what?" Christy asked.

"Well, like lots of things," Joe said, suddenly short on words.

There it was again. Joe never felt a need to impress a woman. In Virginia Beach, there were women who went prowling for SEALs, Frog Hogs as they were known, but in the "Me too" age, Joe had decided they were best avoided. Since most of the intelligent, secure women his age were either married or divorced, there were few, if any, worth getting to know. Joe, being married to the Teams, had long gotten used to his perpetual bachelorhood, much to the disappointment of Anna and his mother; however, when it came to Christy, despite his growing interest, he felt so inadequate around her that he often found himself tongue tied. He was more comfortable conducting a night jump at high altitude over the ocean. Fortunately, Joe was well acquainted with challenge.

"Like what things?" Christy persisted.

"Like, what you've been up to, how your race went last month, how your work's going, and," Joe paused, "some of the things we've been talking about these past few months."

"Ah," Christy said knowingly, "so I *have* had an effect on you!"

"More than you know, Christy."

Chapter 20

Angelo shielded his eyes from the bright fluorescent lights as he walked down the hallway toward Terry's office. His head throbbed from the previous night's coke and alcohol binge. It took two lines just to get out of bed and another two in the parking lot just to make his way into the shop. Glancing at his watch, Angelo quietly cursed knowing he was going to catch an earful from Terry for being late, again.

Reaching the door, Angelo knocked two quick raps, waited two seconds and gave two more. He heard the door unlock and open a crack. He could see the dark eyes and long sharp nose of Johnny "The Blade" Colucci peering through the opening. He gave a disdainful shake of his head and let Angelo in.

"Where ya been, ya deadbeat?" Terry asked, without bothering to look up. He sat behind his desk, which was filled with stacks of bills organized by different denominations that he was feeding into a bill counting machine. The Blade joined him at the desk sorting out another pile of cash.

"I'm sorry, Terry, my alarm didn't go off."

"Did I ask for your excuses?"

"Well, you asked where I was and..."

"Do me a favor and shut up, you meatball. I had to pull Blade in here to help me with the daily count while you was sleeping off your hangover. You think your uncle would be happy if he knew that?"

"No, Terry, I know. Look, I'm sorry. It won't happen again."

"You won't let it happen again, huh? You know how many times I've heard you say that?"

"Yeah, I know, Terry."

"Yeah, you know? You know nothin', dipstick! The Panda puts you in my crew so's I can teach you the business for your uncle and I gotta spend my time babysittin' your stupid, hairy..."

A ring sounded from the loading dock, interrupting Terry.

"Good, that must be your Cousin Shady from the auto parts store," Terry said easing his tone. "Go make yourself useful and let him in. Separate the inventory. You think you can handle that without screwing it up?"

"Yeah, Terry."

"Good, then go do it! And get everything set up in the tool room. Once I'm done here, we've gotta cut and package the coke," Terry said, as Angelo headed out the door.

"You really trust that idiot to handle the coke when you ain't around, Terry?"

"He's stupid, but he ain't that stupid, Blade. Those kilos come straight from Frank's parts store unopened. Angelo knows I can tell if anyone messes with them. He also knows that if he helps himself to the goods, I'll mess his nose up so bad he'll never be able to snort a line, ever again."

"You mean like you did with Jose?"

"Keep a lid on it, Blade. As far as everyone knows, he went back home to Mexico."

Terry didn't like tales being told out of school, especially tales that could bring him unwanted attention. On the other hand, a little "folklore" of what happened when the help got out of line was good for keeping up the honesty among the criminals. Ironic as that sounds.

Just then, a pounding began on the door.

"What do you want?" Terry growled, annoyed.

"Open the door, you mick!"

Together, Terry and Blade winced at the sound of Frank Pandolfino's voice booming through the door. Terry jumped up and opened the door for his boss. He stood as tall as the door. Despite his thin frame, the dark suit and crooked nose gave him an intimidating presence as he stepped into the room.

"Mr. Pandolfino! Welcome to the shop! What can we do for you?"

"Can it, Wood. You know why I'm here."

"Yeah, sure boss, I got your money right here. We were just putting it together to send back with Shady like we always do."

"Not that, you meathead. The other thing," Frank said, as he stared at The Blade.

"Can you give us a minute, Johnny?"

"Yes, Mr. Pandolfino, excuse me." The Blade answered hastily making his exit.

"Pretty good haul for a Wednesday night," Frank said, as he inspected the stacks of currency on Terry's desk.

"Yeah, the summer's ramping up early this year. I think you and Papa will be quite pleased with your cut of the action."

WHACK!

Terry's ear rang from the cupped palm Frank had just cuffed him with.

"You know better than to say that name out loud! What's wrong with you?"

"Geez, Mr. Pandolfino, I'm sorry. I wasn't thinkin'."

"That's right, you weren't thinking! And to top that off, I gotta come all the way over here and check up on you. How come that other thing ain't taken care of yet?"

"What other thing?"

Whack! Now both ears were ringing.

"You know what I'm talking about!"

"Oh, yeah," Terry said, working his jaw to relieve the pressure in his ears. "Look, Mr. Pandolfino, we got right on that one. I'm not kidding. You know that guy that just went over the Falls?"

"Yeah."

"That was him. I mean, come on. Who survives that? We made it look like an accident just like you said, but, don't worry, I got something else going in the hospital."

"Oh, I know you do, and now the police do too," Frank said mockingly.

"What are you talking about?" Terry asked stunned.

"Yeah, that little attempt to kill the mick through his IV? Some nurse spotted the error. Now the police are involved. Attempted murder."

Terry swore. *Is there anything The Panda don't know?*

"Yeah, that's right, Terry. It's a Chinese fire drill, now. You no longer have to make it look like an accident. You just have to get it done and make sure they can't trace it back to us. Or do I need to put someone else on it?"

"No, boss! I can handle it. I swear. Have I ever let you down before?"

"No, you haven't," Frank said, as he looked down on the stacks of currency on Terry's desk. "You run a good operation and your contributions to the family have not gone unnoticed." Time to dangle the carrot. "You might be a half breed, but there are big things in store for you as long as you continue to show your worth to us."

"I like the sound of that, Mr. Pandolfino."

"So that's why I'm telling you to get this taken care of by Saturday at the latest. Capeesh?"

"Yeah, I got it, boss."

"Alright, that's what I wanted to hear. Now, since I'm here," Frank said, looking back down at the cash. "I'll save you the trouble and just collect our share of last night's haul."

Chapter 21

"Roger that, sir. Goodbye, sir."

Joe punched the button to end the call.

"How'd that go?" Christy asked.

"About as well as could be expected, I guess. There's really no easy way to tell your commanding officer you have had two close brushes with death and one of them slipped right past him on national news."

"So what did he say?"

"Commander Harrison is a good chap. He's glad I'm alright, but alarmed that somebody may possibly have tried to kill me. He's probably doing what I'd be doing if it were one of my men; working on a plan of action while notifying his commanding officer. He wants me back down there as soon as possible," Joe finished with a sour look.

"What's wrong?"

"I get why he wants me down there, but I just got here this week and now you're here. I don't want to leave yet."

"I know, I heard you say that to him. What did he say?"

"He said he understands, but that he still wants me down there and that I need to let the authorities flesh this one out, just in case there was something more to it than a medical error." Joe said, with a sigh.

"What are you going to do?"

"I'm working on that," Joe smiled.

"Oh, man. The last time I heard you say that we were handcuffed and being held captive on an island in the Caribbean."

"Hey! It all worked out!" Joe said smiling. "We're both here alive, aren't we?"

"True; although, I think you're running through your nine lives, mister," Christy said, and then winced. "Joe, I'm sorry. I didn't mean to make light of what's happening right now. Please forgive me for being so callous."

"Christy, I could never be mad at you. I know what you meant, and I appreciate it."

"You do?"

"Yes. In fact, this is one of the reasons I'm really glad you came up here. I could really use your wisdom and insight with all of this."

"Really?" Christy asked, her eyes lighting up as she sat up straighter. "With what, exactly?"

"Well, to start, you've given me a lot to think about since last fall."

"Okay, like what?"

"Like, when we met and got to know each other during our capture and escape, I was an atheist. Okay, maybe more of an agnostic. It wasn't that I didn't believe in God, I just had my doubts and didn't really give a flying leap."

"Right..." Christy said, in a manner for Joe to continue.

"Gosh, I'm not even sure how to put this into words. Okay, so those times you were praying on the sailboat and I kind of mocked you?"

"I didn't take it as mocking, Joe, but go on."

"Well, I kind of was and I'd like to start off by saying, I'm sorry. I have come to really respect you as an intelligent and passionate person and I was wrong to think less of you, let alone verbalize anything that may have been offensive."

"Joe, you don't have to apologize. I wasn't offended. I am perfectly used to people having different opinions regarding matters of faith. You were nothing but a gentleman during a time of great danger and, were it not for you, I would have been raped by several cartel members while they filmed it and I would probably be dead by now. I owe you my life."

"As memory serves, you put up quite a fight, Christy. We got out of that mess together. I couldn't have done it without you, but we're getting off topic. What I'm trying to say is, I've thought a lot about some of the things we talked about. You answered many of my questions. You gave sound explanations to many of my objections and, in the interest of being objective, I cannot deny that a lot of what you said makes sense."

"Joe, I'm so glad to hear you say this!" Christy exclaimed. "But you seem to be conflicted about something. What is it?"

"Let's just say that you've opened my mind to the point where I believe that what you say about God, more particularly your Christian faith, is possible, but I still have several hang ups. Being completely honest, although I enjoyed our texts and conversations, I was more interested in talking to you and less interested in the spiritual content. No, that's not right. I didn't mind *talking* about it, but I wasn't particularly motivated to let it change my life. Does that make sense?"

"Yes, perfect sense."

"Really?" Joe asked mystified.

"Yes, really, but please continue, Joe, I really want to hear what you're thinking."

"Okay," Joe said, as he paused to organize his thoughts. "So all of that was interesting, but it was never impactful to me until yesterday. As I was nearing the Falls, I *knew* I was going to die. The reality of God and being a minute away from facing Him was more real to me than the danger I was in."

"Joe, I can't even begin to imagine what that must have been like."

"It was like nothing I have ever experienced. In all the live ops and combat ops, I have always been so focused on the mission and confident in what we were doing that I never thought about dying. Nothing like this anyway."

"Go on," Christy coaxed.

"So now, everything you and I have talked about has taken on a whole new meaning. It's become serious, to the point that I really want to understand it all."

"That's great, Joe! Where do you want to start?"

"Well, let's work through this from the beginning. I understand what is known as the Cosmological arguments for God; that the universe had a beginning, which the leading physicists and even the atheists agree. Call it the Big Bang or what have you. That leaves us to either the universe spontaneously created itself from nothing into an infinitely vast and complex entity or, as you believe, that it was created by God and with a purpose. What I don't understand, is how God came to be."

"Which is a good question," Christy began, "the answer to which is God is infinite and has always been. In other words, nobody created God, He is uncreated and eternal."

"Which doesn't make sense to me," Joe protested. "How can anybody or anything just always have existed?"

"Let me put it this way, Joe. The universe consists of time, space, and matter. Right?"

"Yes," Joe agreed.

"Well, those entities had to have been created by someone or something timeless, spaceless, and immaterial. So to answer your question, if God is going to create time, He has to exist outside of time. He is timeless. If He is timeless, does He have a beginning?"

"No," Joe conceded, "It's just not an easy concept to understand."

"I agree. It's very difficult for us to comprehend anything outside the realms of time, space, and matter. We are finite beings. Consider this, if time had always existed, it would be eternal. Correct?"

"Sure."

"Then, if that were the case, with an eternal past, the present would never arrive."

Joe squinted as he considered what Christy had just said.

"Think about it. The eternal past would never allow us to have arrived at the present. We couldn't exist."

"So that's why you're saying God created time."

"Yes. In order for the material universe to exist, He had to create time, space, and matter; furthermore, it reveals the personal traits of God. He *chose* to create because He wanted a creation to love. He creates and sustains this highly complex universe out of His infinite wisdom and knowledge."

"Okay, that helps. One could still make an argument that you're just using God to fill in the gaps, but what you're saying makes more sense than all of this suddenly appearing out of nothing and for no reason."

"Precisely, Joe, but it's not a 'God of the Gaps' argument. I submit that it's a 'God over all creation' argument. Let's keep in mind that the universe was not only created, but it was extremely fine-tuned in its creation to allow for its creation, as well as to allow for it to sustain. Even the renowned physicist, Stephen Hawking, when remarking on the expansion rate of the universe from its creation, stated that if the expansion rate were off by as little as one part in a thousand million, million, the universe would have collapsed back in on itself."

"Right, this is the Teleological Argument you're referring to."

"Ah! So, you *did* read that book I gave you!"

"*I Don't Have Enough Faith to be an Atheist*, yes, I read it. I took it as a challenge. Yes, the Teleological Argument is the one that got me thinking. I had no idea just how fine-tuned the universe really is. The gravitational forces, electromagnetic forces, speed of light, all being so precise that if they were off by just one part in ten to the one hundredth power, life couldn't exist? It's hard to rationalize those odds by chance when they are statistically impossible."

"Did you know that even Albert Einstein was a firm believer in intelligent design?" Christy asked.

"No, I didn't."

"Yes," Christy nodded. "He was able to understand the universe way beyond most of us and he marveled at the fine-tuning and order. He absolutely believed there was an intelligent and purposeful designer."

"Well, that's what swayed me as well. When I consider an immense universe exploding out of nothing and the improbable odds of every variable being so precisely fine-tuned to sustain the universe and provide the conditions that allow life to exist, I can no longer rationally explain it all to a random chance occurring over billions of years,"

"Same here, Joe, but what really cemented it for me was my medical school classes."

"How so?" Joe asked. "It seems to me that most doctors and scientists tend to favor science over God."

"I believe that's because they box themselves into natural explanations. They will not allow for any explanation other than a natural explanation, even if the evidence points elsewhere."

"Okay, give me an example."

"Let's take the human embryo. A fertilized egg has one complete set of DNA and it divides into matching cells with matching DNA."

"Okay," Joe nodded.

"However, very early into the process, those cells begin to differentiate into specific cells such as; skin cells, epithelial cells of the digestive track which even specialize depending on where in the track they will go, skeletal muscle cells, cardiac muscle cells, smooth muscles cells, nerve cells, and many more. They further find each other and organize into tissues, which organize into organs, which organize into systems, which all interconnect in a vastly complex yet highly functional system. All from one cell. Now, how does that happen on such an organized and complex system? There *has* to be a guiding process to it and it has to come from beyond the DNA since it all arises from one complete set of DNA. Nobody can explain that. I asked my embryology professor and his answer was *"The right gene, in the right place, at the right time."*. I'm sorry but, what? He basically chalked it up to chance which, if true, we couldn't possibly exist as intelligent functioning creatures."

"Okay. That makes sense," Joe remarked.

"And let's consider the DNA," Christy continued. "If you were to walk down a beach and noticed that, scratched into the sand, were the words 'Please help' would you conclude that an intelligent being purposefully wrote that or that the wind and the waves formed those words over time?"

"Obviously, it was purposefully written," Joe answered.

"Okay, so you looked at ten letters and concluded they were purposefully and intelligently placed there. Now, the human genome contains some three *billion* codes precisely arranged to make up some twenty thousand genes that determine the structure and functioning of an extremely complex organism. How does one conclude that a simple message in the stand was intelligently designed, while concluding that the human genome, or even the genome of the simplest of organisms, was a random occurrence?"

"Well, many say it evolved over billions of years," Joe answered.

"Okay, but even the first single cell had thousands, if not millions, of genetic sequences. How did they just suddenly appear when ten letters in the sand could not?"

"I can't answer that," Joe conceded.

"Right. The choices are intelligent design or random chance and you just said you don't think ten letters in the sand could appear by random chance. Now, throw this DNA into the embryological development process which is consistent, complex, and purposefully guided and I can only conclude there is an infinitely intelligent designer creating and guiding these events."

"Makes sense to me," came Anna's voice, as she walked through the door carrying a white paper bag with their lunch.

"Look who I found!" Anna said, looking back over her shoulder as Tony Alendretti, clad in his work attire of khaki utility pants and a teal scrub shirt, trailed in behind her.

"Hey, Tone!" Joe piped up.

"Joe! I snuck out of the ER to grab lunch and thought I'd check in on you. How you holding up today?"

"I'm cooped up and ready to bust out of here, truth be told. Tone, I'd like you to meet a good friend of mine, Doctor Christy Tabrizi." Joe said, as he looked over at Christy. "Christy is an ER doc like you."

"Oh, really?" Tony said delightedly.

Christy stood to shake his hand. Nearly six feet tall, she nearly towered over Tony.

"Where do you practice?" Tony asked.

"I'm in Duluth, Georgia just northeast of Atlanta."

"Are you from Georgia?"

"No, I grew up in Nashville, Tennessee, but I did my residency in Augusta. How about you?"

"I did my residency here in Buffalo. Wait. Augusta? Did you ever get to go to the Masters?"

"Yes!" Christy exclaimed, as her face lit up. "We actually helped staff the medical stations. I got to watch some of the practice rounds and tournament days, as well. That place is amazing! Have you been there?"

"No, hopefully someday. Do you golf?"

"Yes. I actually played with my dad and brothers up through high school, but I only get out a few times a year now. I'd like to play more, but I spend my time doing other things."

"Yeah, like triathlons, Tony," Joe stated. "She just competed in a half Ironman last month and is racing a full Ironman in September." Joe looked at Christy and smiled. "Tony's a marathon runner."

"Oh, really?" Christy asked.

"Yeah, my wife and I usually race one a year. How about you?"

"No. In fact, the only half marathon I've done was the Half Ironman last month in Chattanooga. Running is the part I don't like. I'll do it if I get to swim and bike first," Christy said with a laugh.

"Tony, I'll bet you could smoke a triathlon. You were a good swimmer in high school, and you could do your bike training around the Island," Joe suggested.

"I'd like to one day, but I work too much right now to train like that. What about you, Joe? You're the Navy SEAL, an Ironman would be like a normal day for you."

"Except we don't ride bikes."

"I'll work on him," Christy said, with a wink towards Tony.

They were interrupted by another knock at the door.

All heads turned toward the door where Dr. Bynum stood.

"Afternoon, Ray," Tony said in greeting.

"Tony! Checking up on your handiwork?"

"Nah, just checking in on Joe."

"Well, that chest tube is working perfectly. Thank you for placing that for me," Dr. Bynum said, as he turned his focus onto Joe.

"They called me while I was in surgery and explained what happened, Joe. Suffice it to say, I'm glad you're alright, but I'm terribly sorry that happened.I will not rest until they figure out what happened."

"Wait, what happened?" Tony asked.

Dr. Bynum took a few minutes and explained what he knew about the earlier incident. The three doctors and Anna discussed the matter while Joe listened in. Dr. Bynum then turned back to Joe.

"I'll be in clinic for the afternoon. I have ordered a repeat chest X-ray for you at five. I'll be by around six. If your lung is still inflated,

I'll remove the chest tube. If Tony, here, put it in, it should hurt much less when *I* take it out," he said with a smile.

"Is that so? Well, watch out, Joe," Tony said smiling. "Ray will tell you that you will just feel a little *pressure*," Tony said making air quotation marks with his fingers. "When a surgeon says you're going to feel a little pressure..."

"GRAB YOUR ANKLES!" Tony, Christy, and Anna said in unison.

Chapter 22

Niagara Falls Police Headquarters

etective Lou Peretti stepped off the elevator carrying a thick file folder under one arm and a brown paper bag in the other. He walked back into the squad room and spotted his rookie partner, Detective Kevin O'Keefe, hunched over his desk staring at the computer screen. He appeared just like he did an hour ago when Lou left to go to lunch. Lou smiled, admiring the work ethic his young partner possessed, much like Lou had been when he was a rookie. Not that Lou had slacked off in his later years, Lou had simply learned that the job would never end, but his life one day would. He always put in a hard day's work, but learned to pace himself. Too many good men had burned out early and turned to the bottle, or worse, and lost their families and joy in the process.

Lou loved the job, but he loved his family more. Family was everything. Together, he and his wife, Marissa, had six kids and seven grandkids. They all lived nearby and they all got together on Sundays after church for dinner. It was a dying tradition he and Marissa refused to let go. They had both grown up just a few blocks away in the Little Italy section of Niagara Falls. Back in the early seventies, families tended to remain nearby. Going to "Nonni's" on Sunday was the bare minimum of respect, but it came with great home cooked rewards and lots of laughter. Early on, Lou and Marissa had determined to put their family first. Marissa worked from home and Lou had foregone the after-work gin joints and card games with the boys to spend all of his spare time doting on his daughters, playing ball with the boys in their tiny backyard and, later, coaching their hockey and baseball teams. He and Marissa had sewn good seeds and they were now reaping a good harvest. Lou was subtly trying to instill those values into his young protege.

"No wonder you Irish people are so skinny, you never eat!" Lou said, as he tossed the bag down on O'Keefe's desk. "You said you were gonna get something."

"I know, Lou, but I got the log in info to access the hospital's employee data base and I've been trying to narrow down the search," the slender, fair-haired junior detective said, as he looked up at his senior partner.

"What's in the bag?"

"Lunch, jar-head," Lou said, referring back to Kevin's four years in the Marine Corps before joining the police force.

"Lou, you didn't have to, but thanks. How much was it?"

"Forget about it," Lou waved dismissively. "Show me what you've found so far."

"Pull up a chair and see for yourself," O'Keefe said, as he opened up the bag. "Oh, man! Misty dogs! Thanks, Lou! I'll make it up to you tomorrow," he said, taking a bite.

"So what are we looking at?" Lou asked, as he sat down next to Kevin.

"I used O'Shanick's description of the women who came into his room with the potassium. He might be a squid, but he's a SEAL and he has a well-trained eye for detail. Even though the room was dark and the woman was wearing surgical garb and a mask, he picked up quite a bit of detail; approximate age, height, weight, and hair color. It narrows the list down and I narrowed it down further by starting with nurses and techs who would know how to hook up an IV. I narrowed it down further to who was working that day and reportedly in morning report which, thankfully, occurs at the same time on every floor with the charge nurse keeping record of attendance."

"That helps," Lou commented as he perused the screen. Lou had come of age way before the computer age had hit the department. He would never be proficient with the gadgetry, but he could certainly appreciate their usefulness. Thank Jesus, Joseph, and Mary for a junior partner who could work the things.

"So I compared the list of both the night and day nurses with the list of those who weren't in morning report but there were only four in the entire hospital that weren't at report and none of them fit the description."

"That figures, but it's still a start," Lou said, looking at O'Keefe. "On a hunch, I went back over to the hospital and talked to the charge nurse from each floor. I specifically asked if any nurse or tech had excused herself during report for some reason. You know, claiming she had to hit the restroom or maybe forgot she left a patient on a bed pan so she could duck out and hang the potassium."

"Anything?" O'Keefe asked.

"Two nurses out of all the floors, but none of them fit the description."

"I knew it couldn't be that easy," O'Keefe said, around a mouthful of hot dog.

"It never is, Kevin, but that still helps."

"How?"

"For the moment, let's put all the nurses who were in report aside. I thought about it and it would be too obvious if one had been missing during report. It would make more sense for it to be a nurse who nobody would have missed."

"Like a nurse from another floor or deportment?" O'Keefe asked.

"Well, that's possible, but then their floor would have missed them unless they were on a different schedule. Surgical nurses or other department nurses on a different routine that would allow them to slip away unnoticed would be a list we should look at and," Lou paused to look at O'Keefe, "who else?"

"Somebody not expected to be there. Maybe somebody not working that day but who has the access and skill to pull the job," O'Keefe answered, as he popped open a can of Diet Coke.

"Precisely. We get a list of the nurses who weren't on the schedule that day as well as those from other departments like surgery and start there. We may have to broaden the search to the nurses accounted for in report, but we'll cross that bridge if we have to. There's still a chance it wasn't a hospital employee at all and then we have nothing. The SEAL said the woman was wearing medical gloves, so we won't likely have any fingerprints to work with."

"Alright. You know, it's a shame this local hospital doesn't have the budget for hallway cameras and security systems like some of the more well-funded regional hospitals around here," O'Keefe said, as he began working through the screen pages with the mouse. "Anyway, I'll back out to all who fit the description and narrow it down to those in departments who weren't having morning report at the time. You wouldn't happen to know which departments those are, would you?"

"What do I look like? A chooch?" Lou asked. "Of course, I do. I got it from the nurse administrator on duty. They call her the AOD. Here you go," Lou said pulling a sheet out of his folder and setting it down in front of his partner.

"Alright, so we'll list all of the nurses and techs meeting the description who weren't working today, along with all of the ones who were working today in these departments," O'Keefe said, as he began scrolling through the employee lists.

"Short, curvy, dark hair, that's about half the girls on this computer," O'Keefe exaggerated. "You Italians still own this town."

"We'll narrow it down. It would help if their employee photo showed more than just their face, but we can sort that out. Just narrow down the list and we'll start with that. And what are you complaining about anyway? You married an Italian girl, and a *bella* at that!"

"Who's complaining? I'm just saying we're gonna be here awhile working through this list."

"That's alright, son. It's good practice for you. Odds are this was just some fluke medical error, but it's our job to make sure it was nothing else."

Lou's cell phone began to play the theme to TV's Magnum P.I., the Tom Selleck version. Lou pulled it out and answered the call. He was off a minute later.

"You mean *you're* gonna be here awhile." Lou said.

"Huh?" "O'Keefe asked, without taking his eyes off the screen. "Where are you going?"

"I'm going to Tonawanda. Some guy just reported his boat was stolen. It's been found tied up at Niawanda Park since at least this morning. A black hulled Scarab."

Chapter 23

Tonawanda, New York

*L*ou strode purposefully out onto the dock. Two City of Tonawanda uniformed police officers were still present along with two plain clothes detectives and another guy whom, Lou presumed, was the boat's owner. As he approached, Lou recognized the detectives, the senior detective was the one who called Lou.

"Hey, Peretti! I thought that was a Niagara Falls car pulling up. The rust always gives you guys away."

"At least I'm assigned a car that works, unlike those granny bikes you Tonawanda boys patrol around on. I heard they finally let you take your training wheels off though. What's going on, Tom?" Lou said, smiling as he shook hands with an old friend, Detective Tom Schraven.

"Lou, these are Officers Strassburg and Ketchum."

"Gentlemen," Lou said, as they shook hands in greeting.

"You know my partner, Antonio Mathers."

"Good to see you again, Antonio," Lou said, as he shook hands with the athletic appearing black detective.

"And this is the owner of the boat in question, James Blair."

James stood a good six and a half feet tall forcing Lou to crane his neck up to make eye contact as they shook hands.

"Bring me up to speed, Tom."

"One of the maintenance guys from the park was down here a little after eight this morning cutting the grass and spotted the boat tied up. He didn't think much of it, but noticed it was still here a couple of hours later when his crew finished. He was a little suspicious since it's supposed to be temporary docking for folks trailering their boats, so he called it in. Strassburg came down to check it out and called in the registration number. They tracked down Mr. Blair here and he said he had no idea why it would be here and that it must have been stolen. We had a crew inspect it and dust it for prints. The only thing they found was the ignition for both engines was tampered with, so we are assuming it was hotwired. That's pretty much it in a nutshell, Lou. When I saw your APB over the air about a black-hulled boat, I thought I'd give you a call."

"I appreciate that, Tom," Lou said, as he turned to Blair.

"Mr. Blair, do you mind if I ask you a few questions?" Lou asked, as he opened up his notebook.

"No, go right ahead."

"Where do you live?"

"Right over on Grand Island."

"And what's your profession?"

"I'm a landscaper. I own Busy B landscaping."

Lou asked several more background questions before he began to narrow down on the subject at hand.

"When did you first realize your boat had been stolen?"

"Just an hour ago when the police called me."

"I see," Lou nodded. "When did you last see your boat?"

"On Sunday, we took it out for the afternoon."

"And where do you keep it?"

"Over at Big Six Mile Creek Marina on the West River."

"Does anyone else have access to your boat?"

"No."

"Have you ever let anyone borrow your boat?"

"No, never," the tall man said, shaking his head.

"You said you live with your wife and that you have two grown sons and a daughter. Do they live with you?"

"No, my older son lives in his own house on the Island, my younger son is at sea with the Navy, and my daughter is married and lives with her husband and young son."

"Would any of them have access to your boat?"

"Just my son, but he works with me."

"And you were both working yesterday?"

"That's correct."

"Can you verify that for me?"

"Yes, I can, but why would I need to? This is *my* boat that was stolen."

"I realize that, sir," Lou said apologetically. "The problem is, this boat may have been involved in an accident that nearly killed someone and I have to treat everyone as a suspect until proven otherwise. I have no doubt you're innocent, but I wouldn't be doing my job if I didn't first investigate this thoroughly."

"Murder?" Blair asked incredulously.

"Attempted murder versus merely a careless accident, yes," Lou replied. "You heard about the guy that survived a plunge over the Falls yesterday?

Blair nodded.

"He said he was knocked unconscious when a boat matching this description ran him down while he was sailing."

"Holy smokes! You've got to be kidding me!"

"I'm afraid not," Lou answered shaking his head. "So let me ask you… How long would it take to travel from where you keep your boat tied up to a spot off Cayuga Island?"

"Wide open? Not very long. I'd say about ten to fifteen minutes after leaving the slip."

"And how long from Cayuga to here?"

"About the same amount of time."

Lou wrote a few more things down in his notebook. He looked up and made eye contact with the Tonawanda officers.

"Anybody see anything? Do we have a description of the driver of the boat? What time it arrived?"

"Nothing so far," Strassburg answered.

"Can you do me a favor and ask around? If we can get a description and a time, we might be able to pin this down better. Right now, we don't even know for sure whether or not this is the same boat. How many boats like this are around here?"

"Between here and Lake Erie, a lot," Blair answered. "All types and makes: Scarabs, Checkmates, Bajas, Fountains, Donzis; they're everywhere. Perfect for this area."

"Are there a lot with black hulls?"

"Not that many. Most have lighter colored hulls. I bought this years ago and restored it. It originally had a white hull, but I custom painted it."

"Do you mind if I have a look onboard?" Lou asked.

"Not at all. Be my guest."

Blair jumped in first and helped Lou aboard. He gave a quick tour and stood by as Lou inspected seemingly every detail. Lou leaned out over the starboard side and studied the hull. He looked fore and aft and then turned around.

"The guy said he was sure he was hit by the starboard side. If you were at high speed and ran over a small white sailboat, would you expect to see your paint scratched up?"

"I would think so, if not more damage to the hull," Blair answered. "You don't see anything?"

"No," Lou answered leaning out for another look.

He noted the sleek craft gently tapered over its length to form a sharp bow.

"Mind if I head up onto the bow and take a look?"

"Go right ahead."

Lou hoisted his slightly overweight frame up onto the bow deck. Not a seasoned boater, he struggled to maintain his balance as the boat rocked gently in the current. Wisely, he got down onto his hands and knees as he tried to look over the side to view the forward section of the boat's hull. He grabbed ahold of the low deck rail and leaned out farther. but still couldn't look down well enough to see the hull as it also tapered inward to form the wave cutting deep-v shape. Lou strained to lean out and down enough to where he was able to see the hull revealing several white streaks disrupting the gel coat of the shiny black hull. Deciding to get some pictures, he let go of the rail with his right hand to reach into his back pocket.

"WHOA!"

Lou gave a yell as gravity took over and his weight overcame the stability his other arm provided holding onto the deck rail. In comical fashion, he froze in midair, desperately trying to prevent the inevitable, and then flipped over the side and splashed into the river. Schraven, Strassburg, and Ketchum jumped down into the boat while James Blair leaned over the side and grabbed a hold of Lou's arm as the current pulled him by.

"Grab ahold," James yelled, as the other three men leaned over to help their colleague out of the water.

Together, they worked Lou up onto the gunnel where he was able to swing a leg over. They helped him over and he collapsed into the cockpit.

"Man, is that cold!" Lou pronounced, as the other four men broke out in laughter.

"I'm serious! It's a good thing I'm done having kids," he said, looking around at the other four men laughing.

"What are you laughing at? I could have been killed, or even worse!" The laughter increased.

"You should have seen yourself!" Detective Schraven said, barely able to form the words from laughing so hard. "It was slow motion. Your legs went straight up in the air and you just hung there, upside down, for a few seconds before flipping right in," he said, finishing with a near silent belly laugh.

"Shoot!" Lou said as he fished his iPhone out of the back pocket of his wet chinos. "Not only did I not get pictures, but I probably killed my phone." More laughter.

Antonio stood up and spoke through his laughing.

"That's alright, Lou. I'll get your pictures for you."

"Why don't you let me hold onto you so don't have another repeat," James Blair said, starting after Detective Mathers.

Detective Schraven looked at Lou and sighed after his laughing fit settled.

"There are several white streaks along the bow," Lou told his friend. "This is the boat, Tom."

"Alright. Then I think we will need to send out a press release asking for any information anyone might have in connection with this boat."

"That's a good idea, Tom," Lou said with a nod. "Based on the timeline I got from the victim, we can estimate the time the boat left the marina and the time they tied up here. We're one step closer to nailing the perp."

Chapter 24

Niagara Falls, New York

"Take a deep breath in and let it out," Dr. Bynum coached Joe. "Deep breath in and let it out. Deep breath in..."

With a sudden flash of motion, Dr. Bynum yanked the tube out of Joe's chest. Christy held pressure with a Vaseline-soaked gauze which formed a seal over the open wound while Dr. Bynum finished taping it in place.

Joe had winced, but not made a sound. He noticed a thin streak of blood trailing from his bed and slightly up the wall.

"Is that normal?" he asked.

Bynum glanced over his shoulder and admired his handiwork.

"Yep, if you don't leave a trail up the wall, you didn't yank it out fast enough. I told you it would just be a brief second of pressure."

Christy stifled a giggle.

"I'll bet you enjoyed that," Joe accused.

"Who, me?" She answered, feigning shock.

"Alright, sailor, that should do it," Dr. Bynum said as he stood up. "We'll check a chest X-ray in the morning and, if it still looks good, I'm kicking you out of here, you sandbagger."

"Thank you, sir."

"Anything else you need? You good on pain?"

"I'm fine, sir, thank you."

"Alright then. I'll leave you in the capable hands of this fine young physician," he said, with a nod to Christy as he spun and headed out of the room.

"Fine young physician is right except he doesn't know the half of it," Joe said, as he gingerly sat up. "Let's go for a walk."

"Are you up for it?"

"Um, yeah! I'm sick of this place, I need some fresh air. First, I'm getting out of this thing," Joe said, as he stripped off his hospital gown. He was already wearing cargo shorts courtesy of his sister Marina who had dropped by earlier. He found the t-shirt she had also brought and pulled it over his head, being careful with his new bandage.

"What is R40?" Christy asked, looking at his shirt.

"Are you familiar with the band Rush?" Joe asked, as he slipped into a pair of Hoka One One running shoes.

"A little, my brothers are big fans. Aren't they the ones who play Tom Sawyer?"

"Yes, and about 170 other killer tunes they wrote over a forty year career. R40 was their fortieth anniversary tour. Sadly, it was their final tour, but it was, in my opinion their best of many great tours. Dad turned my brothers and me into fans. We all saw this show together in Buffalo. Anna went too."

"I think my brothers met in Greensboro and saw that show. I've never seen them."

"Well, you missed out. Three amazing, but humble, musicians who always put on a great show," Joe said, smiling reflectively. "But c'mon. Now that I'm not tethered to a vacuum cleaner, let's get some fresh air."

"Hey, Gina, I think your patient's trying to escape!" One of the other nurses yelled back to Gina who suddenly appeared from an inner room.

"Are you escaping, Mr. O'Shanick?"

"Yep. I'll walk or even crawl back to Grand Island if I have to," Joe said in jest. "Nah, I'd miss you too much. Just stepping out for some fresh air. We'll be back."

"Hey," Joe said, whispering to Christy. "Anna has told me how terribly nurses can be treated and how hard they work. Let's come back with some pizzas for them. There's a place right across Pine Avenue."

"I like your style, Joe O'Shanick; I'll spring for it."

"That ain't happening. You might make ten times what I make shooting and looting, but you'll never pay as long as you're with me; besides, it was my idea."

"Split it?" Christy suggested, as they shunned the elevator and took the stairs.

"Nope," Joe smiled back.

"You're a good man, Joe."

"That's debatable," Joe said wryly.

"Bite your tongue, Joe O'Shanick! If I say you're a good man then you are! You have more than proven that to me."

"Whoa, I'm sorry. I didn't mean to set you off."

"You didn't," Christy smiled slightly. "I just won't let you talk like that about yourself."

Christy walked on in silence. Joe was habitually alert and constantly scanning and analyzing their surroundings but was still able to pick up a change in Christy's aura.

"And you," Joe reached out his right arm and pulled her in close. "You have more than proven yourself to me and my trust doesn't come easily."

Christy smiled up at Joe.

"Thank you," she said quietly. "You saved my life and my dignity last year. I owe you a debt I could never repay. I hope you know the feeling is mutual."

Joe gave a gentle squeeze before letting her go.

"Yeah, I do know that," he said genuinely, "and I wouldn't have it any other way."

They reached the pizza shop and walked in, as Joe held the door for Christy. Joe looked around and selected a table towards the back. He took the seat facing the front entrance but had already mapped out where the restrooms were and the kitchen, which would, undoubtedly, have a back entrance. Despite his tactical awareness, Joe felt naked not having a handgun on him, but he was a hospital patient and that was a big no-no, even for special forces operators and, especially, in New York State.

A waitress came and handed them menus. She took their drink orders. Joe ordered iced tea and convinced Christy to try the Loganberry, another Western New York favorite. The waitress set off to get their drinks while Christy looked over the menu.

"I could go for another one of those chicken finger subs, but I want to try the wings and see what all the fuss is about."

"No!" Joe said decisively, causing Christy to look up startled.

"Your first wings will be at my brother Sean's place on the river tomorrow," Joe said more gently. "He won the Buffalo's Best award two years in a row. You'll love them."

"Okay, it's your town. So, what do you recommend here?"

"Do you want to split a pizza?"

"Sounds good, but just a small and I'm ordering a salad. I'm supposed to be training for an Ironman and I haven't worked out all day. I had a sub for lunch, pizza tonight, and wings tomorrow. I'm not even going to be able to fit into my bike shorts by the time I leave here on Sunday."

"Oh, you'll fit just fine. You look terrific. Relax, you're in the junk food capital of the world. You've got to enjoy it while you're here. Where are you staying anyway?"

"At your parent's house. Your mom insisted," Christy said smiling. "But that's tomorrow. I'm staying with you tonight."

"Christy, that's not necessary," Joe began to protest, while he watched a new person walk into the restaurant.

"It *is* necessary, Joe! Anna and I already worked that out. You were nearly killed this morning, whether by accident or by design and we aren't going to allow that to happen again."

"How will you sleep?" Joe asked, watching the man up front out of the corner of his eye.

Joe noticed the man look over at him and Christy. His gaze seemed to linger in their direction. After a few seconds, he looked down at his phone and began thumbing through it. Joe turned his head away while continuing to observe the now fidgety appearing man. He looked up from his phone, glancing directly at Joe. *Have I've been made?*

"...the recliners in the rooms fold out into a bed. I'll be fine... Joe?" Christy asked, noting the cold look that had taken over Joe's Irish green eyes. "What's wrong?"

"Don't turn around. Act natural. There's a guy up front looking at me. I don't like the feel of this. We're gonna need to exfiltrate. I want you to get up like you're heading to the rest room only keep going past it. There's a door leading out back. Take it. I'll be right behind you. Go."

Christy calmly stood up with her purse and headed toward the nearby hall leading to the restrooms and back door. She acted as natural as could be. Joe admired her ability to remain calm no matter how hairy things got. Joe casually pulled a ten dollar bill out of his wallet and placed it on the table. He stood up and made for the back exit as well. On his way, he noticed their friend hastily exit out the front entrance. *Not good.*

Chapter 25

Joe quickened his pace and burst out the door quickly assessing the situation. Christy was right next to him and nobody else was around. Yet. They were standing behind the restaurant in a small access way for delivery trucks and waste management. Joe really wished he had his handgun with him. He looked around and spotted a large squeegee leaning against the wall. He quickly unscrewed the metal handle and started off towards the closer road. The sooner they were in open view the better.

"Joe, what's going on?"

"Some guy back there was staring at me and I'm not taking any chances. He bolted out the front the same time we left out the back. I want to be gone before he gets back here."

"What do you need me to do?"

"Just stay close and follow me. If I tell you to take cover, I mean get behind a dumpster, hide in a door frame or, if you can, run as fast as you can and we'll meet up back at my room."

Joe moved quickly along the wall with Christy directly behind him. Reaching the corner, where the access way met a side street, Joe scanned across the street before taking a quick glance around the corner. It looked clear. He signaled for Christy to follow and button-hooked right, keeping to the side of the restaurant. A short walk and they were back on Pine Avenue. Joe had them cross to the side opposite the restaurant before starting back towards the hospital. Head on a swivel, he didn't spot anything out of the ordinary as they passed in front of the pizza shop. No sign of that guy. It could have just been some nutcase, but Joe wasn't about to let his guard down. They continued on in silent vigilance until they reached the hospital. They crossed over a side street and turned left onto the sidewalk leading down the side of the hospital toward the main entrance.

"I'm sorry about that, Christy. Maybe I'm just a bit paranoid, but when my Spidey sense starts tingling, I find it's usually wise to act on it. I still owe you dinner," Joe said smiling. "Do you mind if we just order in?"

"Of course not."

"Thanks for understanding. Now, if we are ordering, then we are going top notch. There's a place that served the best pizza at The Summit Park Mall we used to go to when I was a kid. The mall has since closed, but the pizza shop relocated and it's out of this world."

"I'm running tomorrow but, after this, I'm going to need to find a bike and throw a ride in before the run."

"My dad rides; he might be able to hook you up. If not, the current is just right for a swim off our dock."

"Oh, really?"

"Yes, did you see it?"

"No, I came straight here from the airport. I haven't been to your house yet."

"Oh, well..."

Joe heard the loud engine coming up behind them. It had the distinctive sound of a muscle car engine amplified by headers and duel exhaust. Joe glanced back over his left shoulder to get a look as the car approached. A chartreuse green Plymouth Road Runner with black stripes in mint condition came charging up the street. Joe's admiration turned to trepidation a split second before the car swerved up onto the sidewalk heading straight for Joe and Christy. With mere seconds until being run over, Joe grabbed Christy and made a lunging dive for the grass. The Road Runner sped by, missing Joe's trailing foot by inches, as Joe and Christy hit the ground. The Road Runner's brake lights came on followed by a loud squeal. The driver shifted into reverse and began to back up. Joe and Christy jumped to their feet and sprinted through a small park in front of the hospital's main entrance. The deep breathing and exertion caused Joe's ribs to scream in protest, but Joe was able to override the pain.

As they burst through the hospital entrance, Joe caught the attention of the armed security guard.

"Call the police!" Joe said breathlessly. "Someone just tried to run us over!"

Chapter 26

"What do you mean, we gotta get rid of my car?!" Angelo pleaded.

"Did I stutter?" Terry glared at Angelo from behind his desk. "Your car stands out like a sore thumb with that ridiculous paint scheme! That guy's probably, right now, giving a description of your car to the cops. Even without a plate number, it won't take them long to trace it right back to you, which means me, The Panda, and your uncle! We ain't taking that kinda heat! Your uncle already thinks you're a knucklehead. What do you think he's gonna do if he finds out you're bringing unwanted attention to his organization?"

"Geez, Terry, he'd kill me. Ya gotta help me!"

"Help you? If you're uncle wasn't the boss, I'd kill you myself for bein' a friggin' idiot! What were you thinkin'?"

"Terry, I thought I could take the guy out. I seen him leavin' the restaurant. I thought I could make it look like an accident and then we'd be back in good standing of The Panda and my uncle."

"You think like a moron, Ange! I told you not to pick a car that stands out and then paint it so it draws even more attention to your fat, hairy self. You need to get it as far from here as possible. Dump it in the lake and say it was stolen or something but, for crying out loud, get it as far away from here as possible!"

Angelo stood awkwardly with his mouth open in shock.

"NOW, you dipwad!"

Angelo turned and hurried out the door, near tears and mumbling an apology.

Terry cursed to himself as he sat at his desk considering his next move. A knock came from his door.

"What?" Terry yelled annoyed.

A rather skinny and young blond girl appeared in the door wearing a black sequined mini-skirt and a silk top.

"Ya ready, Terry?"

"Not yet, sweetheart," Terry said, slightly distracted with no idea what her name was. "Go wait in the break room. I'll come get you in a few minutes. I got something to do first."

Terry noticed the blank look on the girl's face. *Geez, she's been workin' for Marco for a while!* Terry could always tell. The longer they were in the business, the more the drugs took over. Drained the life out of them. They stopped eating, became too skinny, and basically stopped living. It was a short lifespan, but Terry didn't care. They were easily replaced.

Terry opened one of his desk drawers and lifted a plastic pencil tray. Beneath it were several small vials of cocaine.

"Here," he said, tossing one to the girl, who stood there lifelessly as the vial bounced off her chest and landed on the floor. "This will keep you occupied until I'm ready for you."

Realizing what Terry had tossed, the girl bent down and retrieved it. She then turned and headed down the hall. Terry liked his girls to have a little life in them.

Turning back to the matter at hand, Terry sighed and pulled out his cell phone. He dialed the number from memory. This number was not to be stored in his phone. A deep voice answered on the other end.

"Hey, it's Terry. We got a problem."

Frank Pandolfino sipped his scotch while he sat at the Blackjack table. He looked down at the four and the seven that he had just been dealt. The dealer was showing a queen. Frank matched his bet and pointed between the cards indicating he was doubling down. The dealer flipped Frank a nine.

"Are you kidding me?" Frank said annoyed. *First that halfwit Angelo and now this?*

The young female Native American dealer's face remained stone-faced as she dealt out the rest of the table. They all broke trying to best the dealer's revealed face card. Frank was the only one left in the hand. The dealer turned her other card over revealing a ten. Frank muttered an expletive while the dealer took his chips. He immediately placed another hundred dollars in chips for his next bet. The dealer paused to shuffle the decks.

"Frank, the boss wants to see you at his house," came a whisper from his assistant, Jerry "The Bull Dog" Costello.

"Oh, Mother of Joseph, now what?" He said, looking at Jerry, who just shrugged his shoulders. There was no direct communication between Bruno Catalano and his Capos. They either spoke in person or Bruno's underboss, Vincent "The Dazzler" Randazzo contacted the Capo's assistant and relayed the message. It was always a brief message.

"Alright," Frank sighed, as he took his bet off the table before the dealer finished shuffling.

Twenty minutes later, Frank pulled up to the gate at the end of Bruno's driveway. He pressed the intercom switch and looked directly into the camera. The gate doors slowly swung open and Frank eased his car up the driveway. He parked in the designated guest area and walked to the front door where he was, once again, checked over and then escorted out back to Bruno's back porch. Bruno sat in a wicker rocking chair looking out over the expanse of land behind his estate. The sound system had the Yankees game playing. Bruno puffed on a large Cuban cigar while listening to the game. Frank nervously cleared his throat.

"Mr. Catalano?"

Bruno slowly took another puff on his cigar and watched the smoke as he exhaled. After a long silence, he acknowledged Frank.

"Are you trying to give me a heart attack?" Bruno asked, without taking his eyes off his fields.

"Sir?"

"You heard me."

"No, I ain't trying to give you no heart attack. Why would you think that?"

"I give you one job. Whack one guy is all I ask, and you can't even do that."

"But you said..."

"I ain't done talkin' yet!"

Frank swallowed hard and stood in awkward silence. Bruno took another slow puff on his cigar.

"One job. I don't ask much. Your crew makes a good living under the protection I provide for them. Wouldn't you agree?"

"Yeah, boss. Of course."

"Then why is your crew runnin' around like a bunch of street hoods, screwin' up my simple request, and attracting the attention of the police?!" Bruno demanded turning around and glaring at Frank.

"Papa Bruno, I told you, we'd take care of this. You gave us until Sunday. It's only Thursday. We'll get it done. I swear!"

"Is that right?"

"Yeah, Boss, you know we take care of our business."

Bruno continued to glare at Frank.

"You take care of your business?"

"Yeah, you know we do."

"Like that halfwit halfbreed child of my deceased brother..." Bruno said making the sign of the Cross, "...driving his pimped out hot rod down a sidewalk in front of several witnesses trying to run over that Navy chooch? Is that how you take care of your business?"

"Papa Bruno, I just found out about that. I'll handle it."

"What, you knew, and you didn't see fit to inform me?"

"I thought it could wait until tomorrow. I didn't want to disturb you, ya know?"

"My moron nephew just drew the attention of the entire NFPD trying that hair-brained stunt of his and you didn't want to disturb me, or you were too busy losing money at the casino?"

"I was gonna handle it, Mr. Catalano."

"You was gonna handle it? Oh, that's rich!" Bruno took another puff from his cigar as he studied Frank.

"Let me ask you something, Frank. How come I'm more interested in what your crew is doing than you are? Huh? How come?"

"Mr. Catalano, I, uh..."

"You don't have an answer, do you?"

"No, sir," Frank said meekly, looking down at his Ferragamo shoes.

"You know why? Huh? You want to know why? Because I make it my business to know everything going on in this organization!" Bruno emphasized the point by stabbing the air with his cigar. "What I want to know is why you don't take this serious enough to make it *your* business? I can't have one of my crews running around screwing things up for the rest of us. It's not good for business. Know what I mean?"

"Yes, sir, I know."

"Then you need to take care of this thing. The sailor, and my nephew."

"Sir?"

"You heard me. Take care of it. I can't afford the idiot caving when they question him. He needs to go away and so does that ridiculous car of his. I regret the day I let my sister-in-law talk me into letting him start working for me. Is that too much to ask?" Bruno said looking up at Frank.

"No, Mr. Catalano. I'll take care of it."

"No more screw ups, Frank. You've been very good for this business and you enjoy a good life. Screw this up and I'm gonna have to think hard about finding another guy to run your crew. Now go," Bruno said, as he turned his attention back to his fields.

Chapter 27

Niagara Falls, New York

$\mathcal{J}$oe and Christy returned to his room after their close call with the car. A short while later, Detective O'Keefe dropped by and took their statements. Just as they were about to order in, Joe's mother called to inform them that she and Jack were coming over with dinner. Since the day shift had switched over, Joe and Christy decided to order in lunch for the crew tomorrow but they would take care of the night shift later tonight. Joe's parents arrived shortly after, each carrying different items for dinner, one of which was a Filipino dish called Bringhe, a flavorful curry based meal of rice, shrimp, ham and chicken. Maria prepared a large amount and purposefully brought enough to feed the nursing staff, much to their delight as the alluring aroma had found its way out to the nursing station.

Both Maria and Jack were very happy to see Christy. While Maria was busy extracting an update on Daniella's progress at Adult and Teen Challenge, Jack subtly made eye contact with Joe and, with a quick glance in Christy's direction gave a subtle nod of approval. Joe, caught off guard by this, merely shrugged. *We're just friends, Dad. She's out of my league.*

Maria and Christy carried on like old friends catching up. The conversation drifted into talk of Christy's work with the mission in Honduras and the associated parent ministry. Christy and her friends actually wanted to go back down to the clinic but, due to the violent incident they had been involved in, the current state of affairs would not allow them to return. Alternatively, they planned a mission trip to Guatemala City in October. In the meantime, Christy, and her friend, Stacy, an OB/GYN she worked with, were donating their services to a local women's shelter where they ministered to many battered and addicted women. One didn't have to travel abroad to serve. There are people in need in every pocket of the country.

"How long will you be staying, Christy?" Maria asked.

"Just until Sunday. I have to work Monday night."

"Will you be able to join us for church on Sunday?"

"I'd love too. I don't have to be to the airport until four."

"Great. I have Marina's old room all made up for you, but we also have a small beach house down by the dock if you would prefer that."

"No, Mrs. O'Shanick, please don't go to any trouble, Marina's room is more than enough as it is. That's very kind of you both."

"It's our pleasure, Christy," Jack commented.

"Hey, Dad? Christy is training for an Ironman. Do you think you could set her up with one of your bikes?"

"No!" Christy exclaimed in embarrassment. "Mr. O'Shanick, that's not necessary. I'll be fine until I get back. Really."

"No, I'd be happy to set you up," Jack said, as his face lit up. "I have several bikes. Marina rides too. It would be my pleasure. What do you ride at home?"

"My Tri-bike is a Cervelo P2 and my road bike is an S2."

"A woman after my own heart," Jack said. "I only ride Cervelo's myself. How tall are you?"

"Five foot eleven," Christy replied sheepishly.

"I've got a P3 that has a fifty-six-centimeter frame. I think that should suit you just fine. We just need to work out some shoes for you."

"I have shoes and pedals with me. I rented a bike in Cape Cod."

"You're hard core, young lady, I'm impressed."

"A wise man I know one said, *the only easy day was yesterday,*" Christy said, smiling over at Joe.

"Are you going to ride tomorrow?" Jack asked. "I can have it set up for you tonight when we get back."

"No, I was thinking about riding Saturday. Tomorrow, I need to swim."

"How far are you planning on riding?"

"I would like to do a metric," Christy replied.

"Outstanding. I have a great metric course mapped out. It actually comes in a couple miles over at sixty-four miles, but it's twice around the island with a small loop in the middle. Very nice ride almost all of it along the river. If you have a Garmin, I could share it with you, or..." Jack said mischievously, "I could be your guide if you don't mind riding with some company."

"Mr. O'Shanick, I would love that. Thank you!"

"You won't mind having an old man slow you down?"

Christy could tell, looking at Jack's tall wiry build, that she would likely be trying to keep up with him. Joe was definitely a blend of his parents, but his father's height and rugged handsomeness definitely found their way into Joe's gene pool.

"I think it might be the other way around," Christy replied.

"I doubt that," Jack responded. "I'll bet Marina would like to ride with us. Are you okay with that?"

"Of course."

"Then we're set," Jack nodded, before assuming a cinematic voice. "We ride at dawn!"

"Mom, I'll stay home and help dust," Joe said, looking over at Maria in exasperation.

Dr. Bynum had strictly cautioned Joe to avoid any strenuous activity for six weeks. Joe took that to mean two weeks and, at that, he wasn't sure he could wait that long, but he wasn't about to make that thought known to Christy or his mother.

Maria excused herself to use the restroom after nudging her husband that they would need to be heading home soon. It was getting late and tomorrow was another workday. Jack took the opportunity to speak discretely with Joe and Christy.

"Anna told me what happened this morning. What can you tell me?" he asked in a hushed tone.

"Not much, Dad," Joe confessed. "I'm not sure if it's related, but we had another incident tonight though," he added and quickly filled his father in on what happened a few hours ago.

"Any ideas on who it could be?"

"Not yet," Joe said with steel in his voice, "but now we have a bit of intel to work with."

"I'm concerned, son. I think we need to plan out how best to get you home tomorrow."

Just then a loud knock came at the door. Joe looked to the door and instantly recognized the tall, muscular figure, with closely cropped sandy brown hair and a goatee, smiling in the doorway.

"Problem solved," Joe said, smiling at his dad. "Chief! Get in here!"

Chapter 28

"Joey O!" Chief Matt "Rammer" Ramsey boomed in greeting from the doorway. "Looks like you remembered your drown-proof training after all!"

"I could have gone the other way had you been my BUDs instructor, Chief," Joe countered. "Man! It's good to see you!"

"Oh, I found these two homeless guys wandering around and thought they could bunk with you for the night," the Chief said, as he walked in followed by two of Joe's teammates, one a wiry Asian man and the other a blond haired, muscular bulldog with a walrus mustache.

Joe stood, speechless, as he and Chief Ramsey clasped hands and pulled each other in for a hug. Joe then exchanged similar handshakes and brotherly hugs with his two other teammates before introducing them to his family.

"Mom, Dad, you remember Chief Ramsey from the White House last year?"

"Of course we do! Hello, Chief Ramsey," Maria said, as she wrapped her arms around Rammer in greeting.

"And, here, we have Petty Officer First Class Tran Van Truc, also known as Tommy Tran or, most often, Truck," Joe said with his hand on Tran's shoulder. "And this is Petty Officer Second Class Jamie Mueller, better known as The Mule."

Maria and Jack stepped up to greet all three men. Maria surprised Truck by greeting him in Vietnamese.

"Are you Vietnamese, too?" He asked in Vietnamese. They continued on for a minute during which Maria informed Truck that she was Filipino but had learned the language from the many Vietnamese customers who frequented her family's restaurant when she was young. It was good for business.

"Guys, you remember Christy?"

"You mean the warrior lady who rescued our platoon leader from the clutches of Los Fantasma Guerreros? How could we forget!" Rammer said, stepping forward, gently taking her hand and kissing it. "I'm very glad to see you up here, ma'am," Chief Ramsey quietly spoke, as he caught her eye. All three men had been part of the rescue team that intercepted Joe and Christy during their sea born escape from the cartel.

"I'm guessing Commander Harrison sent you?"

"He told us what happened. We immediately hopped in the Chief's truck and were already pulling away before the Commander got done telling us not to get into any mischief," Mueller said with a sly grin.

"You made killer time getting up here from Virginia Beach," Joe said with amazement.

"You know that estimated time of arrival that appears on the GPS? The Chief considers that a challenge," Truck quipped as everyone laughed.

"Do you boys have a place to stay?" Maria asked.

"We're staying wherever the Lieutenant Commander is staying, ma'am," Chief Ramsey answered.

"Guys, I appreciate it. I really do, but that's not necessary. Not up here anyway," Joe responded.

"No man left behind, sir. The mission is to get you home in one piece and we are Charlie Mike," the Chief countered.

"I don't know what to say guys, but, thanks," Joe said in appreciation. There was no point in arguing. He would have done the same for any of them. Truth be told, seeing such loyalty in his men made him exceptionally proud to be their platoon leader.

"Well, Joe will be home tomorrow night and we have room for all of you. I'll cook a special dinner!" Maria exclaimed.

"Ma'am, that's not necessary," Chief Ramsey began to protest.

"Stow it, Chief," Maria said, with mock seriousness, as she cut him off using Navy speak. "You look after my Joe, and I will look after you. No argument!"

"Yes, ma'am," Chief said respectfully and then turned to Joe. "I see where you get your leadership skills from, sir."

"You've got that right, Chief," Jack said appreciatively, as he wrapped his arm around his wife. "Around here, Maria is the commanding officer and I get to serve as her executive officer. But she's right, you're welcome at our place as long as you're in town."

"Thank you, sir," the three SEALs said in unison.

"Well, we have to work in the morning, so we are going to head back," Jack stated. "Are you all planning on staying here?"

"I'll stay here with the Skipper. Truck, you and Mule take my truck and head back to the O'Shanick's and grab some rack time. Plan on meeting back here at 0700," the Chief said with a nod.

"Aye, Chief," they both said.

"Anything we can bring in the morning?" Tran asked.

"Bring our gear and some decent coffee."

"Chief, there's a Tim Horton's right here in the hospital," Joe said.

"Isn't that the place you've been telling me about for years?"

"Yep."

"Then I'll take mine black," Chief Ramsey said as he put a ten-dollar bill in Truck's hand.

"Well," Christy said as she stood up, "seeing as how you're in capable hands, I think I'll head back with your parents and get some sleep myself. Unless you want me to stay?"

"No, Christy. I appreciate it, but you've been up all day and must be exhausted. Go get some sleep. I'll be fine with Rammer."

"Okay," Christy said, as she gave Joe a peck on the cheek and a strong hug. "I'll see you in the morning."

"Thanks for coming all this way," Joe said quietly while holding on to her. "I can't tell you how good it is to have you here."

Maria hugged her son goodbye and the room cleared leaving Joe alone with Chief Ramsey.

"I see what you're doing, Rammer," Joe said looking at his Chief Petty Officer.

"What?" He asked innocently.

"You've got Truck and Mule keeping watch over my family."

Rammer simply shrugged innocently in reply. "Harrison said it's probably nothing but to come up here and circle the wagons, just in case."

"Thank you," Joe said seriously.

"Anything, brother. We got your back."

"I know and I appreciate it more than you know."

"So you think someone might be trying to take you out, Joe?"

"I don't know," Joe said with a shrug. "What happened this morning could have been a simple medical error but they can't figure it out and then we had a little incident tonight and I'm beginning to wonder."

Joe spent the next few minutes bringing the Chief up to speed.

"Any ideas as to who this could be?"

"I'm not sure. The police are looking into it, but at least we have a lead with that car."

"Then let's start there," Rammer said, as he pulled out his cellphone and made a call.

After a few minutes of back and forth on the phone, he ended the call.

"Who was that?" Joe asked.

"That was my old Sea Daddy, Brad Shoemaker. He was my chief back when I was a wee tadpole. Did his twenty and then went on to the FBI. Started off as a course instructor for HRT and went on to become an agent."

"So, what'd you learn?"

"The car is registered to one Angelo Catalano, I have his address here," Rammer said, indicating a writing pad on his armrest. "Here's where it gets interesting. His uncle is Bruno Catalano, believed to be the head of the local Catalano crime family," Rammer said, as he looked at Joe.

"The mafia?" Joe asked sitting up. "I heard they were all but a thing of the past around here."

"Apparently, they're making a comeback. Brad says this guy Angelo appears to be a recent recruit, but the local feds have been watching him to see if he can lead them to his uncle. He has a small time rap sheet: a couple of drug charges for possession and one assault that was dropped when the victim didn't pick him out of a lineup. Several known accomplices who are all suspected of being in a crew headed up by a Frank Pandolfino. That's all I've got for now, but Brad said he would keep working on it."

"That's actually quite a bit, Rammer. But it raises some questions."

"What's that?"

"Well, I have no history with any organized crime family, at least not that I'm aware of that would make them want to come after me. If they are involved, why?"

"No clue," Ramsey responded.

"Exactly. It makes no sense. The only reason I could think would be if they were acting on behalf of someone else. Like the cartel."

"You mean you think Los Fantasma Guerreros could have asked the local mob to take you out after what we did to them this past year?"

"It's a stretch but it's the only reason I can think of," Joe replied.

"Well, decimating their ranks while capturing their leader certainly made you persona non grata with them. Last I heard, Hector Cruz was still at Gitmo. You think he's calling the shots from there or someone below him?"

"Hard to tell, Chief." Joe shrugged. "We nearly took down the entire cartel, but they are extremely well-organized and they have an extensive reach."

The particular cartel they were referring to was Los Fantasma Guerreros or "LFG" for short. Comprised of all former Mexican Special Forces soldiers and Marines, LFG had originally served as the military arm of another cartel before breaking off on their own. Over the past few years, they had ruthlessly taken out rival cartels leaving a trail of blood all across Central America while establishing an extensive reign of terror. Their control of local gangs was not limited to Central America. Many of the cartels had the power and means to extend their tentacles to gangs throughout North America. The fuel sources of this control were the drug and human trafficking trades controlled by the cartels, which gave them dictatorial powers over the gangs dependent on the cartels for supply. A cartel such as LFG need only threaten to raise prices or divert their trade to a rival gang. This threat not only kept the local gangs and organized crime under the cartel's thumb, but allowed the cartels to exact a tax from each gang.

Any member of a gang that refused to pay the tax was immediately targeted by cartel-controlled prison gangs for execution upon incarceration in prison.

Cartel influence was not limited to the gangs and organized crime. In addition to corrupt officials in Central America, there were local, state, and federal officials and politicians in the United States who were under the cartels' influence. Somebody up the chain of command from Joe's platoon had compromised a mission resulting in the deaths of half of the platoon last fall. The offender, either military or political, was, as of yet, still unknown. The corruption was as ubiquitous as it was maddening. It wouldn't surprise Joe or Chief Ramsey in the least to learn that, if these actually were attempts on Joe's life, LFG was behind them.

"Well, that's why we're up here, brother. Just in case there is something going on. We'll keep our heads on a swivel and just maybe do a little hunting while we're up here.

Chapter 29

Terry quietly sipped his scotch as he sat at the bar in the Power City Club. Beside him, Angelo nervously tapped out his cigarette and then immediately lit another one. Angelo knew better than to talk when Terry was brooding. He didn't have to wait long.

"Did you take care of it?" Terry asked.

"Yeah, man, just like you said."

"What'd you do?"

"I sold it to a chop shop over in Buffalo. The one in Kaisertown. Parwalski's. You heard of it?"

"Yeah, I've heard of it. They're small time, but they know to keep their mouths shut. How'd you get back? You didn't tell anyone else about this, did you?"

"No, Terry. I swear. I took the bus."

"You took the bus? All the way here?"

"Yeah, it wasn't easy, but I figured it out with my phone."

"You sure you haven't talked to anyone about this?"

"No! Terry? What the...? Do you think I'm stupid?" Angelo asked, trying to keep his voice down.

"Yeah, Ange, I do," Terry spoke, looking down as he typed in a text message and sent it. "If you were smart, we wouldn't be having this conversation right now. Would we?" Terry said as he tossed back the last of his scotch.

"No, Terry," Angelo sighed.

"You want another one, Mr. Wood?" The young bartender asked, as he spotted the empty glass on the bar.

"No, Geno. Just give me a Genny draft."

"You got it," Geno replied fetching a frosty mug out of an old-fashioned torpedo cooler. He held it under the tap and pulled the Genesee lever, which caused a foamy shot of air.

"Genny's out, Mr. Wood," he said apologetically, "and I don't know how to change the keg yet. I've only been here a week and ain't nobody shown me yet. I'm sorry, sir."

"That's alright, Geno. Ange will get it. He started off here just like you, kid. Ange, go down and replace the Genny keg."

"Since when do you drink Genny, Terry?" Ange asked, as he slid off his barstool reluctantly.

"Since when do you care, halfwit? Go do what I told ya!"

As Angelo hustled off to the basement, Terry sat back down and looked back at Geno.

"Shoot, it'll probably take the idiot an hour just to remember how to do it. Give me another scotch. I ain't waitin' all night."

Angelo muttered to himself as he tromped down the stairs. Arriving in the basement, he walked over to the keg cooler. It was locked. He found the key in its usual hiding spot and removed the lock. Opening the door, he stepped into the narrow cooler. He found the line marked *Genesee*, a local brewery that remained popular among the locals, and traced it to its corresponding keg.

"What the..." Angelo muttered to himself as he realized the line was not connected.

He lifted the keg and determined it was nearly full confirming that the issue was the line had somehow disconnected itself. Angelo reconnected the line shaking his head. He turned and stepped out of the cooler. Angelo froze. Standing before him was Frank Pandolfino with a gun extended toward Angelo.

"Panda?"

"What?!"

"I mean Frank. No! I mean Mr. Pandolfino, sir. What gives?"

"Keep your mouth shut and walk. You so much as utter one word, I'll drop you, right here."

Angelo stared at the silencer attached to the end of Frank's gun and swallowed.

"That way!" Frank indicated with his gun.

Angelo nervously turned and walked toward one of the walls. He noticed that what he thought were built in storage shelves had been rolled to the side to reveal a narrow passageway through the foundation wall. Frank illuminated the passage with his cell phone in his left hand while he kept the gun in his right hand trained on Angelo's back. Angelo dared not look back when he heard the sound of what he presumed was the shelves being rolled back into place behind them. They kept walking for about a minute through the damp and musty passageway until they arrived in a large darkened room. Angelo tried to identify the surroundings of the dark room as Frank rolled another set of storage shelves into place, concealing the passageway. In the dim light cast by the flashlight, he could make out a couple of stretchers and a stack of cardboard boxes. On the far wall he saw what appeared to be a couple of oven doors.

Is that an old furnace? Angelo asked himself. Maybe it was an incinerator. Some of his friends lived in older houses that had old furnaces that looked similar. He turned toward Frank who still had his gun drawn. He nearly spoke, but he thought better of it.

Angelo sensed, more than saw, movement in the dim light behind him. His fear factor instantly went up another level. Suddenly, a sharp sensation wrapped around his throat and his trachea was compressed taking away his ability to breathe. Angelo, instinctively reached for his throat, but the bass guitar string Johnny "The Blade" Colucci had garroted around his throat was imbedded so deep into his skin he couldn't insert even one finger to try and ward off the inevitable.

While Angelo desperately struggled for life, Frank appeared within inches of his face staring directly at him.

"Your Uncle Bruno said to say hello to your dad."

That was the last Angelo registered as his senses faded to black. Colucci held Angelo's lifeless body tight for another minute before lowering him to the floor. Frank turned on the overhead light. He and Colucci quickly placed a large cardboard box next to Angelo's body and opened it. Frank grabbed Angelo's ankles while Colucci grabbed the wrists and they swung him into the box. Colucci quickly removed Angelo's wallet, cigarette lighter and cell phone before taping the box shut and then, together, he and Frank lifted it onto a dolly. Frank moved to a panel along the wall and pressed a button which opened one of the cremation oven doors. He pressed another button and the internal flames ignited casting an orangish blue glow into the room. Colucci pivoted the dolly allowing Angelo's cardboard coffin to line up with the oven door and slid it in. The flames instantly ignited the box as the door slid shut. Frank nodded at Colucci and quietly spoke.

"Omertà."

Chapter 30

Friday

Chief Ramsey calmly watched *Fox and Friends* as Joe emerged from the bathroom freshly shaved and showered. He was clad in a black pair of Lycra boxer briefs.

"Feel better, Joe?"

"Holy crow, yes, Chief. I just realized, that was my first shower since my swim in the Falls the other day. Why didn't you tell me I smelled like the river?"

"Shoot, after the mud pits at BUDs and the decaying rot of some of the jungles we've crawled through? I don't even notice anymore."

Joe stood looking in the mirror and began to remove the tape from the outer dressing on left side of his chest.

"Can I help you with that?" Asked his nurse, Gina, as she walked in.

"I think I can get it," Joe responded cheerfully.

"Well you're really not supposed to remove it until tomorrow in case the wound hasn't sealed. Let me at least make sure you don't re-move the Vaseline gauze," she countered, as she maneuvered in close and began to help Joe with the dressing.

Behind the attractive nurse, Rammer looked up at Joe with raised eyebrows and a mischievous grin. Joe rolled his eyes and gently shook his head while Gina carefully worked off the dressing.

"Hold this, please," she said, as she placed a couple of clean gauze pads over the Vaseline gauze.

Joe did as instructed while he watched her tape the gauze to his chest. She stood much shorter than Joe and he could look down on the top of her head where her thick dark hair was tightly pulled back into a ponytail. He detected a subtle scent of lavender.

"There," she said, as she finished. "Leave this on until tomorrow. After that, you can change it each day after you shower."

Gina stared up at Joe, her dark brown eyes seemed to linger to the point where Joe began to feel awkward.

"How soon can I swim?" He asked.

"What?" She asked lost in thought.

"How soon can I swim? I need to swim as soon as possible."

"Oh," she said, regaining her thoughts as she gathered up the discarded bandages. "Umm, wait at least one week. If it looks sealed over, then you should be fine. If it looks infected, get seen right away."

"Roger that, ma'am," Joe said grin. "The doc said my X-ray looked good. Am I officially discharged?"

"It'll be just a few minutes. I need to finish your paperwork, go over your discharge instructions, and wheel you out."

"I'm good to walk, thanks."

"Everyone gets wheeled out, it's policy."

"I appreciate that, but I'm not that good with rules. I'm walking."

"For crying out loud, Lieutenant, let the pretty nurse do her job, you numbskull," Chief Ramsey chided to Gina's amusement.

"I'll tell you what," Joe said, as he indicated in Rammer's direction, "*He* is the old man. How about you wheel him out. I think he may need it."

"I'll get your discharge instructions," Gina laughed as she walked out.

"Now I know why God made Chief Petty Officers," Chief Ramsey started. "You college boys might be book smart, but you couldn't find your backside if you used both hands."

"What are you talking about, Chief?"

"I'd give anything to have a woman like that show any sign of interest in me. You have her melting in your presence and you're worried about going for a swim. It's called a clue, Joey-O, look into it!"

"What? Her? You think so?" Joe asked astonished.

"Yes, you idiot. You really didn't pick up on that, did you?"

"Maybe, I guess, I don't know."

"No, you don't know, and that's why the Navy sees fit to issue every junior officer a Chief to keep your head in the game. Now if your head was pre-occupied with a certain tall, exotic-looking ER doctor, I might cut you some slack, but as it stands..."

"Christy?" Joe asked astonished. "I can't even go there, Rammer, she's *way* out of my league."

"Is that what you think?"

"Is that what who thinks?" Mueller asked, as he strode into the room with Tran and Christy right behind him.

"Morning, Lieutenant. Morning, Chief."

"Good morning, Joe," Christy said cheerfully, as she gave him a quick hug and a kiss on the cheek.

Rammer caught Joe's eye and gave a knowing nod.

Joe looked down at his semi-state of undress and stammered an awkward response.

"Good morning, Christy. I'm sorry, I just got out of the shower. Let me finish getting dressed.

"Oh, don't worry," she said dismissively. "Reminds me of old times when we swam from island to island together."

Chief Ramsey flashed a toothy grin at Joe.

"Besides, your mom packed a clean pair of shorts and a t-shirt for you," Christy said holding up a small bag.

"Thanks." Joe said, removing the clothing and donning a black pair of cargo shorts and an athletic gray t-shirt with a Grand Island Vikings Lacrosse logo on the front.

"Mule? You stop for coffee?" Rammer asked.

"Oh, shoot, I forgot, Chief. I'll go right now."

"No, Mule, wait," Joe urged. "There's an Italian bakery just up the street. Out of this world donuts and coffee. We'll stop there instead. It's even better than Tim Horton's, Rammer," Joe said looking at his Chief.

"I've been up all night and I'm supposed to trust a cake-eating officer on his idea of good coffee? Alright, sir, you're on."

Gina walked back in with Joe's discharge instructions. She spent a few minutes going over them before offering, one last time, to wheel Joe out to the entrance. Joe assured her he was fine and, after saying goodbye to all the nursing staff, the group made their way down to the lobby. Mueller jogged out to retrieve Chief Ramsey's Ford F-150 pickup. He returned to the covered entrance a few minutes later and relinquished the driver's seat to Chief. They offered the front passenger seat to Joe, who declined so he could sit in back with Christy. Christy, being tall, but athletically slender, chose the middle of the back seat with Joe on her right and Mueller on her left. Rammer turned around holding Joe's personal off-duty concealed carry weapon, a Smith and Wesson M&P Shield .40 along with its concealable holster, and two extra loaded magazines.

"Joe, from here on out, we are going tactical. I thought you might want this."

"Yes! Thank you, Chief!" Joe said, as he inspected the chamber for a round, locked the safety and placed it in the holster.

He put a magazine in each cargo pocket and placed the holster in his waistband. Joe looked at Christy apologetically.

"Are you okay with this?" He asked.

"I'm very fine with this," she answered. "I wish I could have mine here with me as well, but this state has ridiculous laws and it won't honor my Georgia permit."

"You have a CWP?" Ramsey asked, looking in the mirror.

"Yes, I do, Chief!"

"She's a keeper, Joe!" He said appreciatively, as he put the truck in gear and pulled out of the entrance.

Behind them, a young, dark-haired woman in a large sun hat sat on a bench seemingly staring at her cell phone. She watched the truck drive off making sure to watch which direction it headed. Upon confirming the direction, she tapped in a quick text message and pressed send. She picked up her belongings and walked off.

Chapter 31

Terry Wood sat in an old Dodge Caravan parked at the curb on Pine Avenue just past 17th Street. Trina's text came across his phone alerting him that O'Shanick was on his way seated back right with three men and a woman. They were likely his family or some friends from the Island he thought, but the only target was O'Shanick. Colucci and "Paulie P" were pretty good, but if the others got caught in the crossfire? Well, that was their problem.

Terry studied his driver's side mirror, watching for a black Ford F-150 late model. *There it is!* Terry waited for another car to pass and then pulled out into traffic directly in front of the pickup truck. He deliberately drove slow as he watched the 18th street traffic light, willing it to turn yellow. There were cars spaced along the curb making this lane impassable. To Terry's relief, the light turned yellow and he cruised to a stop as it turned red. *Any second now.* Terry snuck a glance in his rear view mirror to witness the carnage.

What the... Terry rapidly swung his head around. *Where the...*

The truck was gone. Terry looked all around. Nothing. No sign of the pickup. The light turned green. Another car was behind him, Terry had to move. He turned right onto 18th and then swung into the parking lot of a Rite Aid Pharmacy. He opened his phone and dialed Paulie P's number.

"Yeah," Paulie P answered.

"The truck was right behind me. Did you see where he went?"

"I never saw no truck, Terry. You pulled up to the intersection, but no truck."

"You've gotta be kidding me, man! Where did he go? Look around you. You see him?"

"No man, nothing."

"Alright, sit tight and keep a watch for him," Terry said as he ended the call and dialed another number.

"Yeah?"

"Blade, did you see the truck?"

"No, just you."

"Shoot, he must've turned down 17th, but why would he do that?"

"Dunno. Whatcha want me to do, man?"

"Stay put a minute. I'm gonna double back and look for him. Be ready if he drives up in front of you. O'Shanick's on your side in the back seat."

"Yeah, I know. Let me know what you find out," Colucci ended the call himself.

Terry pulled out onto Pine Avenue and turned left, heading back the way he came. Approaching 17th street, he immediately spotted the truck parked on the side street next to DiCamillo's Bakery. It appeared empty. Terry turned left onto 17th, traveled a short distance and used a three-point turn to reverse his course. He parked along the curb just before Pine Avenue. This gave him the ideal position to watch the truck on the opposite side. If it turned around and came back out on Pine, Terry could still get in front of him. If it continued on down 17th, Terry could tail him. He took out his phone and texted the update to Paulie P and The Blade.

Chapter 32

"This place has good coffee?" Tran asked.

"Coffee, espresso, cappuccino, donuts, and the beast Italian bread ever. One of my best friend's mom used to get bread from here several days a week. It's the best, I'm telling you," Joe said, as he held the door for everyone.

"Oh my goodness, I'm in heaven," Christy remarked, as she was greeted by the bakery's delectable aroma.

"Yeah, I think you're on to something here, Joe," Rammer nodded in agreement as they all stepped up to the counter.

A pleasant matronly woman greeted them and took their orders. A few minutes later they were all gathered around a park bench out in an open courtyard by the street savoring their coffees and sampling pieces of donuts from an assorted dozen. Christy sat between Joe and Ramsey, while Tran and Mueller stood.

"Joe, is that Italian importer place any good?" Mueller asked, as he studied a storefront just up the block.

"I've never been in there, but it's been around forever."

"I'm going to go take a quick look. I want to see if they have fresh mozzarella to go with this bread I just bought."

"Mule? Are you serious? You know my mother is going to feed you so much you won't be able to fit into your wetsuit!"

"I'll just be a minute. This is like being back in the hood in Philly. We don't get this kind of Italian goods in Virginia Beach, sir," Mueller said, as he walked up the street swinging two loaves of DiCamillo's bread.

As he walked up the street, Mueller scanned the surroundings. It was a natural state of being. Scanning the territory, identifying choke points, concealable locations, avenues of egress and, most importantly, assessing people for potential threats. Across the street, Mueller spotted something out of the ordinary. He kept his face forward and watched in his peripheral vision but he was sure of what he saw. Up on the roof of the Rite Aid, he could just make out a scoped rifle. Mueller pulled out his phone and stopped on front of the sign for the Italian importer. He formed an exaggerated pose as if taking a selfie when, in actuality, he zoomed the camera in on the rifleman and took several HD photos. Acting satisfied, he walked into the import store and took up a concealed position by the window where he could study the man on the roof. Mueller opened his text app and set up a group text for Tran, Chief Ramsey, and Joe. He sent the pictures and a brief message explaining what he was doing.

Christy had just started to retell her experience of when a local gang had raided the women's shelter she and her friends were serving at in Honduras when Joe's phone chimed an incoming text along with those of Tran and Ramsey. Hearing each other's phones chime simultaneously, they all assumed it was a unit text and immediately pulled out their phones. Joe was first to speak.

"Unless the president is in town, that guy is waiting on me. He knew we would be driving right in front of that position and I'll bet someone told him we just left the hospital."

"We should have passed him ten minutes ago," Ramsey postulated. "If he's still there, he must know we made this stop. That means somebody has eyes on us. What do you want to do, sir?"

"If there are eyes on us, we need to move," Joe said, rising from the bench as he texted Mueller while scanning the rooftops. "Let's go through the bakery."

When they arrived earlier, Joe had taken note of a service door on the back of the building just in front of Ramsey's truck. Mueller joined up with them and, as Joe apologized to the staff, they proceeded to the kitchen area and out the back entrance. They quickly climbed into the truck while Ramsey cranked the engine.

"Go straight, Rammer, and take the first left," Joe commanded pulling out the card the police detective had given him and beginning to punch in the number.

"Joe, I think we have company!" Mueller said from up front. "Some dude in a minivan just shot across the intersection and he's on our six."

Joe and Tran looked behind to see the Dodge behind them. It looked to be empty other than the driver.

"Alright, Chief, take the left up here and then the first left after that. We'll see if he stays with us."

Ramsey turned left onto Elmwood and then took another left onto 16th street, taking them back the way they came.

"Yep! He's tailing us," Mueller called from the front.

"What's your plan, Skipper?" Chief Ramsey asked.

"He's probably calling in some more of his goons right now. I say we grab him. It allows us to lose the goons and then we can ask a few questions. Politely, of course." Joe said.

"I like it. Where do you want me to go?" Chief Ramsey asked.

"You guys ready now?"

"Yes!" They answered in unison.

"Then just before we get back to the main drag up ahead, turn left into the alley behind the buildings. Fewer eyes there. If he follows us in, brake hard, Chief. Tran, you, Mueller, and I pop out with our weapons trained and force him out of his car. We'll jump in back with him and bolt. Christy, when we jump out, I want you to get down on the floor."

"Okay," she responded nervously.

"Alright, Chief. Turn left right after this house. Now!"

They turned into the access alley behind several Pine Avenue buildings.

"Is he following?" Ramsey asked.

"Wait one," Joe answered, as he watched the minivan slow to a stop.

"Not yet. He's just sitting there," Joe stated. "Wait! Here he comes. Slow down and draw him in, Rammer."

"Contact front!" Chief Ramsey yelled.

Joe's head swiveled to look out front where he saw a red Dodge Charger stopped in front of the alley on 17th Street. The Charger then turned into the alley as the minivan rapidly approached from behind.

"Hammer after him, Chief! He won't want his pretty little car scratched." Joe commanded.

Chief Ramsey hit the accelerator pedal and the large V-8 engine roared in response as they surged toward the red car. Joe, instinctively, placed his arm in front of Christy to brace her. The Charger loomed larger up ahead as the distance between the two vehicles rapidly closed.

"I don't think he's backing down, Skipper!"

Suddenly, the Charger veered left into a narrow parking alley that opened up between two of the buildings. It nearly clipped one of the buildings in the sharp turn before coming to a stop.

"Stop here, Chief!" Joe commanded, as Ramsey slammed on the breaks.

"Tran, you and Chief get the minivan! Mule, you and I have the Charger! Christy, hit the floor!"

The men jumped out of the truck and took up positions on each vehicle. The Charger squealed its tires and raced up the parking alley where it escaped onto Pine Avenue. The driver of the minivan assessed the situation and began to reverse back down the alley. Joe and Tran gave chase, but the minivan was faster and was back onto 16th street within seconds, where it switched into forward and zoomed out of sight.

Joe and Tran stopped running. Joe looked at Tran and shook his head.

"We almost had them, sir."

"Almost. We'd best get out of here before they come back with more goons."

They arrived back at the truck and hopped in. Christy was already sitting back up when Joe and his men got in and buckled up.

"Chief, turn right out of the alley and then right onto Pine. We'll double back through downtown Niagara Falls rather than go the way they would expect us to go. I doubt that sniper's still there, but why take that risk."

"Skipper?" Mueller asked from the front. "What if we sneak up from behind that drug store and grab the sniper?"

"That's a good thought, Mule, but we don't know if he's still there and we definitely don't know who's with him. I'm not willing to put you guys in harm's way for a bunch of unknowns."

"I ain't worried about that, Skipper. Personally, I'd like to grab the scumbag and work some intel out of him so we can go after the rest of these dirtbags."

"I appreciate it, Mule, I really do. But it just so happens I was able to collect some usable intel back there."

"How's that, sir?"

"New York State is so over-regulated, they require all vehicles to have license plates on the front and back. Got the numbers off of both vehicles. I'm going to call this into Detective O'Keefe, but I think we should move on this ourselves. What say you?"

"Hooyah!"

Chapter 33

Detective O'Keefe's fingers rapidly flew over the keyboard as he updated his report. He minimized the screen and opened the DMV database to confirm the vehicle registration numbers. O'Keefe was a stickler for numerical, as well as grammatical, accuracy in each report.

"Good morning, Kevin," Lou Peretti greeted, as he sat down across from his partner.

"Hey, Lou. How was Ava's graduation?"

"Priceless. I always thought the idea of a kindergarten graduation was kind of ridiculous, but there's something about becoming a grandfather that turns it into a big deal. Thanks for getting a start on this. What'd you find out?"

"Well, for starters, we have three vehicles that have been directly involved with O'Shanick. The Roadrunner from last night belongs to one Angelo Catalano..."

"Catalano?"

"Yep, his nephew and known associate. Believed to be part of Pandolfino's crew."

"Well, that's a good start," Lou remarked.

"There's more."

"More?"

"Yes, sir. About an hour ago, O'Shanick called me personally. Said they spotted a man on the roof of the Rite Aid on Pine with a rifle. He thinks they were waiting to ambush him. A minute later they..."

"They?"

"O'Shanick and his buddies that were taking him home from the hospital."

"Okay."

"Anyway, a minute after spotting the rifleman on the roof, they get into his friend's truck and head off in the opposite direction, but immediately notice a Dodge minivan following them. They nearly got trapped in an alley between the minivan and a black Dodge Charger before they got away. O'Shanick called in with the license plates which I just ran."

"And?'

"The Charger is registered to Paul Pelliteri..."

"We know that name, don't we?" Lou commented.

"Yep, owns "Paulie P's" in North Tonawanda and is a known associate of the Pandolfino crew. Seeing a pattern?"

"Sure. What about the minivan?"

"That's registered to a Marge Miller, age fifty-two, married, works as a secretary. She didn't have any connection, but I called her and guess what I learned?"

"Her van was stolen?"

"Nope. Better. It was in for a new timing chain. Care to guess where?"

"Power City Collision and Auto?"

"Bingo. Terry Wood's shop that he runs for the Catalano organization."

"Can O'Shanick ID the driver?"

"Better than that, Lou, He sent me a picture," O'Keefe said, as he pulled up a cell phone image on his screen.

"By itself, that might not hold up in front of a judge," Lou said, leaning in as he studied the photo, "it's a bit fuzzy through the windshield but, when connected to the auto shop, we just might have something. Kudos to that kid for keeping his nerve enough to get a picture."

"I think between that, the positive ID on Pelliteri's car and Angelo Catalano's car, we have enough to bring them in for questioning," O'Keefe said excitedly. "Heck, with Catalano, we have probable cause to arrest for attempted murder, right now."

"Maybe," Lou cautioned. "They all can make excuses. Catalano could say he accidentally ran off the road answering a text. The other two didn't actually commit any specific crime. We need something stronger. That being said, we have three *known* associates of Pandolfino's crew. This points to either Pandolfino or beyond. We get the soldiers, maybe they talk, maybe they don't. Let's keep an eye on them and see where they lead us. Meanwhile, I think we owe it to O'Shanick to at least give him a heads up on..."

Lou's phone began to ring. He fished it out of his pocket and opened the call.

"Lou Peretti..."

A minute later, he ended the call.

"C'mon, kid!" Lou said as he snatched up his keys.

"What is it, Lou?"

"We just might have our something stronger."

Chapter 34

Grand Island, New York

Christy stood looking in the mirror as she pulled her long dark hair back into a tight ponytail. Glancing out the window, she could see Joe and his three teammates sitting on the dock. Christy had asked Joe about getting in a training swim off his dock. Tran and Mueller said they would swim with her, but she suspected they went out early to discuss the incident they had just encountered. More likely, they were planning what to do about it. Their conversation on the way back had centered around taking care of things themselves. After a bit of discussion, they decided that, as long as they remained vigilant and armed, they would be safe around Joe's neighborhood. They were no longer in Niagara Falls.

Looking back in the mirror, Christy began to have second thoughts about her attire. She was wearing a one-piece navy blue Speedo swimsuit, but didn't feel comfortable wearing that in front of Joe and his teammates. She quickly stripped out of it, threw on a sports bra followed by her Team Endurance triathlon kit consisting of a tank top and bike shorts modified for swimming and running. They were still form fitting, but less revealing. She was going to wear them for her run anyway. It made sense. Satisfied, she grabbed a drawstring backpack with her gear and made her way downstairs, out the front door, and down to the river.

As she crossed the street and walked down the small slope to the O'Shanick's waterfront, Christy heard the guys start to laugh. She smiled. There was a familiarity and a camaraderie about them that stood out. Joe was an officer. More specifically, he was *their* commanding officer, but the familiarity between the enlisted men and Joe was unique. The respect they carried for Joe was palpable, but the formality one expected between enlisted men and their officers was noticeably absent. That was until they were being chased in the truck. All four men became business-like. No, that wasn't right. What was the term? Tactical. They became tactical and Joe went from "Joey-O" to Skipper as if a switch had been flipped. Christy made a note to ask her brother, Jamie, about that. Jamie, a Naval Academy graduate, like Joe, was an infantry 2nd Lieutenant in the Marine Corps, but seemed to describe a more formal relationship with his platoon.

Familiarity or not, Christy marveled at their dedication to one another. Just a hint that one of their own was in trouble and they dropped everything to help. These guys were a rare breed.

Out of curiosity, she tried to sneak up on them. She knew she wouldn't get close, they were SPECOPS operators, but she was up for the challenge. She slowed her pace as she neared the dock, trying to determine how to stealthily walk out on the dock. It didn't matter. In unison, they all sensed her presence and turned her way before she even reached the dock.

"Do you guys have some kind of a sixth sense?" Christy asked, as she approached them on the dock. "I tried to see how close I could get to you before you noticed, and I didn't even make it to the dock!"

"We're frogmen, ma'am," Chief Ramsey replied. "We sensed the vibrations from your footsteps."

Christy stopped with her fists on her hips. "You trying to tell me I'm heavy, Chief?" She said with mock fury, as the other laughed at his expense.

"No, ma'am! You look just fine to me!" Rammer said with both hands raised in surrender.

"You're obviously not married because, at your age, long ago, you would have learned that answer would never be acceptable," she said with a stern look and then broke into a smile, "but I'll give you a pass. This time."

"Thank you, ma'am," Ramsey said, letting out a mock sigh of relief.

"How deep is it here, Joe?" She asked looking down into the water as at gently flowed past the dock.

"About twelve feet."

"So is it safe to dive in?" Christy asked as she began to stretch,

"Yep."

"And I'll be able to swim against the current?"

"Yes. In here, no problem. The further out you go, the stronger it gets. How fast do you swim?"

"I can do two miles in the pool in roughly an hour," she answered.

"With or without fins?" Mueller asked.

"Without."

"That's pretty good, ma'am," he responded. "You gonna swim that far today?"

"That's right. Any of you SEALs care to join me?"

"I'm in," Mueller quickly responded.

"Me too," Truck chimed in. "Joe, do you have any fins?"

"There's a basket of fins, goggles, and masks inside the beach house," Joe said, pointing to the waterfront guesthouse where his teammates were bunking.

"Chief? You swimming?" Truck asked.

"Not now. I'm gonna finish my watch while you swim and then hit the rack for a bit."

"Chief, I would have gladly stayed with Joe last night so you could sleep," Christy said, as she tucked her ponytail up into a bright pink swim cap.

"I'm quite certain you would have, ma'am, but I'm good. Besides, every officer needs their chief to look after them."

"Bite me, Chief," Joe said. "That's an order."

Rammer shared a mischievous grin with Christy.

"Are you ready, ma'am?" Tran asked, as he and Mueller walked up from behind.

"Guys! I'm Christy! It's okay to call me that."

"Just a sign of respect, ma'am. After all, you are a physician."

"Yes, but I'm *not* a white coat wearing prima donna. I have more respect for what you gentlemen do. Christy is just fine, Tran," Christy said, as she finished attaching her waterproof MP3 player to her goggles strap.

"Is that one of those AudioFloods?" Mueller asked.

"Yes," she said nodding.

"Is the sound any good under water?"

"It's perfect. Just like listening on land. The earbuds fit in the ear canal and keep the water out. Would you like to try it?"

"Sure!"

Christy unclasped the tiny iPod and handed the unit over. Mueller fit his mask and set up the MP3 player.

"The earpieces are supposed to stay in even if you dive, but I've never tried that, Jamie," Christy said using his first name.

"I'm not going to risk it with your set," he said, as he began to descend down the swim ladder. He paused and cocked his head as the music began to play in his ears. "Whoa! You like Stevie Ray Vaughan?"

"Of course! Don't you?"

"Yeah. I just don't know many chicks that dig SRV. Sorry, ma'am. Women. Especially doctor women. Well, I mean..."

"Mule, give it up, you're digging a hole," Joe said laughing.

"Sorry, ma'am. You're alright in my book, Dr. Christy. I'll bring these right back," he said, as he pushed off from the ladder and began to breaststroke away from the dock.

Seconds later he transitioned into the Combat Sidestroke and began to work his way through the water. After a minute he returned to the swim ladder.

"Alright, these are cool! I'm totally getting me a pair!" He exclaimed. "Lieutenant Commander, I think these should be standard issue.

"Dream on, Mule."

"Well, it would make our ocean swims a bit less miserable. Here you go, ma'am. Thanks," he said, as he handed the set back up to Christy.

"Would you like to try them as well, Tran?" She asked.

"I'm good, thanks," he said, grinning as he secretly pointed to the back of his head where his own iPod was clasped to the mask strap.

He quickly inserted the earbuds and dove in before Mueller was any the wiser. Tran and Mueller both set out from the dock and settled into an efficient-looking Combat Sidestroke. Christy watched for a moment before commenting.

"I think I'll stick to freestyle."

Having watched Tran dive in with his ear set, Christy decided to try it herself. Having swam in high school, she executed a perfect pike and entry, her lithe figure barely creating a splash as she arched under the water. She emerged with a shriek.

"This is *freezing!*"

Joe and Rammer sat on the dock, laughing.

"It can't be more than sixty-five degrees in here," she said.

"Sixty-one, actually," Joe said smiling.

"You knew? You knew, and you didn't tell me?!"

Joe and Rammer laughed even harder.

"I'm going to get you, Joe O'Shanick!" She said, as she swam closer and splashed Joe and Rammer.

Looking out at Tran and Mueller, Christy remarked, "They dove right in and swam like it was nothing. Was this some kind of a setup?"

"No," Joe replied. "We train in this. They're used to it. The water around Coronado is actually colder than this and we practically lived in it during BUDs. I'm sorry, I couldn't resist, Christy. You should see your reaction! I filmed it for you."

"I'll get you for this, Joe O'Shanick," she said smiling. "When you least expect it, expect it!"

"Give it your best shot, love. Pranking is part of our training. Isn't that right, Chief?"

"I can neither confirm nor deny that rumor," Rammer answered.

"Weak, Chief, weak. Thanks. Okay, I'm sorry, Christy," Joe said, smiling as he stood with her towel. "There's a pool right over in Tonawanda where you can lap swim. It's much warmer. I can take you there right now."

"Thanks, but I'll stick it out. I'm actually starting to get numb. If you guys can handle it, I'll give it a go."

Christy put her head down and stroked out to Tran and Mueller where she settled into a near form perfect freestyle. Joe and Rammer watched for a few minutes in silence.

"God broke the mold when He made that one, Joe. You'd be a fool to let her get away."

"She's one of a kind for sure, Rammer. I just don't think I'm in her league."

"She's here, isn't she?"

"Yes," Joe said contemplatively, "but I think it's as a concerned friend. We bonded during that experience last year, but I don't think it's anything more than that."

"Would you like it to be more?"

"If you would have asked me that last year, I would have probably said no. I thought she was amazing through all that we had been through but, at the time, I thought she was really religious which, to me, was a turn off."

"And now?"

"I don't know, Rammer. She and I have had a lot of conversations about that stuff. I've read several books, listened to podcasts, and even started to read the Bible a little. I'm starting to believe it could all be real. Enough to where I don't see it as religion but, in her case, and admittedly now with my parents, it's a genuine faith for them. They live what they believe. I can respect that."

"I get that, Joe."

"Really? You don't go to church. I've always assumed you were an agnostic, like me."

"No, I believe. I actually prayed to receive Christ when I was a teenager."

"Really?" Joe said looking at his friend in amazement. "I had no idea."

"You wouldn't. I kind of fell away from all that when I joined the Navy."

"Why's that?"

"I don't know," Rammer said letting out a long breath. "I just feel like I can't measure up to God's standard. I've killed a lot of men over the years, some of them with my bare hands. I can still see their faces.

It's combat. We do what we have to do and I accept that. I'm just not sure God does."

"I get it, Chief. Christy and I have had that talk. She can show you scriptures where wartime killing is justified. You and I should talk to her about all this later tonight. It really helped me."

"You serious?" Ramsey asked, looking Joe in the eye.

"Yeah, Chief. I really am."

"Okay, I'm in. It'll be awkward, but I think I need that."

"Copy that, Chief. I need it too."

"Alright, as soon as Tran finishes, I'm heading in to hit the rack," Ramsey said. "When I get up, we need to finish figuring out what to do about our situation with those fellas across the river."

"Chief, I don't want you guys getting involved with that. It's my problem. I appreciate it though."

Chief Ramsey leaned in toward his commanding officer, "With all due respect, sir, it's *our* problem. No man left behind."

"Roger that, Chief," Joe said, with a fist bump.

Chapter 35

Tonawanda, New York

D etective O'Keefe knocked on the door. The house was over a hundred years old, but well maintained, as were many of the surrounding houses in the shaded streets of the old neighborhood just off Niagara Street. A young woman answered the door. Her physical fitness was immediately evident as she stood at the entrance wearing black jogging pants and a purple tank top which accentuated her auburn hair.

"Can I help you, gentlemen?" She said by way of greeting.

"Yes, ma'am," Lou answered as he held up his badge and identification, "I'm Detective Peretti and this is Detective O'Keefe from the Niagara Falls PD. We're looking for Rachel Warren."

"That's me," she said relaxing. "You're here about those two guys?"

"That's correct, ma'am. May we have a few minutes of your time?"

"Sure. C'mon in," she said, opening the storm door.

She led them through a parlor to the kitchen at the back of the house. Both rooms were immaculately clean.

"Can I offer you anything to drink? Coffee? Pop?"

"No, thank you, ma'am; we're fine. We just have a few questions for you, and we'll be on our way."

"Okay," she said, pulling out a chair. "Have a seat. What would you like to know?"

"Well, you responded to our inquiry regarding the boat tied up down at Niawanda Park on Wednesday," O'Keefe began. "We need to ask you a few questions about that, but we'd like to start with some background questions, if that's alright."

"Sure."

"Could you state your full name please?" O'Keefe opening up his notebook.

"Rachel Lea Warren."

"Age?"

"Twenty-six."

"Occupation?"

"I run an online scheduling service. I work from home."

"Does anyone live here with you?"

"Yes, my husband, Jeff."

"And what does he do?"

"He teaches physics and coaches football at the high school."

"Okay, let's talk about the other day," O'Keefe continued, as Lou looked on approvingly.

"You said you think you saw the people getting off the boat?"

"That's right. I saw two guys tie it up and walk off the dock."

"What were you doing down at the park?"

"I was running. I like to run by the river every other day around this time when the weather's warm."

"Was anyone else with you at the time?"

"No."

"You said you saw two men tie up the boat. Was anyone else with them?"

"Not that I saw."

"Can you describe the boat?"

"Yes. Long, like all of those loud fast boats that race up and down the river all the time. I could only see a little bit of the top because the dock was blocking a lot of it, but it was black on the side with a white deck. I saw it again on my way back."

"Where was it tied up?"

"At the docks in front of the concert pavilion."

O'Keefe nodded. So far everything was consistent with what they knew. Now for the gold.

"How close did you get to the two men you saw?"

"Very close. I was running towards them and passed between them on the path."

"Did you get a good look at their faces?"

"Unfortunately, yes. They were practically leering at me."

"Can you describe them?'

"Sure. One guy had sandy blond hair. It was wavy and looked like a mullet, but he was wearing a floppy hat so I can't be sure. He was about six feet tall, overweight, scruffy facial hair, light skin with sunburnt shoulders. The other guy was shorter, dark curly hair cut short, stocky, thick facial stubble. Looked Italian."

"Did they look like any of these guys?" Lou asked holding up photos of Terry Wood, Angelo Catalano, Frank Pandolfino, and Johnny Colucci.

"These two," Rachel said pointing to Wood and Catalano.

"Do you feel confident enough to pick them out of a lineup?" Lou asked.

"Yes. Definitely."

"Is there anything else you remember about them that might help us out?"

"Not really. I was out for a run and the boat caught my eye right before I had to run between the two but, other than that, I didn't really pay much attention."

"You've given us a lot to work with Mrs. Warren," O'Keefe said. "We really appreciate it."

"This is my number," Lou said extending his card out to Rachel. "We may call and ask you to come down and identify these guys in a lineup. If anything else comes to mind, anything that might be of help, please call me."

"I will," she said, as they all stood and went to the front. "I hope you get what you're looking for."

O'Keefe and Peretti walked back out to their car.

"Now we have probable cause, Grasshopper," Peretti said to his partner. "Let's see the magistrate for a warrant and go round them up."

Chapter 36

Niagara Falls, New York

Terry Wood sat with an annoyed look at the interrogation room table. Thus far he had not given any useful information. His attorney, James Rosati, sat next to him, clad in a tailored black Armani suit. His hair was dyed black and slicked back. His left wrist sported a gold Rolex and his right wrist a gold bracelet which complimented a gold diamond pinky ring.

"My client said he was in his office all morning on Wednesday. His head mechanic can confirm this. Your witness must have seen someone who resembles my client," Rosati spoke with traces of his inner-city accent breaking through his attempt at polished English.

"We're still going to require a sworn affidavit from each employee present at the shop Wednesday morning," Peretti answered back, "and your client will remain in our custody pending a lineup this afternoon. If the witness doesn't identify him, and the affidavits confirm his alibi, your client will be released and all charges will be dropped pending any further investigation."

"I think he should be released now," Rosati said, meeting Peretti with a steely gaze.

"No," Peretti replied unintimidated. "Wood isn't going anywhere. In addition to what we've already discussed, we have other questions for him."

"Proceed," Rosati spoke, maintaining his stare.

"Mr. Wood, do you know a Paul Pelliteri?"

"Yeah, I know Paul."

"How do you know him?"

"We've been friends for years. Owns a bar in NT. I sometimes go there."

"When's the last time you saw him?"

"I dunno, a few days ago at his place, I guess."

"Mr. Wood, can you tell us the whereabouts of Angelo Catalano?"

"No clue."

"Is he not one of your employees?"

"Yeah, he is, but he didn't show up for work today. No call, no nothing."

"Do you find that strange?" Peretti asked.

"Not really. He does that from time to time. He's not the most reliable employee. Probably sleeping off a late-night drunk."

"And that doesn't bother you?"

"Sure, it bothers me. Drives me nuts, but his uncle owns the shop. He thinks he can do what he wants and there's not much I can do," Wood said with a shrug.

"What does he do at the shop?"

"He manages the parts and inventory, runs errands and helps out with oil changes, tire rotations. Whatever I need him to do."

"I guess I'm wondering why you wouldn't have called looking for him."

"I called several times, no answer."

"When did you last see him?"

"Yesterday, at work."

"What about last night?" Lou asked.

"What about last night?" Wood asked in return.

"Did you see Angelo last night?"

"Yeah, briefly at the club. He came in and had a beer."

"What club is that?"

"The Power City Club."

"Oh, yes, the social club on Pine. Isn't that where a lot of Bruno Catalano's associates hang out?'

"Hey, I don't know about that. It's just a place for guys to hang out after work, play some Bocce, get away from their wives, play cards, have a few, whatever."

"I see," Lou said, as he made a few notes. "About what time did you see Angelo Catalano at the club?"

"Shoot, I don't know. Probably around eight or nine? The Yankees game was on, but I wasn't paying that close attention."

"And did he say anything to you?"

"About what?"

"Well, there was a report filed of his car running a man and a woman down on a sidewalk by the hospital. Did he happen to mention that?"

"No, but he's a lousy driver. Always looking at his cell phone. It ain't the first time that's happened."

"So he didn't mention that to you?"

"Nope. He didn't say much of anything. Just sat there at the bar looking at his phone like he always does."

"And when did he leave?"

"Not sure. He was maybe there an hour."

"Did he say where he was going?"

"Just that he was heading out. He didn't say where."

"Did anyone leave with him?"

"Not that I saw."

Peretti spent a minute scribbling some notes before shifting gears.

"Do you recognize this vehicle?" He said, holding up an 8x11 photo of the Dodge Caravan that O'Shanick had taken.

"No. Should I?"

"A complaint was filed of this vehicle chasing a truck up 17th and down 16th streets this morning. Do you know anything about that?"

"No, can't say that I do."

"Well, it just so happens, Mr. Wood, that this particular vehicle is currently in your shop for a new timing chain. Does that jog your memory?"

"Maybe, we have lots of vehicles in our shop and I know a couple are getting new timing chains. I don't think anyone was chasing no truck though."

"Oh, is that so," Peretti commented, as he grabbed another photo and held it up. "Well here is a photo taken from the truck being chased as it was chased down an alley between 16th and 17th streets. Recognize the driver, Mr. Wood."

The blow up was slightly blurred due to the windshield, but the resemblance of the driver and Terry were clearly seen. Terry and his attorney stared at the picture for a few seconds.

"Oh, yeah, that Caravan. I took it out for a test drive this morning, but that was it. I wasn't chasing nobody."

"So you were just out for a test drive?"

"That's right."

"And you weren't chasing a truck?'

"Nope."

"But you just happened to follow it up 17th, down 16th, and into an alley where the other side was blocked by a Dodge Charger registered to a Paul Pelliteri, a known friend of yours and associate of the Catalano family. The Charger then chased down the truck and its occupants until they got out and pursued him on foot. At the same time you backed out the other way!"

"Well, yeah, those guys were pointing guns at me!"

"Be quiet, Terry," Rosati said, as he placed a strong grip on Terry's wrist. "Detective Peretti, my client wishes to invoke his Fifth Amendment right at this time."

"And one of the occupants of that truck spotted a rifleman on top of the Rite Aid," Frank continued, standing, his voice rising. "Most notably, one of the occupants of the truck, coincidentally, is the same person who was nearly killed when Angelo Catalano ran him down on a sidewalk. He also was nearly killed by a nurse in the hospital yesterday and just so happens to be the same person ran over by the black hulled Scarab that our witness describes two men resembling Catalano and you, Mr. Wood, getting off that boat!"

"Detective Peretti, I'd like a moment to confer with my client in private," Rosati requested.

"Talk to him all you want, Rosati. Your client is staying right here," Peretti said, as he and O'Keefe walked out of the room.

Peretti and O'Keefe walked in silence until they were back at their desks.

"We need to make that lineup happen ASAP, Kevin."

"Roger that, Lou. I'll get on it right now. What about Catalano?"

"We'll keep looking. He's probably laying low. If we can pin this on Wood, we can worry about Catalano later, but we'll have plenty to obtain a warrant on him."

O'Keefe turned to his phone and began making calls. Lou sat down in his chair, reclined back, and closed his eyes in thought. Four attempts on O'Shanick in forty-eight hours. At least three, if not more, known associates of the Catalano family involved in trying to off him. Definitely a mob hit, but why? O'Shanick was a local, but from Grand Island which isn't exactly Niagara Falls. He had left immediately after high school and has been out of state for fourteen years. Nothing there that would put him in the bad graces of the Catalano family, but here we are. Was it a drunken boating mishap that Wood was trying to cover for? Unlikely. An old score being settled? Lou and O'Keefe had combed the records, nothing turned up involving O'Shanick. Any police record would have disqualified him from the Naval Academy. What was it? How high does this go? Pandolfino? Bruno Catalano? What would those guys possibly have on a decorated Navy SEAL that would make them want to go after him in such a manner? Someone was going to have to talk. Wood, Pelliteri, young Angelo Catalano, someone.

The days of Omertà, where made men and associates adhered to a code of silence, evaporated when Gotti's underboss, Sammy "The Bull" Gravano ratted out all of La Cosa Nostra to save his own skin. Wise guys began singing like birds after that. It was one of several reasons the previous organizations had nearly become non-existent before Catalano took over. Could they get Wood or one of the other guys to talk? Unknown. One thing was for sure, nobody would be talking unless they were facing heavy charges. All the more reason to get Wood pinned down with Ms. Warren picking him out of a lineup. They would find Catalano soon enough.

Chapter 37

Grand Island, New York

Joe deftly worked the throttles to nudge the Sea Ray Sundancer 320 alongside the dock. Tran and Mueller quickly tied her up while Joe shut down the engines. Rammer and Joe hopped up onto the dock and turned to help Christy up, but she had stepped up on her own.

"I thought your dad was a sailor, Joe," Rammer remarked.

"Oh, he is. He keeps his sailboat down at the sailing club where he races and socializes. This little gem was a 30th wedding anniversary gift for my mom."

"Ah, yes, Santa Maria," Christy read off the name painted on the stern, "you once told me your mom is a saint."

"That's right and everyone else knows it too, especially my dad."

The five headed up the dock and reached the steps leading up the hill to the entrance of the riverside establishment Joe's younger brother owned. It was aptly named *Sean O'Shanick's River Pub.* Sean made a tidy living with the year-round restaurant serving fine Irish fare favored by the local residents and boaters. He also ran a small marina, renting out twelve boat slips and performing maintenance during the day. He was the only one of the five O'Shanick siblings not to have gone to college but, with his work ethic and entrepreneurial mind, he was doing quite well for himself. By the looks of things, as they stepped through the door, the Friday lunch crowd indicated that Sean was indeed doing well.

"Hey! Joey-O!" Came a chorus from several old high school friends gathered around the bar situated at the entrance. Joe took a few minutes to greet his old friends, who had just finished eighteen holes of golf at nearby Beaver Island State Park. After breaking away, he led his friends to the hostess stand to get a table.

"Joe!" A petite and blond young woman, wearing khaki shorts and a green *Sean O'Shanick's* t-shirt and apron, was returning from the dining area when she saw Joe and ran into his arms squealing with delight.

"Hey, Abby!" Joe said, as he squeezed her back trying not to hurt his ribs.

"Sean told me what happened! Are you okay?"

"No worse for the wear, I guess. Guys," Joe said, turning to present Abby to his friends, "this is Sean's..." Joe stopped, grabbed her left hand and made a quick check ensuring the diamond engagement ring was still there, "...fiancé, Abby Caldwell. She and Sean have been together since middle school and she's been like a little sister to me for years."

"Well, a sister of Joe's is good enough for me," Rammer said, as he shook her hand gently. "Hello, ma'am, I'm Matt."

They all took turns greeting Abby.

"You must be Christy!" Abby said, looking up at Christy with a beaming smile.

"Why, yes, I am, Abby. It's so nice to finally meet you. I've heard so much about you."

"And you're even more beautiful in person!" Abby replied. "Ina has told me so much about you."

"Ina?" Christy asked.

"I'm sorry, Mrs. O'Shanick. Ina means mom in Tagalog. She likes that better than Mrs. O'Shanick. She says that makes her feel old. She's such a doll and, wow, is she enamored with you!"

Christy blushed.

"Well, she's a very sweet lady. Actually, you put it better...a doll." Christy responded.

"So is it just the five of you, Joe?" Abby asked.

"Yes, unless you and Sean can join us?"

"I wish," she said looking around, "but, as you can see, the summer crowd is starting to pick up and Sean's helping out in the kitchen. I'll show you to your table and let him know you're here."

Once they were seated, Abby took their drink orders and disappeared out front to the bar. She returned a minute later with their drinks and a basket of garlic bread.

"That's from Sean. He said he'll be out in a few. Are you ready to order?"

"Yep. I've been building these guys up about Sean's wings so tell him he's on. Let's get his mini Beef on Weck sampler tray and an order of fifty wings."

"How do you want your wings?"

"Umm..." Joe said looking around the table.

"Hot!" Everyone chorused.

"You too?" Joe said looking at Christy. "Are you sure? We take hot to another level up here."

"I'm half Irish and half Iranian," she answered. "That means I'm feisty and spicy. Bring it on!"

This was met with approving laughter from the guys.

"I like you already!" Abby, said laying a hand on Christy's shoulder. "Coming right up guys!" She said, as she trotted back out front.

"I like her, Joe," Christy said, leaning in.

"Me too. She's been a part of the family forever and she's perfect for Sean. They've paid their dues building up this business. I'm glad to see it's paying off for them and they can finally get married."

"Is the wedding still in October?"

"Yes, they wanted to wait until after boating season so they could get away. Wait. How do you know?" Joe asked.

"Your mother told me," she answered slyly.

"I might have known," Joe smiled, as he shook his head. He may have thought Christy was out of his league, but his mother certainly wasn't going to stop trying.

Joe felt his phone vibrate an incoming text. He retrieved it from his tech pocket and read the message.

"Alright," Joe said turning serious. "Detective O'Keefe texted me and said they have Terry Wood in custody and a witness connecting him to the boat that ran me over. The other guy, Catalano, is still at large but they're looking for him."

"By my count, there are at least three more people involved in this. The police have one. Not good enough," Chief Ramsey commented.

"I hear you, Chief," Joe said nodding in his direction. "You know how I operate. I'd prefer to sweep up every single person involved, but this isn't a foreign enemy we're dealing with. They're U.S. citizens and, for all intents and purposes, we are civilians. We have no right to operate here. We break the law and we can go to jail. I'm not going to put any of you guys in that position. I don't like it, but I think we are going to have to let the police handle it. I trust O'Keefe. He's an honorable combat Marine. His partner, Peretti, seems like a stand-up guy as well, so I'm content to let them handle it for now."

"You really think you can trust them, Joe?" Ramsey asked. "Those mafia types always have some police under their thumbs."

"It's possible, Chief. Every profession has some bad players, but ninety-nine percent of police are honorable, hardworking people just like us. We'll keep our eyes open but we'll have to trust the process. I just don't see how we have any other choice. With Wood in custody, the rest might be laying low."

"Then what should we do, Skipper?" Mueller asked.

"We'll wait and see what the police come up with. Not much else we can do. Meanwhile, I'm going to treat you guys to a nice day on the river.

Joe looked up and saw his brother heading their way, carrying a large tray of steaming wings.

"For now, we'll let the police handle it while we enjoy some of Sean's finest," Joe said as he stood up to greet his younger brother.

Chapter 38

Tonawanda, New York

Rachel fixed her hair in the hallway mirror and grabbed her keys. She stopped to fire off a quick text to her husband, Scott, letting him know she where she was going. She walked out to their detached garage and got into her Honda CRV. Looking both ways, she backed out onto Franklin Street and headed off. She reached Niagara Street by the river and turned right heading toward Niagara Falls. As she did, her phone rang. The dashboard monitor showed it was Scott calling. She pressed the Bluetooth button on her steering wheel to answer.

"Hey, babe," she answered.

"Rachel? What's going on? Your text said something about going to pick someone out of a lineup?"

Rachel could hear the sound of barbells and weights in the background. Scott must have some of his football players in the weight room. Was it after two already?

"Yes," she answered. She loved to toy with Scott.

"Yes? What do you mean? What's going on?"

"What's going on is your wife is now a star witness!"

"A witness? A witness to what?" The concern growing in his voice.

Scott was very protective. Rachel loved to use it to work him up but, deep down, she loved her husband for it.

"Relax, Scott. It's no big deal. I responded to a request the police put out about a stolen boat they found tied up at Niawanda. I saw the guys getting off the boat when I was jogging yesterday and they want me to come identify one of them in a lineup. That's all."

"I don't know, sweetie; I don't like it. I think you should stay out of it."

"Scott! I'll be behind a one-way mirror. They'll never see me. It's the right thing to do. You know that."

"I still don't like it, babe. I at least feel like I ought to come with you. Posi's here. He can run the weight session. Let me come get you and I'll drive you there myself."

"Scott, that's not necessary, I'll be fine. I love that you worry about me, but it's really okay."

"You sure?" He sighed.

"Yes! Go back to your team and show them how it's done. I'll probably be home before you."

"Alright. Please be careful. Text me when you're leaving."

"I will, Scott. I promise. I love you."

"Love you too, beautiful. Bye." He clicked off.

He really did tend to worry, but Scott was a good man, Rachel reflected as she drove over the Erie Canal into North Tonawanda. She was lucky to have him. A former defensive lineman at the University at Buffalo, he was still a rock solid 280 pounds compared to her 120 pounds. She always compared them to an old cartoon where a big tough bulldog was enamored with a little kitten and followed the kitten everywhere to protect it. The bulldog was always happiest when the kitten snuggled up in his arms. That was her Scott to a tee. She would give him a good snuggle later tonight.

Rachel braked to a stop behind a car stopped at a red light in the industrial section of North Tonawanda. A white van pulled up beside her and the side doors suddenly opened. A man wearing coveralls and a black ski mask jumped out wielding a hammer. Frightened, she had enough cool to shift into reverse, only to be stopped by an old pickup truck that had crept up behind her. The masked man smashed her window with the hammer and reached in. Rachel screamed and desperately clawed at his face trying to poke his eyes, but he swung the hammer at her head. The blow stunned her enough to take the fight out of her. The man reached across, undid her seatbelt and dragged her through the window. He deposited her limp body on the floor of the van.

"Go!" Johnny Colucci yelled to the driver, as he secured her wrists and ankles with flex-ties closed the doors, and then removed his ski mask.

The driver sped off with Pelliteri behind them in the car. Back at the intersection, another member of the crew jumped out of the passenger side of the pickup truck and got into Rachel's CRV. He turned right at the intersection and drove behind one of the industrial warehouses where he parked the car leaving the keys in the ignition. He hopped out and jumped back into the waiting pickup truck.

Back in the van, Colucci looked down at his catch. She was still out of it.

"Man! That took all of about fifteen seconds, Marco! That's gotta be a new record!"

"Freaking A right, Blade!" Marco Vona said looking back.

"You sure we gotta waste her, Johnny? A good lookin' chick like that? You know how much she'd be worth a night?"

"I know, Marco. She blows away all the other ponies in your stable, but the Panda was very clear about this. She had the goods on Terry and she's gotta go. No screwups. She goes straight to the funeral home."

"Man! We could take her out of town and sell her. My guy in Manhattan would pay bank!" Marco pleaded.

"Marco! Did I stutter? If we cross up the Panda it'll be us going straight to the funeral home! Don't even think about it."

Chapter 39

Niagara Falls, New York

"Hi, you've reached Rachel! I'm sorry I can't take your call right now, but if you leave a message, I'll get right back to you. Have a great day!"

O'Keefe slammed down his phone in frustration. He had been calling Rachel Warren repeatedly, but her phone kept going to voicemail. She was supposed to have shown up an hour ago. A sinking feeling began to set in. Had someone gotten to her and warned her off? He turned back to his computer and went to a page showing real time traffic calls for the department. Nothing. He went to Niagara County Sheriff's next. Nothing there either. He tried Erie County Sheriff's, City of Tonawanda, North Tonawanda, and even State Police. Nothing. No wrecks, no calls for assistance that matched up. Shoot. O'Keefe leaned back in his chair and closed his eyes. *Where are you?*

Rachel seemed very sharp and organized. Not the type to get lost or forget to show up. Certainly not without calling. This wasn't good. The Catalano organization had proven they were out to kill off a decorated Navy SEAL. Would they be above killing an eyewitness? Not likely. O'Keefe didn't want to accept that. Hopefully, she was fine and there was an explanation. He didn't want to consider the alternative. She reminded O'Keefe a lot of his wife, Loni; young, attractive, fit, hardworking, and organized. They even looked similar. If something ever happened to Loni, O'Keefe would be crushed. All because they asked her to come anonymously pick a thug out of a lineup? No. That can't be. Nobody knew about her. There had to be a reason, O'Keefe thought to himself as he sat up and dialed her number again. Voicemail.

Lou's phone began to ring. O'Keefe reached over to Lou's desk and picked it up.

"Detective Peretti's desk, this is Detective O'Keefe speaking."

"Yes, I'm trying to reach Detective Peretti."

"He's away from his desk right now, may I take a message?"

"Yeah, my name is Scott Warren. I'm trying to find my wife..."

"Mr. Warren!" O'Keefe interrupted. "I'm Detective Peretti's partner, Kevin O'Keefe. We've been trying to reach your wife. She should have been here an hour ago. Do you know where she is?"

"That's why I'm calling you guys. She thought she'd be back before I got home and she's not here. I found this card here with Detective Peretti's number. I've been trying her cell phone and she's not answering. That's not like her. I'm worried, man."

O'Keefe felt that knot growing in his stomach.

"Well that makes two of us," O'Keefe winced. What else could he say? "When did you last talk to her, Scott?'

"When she was driving your way. I told her I didn't think it was a good idea. I wanted to come with her, but she said she'd be fine. I knew I should have come with her!"

"I understand, Scott. I'm married too. I'd do anything to protect my wife. but we don't know if anything happened. Her phone may have died, and she just can't reach us."

"No, you don't know Rachel. She's so organized. She never lets her phone lose a charge. Look man, I'm getting real worried here. You gotta help me find her."

"I'm working on it, Scott. Look, here's what we know. I've checked around and there haven't been any accidents or calls for assistance in the vicinity of her likely route here. So that's good news."

"Good news? I'm worried somebody grabbed her! I'd welcome a minor wreck right now!"

"I understand, Scott. I really do. Look, hardly anyone knew she was connected to this case we're working, so I doubt anyone knows enough to go looking for her. I'm sure there's a good explanation and she'll turn up. Please know, I'm doing everything I can to find her."

O'Keefe looked up as Peretti walked back into the squad room.

"I'm gonna start looking, too," Scott Warren responded, his stress penetrating through the phone. "I'm going to drive your way following the route she would have taken. I should never have let her go without me. If something happened to her, I'll never forgive myself!"

"Scott, I need you to calm down, buddy. We don't know anything yet. Why don't you try some of her friends while my partner and I keep looking on our end. Okay?"

"Oh, I'll be calling them next, but I'm also going to drive around and look for her. Please call me the minute you hear anything."

"You got it, Scott. I promise. Bye for now," O'Keefe said, as he hung up his phone and looked up at his partner.

"We're not going to find her," Peretti spoke quietly.

"What are you talking about?"

"Let's take a ride."

"Lou? What's going on?"

"Just shut up and don't say anything else until we get to my car."

They walked on in silence until they were outside and reached Lou's unmarked car.

"Alright, Lou, what gives?"

"Wood's been let go."

"WHAT?! Lou! Are you freaking kidding me?"

"I wish I was, Kevin," Peretti said, as he guided the car out onto Tenth Street. "The fact is, Wood's been let go and the case has been closed."

"CLOSED? For the love of God, why?"

"It's just the way it is, Kevin. Take my advice and let it go."

"Lou? How can I let this go? You know the facts as much as I do. The Catalano organization has tried to take O'Shanick out four times in two days. Four times! What's more, we know who the guys are who are doing this! Why are you saying we have to close the case?'

"Not my call, Kevin. It came from higher up. Trust me, you need to let it go."

"No, Lou! We're not letting it go. We already have a lot to move on. We can bag these guys and a lot of them at that. That's our job, for crying out loud. How do you expect me to let it go. It's not right!"

"Listen to me, Kevin!" Lou said, as he pulled over to the side and turned to face his partner. "That beautiful young woman is gone! You hear me? Gone! That man you were talking to just became a widower only he'll never have any closure because there will never be a body to bury. No grave to visit. Now, I've lost two partners over my time in the squad because they got too close."

"Too close? To close to what?"

"Let me finish!" Peretti said heatedly.

"Okay, Lou, I'm sorry."

"Look," Peretti said, purposefully toning down his demeanor. "I'm not mad at you, Kevin. I like you. You're an honest cop, a hard worker, and you have a great nose for this business. Maybe too good."

"What's that mean?"

Peretti placed both his hands on the wheel and stared out the windshield for a brief minute before he dropped his head and slowly shook it. With a sigh, he turned back to his partner.

"Bottom line, kid, is Catalano owns this town. He owns the mayor, he owns the city council, and he owns the police. At least the ones he needs to."

"You can't be serious, Lou."

"I'm being completely serious. Now listen to me. I've lost two partners over the years because they got too close to the Catalano organization. They were told to back off, but they refused. My first partner was found floating in the lower river. The second one, Pete, well, they must have really wanted us to get the message because he and his wife were torched alive in their little house in Lasalle. I'm not gonna let that happen to you, kid. These guys are serious trouble. You might think you can take them down, but they won't let you. I've watched too many people go down trying. They haven't touched me out of respect for my dad's family, but also because I knew when to back off. They've let us make some busts, but when they send out a warning, you back off or you won't know what hit you."

"So you're saying they own the police force?"

"No. They own a few guys in the right places. Ninety-nine percent of this department are good people. Only a few are on the take, but they can make life miserable for the rest of us and, if that don't work, the organization will. I'm just saying you gotta know what battles to fight, Kevin. That girl is gone and we've been told the case is closed and to stand down."

"How did they find out so fast? Only three of us knew about Rachel Warren?"

"I assure you it wasn't me, Kevin."

"Then that only leaves Captain Battaglia," Kevin responded quietly.

Lou didn't respond. He simply met Kevin with a blank stare.

"You've got to be kidding me! The chief of detectives is on the take?'

"I'm afraid so, Kevin."

"How long have you known this?"

"Long enough to know to keep my mouth shut and to watch my back, which you will need to do as well if you want to survive this."

"He already knows what happened to Rachel and told us to stand down? It's only been a couple of hours," O'Keefe asked incredulously.

"He told me the word came down from on high."

O'Keefe made a sour face.

"I know, son," Peretti patted O'Keefe's arm reassuringly. "I hate it too, but I've got a family to look out for and I'm three months away from full retirement. You and Loni have a lifetime ahead of you; kids, ballgames, vacations, grandkids, graduations. You're gonna do a lot of good things over the next twenty or so years. Make sure you're alive to do it."

"We need to at least let O'Shanick know," O'Keefe pleaded.

"Not a good idea, kid. You may as well draw a target on your forehead if you do that. Let it go."

Chapter 40

The bright afternoon sun blinded Terry Wood as he emerged from the police headquarters. Having done his bit, Rosati had left for another family job and left Terry to fend for his own ride. Johnny Colucci answered the call and was waiting at the curb in his 75 Corvette Stingray.

"Thanks, Blade," Terry said, as he lowered himself into the passenger seat.

"Don't mention it. This is kind of gettin' to be a routine for us, isn't it? Me pickin' you up from jail? How many times is this, Terry?"

Terry, too tired to talk, sat slumped in the seat and answered Colucci's barb with a one finger salute.

"You're dragging, aren't you, Terry? You need a bump?"

"You got some?" Terry asked.

"Yeah, here," Colucci said, as he produced a small vial of cocaine. "I thought you might be running on empty by now."

"Thanks, Blade," Terry said as he rolled up a dollar bill and opened the vial. "I could've waited until we got back to the shop. You didn't have to risk this coming here to the big house."

"Yeah, I did. The Panda is back at the shop waiting for you. I figured you'd need a little jack before you see him."

"That figures," Terry said, as he snorted half the vial into his nostril. "Is he in a rage?"

"You might say that. But we handled business with the chick that was supposed to ID you in the lineup today, so he's a little better with me and Paulie P, but he's still wanting a piece of you."

"Great," Terry said, as he finished the rest of the vial in the other nostril.

"Ah, don't sweat it, Terry. As long as we keep bringing in the bank, he ain't whacking nobody."

"Blade, you just barbecued Angelo last night. Catalano's frigging nephew! None of us are beyond getting whacked."

"Ange was a chooch who couldn't be trusted. His uncle couldn't stand him. As long as they know we won't talk to no one and we keep making the crew a ton of cash, we're fine. Now wipe your nose. If The Panda even suspects any of us are using the product, all bets are off."

They pulled into the back entrance of the shop and parked by the rear door. Terry winced when he saw that his Monte Carlo was parked in his usual spot forcing Pandolfino to park his Lincoln one spot away from the door. Oh well, none of this was planned. They walked into Terry's office and saw Pandolfino sitting behind Terry's desk talking to Paulie Pelliteri, who was seated on the leather couch. Pandolfino stopped what he was saying and looked up at Terry with a scowl.

"Mr. Pandolfino, I...I'm sorry," was all Terry could muster.

Pandolfino let the silence hang as he continued to scowl at Terry.

"You are sorry, you fat, stupid half-breed," he began. "You're also sloppy and careless. Not only have you boys screwed up this simple assignment I've given you, but now you've brought the heat down on our organization! Mr. Catalano had to call in a couple of favors to spring you and he don't like calling in favors when it's his people who screwed up in the first place. He ain't happy with you, Wood," Pandolfino said and then looked around the room. "He ain't happy with none of us!"

Terry and crew quietly looked on as Pandolfino took his pound of flesh for a few more minutes.

"What now, sir?" Terry asked.

"Your original assignment remains. You're to take out O'Shanick. It ain't gonna be easy. He's holed up with his family, so I would suggest you use his family to smoke him out. Do what you gotta do, but don't get caught. The police have been told to stand down on this one but that's Grand Island and the boss doesn't want to have to call in any favors with the Erie County Sheriff's, so watch your step."

"Mr. Pandolfino, why is it that he wants this O'Shanick guy so bad that he's willing to send the entire organization after him and throw his weight around with the police?"

"You don't know, and you don't want to know. It doesn't matter, Wood. You just do what you're told to do and keep your mouth shut! You hear me?"

"Yeah, I hear you."

"Good. Then get it done!"

Chapter 41

Buffalo, New York

The nonexistent wind allowed the sun to reflect perfectly upon the glass-like water. It had turned out to be a perfect day for boating. The sun warmed the afternoon to eighty-three degrees. Joe couldn't resist the opportunity to take Christy and his teammates up the Niagara River to Lake Erie and show them the Buffalo waterfront.

It had taken decades, but the formerly industrialized city had gradually replaced the waterfront mills and warehouses with a revitalized waterfront and downtown. Approaching the city, one could easily appreciate the vast architecture. Renowned architects such as Frank Lloyd Wright, Louis Sullivan, and H.H. Richardson all had a hand in the city's many distinctive buildings. The gold-topped City Hall with its Art Deco features easily stood out, giving the city it's recognizable city-scape.

They passed the Erie Basin Marina to their left and turned up the Buffalo River, the focal point of the downtown revitalization. Looming ahead to their left was the USS Little Rock, a guided missile cruiser that had served in World War Two. Alongside her were the USS The Sullivans, a World War Two destroyer, and the USS Croaker, a World War Two submarine. The ships were part of the Buffalo Naval and Military Park, one of many downtown attractions. A large waterfront park opened up behind them where scores of people strolled and lounged in the perfect afternoon sun. The long Western New York winters could last into May and the locals were finally able to enjoy the sun and the warmth.

"This is a really cool place, Joe," Chief Ramsey remarked. "It reminds me a little bit of Duluth Harbor back home."

"I've never been there, Rammer, but I can imagine they are similar. Buffalo was a steel manufacturer and ran several grain mills. General Mills is still here and most days it smells like Cheerios and sometimes it smells like cookies. If I'm not mistaken, a lot of the grain and iron ore comes from your town."

"That's right. The iron ore and grain come from all over the Midwest by rail and are loaded onto ships in Duluth. We had our own steel mill too. Now they've revitalized the waterfront to attract tourists and local business, like what we see here. It just dies down tremendously during the winter."

"Surprisingly, the crowds can actually be seen here year-round," Joe said, feeling like a tour guide as they slowly cruised by the waterfront park.

"Excavators uncovered one of the original entrances to the famous Erie Canal in this location. In fact, that's it right there," Joe said, pointing to a narrow canal lined by cobblestone walls.

"A local developer further excavated the old canal into what is now a good part of the park. You can see some of the footbridges that cross the canal in different spots. In the winter, it freezes and people skate all around the park. Up ahead, that large building," Joe said pointing, "is what is known as Harbor Center. The Pegula family that owns the Bills and the Sabres built that where the old Memorial Auditorium used to be. It houses a hotel, two hockey rinks, and much more. They've built up several hotels, bars, and restaurants within walking distance, the Sabres play here and the Seneca even have a casino here, so this place stays busy year round."

Joe steered to starboard and avoided a group of kayakers. They continued on past the arena where the Buffalo Sabres play and past a restored warehouse that now housed several waterfront restaurants. Scores of people were seated at balcony tables as upbeat music drifted down to the water.

"My kind of place, Joe!" Mueller spoke up from the back.

"You guys want to tie up and walk around?"

"Sure!" They chorused.

Joe brought the Sea Ray around and eased her in alongside the pier that stretched the length of the waterfront park. Once again, Tran and Mueller proved their naval skills as they expertly tied the craft to the pier. Christy hopped up onto the pier followed by Ramsey. Joe locked down the boat, pocketed the keys, and climbed up onto the dock as well.

"I'm ready for a beer," Rammer announced.

"Good call, Chief, I'll take point," Tran answered.

Joe hesitated.

"You coming, Joe?" Ramsey asked.

"No, I'm going to take Christy over to that custard stand and let her try another Buffalo delicacy. You guys go on ahead. Meet back at the boat in an hour."

"Aye, sir," Ramsey answered. "C'mon, tadpoles."

"Joe, we can go with them if you want," Christy spoke into his ear.

"I know, but I see them all the time. I haven't gotten to spend much time with you since you got here."

"Oh? I'm honored." She said while smiling.

"Besides, you really do need to try frozen custard. Do you remember me telling you about it, among all the other Buffalo delicacies, when we were trying to eat saltwater ramen noodles on the sailboat in a tropical storm?"

"How could I forget?" Christy smiled.

"Well then, c'mon," Joe said, as he grabbed her hand and led her in a quick run over to a local vender known for its frozen custard.

After paying, Joe led Christy around the Canalside park as they savored their treats.

"Oh my gosh, this is good, Joe!"

"I told you!"

"It can't be good for you," she opined.

"No, but we don't talk about that. It ruins the fun."

"Why are you doing this to me? Pizza, wings, subs, ice cream. I won't be able to fit into my triathlon gear after this weekend!"

"I highly doubt that," Joe said, as he searched for the right words to say. "You just swam two miles and ran nine in under an eight-minute mile pace. You're fine."

He wanted to tell her that she had about as perfectly toned and sculpted a figure as any woman could ever have, but he didn't know how she would take it. She was certainly not a feminist who would take offense, but he didn't want her to think he only thought of her physically. Her appeal was her intellect and her personality, a bold confidence restrained by humility and selflessness. Her striking beauty was just icing on the cake. No, it was more than that. Her beauty was magnified by the beautiful spirit within.

Wait, what?

Was that part of it? Her religiousness had originally been a turn-off, but was that what was the framework of her many appealing qualities? Was that why he found his mother and his sisters so exceptional as well? They were all religious. No, that's not right. They were all genuine in their faith. They all possessed a peaceful, gentle persona, yet were fiercely loyal and selfless. It came naturally to them, like it did Christy. What was that scripture his mom used to pray over him? *Be transformed by the renewing of his mind.* Was that part of it?

"Joe? Joe?"

"Yes?" Joe answered, shaking off his momentary contemplation.

"You look lost in thought. Is everything okay?"

"Everything is great," Joe smiled, "but, yeah, I was just thinking of something."

"What was it?'

"More of a question, really. I'm just not sure how to put it in words," he said, as they arrived back at the waterfront.

"What's it about, Joe?"

"Well, is it odd that an agnostic like me, someone who is normally turned off by religion and religious people, is it odd that I would now find you attractive because of your faith?"

"You mean you didn't find me attractive before?" Christy said, with a mock pouting expression as she placed her hands on her hips.

"NO! I mean, yes, I mean..."

Christy cocked her head to her side in an accusing manner.

"What I'm trying to say is..." Joe paused, as he desperately searched for words.

"Relax, Joe," Christy smiled. "I think I know what you're trying to say."

"You do?"

"Yes."

"Then, in that case, can you say it for me? I seem to be rather tongue tied."

"No, Joe O'Shanick, I'm not letting you off that easy. I want you to tell me what you're thinking. It's okay," she smiled. "I won't bite."

"Alright," he said exhaling, "so, what I'm trying to say is..."

Joe's phone vibrated an incoming call. He decided to ignore it.

"Sorry. Anyway..."

The vibrating stopped after a minute and then returned.

"Joe, take the call. I'll hold your place in this conversation."

"No, this is too important. You're too important."

Christy's eyes opened in surprise.

"Nobody has ever said that to me before," she said quietly. "Alright, Joe, you have my complete attention."

Christy's response brought Joe into focus.

"What I'm trying to say is, I'm beginning to understand your faith."

"Oh," Christy was caught off guard. "Really? Well that's great! How? I mean, what brought this about just now? Was it the ice cream?"

"Yeah, kind of."

"What? Joe O'Shanick! What are you talking about?"

"When you made that comment about gaining weight from all this Buffalo fare?"

"Yes...?" Christy prodded.

"I was going to tell you that you were about as perfect as a woman could ever hope to be, but I stopped myself. I was worried you might take that the wrong way."

"Well, although I don't think of myself as anywhere close to physically perfect, I hold you in the highest respect, Joe, and I wouldn't feel anything other than flattered to hear such a thing from you. You've never been anything other than a gentleman around me and I know your motives are pure. But how does my faith figure into this?"

"I was getting to that. As soon as I stopped and thought about what I nearly said, I realized that what's even more attractive about you is what's inside. You're intelligent, beautiful and confident, but restrained by humility and selflessness. I've seen you fight off an attacker and even pick up a rifle and shoot to survive, but you're first and foremost, a healer. You're remarkable in so many ways, but you also remind me of my sisters and my mother and that's when it hit me. It's not at all about being religious with you guys. There really is a genuine faith going on inside of you guys. It's real, isn't it?"

"Yes, Joe, it's very real."

"That's what I'm starting to get. You've got to understand, I've fought in Iraq, Afghanistan, and now Central America. I've seen terrible things done in the name of religion. Even here, most of the people I've known that have been religious have been terrible people in many respects. I wanted nothing to do with it. You're different. My mom, Marina, Anna, even my dad, you're all different. It's not something superficial with you. It's not a religion with you. It's something very real. Your faith is real. You live it."

"You are starting to understand it, Joe, but you're missing a key point."

"Okay, what's that?"

"The point is, it's not me who lives it, it's Christ in me. By myself, I'm nothing of what you just described. I'm sinful, self-centered, and ugly. It's when I die to myself and let Christ live through me that those qualities begin to show. It's not even faith."

"What? It's not faith? Then what is faith?"

"Faith is believing in and acting upon the evidence of what we know to be true. Yes, I follow Christ because I have faith in Him, but that faith is based on evidence. Evidence that causes me, and your mother and your sisters, to *know* that He is real, to know that He is who He said He is and that He is the way, the truth and the life. That's what motivates me to live for Him, but living for Him means allowing Him to live through me."

Joe looked quizzically at Christy, as he processed this information.

"You're looking at me funny, Joe. Does this make sense to you?"

"Actually, a lot of it does, yes. I'll be honest and say that I have come around to believing a god likely exists, but I'm not to the point where I can definitely say it's the Christian God or Jesus. Having said that," Joe said holding his hand up in defense, "I see that your faith is real and how it affects you, which adds a lot to what you're telling me. I need more convincing, but you've made me open my mind. All that to say, religion used to be a turn off for me but, in your case, your genuine faith makes you even more appealing."

Christy looked up at Joe, speechless.

"Thank you, Joe," she managed quietly.

"But I won't lie. You can absolutely rock a triathlon suit!"

"Joe O'Shanick!" Christy said, as she began to playfully pound on his chest.

"Hey! What do you want me to say?" he said laughing, "I'm being completely honest!"

His phone began to ring again.

"You better see who that is."

"What? And spoil the moment?"

"I'm serious, Joe. There's a lot going on with you. Take the call. It could be important. Please?"

Joe looked down and didn't recognize the number.

"It's probably someone calling to extend the warranty on my truck," he said, as he punched the receive button.

"Hello?"

"Lieutenant Commander?"

"Yes?"

"This is the Second Marines grunt that you met yesterday. Do you remember me?"

"Yes, I do," Joe answered, perking up to the fact that Detective O'Keefe was being elusive.

"Good. I need to talk to you about something, but it would be better if it were in person. Is that possible? It's rather urgent."

"Yes. When?"

"Where are you now?"

"I'm up in Buffalo at the waterfront park by Canalside."

"I can be there in twenty-five minutes."

"Okay, I'm in a white Sea Ray Sundancer tied up close to the concert stage."

"On my way."

The line went dead.

"Who was that?"

"Detective O'Keefe. He's on his way. Didn't want to talk on the phone."

"That doesn't sound good."

"No, it doesn't. Let's head back to the boat." Joe said, as he turned and led Christy back down the pier.

"Should you call your teammates? I'm sure they'll want to know what's going on."

"Oh, they definitely would. That's the problem."

"Why is that a problem?"

"Because those are the most loyal operators a platoon leader could ever hope to have."

"That sounds like a good problem to have," Christy said, as she stepped onto the boat.

"It is," Joe said stepping down behind her. "But those guys don't deserve to get caught up in this. It's not a combat op where we are ordered to engage and kill the enemy. We're dealing with mobsters, but they're American mobsters and, like it or not, they're afforded equal protection under the law. We can't just go after them and take them out. We'd end up in jail. My guys' lives would be ruined. I'm not having that. No. I'm not sanctioned to operate under these circumstances, especially in New York State where you can't even stand your ground. As much as I hate it, I have to let the police fight this battle for me. Let the boys relax. You and I can see what this is all about. Maybe it's good news," Joe said, without conviction.

As it turned out, Ramsey, Mueller and Tran returned to the boat before Detective O'Keefe arrived.

"I didn't hear any sirens," Joe said, by way of greeting when they all stepped back on board.

"You didn't give us enough time to get into any real trouble, Skipper," Mueller replied.

"Mule, I kept watching the Skyway wondering when you were going to dive off," Joe said, as he pointed to the landmark bridge towering high overhead.

Mueller looked up.

"That might be pushing it a bit, sir, even for me."

"Glad to know you have a limit, son," Ramsey remarked.

"I might be fearless, Chief, but I ain't crazy."

"That's debatable," Tran remarked.

"Maybe so, Tran, but I do hold the record for the highest water jump in the platoon jumping off that oil platform in the Gulf. I call that inspirational."

"Well, when your IQ falls short of your record jump, I call that a deficiency, Mule," Tran quipped back as the others laughed.

"Excuse me. Lieutenant Commander O'Shanick?"

At once, everyone looked up to see Detective O'Keefe standing above them on the pier.

"Good afternoon, Detective, c'mon aboard. Guys, this is Detective Kevin O'Keefe. Detective, these are my friends, Matt Ramsey, Tommy Tran, and Jamie Mueller. You've met Dr. Tabrizi."

"Nice to meet you all," O'Keefe said, as he shook each one's hand while giving each a quick eye survey.

"Have a seat, Detective. Can I get you something to drink? There's water, Body Armor, and pop."

"I'm good, thanks. I can't stay long."

"I respect that. So what did you want to talk about?"

O'Keefe looked around uneasily.

"Everyone here can be trusted, Mr. O'Keefe. I trust these guys and this gal with my life. You're safe to speak freely."

"They're teammates, aren't they?" O'Keefe asked looking around again.

"Yes, but let's keep that amongst us, if you don't mind," Joe answered.

"Absolutely. I could just tell. I did four years as a grunt officer in the Corps. I know special operators when I see them. Actually, I'm glad they're here. You've got a serious problem..."

Chapter 42

Grand Island, New York

" **T**ell your dad I said 'Hi.' It was good seeing you again, Joe!'"

"I will, Dan. Good seeing you too!" Joe yelled back, as they pulled away from the dock.

On the way back from Buffalo, they stopped to top off the fuel tanks at a local marina just upstream from Sean's restaurant. The owner was a friend of the family and, ever the loyal friend, it was the only place Joe's father visited to fuel his boat.

Joe's team wanted to discuss the shocking information Detective O'Keefe had dropped on them, but Joe wanted to get on their way first. The ride back from Lake Erie had been fast and loud, making for difficult conversation. Pulling away from the dock, Joe eased the craft out into the channel and kept to a slow cruising speed that would allow for conversation.

"Christy, would you mind steering for a while?"

"Sure," she said, as she pivoted in the raised seat opposite Joe, extending her long legs to the deck, and stood up.

Joe stood aside as she stepped in behind the wheel.

"Okay, just keep us in the center of the river. I need to talk this matter over with the guys," he said quietly. "When you get to the bridge, go under the center span."

"Will you stay next to me?" She asked.

"Yep."

"Good."

"Why? Are you nervous about handling the boat?"

"Nope. I just want to be next to you," she said, as she looked up with a pleasant grin.

Joe smiled back, reached with his right arm and pulled her in for a quick hug. With a sigh, he let go and turned around to face his teammates.

"Alright guys, picking up where we left off, I appreciate and I'm deeply moved that y'all are willing to head down range and engage these mobsters, but it's a civilian matter and you could all end up in prison. You and your families could be targeted. I cannot, in good conscience, let you do that. So far I'm the only one they're after, and I'm willing to accept that and keep it that way."

"With all due respect, Skipper," Chief Ramsey started, "that's not your choice. We aren't leaving you here to fight this on your own. We just need to figure out a way to bag these street rats without landing us in prison."

"I'm with the Chief, sir," Tran spoke up. "No man left behind."

"That goes for me too, sir," Mueller added.

"Guys, your careers and your futures could be at stake. I get sick just thinking about that."

"Skipper, you've ran into enemy gunfire and dragged me, personally, out of harm's way when I went down. I wouldn't be here today if it weren't for you. You've kept us all safe over the years. If it was any of us in your shoes, you'd be the first one to step in and that's how it is with us. We've got your six."

"Alright then," Joe said as he eyes watered with pride. "Let's figure this thing out. And guys? Thank you."

"We wouldn't have it any other way, sir," Rammer replied. "What do you see as our options?"

"I think what we need to do would be to start with these guys Wood and Catalano and work our way up the food chain until we find out who put out the hit on me and why. I'd love to neutralize the threat along the way, but that's not an option. We need to remove each one from the fight and get them to talk. Thoughts?"

"Snag and bag," Ramsey suggested.

"Okay, Rammer, go with that."

"Well, sir, the way I see it, these guys are crooked to the teeth. We collect intel, roll them up, bag the evidence, and use it against them. We get them to talk and we work our way up. What can they do? Call the cops on us? We take them down with the evidence we collect. Come after us? They already are."

"You sure they'll talk, Chief?" Tran asked.

"Yeah, Truck. We aren't dealing with radical Islamists like we did in the sandbox and Afghanistan. These are street punks with cash and they want to enjoy it. Getting them to talk won't be hard. We just need the right leverage; a bullet to the groin, a major bust with prison time, geez, some of these guys might even squeal if you twist their arm. They run with a mob. Very few of them can handle themselves on their own."

"Well, we've got the names of three foot soldiers: Wood, Pelliteri, and Catalano. We start following them to get some intel and then plan our attack. We're going to need cameras, scopes, comms gear and more. We need to come up with all of that."

"We've got it covered, Skipper," Tran answered.

"You do?" Joe asked surprised.

"Yes, sir. When Lieutenant Commander Harrison gave us your sit-rep, we did a quick load out. It's all back at your beach house."

"Freaking awesome. Good thinking, guys!"

"So standard sneak and peaks and snatch and grabs," Ramsey summarized. "Nothing we haven't done before."

"My concern is who we are handing them over to. If the police are compromised at the upper levels like O'Keefe told us, how can we be sure that these guys will even be prosecuted?"

"Good question, Skipper. What are our options there?" Ramsey asked.

"I'm wondering if we can't reach out to your former sea daddy, Shoemaker. Organized crime is the FBI's purview. What if we hand these guys over to them packaged up with a box full of evidence?"

"What if we just ghost them and save the taxpayers millions of dollars in trials and imprisonment?" Mueller asked.

"I hear you, Mule. That would be far easier and society would be better off, but we would eventually be rolled up for this. They would certainly come after me for questioning and I can't lie under oath. I won't lie under oath. We can't do that. We have to figure out a way to roll these guys up without crossing the line."

"Sir, with all due respect, we do this kind of thing all the time. We infiltrate, shoot, loot, and exfiltrate without leaving any clue as to who we are."

"Correct, Mule, but that's in wartime scenarios where we are ordered to do so. This is not a war, at least not in the traditional sense, and there is a Constitution protecting their rights. Something we gave an oath to support and defend."

"Roger that, sir."

"Having said that, we have skills that can be used to bring these scumbags down and put them away. Rammer, reach out to your sea daddy. Find out who we can work with to accomplish this. We're not looking for any credit or recognition. They can have everything. We're just offering our skills to find these guys and get them off the street. All we want is to neutralize the threat and find out where the hit order came from."

"You got it," Ramsey said, as he pulled out his phone.

"Sir? Would another option be to pull back to Virginia Beach and see if they follow you down?" Tran asked. "We could handle them much easier down there and you would be in a defensive position which allows more options within the law."

"That's good thinking, Tran, and I actually considered that option, but I'd prefer to stay here where I can monitor them while we work the problem."

"Copy that, sir."

"Shoe! Matt Ramsey, here..."

Joe turned his attention back to Christy, who looked quite content at the helm.

"You okay?"

"Yes, I love this boat!"

"It is quite nice," Joe nodded, "but I was referring to everything going on."

"I'm okay. I hate that this is happening to you and I hate that you and your team are having to handle this yourselves, but I know this is what you do. Hearing you talk through it all actually makes it a little easier to deal with. It just makes me sick that the police are so corrupt."

"Only a few. The majority are fine. Every organization has their bad apples. Even our professions."

"Good point. It still seems like a major injustice is being committed and the law abiding are the ones who are hamstrung by rules."

"Story of my life, Christy. The Taliban, ISIS, Al Qaeda, the cartels, none of our enemies wear uniforms or fight fair. It's the same for you doctors."

"What makes you say that?"

"You."

"Me?"

"Yes, weren't you the one who told me that patients don't read the textbook?"

"Ah, touché! Yes."

"Right? You told me patients never present like the textbook says they should. Back pain can be an aortic aneurism and dizziness with no other symptoms can still be a heart attack."

"Wow, Joe! You really do pay attention when we talk on the phone!"

"I even take notes!"

"You do not!" Christy said, as she backhanded him in the stomach. "Oh! I'm so sorry! I forgot about your ribs! Are you alright?"

Joe looked out to the river without answering.

"Joe? Answer me! Why won't you answer me?"

"I'm trying to decide which answer will get me the most sympathy."

"You're going to get another backhand, is what you'll get! Now seriously, are you alright?"

"I'm fine. Ribs really don't hurt much at all. I am concerned about you though."

"Why's that?"

"I don't know how far these mobsters will go to get to me. Until we round them up you could be in danger. You'd be safer if you were somewhere far from here."

"Are you saying you want me to leave?"

"Only because I'm concerned for your safety; otherwise, no. You being here has been therapeutic in many ways. I love having you here. My family loves having you here. I want to pick up where we left off earlier. There's a lot I need to talk to you about and..."

"Then I'm staying right here," Christy said firmly.

"Christy, I just wish it was under better circumstances. With what we are planning, I may not be around much, and I can't guarantee your safety."

"I'm not asking you to. Ever since I arrived, I have loved every minute being here with you *and* your family. I don't want to leave yet. And, you said it yourself, there is a lot we need to talk about," she finished with a smile.

"You're sure?"

"Yes. I feel safer here with you. But I do still have to leave Sunday. I work Monday."

"Okay," he said, pulling her in close, "and thank you. It's really good having you here."

They passed the Edgewater section of Grand Island marked by the smokestack of a sunken ferry boat that still protruded out of the water decades later. They would soon be in front of Joe's dock.

"We're almost to my parent's house. Do you want to take her in?"

"Um, that's a no. I would feel terrible if I rammed your dock. You take over," Christy said, handing over the helm. They traded spots allowing Joe to be next to the throttles. Joe was pleased to see she chose to stay right next to him.

"Good news, Skipper," Chief Ramsey said, as he hung up his phone.

"What's that, Chief?"

"Well, as you know, we can't kick down doors, we can't shoot, and we can't loot. What we *can* do is collect intel, recon, and hand it over to the FBI for them to act on. Shoe says they will welcome that, and we can even act in a role as Confidential Human Sources, which we can use to get inside some of these organizations for up close intel."

"Well, that's a start," Joe said, as he started easing in to shore.

"Yep, and he's going to reach out to a buddy who works the field office up here that we can link up with."

"Sounds like a good start, Chief," Joe said, as he swung the boat around to approach the dock from downstream. "I have one concern."

"Shoot."

"I'm concerned they may come looking for me at my parent's house. I'd like to set some sort of security for them, but we're a few operators short."

"Problem solved, Joe. Take a look at your dock."

Chapter 43

"Mrs. O'Shanick, that was the best meal I've had in years. What was the name again?" Ramsey asked.

"Mechadong Baka, Chief. Filipino Beef Stew. I'm so glad you liked it."

"We all liked it, ma'am," Petty Officer First Class Ken "KK" Kowalski answered. "Can you please teach your son to cook like this?"

Kowalski was one of the new arrivals who had been swimming around the dock earlier when Joe and the rest of the team had returned on the boat. Along with Kowalski were Petty Officer Second Class Eddie Sierra, and Petty Officers Third Class Ricky Moreno and Carter "Crazy Cartso" Stinnet. Chief Ramsey had discreetly called them the night before when he learned of the attempted hits on Joe. Ramsey immediately presumed they might have a small war on their hands, but he also knew Joe would not want to involve his team in a personal matter. Ramsey respected his commanding officer, but this was going to require the entire team. The look on Joe's face when they returned to the dock confirmed for Ramsey that he had made the right call. There was strength and security in the wolf pack.

"Joe *can* cook, Mr. Kowalski. He is a wonderful cook. I taught him myself."

A collective outrage went up from around the table.

"What?" Carter Stinnet said, as he looked at Joe with an accusatory look.

"How come you never cook for us, Joey-O?" This from Eddie Sierra.

"Thanks, Mom," Joe said rolling his eyes. "I think you just initiated a mutiny."

"They should and I'll join them! How many times have I told you that cooking a good meal for others is a show of love and respect? You don't cook for these boys? You should be ashamed of yourself," Maria said, as she approached Joe holding a large wooden spoon in a threatening manner.

"Get him, Mrs. O'Shanick!" Mueller yelled.

"Oh, Joey-O's gonna get the spoon!" Ramsey howled, as Joe mock-ducked from his mother while the others laughed.

"Just a warning this time, mister!" Maria smiled at the team. "This is my favorite spoon. I've broken many of these on Joe in the past."

"Rumor has it, Mrs. O'Shanick, that an instructor busted a paddle over Joe one time in BUDs," Ramsey answered back.

"There! You see, Joe? I was toughening you up. Now you better start cooking for these nice boys or I'll get one of those paddles!"

"I think you should listen to her, sir," Tran suggested.

"As your CPO, I agree, Joe," Ramsey added. "Now, how about we show some gratitude by policing the kitchen for Mrs. O?"

In answer, the men all stood up and began to clear the table. Maria began to protest.

"Thank you, boys, but in this kitchen, I'm the CO and I'm not letting you men, who serve our country and keep my Joe safe, do any work tonight; besides, you'll probably break all my dishes. Joe's sisters and I will take care of it. Now go outside and relax. Make Joe build you a fire down by the river."

The men thanked Mrs. O'Shanick and began to head outside. Christy hung back to lend a hand.

"No, Christy, we've got it." Maria soothed. "You're our guest. Go on outside and relax."

"I will in a bit. I've been with the guys all day. I want to spend some time with the girls, and I want to help."

"Well good, you can help me with the table then," Marina offered.

"And after that, I need you two young ladies in the garage," Jack said, as he passed through the kitchen. "We need to set one of the bikes up for Christy and then we can get everything ready for our ride in the morning."

"Are you sure that's a good idea, Mr. O'Shanick?" Christy asked. "I mean, I want to ride but maybe we should wait until all of this blows over?"

"Good point, Christy. I think we should be safe on an early morning ride away from Niagara Falls but let me talk to Joe about it. I doubt anyone would come after us, but if they did, they'd have to get through me before they got to you or Marina.

"Sounds good," Christy answered. "I'll go with what Joe says. I would love to get in a good ride, but only if he thinks it's safe. I don't want to put anyone at risk for my sake."

"Are you kidding me?" Jack asked. "Marina and I ride all the time. We're looking forward to this. Tran rides. Maybe we should have him ride with us to be extra safe. How's that sound?"

"I like it," Christy smiled. "A good ride might just be what we all need."

"That's what I'm talking about," Marina chimed in as she gathered up some plates. "I ride or do Pilates every morning before work. Keeps me relaxed so I don't get cranky."

"You mean less cranky," Jack said teasing his daughter.

"So what was the Half Ironman like?" Marina asked, ignoring her father.

"It was actually a lot of fun!" Christy answered.

Anna shared a quiet smile with her mother as Christy and Marina cleared the table while engaging in a conversation about bikes and fitness.

"I like her, Mom," Anna said quietly as they stood side by side at the sink.

"Me too. She's good for our Joe."

"I just hope he realizes that," Anna replied.

"Joe is smart. I think he does."

"We have tactical vests, comms, night vision, weapons, motion sensing trail cameras, flash bangs, and just about anything we need, Skipper," Ramsey summarized after pooling all the gear that had been brought up. "How do you want to do this?"

"I want to keep four men around here at all times. They're after me, not my family but I'd rather play it safe. Set up motion detectors and cameras to cover a perimeter. Use two-man watches, four-hour rotations. Eddie and Ricky, I want to have you guys get inside their auto shop tomorrow. We'll pose you as Mexican nationals having trouble with your truck. Get inside the shop and have a look around. O'Keefe has reason to believe it could be a center of operations. Grab some rack time for tonight."

"Copy that, Skipper," Eddie Sierra answered.

"KK, I'd like to conduct some recon tonight. I think we should start with the auto shop, but I also want to get a picture of where these guys live. Not just Wood and Catalano, but their bosses all the way up to Big Catalano."

"Joe, if I may make a suggestion?" Ramsey asked. "Why don't you hang back here with your family and have Cartso roll with KK?"

"I appreciate that, Rammer, but if I'm sending people outside the wire, I think I should be one of them."

"Joe, we all respect that you prefer to lead from the front, but your family will feel more secure with you here. You're still recovering from your injuries. Let them handle this one. I also like the thought of you coordinating everything from the base."

"Chief, really, I'm fine and I know the area."

"I know, but there's also the concern that they're looking for you and know what you look like. If anyone sees you out, or any of us who were there earlier today for that matter, and especially if we're found somewhere we shouldn't be, they can blow this back on you. KK and Carter are less recognizable."

"Good point, Chief. Alright, Kowalski, you and Carter hang back when we're done here, and I'll brief you in on the area."

"Aye, sir," the tall-blond haired Kowalski answered.

"Be careful out there. Avoid any engagement. We have no legal cover and this state is militantly anti-gun and borderline pro-criminal with their laws. I have a legal permit to carry here, but y'all don't. You can be arrested if found with a weapon. I won't tell you not to carry, but I strongly advise against it. If they come after us here, we have more of a self-defense option but out there, we have nothing."

"So what you're saying, sir," Carter Stinnet spoke up, "is, once again, we have to play by the rules while the bad guys don't."

"That's about the short of it, Carter," Joe answered. "Nothing we aren't used to. We just have to outsmart the bad guys. Good thing the Navy has invested a lot in our training."

"Since we can't put bullets in their heads, what *is* our objective, sir?" Kowalski asked.

"The objective is to get these guys behind bars. We roll them up, collect evidence, and drop them into the laps of the FBI. Chief? Would you mind bringing us up to speed on the FBI's involvement?"

"Yes, sir. I just spoke to the local FBI agent about a half hour ago. He's with the Buffalo Field Office and has been investigating the Catalano organization for over a year. We can actually function as Confidential Human Sources where we collect intel they can use to make a bust. He has a lot of useful intel that he would not normally share, but will make an exception for us. In short, we cannot break any laws, and we can't violate their Constitutional rights, but anything we learn through observation, recon, or revelation can be used to help roll these guys up."

"Chief, does this guy know how many of us are here?" Mueller asked.

"Not an exact number, Mule. Why?"

"I'm just thinking. Let's say he thought there were just four of us. We let him see those four doing something legal while the other four infiltrate the targets, ghost the tangos, and bolt. Problem solved and nobody can pin it on us. We'd be doing the taxpayers a favor."

"As tempting as that sounds, Mule, you would then be guilty of murder. As simple as it may be, it's not an option," Joe admonished. "I appreciate it though."

Joe wished it really were that simple. Those were good missions in Afghanistan and Iraq. It would quickly solve the problem here as well. The mobsters really did a lot of harm to individuals and society as a whole. Drug and human trafficking destroyed lives, families and were the main cause of violent crime. Back in his mother's home nation, the president of the Philippines, with the support of a majority of Filipino citizens, actually urges civilians and police to execute drug dealers. Simple in thought, Joe surmised, and quite appealing in some ways, but he was also quick to recognize that, without a Constitutional restraint, it could get out of hand quickly. The Constitution is what sets the United States apart and above all other nations. If people start selectively obeying it, the nation will devolve into a cesspool of lawless anarchists that will eventually be ruled by tyrants. Safe to say, the Founding Fathers knew what they were doing when they wrote that amazing document.

Joe looked around the table in the beach house where his men were gathered. They were all in for him. He was all in as well. This meant that he had to ensure none of his men became casualties...or convicts. *There has to be another way!* Joe thought. Then an idea dawned on him.

It was apparent that the Catalano organization was fully committed to seeing this through. They were boldly going after this with no concern over the police. They knew where his family lived. What would stop them from coming after him here? Nothing. In fact, it was the obvious play. Joe decided to exploit that. First, he would have to read his family in on everything.

Chapter 44

"*L*ook out for the deer!"

"I got it," Johnny "The Blade" Colucci calmly responded.

A doe and her five fawns pranced across the road and disappeared into the woods of Buckhorn State Park. Colucci looked over at his boss and hid his annoyance. Jerry "The Bulldog" Costello was Frank Pandolfino's assistant. Out of frustration, Frank had sent him along to ensure the hired help stopped operating with their recently developed incompetence. Colucci was inwardly furious. He preferred to operate alone. He certainly did not need The Bullfrog (a name Colucci secretly called Costello as a result of the annoying man's late middle age yielding a hefty torso with ridiculously skinny legs) babysitting him on what could have been a simple stealth mission.

"You didn't even slow down, Johnny!" Costello admonished. "If you'd a hit those deer we might be sitting on the side of the road explaining a broken van and no bodies to Frank."

"I told you I had it, Jerry. Did we hit them?"

"No, but you was close. And watch your mouth, you chooch! Don't forget your place in this organization! If it wasn't for you and your clown friends screwing this one up, we wouldn't be driving around Grand Island on a Friday night. You sure you know where you're going?"

"Yeah, I know where I'm going. This road turns into East River Road. See? Right there," Colucci pointed to a road sign for Baseline and East River.

"Alright," Costello said lowering his tone, "I was just checking. You and me are gonna take care of this job and be done with it. It shoulda been done already. I don't want any more screwups."

"We'll get it, boss."

They drove on in silence through the quiet residential area.

"Man, I haven't been over here in years," Costello remarked. "The guy who owned the landfill used to have a big mansion over here. My old man ran with him. Used to bring me over here when I was a kid. That's it right there," he said pointing to a large gated house on the left. "Except that ain't the same house. I heard somebody tore down the old one and built himself a new one. I don't know why. The old one was nice. Rumor had it, Robert Redford almost bought it."

"The actor?" Colucci asked, to show he was listening.

"Yeah, they filmed *The Natural* here in Buffalo at the old Rockpile. You know, where the Bills and the Bisons used to play before they got their own stadiums. Somebody showed him that house on the river and he nearly bought it until word got out, then he bailed. People just can't keep their mouths shut."

"Okay, we just passed Stony Point Road," Colucci stated, as he sat up straighter, "we're getting close."

"Aren't you gonna slow down?"

"No."

"Why not?"

"Because I'm trying to look like any other schmuck driving down this road. Driving slow draws attention." *How did this moron become Frank's assistant?*

"We're close," Costello said, as he read the street numbers on the mailboxes. "Should be the next house. Hey, look at that!"

Both men's eyes were drawn to their left where a bonfire was blazing down by the river. The glow of the fire illuminated a small guest house. The silhouettes of several people could be seen around the fire as Colucci continued on by.

"It can't be that easy," he said, rounding a turn and pulling over onto a vacant lot.

"Maybe it is, kid.Let's make quick work of this and we can be back at The Power City Club sipping scotch in half an hour."

Colucci dimmed the lights and backed the van onto the lot leaving it pointing back out to the road. They got out of the van, walked around back and quietly opened the doors. Both donned black coveralls with matching black ski masks. Both pocketed their preferred sidearms. Costello picked up a fully automatic AK-47 he had loaded at home. Colucci opened up a padded gun case and removed a Remington R-25 7mm scoped hunting rifle and screwed on a custom-made silencer. He inserted a magazine and quietly chambered the first round. He didn't plan on needing a second magazine, but he pocketed one just in case. They quietly shut the doors and made their way down to the river.

Upon reaching the river, they could see the flickering light of the fire. Sound travels well along water and they could clearly hear two male voices talking. It sounded like they were arguing about hockey. Colucci and Costello picked their way among the various waterfront beach houses and sheds until they came to a border hedge two lots away from O'Shanick's waterfront.

"Okay, Blade," Costello whispered, "I'll cover you from here. Make sure that's our guy. If not, we'll go take a look at the house. If it is, waste him. Once you take out O'Shanick, make tracks for the van. If anyone's chasing you, I'll hose em' down and buy us some time. You better have that friggin' van running and ready to go when I get there."

"I will, Jerry, I swear."

"Make sure it's O'Shanick you got in your sights."

"Yeah, Jerry, I know," Colucci hissed in exasperation.

"I mean it, kid! Don't screw this one up!"

"I won't, Jerry. Trust me."

"Alright, then get going."

Colucci gingerly stepped onto the break wall and around the hedge. He spotted a deck box on the adjacent dock where it met the shore and slowly edged toward it. The voices by the fire were louder now with no objects between them to block the sounds. He slowly crawled toward the deck box keeping low to the ground so as not to be seen behind it should they look his way. Upon reaching the box, he carefully raised himself up enough to look over it. Colucci saw six people around the fire. The late spring air had cooled into the upper fifties. Two men, wearing jeans and flannels were animatedly arguing while the others, clad in hoodie sweatshirts, quietly listened.

Colucci was actually breaking a sweat in his coveralls as he quietly set his rifle down on the deck box and peered through the scope.

He was only about forty yards away. It would be an easy shot. It just had to be the right shot. The Blade used the scope to search out his prey. He sighted in on the man who was speaking first. Rugged face with a goatee. That wasn't O'Shanick. He moved the scope over to the other man in the conversation. The glow of the fire lit up his face. Good-looking guy, dark hair…that was him. There was no mistaking it. With practiced ease, Colucci began to slow his breathing as he centered the crosshairs between O'Shanick's eyes. He slowly moved his finger to the trigger to begin the gentle squeeze. Suddenly, everything went black.

Chapter 45

*E*ddie Sierra secured Colucci's wrists and ankles with zip ties while Ricky Moreno secured the rifle and slung it over his shoulder. The two men carried the limp Colucci into O'Shanick's waterfront beach house. A minute later, Chief Ramsey and Jamie Mueller arrived carrying a similarly bound Costello. The men's wallets, cell phones, and weapons were handed over to Joe who gave them a quick once over. Both men were groaning as they slowly came around. Joe stood looking at both men as he sized up the situation.

"Stuff a rag in both of them and tape their mouths shut," he ordered.

"We should keep them separate too. Mule, Rammer, take the fat old guy out and stash him down below on my dad's boat."

"How 'bout we move the skinny guy instead, Joe?" Ramsey asked.

"Good copy, Chief," Joe smirked, "Move slim to the boat and keep the whale here."

"Tran?" Joe spoke into the throat mike of his squad radio, "Anything else moving out there?"

"Negative, Joe. All clear."

"Good. Remain sharp. Eddie and Ricky are coming back out."

"Roger that, sir."

"Thanks, guys," Joe said, addressing Sierra and Moreno, "I can handle him from here. Go help Tran with the perimeter watch. Chief, once you and Mule get slim squared away, I'll need you back here."

"Aye, Skipper," Ramsey nodded as he and Mueller carried Colucci out the door.

Joe pulled a black balaclava over his face and stood over Costello as he slowly came around. The man's eyes began to flicker. He looked around, briefly making eye contact with Joe and then looked down and away.

"I know you can hear me, look at me."

Costello continued to feign confusion.

Not wanting to play games, Joe kneeled to the floor, placed his knee on the inside of the man's shin and pressed down hard. The man gave out a pained bellow that was muffled by his gag.

"You awake now, tough guy? I said look at me."

Costello responded by looking in Joe's direction as his eyes winced with pain. Joe let up, but he kept his knee in place.

"Are you listening?"

Costello nodded.

"Good. We know who you guys are. You may think you know something about killing people, but we are *trained* killers. You and your buddy, Colucci, could both be dead right now. Do you realize that?"

A slight nod.

"Do you realize we could still kill you and claim self-defense or just get rid of you and nobody will ever know?"

Another nod.

As a Navy officer and a law-abiding citizen, Joe wouldn't kill them. but he wasn't going to let Costello know that.

"We also have night vision film of you and your buddy setting up to shoot six people sitting around a bonfire, photos, weapons, and all the proof we need to hand you over to the FBI."

This resulted in a slight startled reaction from Costello.

"That's right, Jerry, we know your organization owns the locals. The feds have developed quite an interest in you. They will actually put you away. So you know what that means? It means we have options. None of them are good for you, but one keeps you alive and may get you witness protection. The choice is up to you. It's simply a matter of telling us what we want to know. Do you think you can do that?"

Costello didn't respond.

"Oh, you're not sure? Let me help you with that," Joe said, as he ground his knee into Costello's shin.

Costello let out a muffled scream as he writhed around under Joe's knee. Joe let up briefly and then ground back down into the man's shin for another twenty seconds before letting up. Ramsey stepped back into the beach house. He, too, was unrecognizable in a black balaclava.

"Ah, just in time. I was just about to ask our friend here if he is ready to talk. Would you mind working his gag?"

"Shoot, yeah," Chief Ramsey responded.

"Are you ready to talk, Jerry?"

Costello responded with a slight nod.

"That's better. Now, if you try to scream, my friend here stuffs the rag back in your mouth and I will give you something to scream about. Play it cool and we'll all get along. Do you see how that works?"

Another slight nod.

"Good," Joe said and nodded for Ramsey to remove the gag.

Ramsey sat Costello up, ripped the duct tape off his face and pulled out the rag, which was actually a cravat from his med kit. He then looped the cravat under Costello's chin and crossed the ends over the top of his large head.

"Now, we are going to start with some basic questions and work our way up. You should know that we have done our homework. We know a lot about you and your organization; therefore, we will ask many questions we already know the answer to, to see whether or not you're lying. Since you don't know how much we know, you may want to be careful with your answers. If we catch you lying, the gag goes back in. Why? Because even though there is no one around to hear you scream, we don't care to hear it ourselves. And you *will* be screaming. Am I clear?"

Costello nodded.

"Let's start with who you work for. Who's your immediate superior?"

"Bugs Bunny, you friggin' mutt!"

Ramsey gave the cravat ties a sharp yank causing Costello's jaw to slam shut. Joe followed by once again grinding his knee into

Costello's shin for a full minute. Costello broke into a heavy sweat as he writhed in agony. Joe nodded at Ramsey and they both let up. Another minute passed before Costello had his breathing under control.

"You've got one more chance, Jerry. Are you going to cooperate?"

A weaker nod this time.

"Alright, let's try it again. Who do you work for?"

"Frank Pandolfino."

"Ah, that's better. See how easy that was? Now, of course, we knew that, but you didn't know we knew that."

The bold look of defiance had vanished from Costello's eyes. Everyone had their breaking point, even the toughest warriors, but Costello seemed to have quickly lost the will to fight. Time to reinforce that.

"Would you like a little water?" Joe asked, holding up a bottle of water.

Costello nodded in defeat. Joe held the bottle up as Costello took a long drink. He nodded and Joe pulled the bottle away. The man took a deep breath and exhaled, dropping his double chin to his chest. After another deep breath he looked up at Joe and sighed in resignation.

"What do you want to know?"

Chapter 46

*J*ack O'Shanick grinned as he tossed the ace of spades down on the table. Maria frowned as she tossed the jack of spades; followed by Anna with a queen of spades. Christy nonchalantly tossed a queen of diamonds and grinned at Jack.

"Euchre!" Maria yelled triumphantly.

"You've got to be kidding me!" Jack responded in exasperation. "I had both Bowers and the king of trump along with the ace of spades. How did you pull that off?"

"I had the other four trump cards," Christy responded with a shrug.

"She's being modest, Jack. We have a new Euchre shark in the house!" Maria said, as she reached across the table to fist bump her partner.

"We'll see. The game's not over yet," Jack said. as he finished gathering the cards and passed them across to Anna.

"Oh no!" Maria exclaimed, as she intercepted the deck. "You're not stealing my deal. Give me that!" She playfully threatened Anna with a backhand.

"Good eye, Mrs. O," Christy exhorted.

"Years of practice, Christy. When it comes to cards, my family is as sneaky as they come."

"Taught them everything I know," Jack proudly proclaimed.

"Yes, but you forget," Maria said, as she began shuffling the cards, "you cannot outsmart us Asians."

"Don't I know," Jack said, as he looked across the table at his daughter. "Anna, are you okay, sweet pea? You're unusually quiet."

"I'm just worried about what's going on with Joe. I hate sitting in here all helpless like this."

"I know, darling. This is *our* Joe being threatened and my instincts are to take care of matters myself, but I also know that I'm nowhere near as capable of handling this as your brother and this is how he and his teammates think it should be handled. We have to trust them."

"I know. It's just hard, Dad," Anna said, as she looked down and stirred her tea.

"Anna," Christy said, as she placed a hand on Anna's, "I'm one of the few people who has gotten a glimpse behind the curtain of Joe's world. I've seen him in action. I wouldn't be here today if it weren't for him. He has the strategic intelligence of a surgeon and the fight of a tiger. He and his teammates *will* finish this. You can count on that."

"I know that," Anna replied near tears. "But that's my big brother and somebody is trying to kill him. Why? What has he done? He puts his life on the line for our country and somebody wants to kill him?"

"I don't know. The world is full of cruelty and evil. I see too much of it in the ER. Since the beginning of time bad people have done bad things. But there are always good people who do good things. People like Joe, and Chief Ramsey, Tran, Mule, KK and all the other warriors with nicknames who God uses as instruments of justice."

"But God still allows bad things to happen to good people. I don't get that!" Anna objected.

"You're exactly right," Christy answered. "He does allow bad things to happen. One thing I have learned, however, is that God has a sovereign will and it will not be moved or changed. A will of which we are all a part of. However, He also has a permissive will. We may not always know why He allows things to happen, but His permissions have a purpose. He permitted Joseph to be sold into slavery and wrongfully accused only to put him into a position where Joseph could preserve the Israelites during a time of famine. He permitted His Son to be crucified on a cross to redeem mankind. We don't know why this is happening. but there *is* a purpose and we know that Romans 8:28 tells us that He works all things together for the good of those who are called according to His purpose."

Maria stopped shuffling and shared a quiet smile with Jack.

"But Joe's not a Christian. He admittedly says so," Anna replied. She couldn't bring herself to openly say he was an atheist or even an agnostic. "What if he isn't one of those who are called."

"He's called," Christy answered reassuringly. "He hasn't answered yet, but he's getting closer."

Maria reached across the table and grabbed Christy's hand, "Yes! I believe this too!"

"Really?" Anna asked.

"Yes," Christy said looking around at all three O'Shanicks. "God is doing a work in him. He is no longer an atheist. He believes in Jesus, he just hasn't accepted Him…yet."

"Well, what if these mafia people get to him first?"

"I don't think that's going to happen. He's survived combat, capture, a near poisoning, and a trip over Niagara Falls. He and his teammates have faced far more dangerous situations than this. He'll be fine."

"I hope so, Christy. I love all my brothers, but Joe has always been like a superhero to me."

"He's a hero to me too, Anna. Let's get him through this and we'll keep working on his salvation."

Anna smiled at Christy. "That's a good plan. I'm in. We'll gang up on him! Mom will too."

"I'm already in," Maria spoke up. "Who do you think made the call to get Christy up here?"

"You? Yes, of course. I should have known," Anna answered. "Alright, Mom, deal the cards already."

Jack looked on contentedly as his wife dealt out the next hand. He had been aware of Maria's admiration of Christy ever since they had met at the White House last fall, but he hadn't fully understood why. He saw it now. Any man would be blessed to have a woman like that in his life. Jack wasn't one to play matchmaker like Maria and Anna, but he certainly wouldn't mind if Christy, one day, became a regular around their table.

Chapter 47

"Anything else?"

"No, Mr. Costello, I think that about covers it for now. You've been very helpful," Joe responded.

They had questioned the man for over an hour. Ramsey wrote down three pages of detailed notes. He had also recorded the entire conversation using a laptop which he had opened, ostensibly, to refer to a database from which they asked questions. The video limited the imaging of Costello from the neck up.

"Our deal's still good? You're not gonna renege on me, are you?" Costello asked with concern.

"No, a deal is a deal. If your information checks out, you'll be handed over to the FBI in the morning. We're keeping you here tonight in case other questions arise. I'm gonna talk to your buddy, Colucci, for a bit," Joe said, as he opened his knife and cut the zip tie around Costello's ankles. "Before I do that, you've earned a trip to the head. If you promise to behave, I'll cut your wrist tie and move your hands to your front. One wrong move and we go back to being hog-tied, but I think you're wise enough to know trying anything isn't going to be good."

"I'm done, man. I'm as good as dead with the organization. I'm not gonna cross you up now."

"That's what I wanted to hear," Joe said, cutting the wrist tie and standing back with his Smith and Wesson .40 pointed at his captive.

He led Costello to the full bath and allowed him to relieve himself with the door open. After washing his hands, Costello dutifully stood in front of the door with his hands clasped. Ramsey applied a zip tie and cinched it tight. They led him into one of two small bedrooms. Joe guided him to one of two twin beds that lay adjacent to opposing walls. Ramsey had looped two zip ties together and secured them to the bed frame. Once Costello was on the bed, Ramsey secured his leg to the zip ties.

"I'm sorry about the inconvenience, Jerry, but you did try to kill us tonight," Ramsey admonished. "At least you get a mattress. I strongly caution you to behave. We can still claim self-defense if anything were to happen."

"I told you, I'm hosed. Just get me to the Feds. I won't try anything."

"Fair enough. I'm leaving the door open and the light on but try to get some sleep. You've got a busy day ahead of you."

Joe and Ramsey reconvened at the table in the eat-in kitchen that made up one end of the open beach house. Ramsey had the notes arranged for them to go over.

"So what we've learned is that he is second to Pandolfino and that the hit order came from above which points us to Bruno Catalano. What we don't know is why. Catalano doesn't know me and would have no reason to go after me."

"As far as you know," Ramsey offered.

"Right, but my operating theory is he's doing this as a favor to someone else. My guess is Hector Cruz or somebody else in his cartel."

"Is there anyone else you can think of?"

"Well, it's not like we go around the world as good will ambassadors, but nobody else comes to mind. I think we should just ask Catalano."

"And there lies the problem," Ramsey replied. "We still don't know where to find him. Fat Jerry says he has never been to Catalano's house and has no clue where he lives."

"But we know where Pandolfino lives and *he* will know where Catalano lives."

"Yeah, but Joe, you said yourself we can't go kicking down doors and threatening people. How are you going to get to these guys without breaking the law?"

"I have no idea," Joe said with a shrug, "but that doesn't mean we can't think of something. We just have to keep working the problem. I'm going to step outside and call KK. I'll have them recon Pandolfino and then I'm going to have a little chat with our other friend. I'll send Mule in for you. Bring the laptop and your notepad."

Joe pulled out his cellphone as he stepped out of the guest house. He punched the speed dial for Kowalski who picked up on the second ring.

"Pueblo's Paper Hangers, how can I help you?"

"That's funny, KK. What do have so far?"

"Well, this auto shop keeps some funny hours."

"Yeah? How so?"

"There were several cars that came and went earlier. All pulled into a garage bay and left a few minutes later. That died down and then some pimp-looking guy brought two young girls in with him. He just left the place without the girls."

"Prostitutes?" Joe asked.

"Either that or the night mechanics are skinny girls in really tight mini-skirts."

"Okay, anything else?"

"Yes, your guy Wood left on foot a half hour ago and walked a few blocks down the street to a place called The Power City Club."

"Yeah, I know that place. That's a private club where the mob hangs out. That's right where we were today when Wood chased us. Colucci was waiting up on the roof of a nearby drug store, with a rifle."

"You want us to go check out that club?'

"Negative. I need you to go find Pandolfino. Our intel says he frequents the casino. If he's not there, he could be at that club or he's home. He lives on Cayuga Island. Has a house on the river almost across from our sailing club. He drives a Lincoln Town Car. I'll text you the license along with his house address. Let me know what you find. We may have to pay him a visit."

"Good copy, sir. Anything else?"

"That's it for now, KK, thanks."

"You got it, Skipper."

Joe ended the call and pocketed his phone. He stepped onto the dock and walked out to the slip the *Sea Ray* was moored in. Stepping aboard, he pulled his balaclava back down and headed below.

"Well how goes it there, Blade?" He said, addressing the bound man lying on the deck.

"Is Johnny behaving for you?" He said to Mueller without using his name.

"Yep, but he isn't very chatty."

"Well, we may not need him to be. His boss, Fat Jerry just sang like a canary so I don't think Colucci here is going to be much use to us. Why don't you go trade places, so you can entertain Jerry for a while."

"I'm on it," Mueller said, as he climbed out of the cabin and stepped out onto the dock.

Joe ground the heel of his boot into Colucci's shin which yielded a muffled bellow through his gag.

"Now that I have your attention, Johnny, I'm going to make this real clear. I have you on night vision video preparing to take a shot at a group of people around a bonfire. It's enough for the FBI to put you behind bars, especially considering your long rap sheet. You have quite the talent as a hired killer, don't you?"

Colucci just stared back without as much as a nod.

"Well, seeing as how we caught you, that remains in doubt, but the feds certainly have an interest in some of your past endeavors. Now, if you prove helpful to us, maybe the feds will go easy on you and let you into Witness Protection if you're willing to turn over the organization; otherwise, we can take a boat ride down by the Falls and *you* can see what it's like to drop over them. Maybe you'll get lucky too and survive the fall. Oh, rats," Joe said, as he snapped his fingers in mock disappointment. "We can't venture into Canadian waters, so I guess we would have to make it the American Falls. That's the one with all the boulders at the base. That'll leave a mark. Won't it?"

Joe looked over his shoulder and saw Chief Ramsey step down into the cabin.

"Ah, good. We can get started..."

An hour later, Joe and Chief walked Colucci off the boat and led him into the cabin. Colucci didn't break as quickly but, as best as they could tell, he knew less than Costello. That didn't come as a surprise. Colucci may have been tougher, but he was lower in the organization than Costello. Mueller helped Joe secure him in the other guest room while Ramsey called the FBI agent. After a brief discussion, Ramsey ended the call.

"Special Agent Jennings will be here within the hour."

"Good," Joe answered, as he finished donning his tactical kit and walked over to the table holding the computers. "I'll copy what we have onto a thumb drive for him."

"Tell you what, Joe, how about I do that, and you check in with your family."

"Good copy, Chief," Joe said realizing the Chief was right. "You guys want anything while I'm up there?"

"Coffee would be great," Ramsey answered.

"What was that dessert your mom served?" Mueller asked.

"Silvanas?"

"Yes! A couple of those and some coffee."

"Same here, Joe," Ramsey added.

"I'll see if there are some left," Joe said, as he turned to head out the door.

"Echo One coming out. Heading to the big hooch," Joe spoke into his microphone to alert the guys out on watch.

"Copy, Echo One," Tran answered.

"Anyone want some coffee or a Bang?"

"Coffee. Your mom's coffee. No offense, Skipper," Tran replied.

"Same here, Skipper," Eddie Sierra replied.

"Me too, Skipper," from Ricky Moreno.

Joe walked around to the back yard, crossed over his father's grilling porch and, noticing that most of the lights were off, quietly entered the empty kitchen through the back door. Joe saw a dim light being cast from his mother's sunroom and went to see who was up. Christy and his mother were seated beside a small tea table at the far end. Each held a mug of tea. A lone scented candle cast a soft light.

"Euchre game end already?" he asked.

"Yes. Anna has to work in the morning and your father wants to get a good night's sleep. He's worried he won't be able to keep up with Christy on the bike."

"I think it's going to be the other way around," Christy commented. "But we're wondering if we should even go. Your father thinks it's okay but said he would talk to you about it. He thought maybe Tran could ride with us just to be sure."

Joe paused for a moment as he contemplated whether or not they would be taking a risk going for a ride. He concluded that the organization was after him, and it might be preferable to have his family elsewhere and out of the line of fire, but it would be a good idea to have someone with them just in case. Tran was an avid cyclist. He would talk to him about that.

"Well, who won?"

"Christy and I beat them three straight," Maria said with a sly smile. "She's a shark."

"More like your mom is the shark, but we are the new Euchre queens!" Christy exclaimed.

Together the two mimicked dancing in their chairs as they quietly sang "Euchre Queens, sharply skilled, we are quite the team!" to the tune of ABBA's hit song *Dancing Queen*.

Joe rolled his eyes as the two broke out into laughter.

"Please tell me you didn't do that at the table when Dad was here."

"Oh, yes we did!" his mother said, giggling with her hand on Christy's forearm. "And it drove him nuts. He's so competitive."

"So what have you been doing since?"

"We're just talking," Christy answered with a grin aimed at Maria. Looking back at Joe more seriously, "How are things going with you guys?"

"So far, so good," Joe answered, not wanting to alarm his mother by revealing too much. "They sent me in here for some coffee, actually."

"Oh!" Maria exclaimed, standing up. "I'll go make some for you."

"No, Mom, that's okay. I was planning on making it."

"Nonsense, Joe! I'll get it. You and Christy have hardly seen each other, and she came all this way just to see you. Now sit down," Maria said, as she walked out of the room.

"Can't say no to that," Joe said, as he settled into the chair and leaned his civilian version M-4 against the wall. He looked over at Christy.

"I'm so sorry this is happening. I'd much rather be in here with you. I hope you know that."

"I do, Joe. This is a terrible situation, but it's not your fault. You don't have to apologize to me. I totally understand. In fact, I'm grateful that you and your team are handling it."

"Really?"

"Yes, really. Besides, I really enjoy your family. We had a great time tonight and I absolutely love your mom."

"Okay, that makes me feel better. I still wish we could all relax together but, it is what it is. I can't let this threat linger. Maybe we could come up here again, later this summer when everything is back to normal?"

"Yes. I'd like that a lot."

"So would I," Joe sighed.

"So," Christy said lowering her voice, "are you guys getting anywhere?"

"Actually, yes," Joe said, leaning in and speaking quietly. "Our little bonfire trap with the dummies worked. We caught two guys sneaking in with rifles. Got them on film setting up to take shots. Also got a lot of actionable intel out of them. FBI is coming to arrest them as we speak."

"Are you serious?" Christy nearly hissed with alarm. "I didn't think they would actually come here. Good thing you did. Do you think that's the end of it?"

"I wish," Joe said shaking his head. "We confirmed that the hit order comes from the very top of that organization. A *big* organization. It won't stop until we cut off the head of the snake. The problem is getting to him. Even then, I think the guy is acting out a favor for someone else."

"Who? The cartel?"

"Maybe. I'm still trying to figure that out. We won't know until we get the top dog to talk."

"What about the guys you caught? Can't they tell you?"

"They don't know. They're just following orders."

"Can't they tell the FBI who ordered the hit?"

"They can tell them their boss gave them marching orders, which is something, but they didn't get the order directly from the main boss. We either need their Capo to rat out Catalano or somehow bust Catalano and get him to confess. Both are long shots."

"Do you think they will try again tonight?"

"I hope not, but if they do, we'll handle it."

"Coffee's ready, Joe," Maria said, appearing in the arched entrance.

"Thanks, Mom," Joe said as he stood, picked up his rifle and slung it over his shoulder.

"I think I'm going to call it a night, Mrs. O'Shanick," Christy said, as she stretched her toned arms high overhead. "I've got a metric ride with your husband in the morning and he'll be looking for revenge."

"Nah, he talks smack, but deep down he's a true gentleman," Maria said as she approached. "Now give me a hug."

The two embraced warmly and Maria stood back, looking up as she held Christy's face in her hands. "You're as beautiful on the inside as you are on the outside. I enjoyed talking and praying with you tonight. I hope we get some more time together tomorrow."

"I'd love that, Mrs. O'Shanick."

"Please call me Maria or, even better, call me Ina. That means "mom" in Tagalog."

"Yes, Ina, thank you," Christy said, as she hugged Maria one more time.

"Joe, come find me in the kitchen," Maria said as she turned and walked out of the sunroom.

"Ina? Wow, Christy. That means she considers you one of her own." Joe said as they walked to the stairway together.

"Something tells me she's like that with everyone."

"She is, that's just her way, but she really does think the world of you. I can tell."

"Oh, really? And how can you tell?"

"Because my mother is a wise lady who knows a good thing when she sees it. And she happens to be right."

"Thank you, Joe," Christy said, as she stood at the base of the stairs, looking in his eyes with a pleasant smile.

Reaching out, Christy pulled Joe in and hugged him tight.

"Be safe. I'm praying for you," she whispered in his ear.

"Thank you. I will. I'll see you in the morning."

Christy turned and started her ascent. Joe lingered, watching longingly as she gave a final wave and disappeared upstairs.

Chapter 48

"*F*eds are five mikes out, Joe," Chief Ramsey announced pocketing his phone.

"Roger that, let's get Johnny and Jerry up to the street."

Joe helped Ramsey and Mueller get Costello and Colucci up and secure their hands behind their backs. They frog-marched them both up the small grass incline to the street and across to the driveway. They remained silent. There was nothing further to say.

A minute later, two vehicles approached, a white Ford Explorer and a blue Ford Escape. They slowed and pulled into the circular driveway. Two men got out of each vehicle.

"I'm looking for Master Chief." Special Agent Matt Jennings said, being careful not to use any names.

"That'd be me," Ramsey stepped forward with his right hand extended.

"Special Agent Jennings," he said shaking Ramsey's hand.

"This is my CO, Joe O'Shanick," Ramsey said as Joe stepped forward.

"Joey-O! I thought this was your house! How are you?"

Joe, caught off guard, squinted trying to identify the agent in the dim light.

"It's me, Matt Jennings. I graduated with Sean."

"Oh, Matt! Man, I'm sorry. I didn't recognize you at first. What's it been, about ten years?"

"That's about right. Last I saw you was graduation week at the Naval Academy. I was a rising Second Class Midshipman at the time. Sean tells me you're still in?"

"Yeah, that's right. You went into the Marine Corps, right?"

"Yep, did my four as a grunt officer and then jumped to the FBI. I saw Jacob and your dad this morning, as a matter of fact, at the Island Band of Brothers."

"Yes. The men's Christian group that meets at Tim Horton's? Your dad heads that up, right?"

"Yep. You should come next week if you're still in town."

"Yeah, well, it all depends on how things turn out here with all of this."

"Well, we'd love to have you. I see Jerry Costello and Johnny Colucci in flex cuffs. What's the story?"

"Apparently, there's a hit out on me and they came here to collect."

Joe and Ramsey spent several minutes briefing Special Agent Jennings on the events of the past few days as well as the past few hours. Joe showed video of the incident on his phone.

"That's conspiracy to commit murder right there all by itself," Jennings said, being sure Costello and Colucci could hear him. "With the right judge, that alone can carry a life sentence, but if word gets out that they snitched on the organization, that will be a relatively short period of time. Bill? Greg?" Jennings said addressing the agents with him. "Read them their rights."

Jennings turned and read Costello and Colucci their Miranda rights before securing them into the back seat of each vehicle.

"Joe, let's take a walk."

Joe led Jennings to the far end of the driveway before he turned and faced him.

"Joe, this is good work. We've been trying to pull down this organization for years. They're very good at staying out of custody. What you have here should give me enough to put them in prison for a long time, but you and I know they're just cogs in a much larger machine."

"Understood, Matt."

"That means, you're still not in the clear. The price on your head still stands."

"I know."

"I want to use them to root out the entire organization and take them down. In order to do that, I might have to offer witness protection. That means these two gunmen would go free."

"I'm aware of that."

"Are you okay with it?"

"If it means taking down Catalano and the organization? Absolutely. The only thing I'm after is removing the threat, especially to my family. The thing is, I think Catalano is doing this as a favor for someone else. I want to know who."

"I'll do everything I can to find out for you but, keep in mind, anyone who can get Catalano to do a hit job is a big player."

"I'm well aware of that, but that threat will still have to be dealt with no matter who it is. We can't neutralize a threat when we don't know who it is."

"I follow you, Joe."

"Can I ask you a question, Matt? Off the record?"

"I think I know what you're going to ask, Joe. If I were in your shoes, I'd be asking the same thing. My official answer is, do what you've been doing. Keep your head on a swivel, gather intel and evidence, and turn over anyone you catch just like you did here. Let us roll them up. Anything more than that and you could get yourself in legal trouble you don't want."

Joe closed his eyes and sighed with frustration.

"I hear you, Joe. Personally, I'd be just as happy for you guys to kick down Catalano's door and put a bullet in his head along with every other wise guy in his organization. It would be swift justice and save the taxpayers a fortune. Unfortunately, the law doesn't allow that, especially in New York State where the government is soft on criminals and tougher on law-abiding citizens trying to defend themselves."

"I know. I told my men that earlier tonight. It's just frustrating. We could end this before the morning, and everyone would be better off."

"Well, let's do this. I'll stay on Catalano's organization and keep you informed of everything I hear, and you do the same."

"I guess that's all we can do for now, Matt," Joe said offering his hand to shake.

Jennings walked back to his fellow agents and spoke a few words. They got into their vehicles and headed out. Joe headed back down to the beach house with Mueller and Ramsey. They stowed the bonfire dummies away and made sure the fire was out.

Ramsey and Mueller would stay up on night watch. Ramsey would spend the first three hours on the grounds while Mueller would stay in the house keeping watch over all of the motion sensing cameras. Ricky and Eddie would turn in to rest up for their recon in the morning. After quickly agreeing to ride with Christy, Marina, and Jack in the morning, Tran hit the rack. Stinnet and Kowalski were monitoring Pandolfino's house and reported in that he had returned home recently and all was quiet. They set up a few motion sensing cameras and would return to base in a couple of hours if there was no further activity.

Joe walked into the house with mixed thoughts. They made progress, no doubt, but the threat was still there. It was a cruel twist of irony that the legal system prevented Joe and his team from proactively working the problem which left them sitting ducks. One wrong move and the criminals were turned loose to continue their reign of terror while good men went to prison.

He had every bit of confidence that Special Agent Jennings would do everything he could to bring the Catalano family down, but would it happen soon enough? If Joe went back down to Virginia Beach, would they follow him? Would they use his family to get to him? A lot of what ifs. Too many variables made for difficult defense. The best defense was a good offense. The answer was to go on the offensive and take out Catalano. The problem was how. *Work the problem, O'Shanick!* That axiom had been ground into him in the grating sand and cold waters of BUDs. It was a central theme of their continuous training. Every evolution had an objective guarded by a problem. They were trained to work the problem and achieve the objective. If the problem couldn't be attacked one way, they figured out another way. There was always another way.

Joe quietly passed Marina's old room where Christy was staying. He looked at the bottom of the door, hoping to see a sign that the light was on. Darkness. He was tempted to knock anyway, but he refrained.

It wouldn't be right. It wasn't that he had inappropriate motives. Far from it. He actually had been going out of his way to show a genuine level of respect and decency. He just needed Christy's perspective. As an emergency physician, she was also trained to rapidly assess a situation and process the data to make life and death decisions. Very similar to what Joe did, and with similar consequences, but in an entirely different arena; however, she seemed to accept her limitations and temper them with her faith that yielded a serenity and acceptance. Even when being shot at by cartel warriors and escaping in a tropical storm, she had maintained a cool focus. Joe's training created a focus under fire, but he was having a fit over his limitations right now.

Joe laughed at himself when he considered the irony as he set his rifle down and began removing his tactical kit. Months ago, he found it annoying that she would take the time to pray while they were being pursued and now he envied the peace her faith produced. She wasn't one of those "holy rollers" who ran around putting their religion on full display only to treat people terribly when they thought no one was paying attention. There was a reason that restaurant servers dreaded working Sunday afternoons. Quite the opposite, there was a genuineness with Christy and her peaceful aura was so real as to be tangible. He could use that right now. One wrong action could land his team in prison. Conversely, too much inaction could get his family, and even his team, killed. There was no peace in any of that.

Joe slipped into his old bed fully dressed. Despite his responsibilities, sleep usually came easy for him. Even in combat, the objective and the methods were clear enough that he could sleep on a noisy helicopter approaching a landing zone. The unrest of the current situation made sleep elusive tonight. He was mentally working the problem, but the variables beyond his control seemed to conceal the solution. Christy would tell him this is the perfect reason to pray. His mom would tell him the same thing. *Dad? Yep, him too.* Joe admitted to himself.

He turned on his side as he mulled it over. A few months ago, he wouldn't have even considered prayer. Since high school, he had been skeptic, if not an atheist. Conversations with Christy and some directed reading had challenged those beliefs to the point where, albeit kicking and screaming, he had to acknowledge that there likely is a god and it very well could be the God of the Bible. The thought certainly dawned on him moments before going over Niagara Falls. Joe had seen the evidence in Christy, his parents, his siblings. They didn't appear to be faking it. But, did that necessarily change anything for him? *If I start praying and going to church, will this give me that kind of peace? What are you talking about, Joe? You're a Navy SEAL for crying out loud and an officer no less. Snap out of it and start acting like one! Work the problem and be at peace with that!*

Joe turned over in his bed. He tried to work the problem by thinking through different scenarios and contingencies. The conflicting thoughts darted in and out of his mind making solutions elusive. Sleep seemed just as elusive, but it eventually came.

Chapter 49

Christy thumbed the gear shifter at the leading edge of the aero-bars which produced a quiet, metallic click and the resistance dropped. She increased her cadence as the road began to rise leading to the overpass. As the incline increased, Christy rose off of the bike saddle and began a standing climb. Many triathletes preferred to remain seated in the aero position as much as possible but Christy, not a fan of saddle sores or numb nether regions, welcomed the change of positions. Marina smoothly worked the climb on Christy's left while Tran and Mr. O'Shanick stayed right in close behind them.

They crested the top of the overpass and she settled back into the aero position as she shifted back down into faster gears. The shifting was smooth and her speed picked up rapidly. As they reached the bottom of the hill, they were still accelerating. Christy snuck a glance at her Garmin watch and saw they were at 36 mph. She dug in, working her cadence, allowing momentum to maintain their speed. The group maintained a tight pack as the parkway brought them out of the wooded state park and began to parallel the river.

"Is this the West Niagara River?" Tran asked.

"That's correct. We're heading upstream. A mile downstream is where the East and West Rivers join back up a few miles before the Falls," Jack answered. "This parkway is closed to cars for the next twelve or so miles so we have it all to ourselves."

"It's beautiful!" Christy remarked, looking at the glassy surface of the river lined with trees on each side. "Is that Canada across the river?"

"That's right. In fact, the official border is just off our shore. That's nearly all Canadian water you're looking at."

As their speed began to slow, Christy felt the resistance begin to increase. She shifted out of the 11 gear and down through 12, 13, 14, settling into 15. Her cadence came back up into her preferred range of 90-100. They road along in silence for a few minutes. The resistance seemed to increase. Christy had to drop another gear to 16 to maintain her cadence.

"Grand Island doesn't have many hills, but it sure has a lot of false flats!"

False flat is a cycling term for a long mild incline, imperceptible to the eyes, but definitely perceived by the lungs and legs.

"Worse part is," Marina spoke between breaths, "no matter which direction you ride, it always feels like you're on the same false flat!"

"What's it like where you ride, Christy?" Jack asked from behind.

"Beautiful rolling hills. All work uphill and all reward downhill!"

"It's like that south of here," Jack responded. "My brother, Tom, lives in Colden near the ski resorts. He moved there just so he could ride every day in the hills. Loves it."

"Well, if I lived here, I'd learn to love the false flats. I wouldn't want to give up this river."

"You've got that right!" Marina exclaimed.

They continued to ride on. The false flat seemed to go on forever. They all had to drop another gear or two before finally cresting the peak and getting a little boost from a gentle decline. Before long, Christy was back into the 11 and they were cruising along at a brisk pace.

"Christy, are you still okay with us riding in close to you like this?" Jack asked.

"I'm okay. I don't ever draft ride, especially on a triathlon bike, but I can't see you guys behind me, so I'm good. Thanks."

"Out of sight out of mind," Tran added from behind.

"Exactly, Tran! Just don't expect me to draft behind you guys."

"Don't worry, Christy, they won't ask you." Marina teased. "They get the easier ride having us cut a path through the air for them."

"Oh, is that it?" Christy asked.

"Hardly!" Jack spoke up. "You two little skinny-minnies don't punch much of a hole through the air. Now, if *my* fat butt was out front, you wouldn't even break a sweat!"

"Yeah, right, Dad. He still fits into the plaid pants he wore in high school!"

"Plaid pants, sir?' Tran asked mockingly.

"She's joking, son."

"No, I'm *not*!" Marina yelled back.

"That was middle school!" He yelled back. "But our Navy uniforms still had the bell bottoms back then."

"We still have them in our crackerjacks, sir."

"Good to see some traditions don't die..."

Christy rode on in silence as Jack and Tran talked on about the Navy. Their banter was enjoyable. Christy could see a lot of Jack in Joe. Both were tall, lean, and muscular with rugged good looks and dark features. Both were serious men, committed and loyal, but seasoned with humility and a sense of humor. Very pleasant to be around. And safe. Jack was as gentle and caring around Maria and their daughters as Joe was around Christy. Yet Christy recalled how Joe had skillfully and ruthlessly killed cartel soldiers to protect her. Beneath that quiet exterior, a fierce warrior lurked within. A trained warrior with discipline. One who could protect and nurture as skillfully as he could hunt and kill. She admired that. Actually, she was attracted to that.

For some reason, a predominant cultural theme was to discourage men from being traditional chivalrous males. "Toxic masculinity" was the term they used. Christy had no use for the cultural trend to emasculate men. Sure, brute chauvinism could disappear and she would never miss it, but a confident warrior, one who put others before himself out of respect and humility, was far more attractive than some bookish social media warrior clad in skinny jeans and intellectual glasses.

She couldn't deny the attraction. It started last year when they escaped from the cartel. It grew over the past nine months as they kept in touch from a distance. Ever since high school, her life had been so busy and focused; high school sports, volleyball player at the University of Tennessee, medical school, residency, and work that she had suppressed any interest in men. She didn't want anything to derail her.

There had been some prospects along the way; however, her father and her brothers had shaped her perceptions of what a man should be and nobody had yet to measure up.

That is until now. Joe was nearly everything she was looking for in a man. She had tried to ignore that developing reality over the past year, but the last few days made it undeniable. Having nearly lost him to the several attempts on his life made it all the more apparent. She felt so natural around him. And his family. Yes, his family had opened their arms to her and they felt like an extension of her own family. That was an intangible. Yes, her feelings for him went beyond those of a friendship, even a friendship born in traumatic events.

Was that feeling mutual? It was hard to tell. He certainly made her feel special and appreciated. He had put his arm around her a few times, held her tightly, and hugged her more than a causal embrace, but Christy had seen Joe treat his mother and sisters like that too. Maybe that was just his way. He was a tough read; introverted, but friendly and willing to talk. Was she over analyzing this? Hopeful?

Should I be hopeful? We're not equally yoked. I know better. Christy thought to herself as she downshifted into the 15 gear in response to another false flat.

She remained down on the aero-bars as the road gently curved left and they moved away from the river. The early morning sun was just starting to edge up over the trees. The temperature had begun to rise yielding a fine layer of sweat on her arms and face. Her heart rate monitor showed her pulse steady in the 140's. A pace she could hold for hours. Christy was dialed in.

"Christy and Tran," Jack called out, "Just to let you know, the bike parkway ended back there so we have to watch for cars again, but I don't expect many down here."

"Good to know, thanks," Christy acknowledged.

Jack and Tran continued their conversation, seemingly unaffected by their workout. Marina quietly pedaled along as she focused on the road ahead. Christy's thoughts returned to Joe.

We're not equally yoked.

She couldn't shake the thought. They had much in common. They had a great friendship and Christy sensed it could easily be more than that. She felt completely at home with Joe's family and he would be at home with hers. She was increasingly drawn to him, but there was one fundamental problem. It wasn't their vastly different careers. It wasn't the fact that her income was far greater than his. Joe's value was immeasurable regardless of his income. It wasn't the reality that he could be killed doing his job.

The problem was spiritual. To many, that would seem like a trivial issue. Not to Christy. Christy was not religious. She was a follower of Christ. Christ was the center of her life and no man, person, object, or career should supplant Christ. That wasn't some legalistic dogma. It was a fundamental truth. He is Creator God, the One who died for her sins, the Lord of the Universe, and the Lord of her life. Christy fully accepted that because Christ was more than a character in a book. He was very real in her life.

Accordingly, no man could replace Him. She wanted a man that would serve Him *with* her. A helpmate, a partner and a complement. Weak where she was strong and strong where she was weak. It wasn't a snobbish, holier than thou attitude. It was a biblical reality. An unbelieving spouse could potentially draw the believing spouse away from Christ. As drawn as she was to Joe, that was a compromise Christy was unwilling to make. Joe had come a long way and he was supported by a loving Christian family but he was not, himself, a believer. *Not yet?* Yes, he could certainly make a commitment to Christ, but he hadn't as of yet. Was that a foregone conclusion? No, not really. Could she wait? Yes. She had waited this long and there was no one else who held her interest. Waiting was possible.

That's if he's even interested. That question remained. If he showed interest, their faith difference would eventually become a conversation. That could be awkward.

"Yes, Joe, you're everything I've ever wanted except..."

How do I even put that into words? Christy wondered to herself. *Would he understand? Maybe we could let things progress naturally and he would grow into a believer along the way?*

Christy wanted to believe that, but knew it was a risk. She would have to...

"Car!" Jack's call interrupted her thought.

The foursome merged into a single file column and hugged the right side of the road. A white panel van passed them politely giving the cyclists a wide birth.

"Thank you!" Jack yelled as they all waved to show their appreciation.

The driver waved back. Probably a fellow cyclist, Christy thought. Many motorists weren't so polite. Many even drove dangerously close out of annoyance as they passed, considering cyclists a nuisance on the road. To be fair, some cycling groups remained in a side by side grouping rather than moving to single file making it difficult for motorists to pass. If both sides showed a little courtesy and respect, accidents would be far less frequent.

"Another car!" Jack announced.

The foursome remained in their column as they maintained their pace. Christy remained in aero which naturally limited her ability to finely steer the bike. Not a problem for straight riding but, since she was hugging the edge of the road which had a raised curb, she had to concentrate all her efforts to avoid swerving into the curb. As such, she couldn't look back to spot the car approaching from behind. Out of practice, she listened as it approached, anticipating when the car would pass so she could ease away from the curb. What she heard next made her skin crawl.

The sickening crunch of metal and carbon was followed by a shocked yell by Jack and a loud curse by Tran. Christy reflexively looked back and was horrified to see both men tumbling through the grass on the side of the parkway, their bikes a twisted mess. A battered old pickup truck continued on just behind Marina who was also looking back. Two men sat inside the cab, both wearing ski masks.

The sudden realization of the situation created a huge adrenaline surge in Christy. It was the body's way of preparing for the fight or flight response to danger. Christy's instinct caused her to sit up out of aero, grab the brakes, and squeeze hard. Flight was not even a consideration. There were men down and the physician in her took over.

Christy unclipped her bike shoes from the pedals as she came to a stop. As she hopped off the seat, she saw the white van a few yards in front stopped at an angle that blocked the road. Two men in black ski masks were charging in her direction.

"Run, Christy!" Marina yelled as she dismounted her bike.

Both women began to run but were encumbered by their bike shoes. The pair from the van quickly reached Christy and tackled her to the ground while the pair from the truck did the same to Marina. One of the men landed on Christy's back knocking the wind out of her. Christy tried to fight him off, but she was face down and his weight made it difficult. He slammed her face into the ground and held it there while the other man twisted her arms up behind her and secured them with zip ties. Christy could hear Marina struggling with the other two. She must have bitten one of them as she heard the man curse at her for biting him while he slapped the side of her face and punched the back of her head.

Christy summoned every bit of strength she had and tried to twist and turn under the heavy man while kicking wildly with her legs. The metal cleat on her bike shoe made contact with the other man's face. She heard the sickening crunch of cartilage followed by a loud curse. She hoped it was the other man's nose and kept thrashing about.

"Oh! She's a wild one, Marco! We need to keep her for your stable!"

"Shut up, you fat idiot! Hold her steady while I get her legs!"

Christy kept kicking, but eventually the other man was able to hold her legs down with his weight and secure them with another zip tie. She kept trying to thrash about, but it was futile.

Tran hit the ground hard and tumbled several yards before finishing on his back. He was still processing what had happened while his subconscious was already reacting. He immediately rolled to his right and saw the crumpled heap that, seconds ago, was a racing bike. He saw Jack sprawled in the street in front of the truck. He was not moving. Two men in ski masks raced past him, heightening his alarm. Tran looked to where they were running as he pushed himself up onto his knees. He ignored the sharp pain in his left shoulder as he saw four men wrestling Christy and Marina to the ground. Tran jumped up onto his feet and immediately stumbled. The searing pain in his right lower leg registered a split second later. His shoulder got in on the act a second later when he used his hands in attempt to break his forward fall. Something was definitely wrong. It would have to wait.

Tran rose his feet again and, ignoring the pain in his leg, hobbled over to Jack's prone figure. Before they left, Jack had confided in Tran that he always carried handgun when biking. Due to the extreme laws against non-licensed carry in New York, Tran opted not to carry his. He would have no legal protection. He reached into one of the pockets on Jack's bike shirt and retrieved a Glock 43. Six rounds, maybe seven if an extra round was chambered. *Not enough,* he thought, as he recalled that New York Safe Act that limited the number of rounds a civilian gun could carry to seven or less. *Like the criminals will care.* Tran pulled back the slide and confirmed a round was in the chamber. He quickly checked the other pockets for extra magazines, but came up empty. He turned and began to hobble towards the women who were both doing their level best to fight off the masked men trying to secure them. He immediately stumbled. His lower leg was throbbing severely and bent at a grotesque angle.

Override! Charlie Mike!

Tran stretched out into a prone position and extended the Glock in front. His left shoulder screamed in protest. Tran quickly assessed the situation. They were about thirty yards away. Too far for a tiny handgun. *Would they know that?* Tran quickly weighed the risk/ benefits of trying to move in closer on one leg as opposed to staying put and trying to stop them from where he was. Neither option was promising, but he currently had the drop on them and there were no weapons in sight. Tran aimed at the closest man and fired twice. The man was straddling Christy's back when one of the rounds caught him in the shoulder and knocked him off. Tran adjusted his aim and fired two rounds at the man next to him, but both shots missed as the man dropped to the ground. The distance was just too far; nevertheless, he had them in a brief state of shock. Time to capitalize.

"Down on the ground! Hands on your head!" He yelled.

All four men were down. Tran, painfully, pushed himself to his knees. He would have to move in to cover, and fast, before they realized their advantage and countered. He sprung up onto his good leg and began to hop closer. A shot rang out. He instinctively dove to the ground as he felt the round pass closely by. A second shot rang out striking him in his right shoulder. Both shoulders screamed in protest as he summoned all of his strength to control the handgun while searching for the source of the gunfire. Another shot rang out, spraying dirt and grass as it struck the ground in front of Tran's face. Tran located the source and reflexively adjusted his aim. He was midway through trigger pull when he froze. The shooter was prone behind Christy, holding his hand gun steady on her back. Tran couldn't risk the shot. His target profile was too small and the distance still too far. He could easily hit Christy if his aim was off. The ski mask magnified the sinister look of the shooter as he locked eyes with Tran and fired.

Chapter 50

*C*huck Haltiwanger held up the smallmouth bass as Dickie Dwyer took a picture.

"I'd say that's about a three pounder, Dick!"

"Easily, Chuck."

"I hate that I have to throw her back in. Two more weeks and she would be mine."

"Two more weeks and she won't hit anything. They know when the season opens."

"Ain't that right," Chuck said as he kneeled down on the concrete pier.

He kissed the bass on the head. "Go get your grandpa!" He said encouragingly as he gently released his catch back into the river.

Chuck quickly rinsed off his hands in the river and jumped back up onto his feet. He picked up his pole and began to inspect his jig lure when his two-way radio sounded a call.

"Grand Island, please respond, EMS call, West River Parkway, just west of Beaver Island Traffic Circle. Two adult males unresponsive after apparent bicycle versus car accident. Car is believed to have left the scene."

"That's me, Dick, I gotta go. You comin' or stayin'?" Chuck said, as he secured his hook and closed his tackle box.

"I'm coming with you," he answered packing up his tackle box as a thought struck him. "Wait! That's close by! Like right where we heard those gunshots a few minutes ago!"

"You're right! I thought that was just somebody shooting in the woods. C'mon!"

They ran off the old pier, up the hill and across the bike path/ parkway, crossing a grassy strip until they arrived at Chuck's heavy duty pickup truck, parked on the side of West River Road. They tossed their fishing gear in the back and got in. Chuck fired up the truck and immediately turned on his blue flashing lights, signaling his status as a volunteer firefighter responding to a call.

They arrived two minutes later. Chuck parked his truck on the grass and they jumped out. He grabbed a med kit from the back seat and ran up to the scene. Two younger men, both in cycling kits were kneeling beside a man sprawled in the street. Multiple sirens could be heard approaching.

"What have you got?" Chuck asked, as he knelt down beside the man.

"We rode up and found these two sprawled out," the taller man said. "There's another one over there. He's unconscious, but this guy's starting to wake up."

Chuck glanced over and saw the lifeless appearing form of another cyclist laying prone. He looked down at the man moaning at his feet. *Airway, breathing, circulation.*

"Dick, go check on the other one," Chuck said as he kneeled down. He looked up at the taller cyclist.

"What's your name?"

"Bill," he replied quickly.

"Bill, can you help me by supporting his head. I don't want his neck moving. I'll get his helmet off."

"Okay."

With the man's help, Chuck removed the bike helmet. They gently rolled him onto his back, taking care to keep his spine immobilized.

"Sir? Can you hear me? Sir?"

The man moaned in response.

"Sir?" A little louder as Chuck rubbed the man's sternum with his knuckles.

"Yeah?" The injured man answered weakly.

"Sir, open your eyes."

The man blinked rapidly as his eyes fluttered open. Chuck instantly recognized the man.

Shoot! That's Jackie-O!

"Chuck?" Jack asked in confusion.

"Yeah, Jack, it's me. What the heck happened?"

Chuck was a few years younger than Jack, but Grand Island was still a small town and he had known him most of his adult life. Working for the town highway department, he often interacted with Jack and his construction company, but they were also friends socially.

"I…I'm not sure. I think someone drove into me. How's everyone else?" Jack asked with growing concern. He tried to sit up, but Chuck held him down.

"Easy Jack, try not to move until the paramedics get here and check you out."

"No. I'm okay, Chuck. Where are the others?" Jack asked with increasing alarm. "There were four of us. Marina and two of Joe's friends! Where are they?"

Chuck looked and saw Dick kneeling next to the other cyclist. He didn't see any others. Two more volunteer firefighters pulled up, immediately followed by the paramedic truck from the station. He saw six bikes, two of them likely belonged to the two good Samaritan's, but he didn't see the other two riders.

"I see one other rider from your crew, Jack. Maybe the others went to get help?"

"Yeah? Maybe that's it," Jack said, still seeming dazed. His eyes suddenly went wide with fear.

"No!" He exclaimed as he struggled to sit up. "Marina, wouldn't have left. She has her phone, she would have called for help! Where is she? Marina! MARINA!"

The paramedics pulled up and jumped out of their truck. Chuck immediately recognized that one of them was their medical director, Dr. Chris Krasinski, an Island native and paramedic who had gone on to become an emergency medicine physician. He practiced in a couple of local hospitals, but he also liked to ride with his department paramedics on certain days off. Chuck looked over at Dick who looked back and grimly shook his head.

"Chris!" Chuck and Dr. Krasinski had been friends since high school. "I've got Jack O'Shanick here, but he seems stable. Go check the other guy first."

"Dick! Two others were riding with Jack. One is his daughter, Marina. See if you can find them."

Dick and a couple of the volunteers spread out and began looking in the woods and along the parkway. Chuck turned his attention back to his friend.

"Jack, where all do you hurt?"

"I'm fine, Chuck. We need to find Marina and the others!"

"We're on it, Jack. Let me check you over."

Chuck spent the next minute working a quick head to toe exam. Jack likely had a concussion, but other than several abrasions and bruises, he seemed to be intact. He would still need to be checked out at the hospital. Against Jack's protests, they continued to protect his cervical spine.

An ambulance pulled up and the EMT's emerged. They opened the back doors and pulled out a stretcher and spinal board. Dr. Krasinski jogged over.

"Pack this one up guys, I'm gonna fly the other one."

"Do you need anything from us, sir?"

"Negative, we're starting an IV and boarding him ourselves," he replied as he kneeled down next to Jack.

"Jack? Chris Krasinski here. What the heck happened?"

"I'm not sure, Chris. I think someone drove into us. Marina and two of Joe's friends were with me. Where are they?"

"We're looking for the two girls, but who's the guy you were with?"

"That's Joe's friend, Tran Van Truc. He's a Navy SEAL with Joe. Is he okay?"

Krasinski wrestled with how much to reveal.

"He's been shot, Jack. Multiple times, including one to the head. He's alive, but he's in bad shape. I'm flying him out."

"The girls!" Jack yelled, as he broke the grips and bolted upright. "Marina and Christy! We have to find them!"

"Jack! Lay back down. You're injured too!" Chuck admonished.

"Screw that! I'm fine!" Jack said, as he reached back into his bike jersey pocket and retrieved his phone.

Chuck and Dr. Krasinski tried to lay him back down, but he swatted their hands away as he punched in a number and held the phone up to his ear. Turning his head, he got a glimpse of the scene.

"Joe! It's me, Dad. We were ambushed. Tran's been shot and I think they took Marina and Christy...I don't know, they rammed me on my bike and I was knocked out. I didn't see what happened...Yeah, I got my bell rung and I'm a bit banged up, but I'm okay...They're taking me to NCMC to get checked...No, I didn't see the car, he hit me from behind...Tran's unconscious. He was shot several times, they think. They're flying him out...I don't know, son...I'll have them call you, but you need to get the police and Matt Jennings on this now, they might still be on the Island. Maybe they can shut down the bridges! Yes...I understand, son, please be careful...Yes! Get them back!"

Chapter 51

*J*oe disconnected the call. Anticipating a busy evening, Chief Ramsey had convinced Joe to grab some rack time while Christy and his family were biking. He was wide awake now. He immediately called the Sheriff's Department who informed him that Chuck Haltiwanger had already informed them of the hit and run. They were notifying state police and dispatching several units to cover the bridges. Joe did the math as he ran downstairs. It would only take five minutes to get over the South Grand Island Bridge from the Beaver Island Circle. Ten minutes if they went over the North Bridge. Not enough time to catch them. Complicating matters, there wasn't even a vehicle description. Every minute that transpired translated to a larger search area and a decreased chance of finding Christy and Marina. He and his team needed to handle this.

Joe searched the house for his mother, but she was nowhere to be found. She would want to know what was going on. He walked through the garage and her SUV wasn't there. He recalled her saying she would be going to her boot camp class. Just as well. He needed to form a plan with the team and execute it ASAP. Joe was suddenly struck with concern that they may have gotten her too. Doubtful, she was at a park with a dozen other woman. Nevertheless, he couldn't be sure. He would call to check on her and fill her in.

He finished strapping on his tactical vest and keyed the radio mike.

"Echo One heading to beach house. All hands fall in on me."

Joe stepped up onto the covered porch and entered. Moreno and Sierra were studying overheads and street layouts of Niagara Falls on a laptop, while Chief Ramsey was rousing Kowalski and Stinnet. Mueller followed in shortly behind Joe.

"Alright guys, listen up. Our mission parameters have just changed."

"What's up, Skipper?" Kowalski asked.

"The bike crew was ambushed. My dad was hit by a car. He's banged up, but says he's okay. Christy and my sister are missing and presumed abducted. Tran was shot multiple times and is being flown to the trauma center."

Joe paused as the information was processed by the team.

"Whiskey Tango Foxtrot." Ramsey solemnly spoke as the others grimly nodded.

"My first thought too, Rammer," Joe nodded. "They asked me if I thought it was safe for them to ride and I thought it was. I royally screwed that one up. That's on me, but I can't dwell on it now. I've got to make it right. Here's the deal. I'm going after them. My sister and Christy's lives are in the balance, let alone what else these scumbags might do to them. It's my fault they were taken, my fault that our teammate is clinging to life in a helicopter right now. I'm probably going to go to prison for what I'm going to do, but that's trivial compared to the bigger picture. I can live with that. What I cannot live with is what happened to Tran and what could happen to Christy and Marina."

"Do you have an op in mind, Skipper?" Ramsey asked.

"Yes, I'm going after Pandolfino. He'll know where they are. He either tells me or I use him as bait. Once we have Christy and Marina back, I'm taking the organization down. I'm not stopping until I get to Catalano. By the time I'm done with him, he will be begging to go to prison. And *then* I'll get him to cough up the source of this hit order."

"How do you want to get Pandolfino?"

"By water."

"Come again, boss?" Ramsey asked.

"By water. I need to move now. KK and Carter said he got back late and may still be home. The bridges are being held up as they search vehicles so I can't go by truck. We have an aluminum john boat for fishing. I'll take that."

"Skipper, you're speaking in the first person singular," Stinnet pointed out. "Are you planning on going this yourself?"

"One, yes, I'm flying solo on this, Carter. Two, did you get an English degree while you were rehabbing your injuries this past year?" Joe said trying to deflect. "What's with this first-person singular business?"

"I might have taken an online class or two for some college credit," Stinnet grinned, "but that's not important right now. I'm concerned about you going down range by yourself. This should be a four man op. KK and I know the area, we'll go with you."

Kowalski nodded in agreement.

Joe held his hands up in protest. "Guys, I appreciate it, but I've said all along, I'm not doing anything to jeopardize your careers and certainly nothing that will land you in prison. I won't have that; besides, I need someone to stand watch here and look after my family. I also want someone to take my mom to the hospital to check on my dad. We also need to check on Tran. There's plenty to be done."

"With all due respect, Skipper, that's just it," Stinnet responded. "They not only went after your family, they went after and took out our teammate. My loyalty is to this team. I'm not standing down."

"Stinnet's right, Skipper, I'll do whatever you want, but I'm all for taking these scumbags out," Kowalski added.

"Guys, I can't ask you to do that."

"Who said anything about asking, Joe?" Chief Ramsey spoke up. "We're all in. It's not even a question."

"That's right," Moreno added.

Joe looked around the room. He saw a bunch of determined faces nodding.

"Alright," Joe sighed. "I can't stop you guys and, in all honesty, I'd do the same thing for each of you. Having said that, I have no legal authority. If we are caught, I can't do anything to save your careers or keep any of you out of prison. Does everyone understand that?"

They all answered in the affirmative.

"Guys, I'm beyond humbled and grateful. To each one of you, I thank you and my family thanks you."

"We wouldn't have it any other way, Skipper," Ramsey stated.

"Alright, then. If we're in it together, we plan it together. Here's what I think our objective should be..."

Chapter 52

Cayuga Island, Niagara Falls, New York

Ramsey reduced the throttle and the aluminum fishing boat quickly settled down into the water as it slowed. Joe dropped the bow-mounted trolling motor into the water and began to gently steer them in close to the docks. He looked down to ensure the boat's registration numbers were concealed by a minnow net he had placed in such a manner as to drape over the bow. Kowalski and Stinnet had already cast their lines, assuming the look of four friends out fishing. Ramsey cast his line and began jigging it in while Joe tried to look like he was tying on a lure. Using the foot pedal, Joe maneuvered the boat in close to shore, weaving around the docks as the others fished.

Frank Pandolfino's waterfront approached. Joe and his team silently assessed the house and back yard as Joe maneuvered the boat up against the shore break-wall. All clear. The break-wall rose four feet above the water allowing the boat to be concealed from anyone who might happen to look out of the house. Joe and Stinnet tied the bow and stern to cleats mounted on the wall. They peered over the wall and studied the house. Nobody could be seen in the windows. Joe gave a silent nod, pulled down his balaclava and rolled up onto the grounds with Stinnet and Kowalski. Ramsey remained in the boat with the outboard engine idling.

Handguns at the low ready position, they stealthily kept to the cover of the several willow trees lining the eastern side of the yard.

The early morning sun cast large shadows which they also used to their advantage. Kowalski led them to a side entrance to the garage. Stinnet made quick work with his lock picks and they were in. They moved to the door leading into the house and Stinnet checked the knob which was unlocked. He quietly turned the knob and gently eased the door open. It led into a utility room which opened into the kitchen. A security panel box was adjacent to the door, but it was not activated. Helpful.

Joe keyed the mike to their inter squad radio. "No alarm, Rammer, stand by."

"Good copy, Skipper."

The lights were off and, to Joe's relief, there was no smell of fresh coffee. The kitchen opened into a large living room with a grand view of the Niagara River. A hallway at the far end led to several bedrooms of the large ranch style house. With well-choreographed movements, the trio methodically cleared each room on their way to the presumed master bedroom at the end of the hall.

During last night's interrogation, Costello revealed that Pandolfino was divorced, but was known to avail himself to the girls in their prostitution ring from time to time. Other than that, he lived alone. As they approached the closed door, Joe hoped last night was a night off for Pandolfino. Kowalski and Stinnet reported that he appeared to be alone when he pulled into his garage.

They formed up on the door through which snoring could be heard. Stinnet quietly worked the knob and opened the door. Peering through the gap, he saw Pandolfino soundly asleep, but he was not alone. There were two women sprawled on the king-sized bed as well. Stinnet led the team into the room. They quietly moved to each side of the bed. Joe saw a back of crack rocks and a large bag of cocaine on the nightstand, along with a bong and a bag of weed. A bottle of Johnny Walker Black was on the stand next to Pandolfino, who was sound asleep next to the two very young girls. Young teenagers by Joe's guess. Neither was wearing anything. Pandolfino, thank God, was wearing black silk pajama bottoms. Two large gold chains dwelled within the thick graying hair on his bare chest.

Stinnet pulled a precut strip of duct tape off his thigh and held it over Pandolfino's mouth. At Joe's nod, Stinnet secured the tape while

Joe simultaneously punched Pandolfino in the groin. His windless gasp was muzzled by the duct tape. They flipped his temporarily incapacitated form over and Kowalski secured the mobster's wrists behind his back. Joe grabbed Pandolfino by his thick hair and pulled his head up. The man's head flopped down leaving Joe grasping a large toupee. He grabbed the remnants of Pandolfino's hair at the base of his skull and yanked the man's bald head up.

"You might think you're in pain now, but this is nothing compared to what you will feel if you try to resist us," Joe said, adding a painful yank to emphasize his words.

He rolled Pandolfino to his side and sat the tall, thin man up. Grabbing his wrists, Joe yanked the man up to a stand and began to march him out of the room.

"Cartso, get some photos of the girls and the drugs. Have a look around for any usable evidence while KK and I have a little chat with our Italian friend here."

"Copy that."

The two girls slept on. Joe and Kowalski marched Pandolfino down to his basement. They sat him down in a chair and zip tied his ankles to the chair legs. Kowalski opened his iPhone and held it up in front of Pandolfino. He played an edited video of Costello's confession while Joe grabbed a pair of pliers from a generously apportioned work bench nearby. After the video finished playing, Joe clamped the pliers to the nail bed of Pandolfino's right great toe and slowly applied pressure. Pandolfino let out another muffled bellow.

"Have I got your attention, Frank?" Joe asked as he released his grip,

Pandolfino met Joe's eyes with a steely stare.

"I'll take that as a yes. Good. I'm gonna make this so simple even a Neanderthal like you can understand. The tape comes off your mouth and you stay silent. You speak only to answer my questions, which you will do truthfully or you'll find out just how many pounds per square inch of pressure a pair of pliers can apply. Can I make it any simpler?"

Pandolfino continued to stare.

"I'll take that as another yes. Tape coming off. Don't disappoint me..."

Kowalski ripped the duct tape from Pandolfino's mouth. Pandolfino immediately began a tirade of colorful threats and insults. Joe gently applied pressure to the man's toe which got his attention. While distracted, Kowalski rapped Pandolfino hard on his left kneecap with a large adjustable wrench. A loud bellow ensued.

"I told you to keep your mouth shut!" Joe scolded, as he squeezed hard on the pliers.

Pandolfino stopped bellowing and began to grunt through gritted teeth.

"I'm not letting up until you promise to be a good boy, Frank!"

"Okay, Okay! Stop!"

"You gonna tell me what I want to know?"

"Yes!" Pandolfino gasped.

"Alright then," Joe said, as he relaxed his grip.

Kowalski stood off to the side as he activated the video recorder on his cell phone. He placed it back in a special pocket on his tactical vest and nodded at Joe.

"You just watched your right hand man sell you out. We know a lot about you and your organization, Frank. Enough to turn you over to the feds, just like we already did with Costello and your boy Colucci. So, in actuality, there isn't much I need from you. Except for one thing. Where are they taking the two women they abducted this morning?"

"What women?"

Joe squeezed the pliers, "Wrong answer!"

"I swear I don't know what you're talking about!" Pandolfino grunted in agonizing pain. "What women? What kidnapping?"

"Don't try me, Frank!" Joe yelled keeping the pressure on.

"I don't know what you're talking about! I friggin' swear!"

Joe let up on the pliers. Pandolfino gasped in relief. He was in a full sweat. Joe was starting to believe him, but he had to test him.

"Alright, Frank. Let's try this again. I'm going to ask you some questions of which I already know the answer to some. I'll give you one chance to tell me the truth. Don't screw it up."

Joe quickly led him through a series of questions of which he had already gotten the answers from Costello and Colucci earlier. Pandolfino answered truthfully.

"Alright, Frank. Next question. Who have you guys been trying to kill these past few days?" Joe applied a slight amount of pressure as a reminder of what would happen if Frank lied.

"Joe O'Shanick, which I'm guessing is you."

"I can neither confirm nor deny your guess, Frank. Why are you after O'Shanick?"

"I don't know. I'm just following orders."

Joe squeezed the pliers. "You expect me to believe that? You admit to trying to kill O'Shanick, but you don't know why? Try again, Frank!"

Frank screamed in pain. "I'm telling you the truth, I don't know! It was an ordered hit!"

"So Catalano ordered the hit?"

"I didn't say that."

"You just said it was an ordered hit, Frank," Joe said, as he applied pressure to the pliers.

"It was! I swear!"

"Then who ordered it?"

"I don't know."

Joe squeezed harder. "Try again, Frank!"

"I don't know! I get an order and I see that it's done. I don't question it.!"

"I'm not an idiot, Frank!" Joe said, increasing the pressure. "I know you work for Bruno Catalano. If you got a hit order, it came from him."

"Then why are you asking me?"

"I think you know why, but we're not done here. Someone went after O'Shanick's family not even an hour ago. They killed one of his friends, severely injured his father and kidnapped two women. I want to know who did this and where the women are. NOW!" Joe said, as he gave the pliers a sharp squeeze.

Pandolfino bellowed in pain. Joe kept the pressure on. This man was very well behind the disappearance of Christy and Marina. Joe was not a heartless monster, but Pandolfino would not see an ounce of mercy until Christy and Marina were safe. Pandolfino continued to scream in agony. Kowalski held a shop rag over the man's mouth to mute the screams. After what seemed like a lifetime to Pandolfino, Joe let up and let the man catch his breath. He appeared thoroughly worn down. Joe hoped he was close to breaking.

"You ready to talk now, Frankie?"

"I'm tellin' ya, I don't know nothin' about no hit this morning. You gotta believe me. Whatever went down, I had nothing to do with it!"

Stinnet's voice crackled in Joe's earpiece, "Skipper, I've got something you need to see."

"Copy, on my way."

Joe looked at Pandolfino. "I'll be right back, Frank. We're not done here."

Joe took the stairs two at a time as he charged up to see what Stinnet had found.

"Where you at, Cartso?"

"Bedroom."

Joe walked back to the bedroom. He entered and saw the girls were still sound asleep. A dresser drawer was opened as was the drawer to one of the nightstands and television armoire. Stinnet stood by the nightstand holding a smartphone.

"What do you have?" Joe asked quietly.

"Plenty, boss. This guy has a large stash of coke and heroin in here in addition to what was left out earlier. The armoire over there is loaded with home-made DVD's that all have different girls names written on them with a Sharpie. I found three hidden cameras all pointed at the bed..."

"Upstanding member of society, isn't he?" Joe commented.

"Yeah, boss, but the reason I called you is this," Stinnet said, as he held up the smart phone.

"Is that Pandolfino's?"

"Sure is and a call just came in from Terry Wood."

"Did you answer it?"

"Shoot no. I didn't want to tip them off. But I was thinking..."

Stinnet was interrupted when the phone emitted a soft train whistle sound signaling an incoming text. Both men looked at the screen and caught a quick glimpse of the text as it lingered on the screen before disappearing.

Call me when you get this. Haven't heard from Costello or Colucci but all seemed normal at O'Shanick house. Four people left his house on bikes. Our man wasn't one of them but we whacked two guys and nabbed his girlfriend and another chick. We thought you could use them as trade bait. Keeping them at the stable. Let me know what you want to do.

Joe let out a rare curse word as the text disappeared and the screen locked out requiring a passcode.

The stable?

Joe first thought of the horse stables just up the road from his parent's house. but quickly discarded that thought. Today was Saturday, a popular riding day. No way would they be held at any horse stable. Joe looked down at the two girls passed out on the bed.

Wait a minute. Might stable be a reference to where they kept the girls they were prostituting? It had to be!

"Carter, quick! We need to wake these girls up!" Joe said, as he leaned over and began to shake the dark-haired girl closer to him.

Stinnet went to work on the blonde next to her. Both stirred slightly, but neither would wake up. Joe switched to a painful sternal rub but got little in response.

"Shoot! They could be out for hours. We don't have hours!" Joe said out loud, as he quickly worked the problem.

Joe used the butt of his handgun and smashed the large mirror perched over a large oak dresser. He reached into one of his vest pockets, pulled out an old model iPhone and handed it to Stinnet.

"This is a burner phone. It's untraceable. Catalogue everything incriminating with the camera. The girls as well. When you're done, try to rouse them again. Let me know if you get anywhere."

"Aye, Skip."

Joe hurried out of the room and back down to the basement. Kowalski was standing beside Pandolfino who was in a profuse sweat.

"You've been holding out on me, Frank. Care to explain why Terry Wood just texted you about ambushing O'Shanick's family and kidnapping two women?"

"Do I look that stupid to you? Nobody sent me no text. You're trying to get me to talk about somethin' I ain't got nothing to do with."

"Is that a fact? Well, why don't we open your phone and see for ourselves. What's your passcode, Frank?"

Frank didn't answer.

"Frank? I asked you a question. What's your passcode?"

The sweat poured off Pandolfino's face. He appeared close to breaking. Joe kneeled down and picked up the pliers. Pandolfino nervously tracked Joe's movements.

"Frank?" Joe asked, placing the pliers in position.

Pandolfino continued to sweat as he quickly assessed his predicament. He knew he was hosed. It was simply a manner of choosing which hill to die on. A look of resolve came over his face. Joe sensed the change.

"Go ahead and do it, you mick," Pandolfino growled. "You can twist my toes completely off, but I ain't never gonna give that information to you."

"Let me tell you something, Frank," Joe replied, as he cranked down hard on the pliers. "There are four lives that are much more important to us than your miserable existence! Two are in the hands of your slimeballs right now. I don't care how tough you think you are, we *will* get it out of you!"

Joe kept the pressure on as Pandolfino writhed and screamed in agony. Kowalski wrapped a towel around the mobster's face to muffle his screams. Joe was calm on the exterior but, internally, he was in a rage. Christy and Marina's lives hung in the balance. The chances of finding them before they were harmed diminished with every passing second. Joe was no fan of torture. He had been subjected to it, to some degree, in Survival, Evasion, Resistance and Escape (SERE) training. He preferred to just kill the enemy, but the mission was paramount and, especially with Christy and Marina being the mission, nothing was off the table. He would deal with the psychological and, likely, criminal fallout later. Joe kept the pliers clamped down a few seconds longer and then let up.

"You ready to try that again, Frank?"

Pandolfino took a minute to catch his breath. Again, his face went from near exhaustion to angry determination. He began with some very colorful words and finished with a few threats.

"You should have let us kill you when you had the chance. If you'd have just drowned in the Falls, your sister and girlfriend would be fine. Yeah, that's right. I know it's you, O'Shanick, behind that balaclava."

Joe didn't acknowledge. He just stared icily at the middle-aged man sweating before him.

"You can torture me all you want, but you won't kill me," Pandolfino said with growing confidence. "You can't kill me! You're a friggin' Boy Scout Navy SEAL who plays by the rules. There ain't nothing you can do to me that's gonna make me break Omertà and have to run from the family the rest of my life. Every minute you waste here ain't gettin' ya nowhere. Meanwhile, your sister and girlfriend? Well, let's just say they are going to be the prized ponies in that stable. Are you really gonna waste time here with me when you should be out looking for them?"

Joe slowly stood. He silently looked around the room.

"Yeah, that's right. You're a smart guy, Joe. You know you've got a problem with me here. I can tell the police you broke into my house, threatened me at gunpoint, assaulted me and tortured me. You know what they do to guys who do that? They put them in prison, Joe. Guys like me? We own the prisons. You have no idea the kind of fun the inmates will have with a pretty boy like you, Joe. The only way to keep me from talkin' is to kill me and we both know you ain't gonna do that. Meanwhile, your sister and girlfriend will be working for me, making me a ton of cash, until they're no longer desirable, which doesn't take long before most girls are used up and discarded. Oh, and now you've forced me to have to off the rest of your family too. But that's okay, the world won't miss a few micks now, will it? You guys breed like the halfwit gerbils you really are. I'll be doing the rest of us a favor. Is that what you want, Joe?"

Joe just stood staring and didn't answer.

"Cat got your tongue, Joe? Yeah, I don't blame you. You're not so tough when I'm holding all the cards, are you, ya half-breed?

Now, if you cut these ties and release me, maybe we can work us out a little deal."

"That's not going to happen," Joe said in a factual manner.

"Is that a fact? Well, the way I see it, the only way you're getting those two bellas back is through a trade. You for them."

Joe stared at the man in silence.

"You see, with one simple call or even a text, I can have those girls delivered anywhere you want. Your lackey here can go pick them up while you stay here with me, only *you're* the one tied to this chair."

"You've got to be kidding me," Joe answered.

"Nope," Pandolfino shook his head with growing confidence. "That's the way it's gonna happen if you ever want them back. You're the one we've been after. As much as those two little fillies would make a profitable addition to our stable, I'll trade them to deliver your head. Think about it, Joe. Your family will never hear from us again. Your life for theirs. It's really not that hard a decision for a Boy Scout like you, is it?"

"So I'm just supposed to switch places with you and let you kill me, yet trust you to keep your end of the bargain?"

"That's right, tough guy. You send your lackey here to the drop off spot and, just to prove I'm a sport, I'll stay where I'm at until they're ready to make the exchange. You cut me loose and hand me your gun. Once I've got you tied up, I give them the word and they release your girls."

Joe looked up and saw Kowalski standing behind Pandolfino, slowly shaking his head. It was suicide, but what choice did he have? Pandolfino feared his organization more than he feared what Joe could do to him. Joe had lost his leverage and time was running out. Even if he took out Pandolfino, located the girls, kicked down the doors and rescued them, the Catalano family would continue pursuing Joe and likely his family until they got what they were after. Joe could end it all now if he simply surrendered. Christy and Marina would be returned and his family wouldn't have to spend the rest of their lives looking over their shoulders. *Or would they?* He couldn't trust them. They would want to remove anyone who could identify them or pin Joe's death on them.

Joe quickly sorted out the options. The reality was, there would only be two outcomes. He would either face a lengthy prison sentence or he would be killed by these mobsters. Neither was a good option. He would likely be a target, but he could handle himself in prison; however, he couldn't handle the thought of not doing everything in his power to protect Christy and his family. They were the mission. If he could just buy them some time. What did Christy write to him last year? Yes, that bible verse.

Greater love has no man than this, that he lay his life down for another.

Joe exhaled a sigh of resignation. "Alright, Frank. How do you want to do this?"

Chapter 53

Grand Island, New York

"Just a few more! Don't give up!"

A dozen women poured sweat as they worked through a set of ten burpee tuck jumps. The early morning cool air was rapidly warming with the sun as this outdoor session neared its conclusion. Leading them was a petite dynamo named Anita. Similar in age to Maria, Anita could outlift and outlast any of the women in her boot camp class, even some who were half her age. Maria didn't consider herself as fit as Anita, but was pleased to finish the last tuck jump with her knees still high in the air.

"C'mon ladies! One last trip up the hill!"

A collective groan sounded as the group followed Anita in one last sprint up the hill at Veteran's Park. Maria gasped for air along with the rest of the class as they ascended the hill for the tenth and final time. *Thank God!* They neared the top as Anita lightly skipped back down.

"Remember, you'll pass out before you die!" She sang out as they rounded the top and followed her back down.

They reached the bottom with a collective sigh of relief. The hour-long Boot Camp was finally over. They were exhausted, but the tangible feeling of accomplishment was worth the pain and fostered a camaraderie among the variously aged women.

They spent the next ten minutes stretching and cooling down before breaking apart and heading to their various cars and SUV's.

Maria and a couple of other women, Laurie and Joan, helped Anita gather up several instruments of torture; medicine balls, dumbbells and jump ropes. After depositing the items in the back of Anita's SUV, Maria addressed them.

"Would you guys mind if we held our Bible study at the Tim Horton's this morning? Joe is in town with several of his Navy teammates and it would just work better this morning if we met somewhere else."

"I'm all for that, but we could also meet at my house if you guys prefer," Anita offered.

"Are you out of your mind?" Joan challenged. "If we meet at your house, you'll make us all ride the exercise bikes and elliptical machines on your porch of terror while we hold our study. I vote Timmy Ho's."

"You're probably right," Anita said with a laugh. "Alright, Tim Horton's it is, but coffee only! *No* donuts!"

"Oh, we are *so* having donuts and I'm buying!" Maria chimed to Laurie and Joan's approval as she turned and headed to her SUV.

A few minutes later they were seated at a table in the popular donut chain's restaurant at the south end of the Island. Maria reached into her small purse and donned her reading glasses. She took out her iPhone to open her Bible App and noticed she had several missed calls and texts from Joe and her husband. A look of concern crossed her face as she opened the texts.

"Maria, is everything alright?" Anita asked.

Maria looked up at the table in shock. Her mouth hung open as tears welled up in her eyes.

"Maria! What's wrong?"

"Somebody tried to kill Jack," she spoke barely able to get the words out.

"What!?" Anita gasped. "How?"

"He was hit by a truck when they were biking. He's at NCMC. but Marina and Joe's friend Christy are missing! Oh, dear God, no!" Maria began to sob.

"Let's go!" Anita said, abruptly standing from the table. "I'll drive."

Chapter 54

Niagara Falls, New York

The room smelled of a pungent mixture of mold, cigarette smoke, and cheap air freshener. It was one of many similar rooms making up the modest cheap motel, easily overlooked and conveniently located near the interstate. The motel was owned by the Catalano organization through a shell corporation that existed on paper only. The rooms were rented out nightly to various clientele; truck drivers, families on a budget, and, frequently, homeless people. An entire wing was devoted to rooms that were rented by the hour. These were ostensibly used by couples looking for a discrete location for a tryst. They were more often rented by desperate men looking to pacify their lusty urges.

Having lost significant income from traditional ventures such as labor unions and illegal gambling, the organization had turned to the drug trade and, increasingly more so, the growing human trafficking trade to build their empire. Marco Vona had solidified his standing in the organization by running a very profitable prostitution business as a part of Frank Pandolfino's crew. A couple of tech savvy associates helped him create an online escort service discreetly providing women, girls and even young men to clients with the means to pay. Marco's techs had been among the first to create phone apps for easier and discreet access to the service. Aside from the girls who were sent to work the truck stops, there were no streetwalkers. Technology had removed the need.

The girls were kept, four to a room, on the upper level of this wing of the motel; an area known as "The Stable." The lower level was reserved for the rooms rented by the hour. Renters paid a standard hourly rate, but, if they paid for the "Adult Entertainment" package, one of the girls was provided. They either paid cash or it would show up on their credit card statement as a simple motel room charge.

Additionally, there were several dozen women who voluntarily worked as escorts for Marco due to the convenience of the online service as well as his protection. They came and went as they pleased and tended to fetch better prices due to their looks and "professionalism." The Stable was different. Most of the girls in The Stable were little more than property to the organization. About half were runaways or girls who had been abducted and forced into prostitution. The other half were illegal immigrants who had begun with the Central American Cartels or were imported from Europe or Asia. Many were forced into prostitution to work off their debt for the privilege of being brought to the United States. Others had been sold to the cartels by their own families. Many arrived already addicts. Those that weren't were quickly made so by Marco and his associates. Their addictions made them easy to control and kept them from running away. They rarely had to use force. They were cheap labor and they produced high profit margins.

Christy and Marina sat together on one of the beds, they held each other's hands as they earnestly prayed for Marina's dad, her family, Tran, and for the safety of Joe and his men. They had been kept blindfolded the entire drive and, only after being shoved into the room, were they able to remove the hoods that had been placed over their heads. Marina had made an attempt to look out the single window, but could not tell where they were. The solitary door was locked from the outside and the windows of the upper lever rooms had been replaced by reinforced plexiglass. They could not be broken. Christy and Marina had already tried.

"...Lord, our strength is in you. You are our fortress, our redeemer and our salvation. Give us wisdom and strength to face our captors and help us to trust in you for the battle is yours. We proclaim your Word in which you said that no weapon formed against us shall prosper. We thank you in advance for the good work you will do. It's in Jesus' name we pray. Amen."

As Christy concluded the prayer, she and Marina shared a hug. Marina was still tearful regarding their situation, but more so over the unknown status of her father. For all she knew, he could very well be dead. Christy had tried to reassure her, but had very little to base her reassurance on. She needed to take her mind off of the situation. But how? *Work the problem. Keep moving.* Christy could hear Joe's voice speaking those words. She vividly recalled a similar situation when she and Joe were being held captive in a bungalow on a small Caribbean Island off Belize. He kept trying to plan their escape.

Christy rose to her feet and began to inspect the room. The other bed was messed as if someone had slept in it. The tiny bathroom was a mess. Several items of tawdry women's lingerie hung on the shower curtain rod and the vanity was full of women's make up. Several wigs were arranged on top of the dresser. The closet had several skimpy outfits and the dresser drawers were about half full of jeans and t-shirts.

"What are you looking for?" Marina asked.

"I'm looking for anything that will help us get out of here. I think someone lives in here. There are a lot of clothes. It looks like she's been here awhile. Kind of sleazy...oh."

Christy caught herself in mid-sentence as the realization hit her.

"Oh? What's oh?" Marina asked.

"She might be a prostitute."

"Really?"

"Yes, I have been involved with a human trafficking ministry since last year. It fits the pattern. If she lives here, she's either an addict trying to support herself or she's being kept as a sex slave," Christy said, as she opened the nightstand drawer while continuing to inspect the room. "I don't see any drugs or paraphernalia, so I'm guessing she's a slave."

"What makes you say that?"

"Because if she were practicing solo, she would have her own supply in here. If she was being controlled, her pimps would only give her one fix at a time. That way she does what they tell her. Plus, they wouldn't leave her with enough to run away with...or overdose."

"Oh my gosh, Christy. What a sad reality. To be controlled in such a manner where your best options are to run away or to kill yourself."

"You're right, Marina," Christy said with a slow shake of her head. "It's pure evil what these barbarians do to these young girls. It's demonic. It's even worse in Central America."

"Isn't that what you were doing down there last year? Working in a ministry that helps those women?"

"Yes, I went with several of my friends."

"And then you were attacked and held prisoner?"

"Yes," Christy said, as she sat down in the chair opposite Marina. "It was horrible, and then half of Joe's platoon were killed trying to rescue us. I can't get over that," Christy said with tears starting to form.

"I don't know how anyone could get over that, but you can't blame yourself, Christy. You were serving in a dangerous place. Performing a vital ministry. Joe said it was terrible what happened to his men, and even worse what happened to several of the women working in that mission, but that his platoon willingly ran into harm's way knowing they were going in to rescue brave women serving in such a capacity. He said it was a righteous op. His words," Marina said giving a consoling smile.

"He really called it that?"

"Yes. Joe says they get called to make a lot of bad ops chosen by self-serving bureaucrats, but a righteous op is one where the beneficiaries are good people doing good things. He so looks up to you, Christy. We all do."

"I don't know what to say, but thank you. Actually, it's more the other way around. I really admire Joe and all of you. There is such a strong family dynamic and I see so much of that in Joe."

"So forgive me if I'm getting too personal, but I'm curious...and hopeful. Is there something going on between you and my brother?"

Christy shrugged and said, "Yes, kind of...I don't know."

"What do you mean, you don't know?"

"Well, I mean, yes, there is something there. I think we're both interested but, it's complicated," Christy said, as she looked down at the floor with a grimace.

"Would it be less complicated if I told you I thought my brother is enamored with you?"

Christy looked up, startled. "You really think so?"

"Yes," Marina sad with a laugh. "I know my little brother. I've never seen him like this before, ever. He's always been so introverted and focused. No woman has ever held his interest before. But, with you? Oh man!"

"Really?"

"Yes, Christy! And I don't think you'd be up here if you weren't interested in him, so I'm not understanding why you think it's complicated."

"It *is* complicated, Marina," Christy said quietly. "Yes, I find your brother amazing and quite appealing. I've never met anyone like him. To any woman, he would be a dream catch."

"But?" Marina prompted.

"But, I'm a believer and he's not," Christy said bluntly. "We're not equally yoked."

"Ah, yes. Got it," Marina nodded in understanding. "Yes, that is an issue."

"It's really *the* issue," Christy replied. "Christ is the center of my life. I cannot be with any man who won't serve Christ side by side with me. The Bible is very clear on that and I firmly believe it."

"You're right, Christy. I strayed from my faith while I was in college. I rededicated my life to Christ shortly after TJ and I were married, but he wasn't a believer at the time. We struggled for several years, but he accepted Christ three years ago, thank God, and it has been much better since. I wouldn't recommend an unequally yoked marriage to anyone."

"How did TJ come to Christ?"

"I think my family had a lot to do with it. They loved him and accepted him and demonstrated Christ in how they live. He saw that it was genuine and not some form of religion. He despises religion. I kept telling TJ that Jesus spoke against religion as well and that there is a *huge* difference between being religious and actually being a follower of Christ. He didn't see the difference at first, but he eventually grew to understand it. My dad and Jake really took him under their wings and mentored him. I really think Joe's not too far away either."

"I think Joe has come a long way, too," Christy agreed. "He was quite the skeptic last year when we met, but we have had many conversations since then and I think he now believes in Christ and even understands what salvation really means. He just hasn't gone the distance, yet."

"Key word, 'yet'," Marina said with a smile. "We just need to keep working on him."

"I sure hope..." Christy was abruptly interrupted when the door was kicked open. In walked Marco Vona and Terry Wood, both wielding guns and lascivious looks.

Chapter 55

erry Wood gave off a menacing leer which revealed crooked teeth, rotted from crystal meth. They had just received a text from the Panda informing them that he would be arriving shortly with O'Shanick in the back seat and, upon arrival, they were to release the girls to a truck that would be waiting across the street. Upon doing so, O'Shanick would surrender to the Panda.

Terry and Marco agreed that they were entitled to a few minutes of pleasure with the girls before releasing them. Screw O'Shanick. He'd be dead soon anyway. There wasn't anything he could do about it. Before coming up, they played a quick game of Rock, Paper, Scissors to see who got first pick. Wood won two out of three. He eyed both girls, *women actually,* in their form-fitting biking apparel, and decided on Christy even though he found both extremely desirable. Both were shapely, exotic brunettes, but Christy's height gave her the alluring appeal of danger.

"Tall one's mine, Marco," Wood spoke before pointing his gun at Marina. "You. That bed, clothes off. Now!" He commanded pointing his gun at the slept-in bed.

"No!" Marina shouted back as she and Christy locked arms.

A deafening explosion erupted from his gun as he fired a shot into the pillow on the bed they were standing beside. Christy gasped, and Marina let out a short scream.

"Did I stutter!? Next one goes in your knee! Get over there now!"

Trying to keep her distance from Wood, Marina gingerly climbed over the bed and stood in front of Marco, beside the other bed.

"You heard the man, take it off!" Marco ordered.

"Take it all off!" Wood added maliciously, causing both men to laugh.

Marina stood frozen as tears silently flowed down her face.

"Now, don't do that, beautiful. You know you want me," Marco soothed. "Now get on with it!"

Marina continued to cry as she began to shake. Marco back-handed her across the face causing her to fall on the bed.

"You've got two seconds to get up and undress before I rip those clothes off of you myself, you little tramp!"

Marina stood back up and, with trembling hands, awkwardly removed her bike jersey.

"Now we're talking. Keep going," Marco said encouragingly. "Terry, I'll go first while you cover them."

Marco placed his gun down on the dresser and began undoing his jeans. Wood, ever mindful of the time, decided to have Christy get ready.

"You too," he said. "Clothes off, now."

"No," she spoke through gritted teeth. "I'd sooner die than give it up to an animal like you."

"That can be arranged, sweetheart," Wood said as he stepped closer and placed the barrel of his Glock on Christy's forehead. "Now do it!"

"Okay, okay!" Christy said, holding her hands up beside her face in surrender. "Please don't shoot me," she whimpered.

Wood snickered. "That's what I thought. Real tough babe. Just do..."

Christy's right hand circled up in a rapid blur of motion making contact with Wood's gun hand as she simultaneously stepped to her left. Her right hand clamped down on top of his gun while her left hand grabbed his forearm. She instantly pulled Wood into her and used her weight to bend Wood's hand in at the wrist until he lost mechanical advantage and his grip loosened. Christy yanked the gun down and away and then used her left elbow to deliver a savage blow to his nose. She jumped back, arms extended in a firing position and fired a shot into his chest. It happened so quickly that Marco, who was distracted by the sight of Marina undressing, was taken by surprise by the loud report of the gunshot. He quickly turned around and grabbed his gun off the dresser but Christy fired, knocking him into the wall as the round struck him in the side of his chest. She fired twice more and his lifeless body collapsed to the floor. She turned her attention back to Wood, but her round had struck him dead center and he too was lifeless.

"We've gotta get out of here now!" Christy exclaimed, as she sat down on the bed and began unfastening her bike shoes. "Get your bike shoes off so we can run! Can you handle a gun?"

"Yes! I got my CWP a few years ago. Joe and Dad insisted." Marina replied, as she pulled her bike jersey back on.

"Good! Grab that one and let's get going," Christy said as she stooped down to check Wood for extra magazines. "Check him for extra ammo."

Neither man had an extra magazine. Christy did retrieve the key to open the door which had been altered to only unlock from the inside by key. The two stood and cautiously approached the door. They opened it with their guns extended, but no one was standing outside. There was nobody on the outdoor walkway so they ran to the nearest stairway. Peering down, they saw no one and quickly descended to the parking lot level. Reaching the bottom, they broke into a run for the main road out front. They were approaching the motel's lobby when two men bolted out the door.

"Hey! Where do you think you're going? Stop or I'll shoot!"

Christy looked in the direction of the voice and recognized the face as that of the man in the Dodge Charger the other day. He was accompanied by another man. Both held guns pointed at Christy and Marina. They were twenty yards away, but directly in the way of Christy and Marina's path of escape. To her left was a pool surrounded by a low fence which offered little in the way of protection.

"Marina! Quick! Between the cars!" Christy yelled out as she cut to right.

Shots rang out as they dove for cover beside a Honda Pilot. Christy heard the sound of running feet. She quickly peered around the back of the Pilot and fired two shots forcing the two men to duck behind a battered pickup truck a few parking spaces away.

"Are you okay?" Christy asked Marina.

"I'm fine. How do we get out of here?"

"I'm working on that," Christy answered breathlessly.

"My brother always says that!"

"Just stay down for a second and cover the right side. I'm gonna take a look."

Christy quickly rose high enough to peer through the Pilot's windows. The windows had an aftermarket tinting that were too dark to see through. She quickly glanced around the back end of the vehicle but didn't see either man. From behind, Marina fired her weapon.

"Missed him! They just tried to come around this side, Christy! I think they're heading back the other way!"

"Got it! You watch that end and I'll cover this end!"

Christy watched as the Dodge Charger man peaked around the back of the truck. She waited as he began to sneak her way hugging the truck's tailgate. He reached the clear and Christy fired. The man spun and fell out of sight as he emitted a slew of cuss words. She saw a Lincoln Town Car turn in off the street before she ducked back behind the Pilot.

"I hit one, but I don't think I killed him! We've got to get the other one, but I think more just pulled in!"

"I'm watching for him," Marina replied, as she slowly rose over the hood.

Several gunshots rang out as she ducked back down. She glanced over at Christy.

"Marina! Behind you!"

The other man materialized at the front of the car. His gun pointed down at Marina. Christy fired two quick shots. The first struck the man in his chest, the second missed. His gun fired at the same time Christy's round impacted his chest knocking him back into a door. He collapsed in a lifeless heap.

"Marina! Are you okay?"

Marina lay on her back; a small pool of blood began to spread on her left chest. She was hyperventilating and speaking in gasps.

"Can't...breathe...got me..."

"No!" Christy exclaimed as she quickly moved to Marina's side.

Suddenly, the Dodge Charger man appeared from around the back of the Pilot. His right shoulder hung limply but his left arm was extending in Christy's direction. Christy quickly raised her weapon and pulled the trigger.

Nothing. The slide was locked open. She was out of ammo.

Chapter 56

hristy cradled Marina's head in her lap and held her hand as she realized they were both about to die. As the man's gun rose to meet her, Christy had one of those experiences where one's life flashes before one in an instant. Only it wasn't her past life. It was her future, or what it might have been. She saw a life with Joe and his family. She saw young children swimming off the dock at the O'Shanick house in the summer and playing in the snow in front of a beautifully decorated house during Christmas. Christy looked down at Marina, gasping for air. It wouldn't be long for her. They wouldn't even have to shoot her again. Marina could have been her sister in-law, but now that day would never come. Neither one of them would ever have children. The visions faded. At least they would meet their Lord together. Christy held Marina's hand tightly as she looked up to face her killer. In slow motion, she saw his finger tighten on the trigger.

The man's head exploded in a cloud of pink and he collapsed to the ground. His gun fired harmlessly into the Pilot.

"Christy! Don't shoot! It's me!" Joe yelled as he raced around the corner.

"Joe!"

"Yes, it's me! You're safe now!" Joe froze as he spotted Marina. His eyes bulged.

"Joe, she's been shot! We've gotta get her to the ER right now!"

Joe turned and gave a loud whistle along with a wave. Seconds later, Eddie Sierra braked to a rapid halt beside Joe. Ramsey, Kowalski, and Moreno all appeared on foot right behind him.

"Marina's been shot! We need to medevac her now. Help me get them in the back of the truck!" Joe said as he scooped up his sister and carried her to the back of the Toyota pickup. "Christy, are you hit?" He called over his shoulder.

"No, I'm good!"

"Thank God! Will you help me with Marina? She needs you!"

"Of course I will!" Christy said, as she vaulted the side of the truck and landed in the bed. She helped Joe load Marina in the back.

"Rammer, get in back and help Christy!" Joe said, as he ran up to the driver's side door. "Eddie, slide over and let me drive."

Sierra climbed into the passenger seat as Joe opened the door. Joe hopped in a craned his neck out the window to Kowalski and Moreno.

"KK, you, Carter, and Ricky take Pandolfino back to his house and get him to cough up Catalano. Call me as soon as you know anything."

"On it, Skipper!" Kowalski replied as he and Moreno turned and ran to the Lincoln Town Car where Pandolfino was still restrained in the back seat under the watchful eye of Carter Stinnet.

Joe put the truck in gear and reversed into a turn in front of the courtyard pool area. He then shifted into forward and sped out the entrance turning left onto Niagara Falls Boulevard. A minute later, several police cars sped past them heading towards the motel with lights and sirens engaged. Joe didn't let up on his speed and the police didn't seem to care. He found himself praying for his sister and for green lights as he merged onto Pine Avenue less than a mile from the trauma center.

"Christy, how's my sister?" Joe yelled back through the open sliding rear window.

"She's hanging on, but we need to get there fast!"

"I'm working on it!" Joe yelled back.

"Stay with me, Marina! We're almost there!"

Marina looked Christy in the eyes. "Pray." Her breathing was so rapid and shallow, Christy sensed more than heard what Marina said.

"You got it," Christy answered quietly, as she squeezed Marina's hand tighter and closed her eyes in prayer. "Heavenly Father, we ask, in the name of Jesus, for your healing touch over Marina right now.

Please guide the hands of the doctors and nurses who will soon be providing care for her. Take all pain from her, restore blood flow to all vital areas and work a miracle in her. We also ask for healing for her father and Tran. It's in your mighty name we pray. Amen."

As Christy opened her eyes, she saw that Chief Ramsey had laid his hand upon Marina's shoulder and prayed with her. He looked at her and gave a brief nod.

"Hold on back there, we're turning in!" Joe yelled.

He turned the truck down a side street and turned into the ambulance entrance. He blared the horn as he brought them to a quick stop. A security guard came out the sliding glass doors.

"Hey! You can't park here! This is for..."

"I'm an ER doctor and I've got a female with a gunshot wound to the chest!" Christy yelled in an authoritative voice. "Hold those doors open and tell your charge nurse to get a stretcher!"

Christy and Ramsey hopped out and helped Joe get Marina out of the truck bed. Joe scooped his sister up and ran through the doors with Christy in the lead. Christy instinctively spotted a nurse.

"Gunshot wound to the chest! Where's your trauma bay?"

"This way!" the nurse said, as she took off in a trot and yelled, "I need a doctor to room 2 now! Activate a Level 1 Trauma now!"

Joe followed the nurse and Christy into the trauma bay. Marina was unconscious and hung limp as he deposited her on the stretcher and quickly backed out of the way. Christy grabbed an ambu bag off the adjacent wall and hooked it up to the oxygen tree which she turned all the way up.

"Can somebody set up an airway for me? I need an 8.0 endotracheal tube and a size 3 Macintosh blade, please. Let's also get respiratory and X-ray, in here please."

Christy's voice was calm, but authoritative. She was in her element doing what came naturally to her after years of training and experience.

"Let's have large bore IV's in both arms with Normal Saline going wide open, please."

The direness of the situation, along with Christy's command and knowledge, convinced the nurses to disregard the fact that a strange woman in biking apparel was ordering them around and they sprang into action. Like a finely choreographed dance, the nursing staff and techs were already busy at work. A nurse was at each arm starting a large bore IV while another nurse was hanging and prepping IV bags. One tech was hooking Marina up to the monitor to obtain vital signs while another tech was using a pair of trauma sheers to cut off Marina's clothing. The respiratory therapist had arrived and was setting up the items Christy called for to insert an airway.

"What do we have, guys?" Dr. Tony Alendretti asked, as he hustled into the room.

"Gunshot wound to the chest, unresponsive," Christy answered. "Do we have vitals yet?"

"Heart rate is 140, BP 70/32," the tech answered.

"Start Type O negative blood, please," Christy ordered in her calm manner. She looked back up at Dr. Alendretti as she began breathing for Marina using the ambu bag and a face mask. "I'll handle the airway if you want to take a look at her."

Dr. Alendretti looked back puzzled at the familiar woman ventilating his patient while clad in biking kit.

"Oh, you're Christy!" He exclaimed.

"Riiiight!"

"Yes," Alendretti snapped back into clinical mode. "If you could handle the airway that would be a huge help," he said, as he began to listen for lung sounds with his stethoscope.

"I need the chest cart now, please! Has anybody heard from Dr. Bynum yet?" Alendretti asked.

"He's still in the OR with that MVC patient," the charge nurse answered.

"Tell him what we've got and that we may be cracking her chest!"

Alendretti quietly uttered a curse word before looking at Christy. "I think she's got a hemothorax," he said, referring to a large amount of blood filling up the left side of her chest and restricting the ability of the lung to expand. "I don't hear any breath sounds on the left and she has blood oozing out of that wound," he said, pointing to the relatively small hole just to the left of Marina's sternum.

"I'm gonna throw in a chest tube, but if it's as bad as I think it is, we're gonna have to crack her chest."

"I think you're right," Christy said in agreement. "I'll get her intubated and then I'll come over there and give you a hand."

Joe watched on in silent horror. He had enough medical training and had seen far too much combat related trauma. He knew exactly what was happening. He also knew that the best thing he could do was to stay out of the way and let Christy and Tony take care of business. Actually, there was one thing he *could* do.

"Lord, please don't take my sister," he began to pray quietly. *"It's me they were after, not her! You know I agreed to trade my life for her earlier and I'll still give it for her now! Please, please don't take my sister..."*

"Bag for me, please," Christy asked.

The respiratory therapist took over bagging as Christy readied the laryngoscope blade and the endotracheal tube.

"Okay, let me take a look."

Christy used her right thumb and forefinger to open Marina's mouth. She placed the laryngoscope into Marina's mouth and used it to sweep the tongue out of the way before advancing the curved blade further into the oropharynx. Christy then positioned Marina's head into the "sniff" position to optimize viewing of the vocal cords. Using the laryngoscope, she lifted Marina's tongue and jaw up and away allowing her to see the vocal cords. Unfortunately, they were obscured by blood pooling in the oropharynx. Christy grabbed the suction probe and quickly suctioned the blood out.

"Tube," she said, holding out her hand.

The respiratory therapist handed Christy the endotracheal tube which she then inserted into Marina's throat and past the vocal cords into her trachea.

"That should have it. Balloon up and bag, please," Christy ordered to which the RT inflated a small balloon at the tip of the endotracheal tube to hold the tube in place and protect the airway from aspiration. The RT then connected the ambu bag to the tube and resumed ventilations. One of the nurses gave a quick listen with her stethoscope.

"I don't hear anything on the left, but there are breath sounds on the right."

Christy checked the markings on the tube.

"We're 21 centimeters at the lip so I don't think we're in the right mainstream. We probably just can't hear the left lung due to the hemothorax," Christy concluded out loud.

"Starting the chest tube now," Alendretti announced, as he made a small incision just above the sixth rib on the left side of her chest.

"Can you take over here?" Christy asked the respiratory therapist, who nodded.

"I'll come help you, Tony," Christy said as she stepped away from the head of the bed. "May I please have a sterile gown and a pair of size seven gloves?"

"Would you like something for your feet?" A young tech asked.

Christy looked down at her feet and remembered she had ditched her bike shoes back at the motel. Her feet were barely covered in ankle socks.

"Yes, please," she answered with an embarrassed smile. "Thank you," she said quietly.

One of techs opened up a gown and helped Christy into it while Christy quickly donned a pair of sterile gloves. She stepped over to the sterile table as Alendretti inserted a large hemostat into the incision and bluntly dissected through the muscle between the ribs. Seconds later, the hemostat broke through and blood began to trickle out. He opened the hemostat to increase the size of the hole and blood began to pour out. He removed the hemostat and placed his finger in the hole to mark his place although it was not usually necessary in patients as lean and fit as Marina.

"I've got your tube loaded," Christy said as she handed Dr. Alendretti another large hemostat clamped to the first fenestrated hole on the leading edge of a large chest tube. Using his finger as a guide, he inserted the chest tube and advanced it until all the fenestrated holes were in the chest cavity. Blood poured out of the tube soaking his pants and shoes until the nurse could hook the open end of the tube to the pleur-a-vac. Alendretti and Christy watched in horror as the pleur-a-vac suctioned blood out of Marina in an alarming volume. The container filled up within seconds and blood began to run onto the floor. The level of blood loss was well over a liter and likely two or three. Christy glanced up at the monitor. Heart rate was still in the 140's despite having a good airway. Her clinical knowledge told her she was looking at the heart rate of a rapidly hemorrhaging patient. Marina's blood pressure had dropped to a precariously low 63/30. Christy and Tony's eyes met.

"We have to crack her chest," he spoke somberly.

"I agree," Christy replied. "Let's do it."

"She needs more blood and let's start adding platelets and FFP in a one to one to one ratio. Let's give her 1000 milligrams of Tranexamic Acid as well. We're opening her chest."

A collective gasp left the room briefly devoid of voices. The only sounds were the mechanical sounds of the ventilator and the monitor alarms. Cracking one's chest in a penetrating trauma situation was a heroic attempt to locate the bleeding source and fix it, if possible, in a patient who was seconds away from death due to internal hemorrhaging. In the movies and TV shows, it was often depicted as successful. In reality, it was the medical equivalent of a Hail Mary pass in football. One last ditch attempt to save the patient, but it rarely succeeded. Christy had performed only two thoracotomies, the proper medical term for cracking a chest, in her career. Both had been in residency and neither patient had survived. Dr. Alendretti selected a scalpel from the chest cart and looked at Christy. She could see the concern in his dark brown eyes as they peered over the mask.

"Here we go," he announced as he turned and began the incision at Marina's breastbone, following the top edge of the sixth rib and extending the incision all the way to the chest tube incision in her left side.

Christy briefly made eye contact with Joe. A silent communication signaled their mutual understanding of the severity of the situation despite each person's stoicism under the circumstances. Clinical stoicism in Christy's case and tactical stoicism in Joe's case. Vital tools of the trade for each of them. Inwardly, Christy fought hard to maintain her composure. She silently prayed while she pushed back her emotions and handed a rib separator to her colleague.

Joe may have appeared calm on the exterior, but, inwardly, he was a wreck. He was quite aware that his sister was very close to dying on the table in front of him. He was even more cognizant that her death had nothing to do with anything she had done and everything to do with who her brother was. Joe had spent years training and fighting against a very tangible evil that caused people to do evil things. There were many reasons he did so; love of country, duty, a sense of honor, but also so that his family, whom he loved beyond measure, would never have to experience the evil he had seen and experienced. Ironically, that evil had come full circle and was visiting his family right now. He looked at his sister, the innocent victim of his world. He looked at Christy and Tony, two people he trusted completely, desperately trying to right this wrong, but they too were human and there was only so much they could do.

Dear God please don't let Marina die! I know I have no right to ask you for anything. I'm the one who was wrong. I thought I was strong enough on my own and didn't need you but I'm here now! I need you to do something I can't do, something no human can do. Please save Marina. She had nothing to do with this. Why should someone innocent have to die when it's others who are evil? Why...

Joe was struck by a sudden revelation. Something he never thought about became very clear to him. Marina was still in critical danger and he, desperately, continued to pray for his sister, but he now prayed with a better understanding. As Joe prayed, he saw Christy and Tony dialed in, doing what they were trained to do, and he was comforted knowing that Marina was in good hands. Very good hands.

"Rib spreaders," Dr. Alendretti called out.

Familiar with the procure, Christy anticipated each step. She already had the large contraption in her hands and held it out. He took it from her and inserted what looked like a closed vice in the space between Marina's fifth and sixth ribs. He rotated a crank and it quickly spread the ribs apart bringing her left lung and her rapidly beating heart into view.

"Cross-clamping the aorta. Mark the time," Alendretti said as he applied the clamp, temporarily shutting down blood flow to the lower extremities and viscera in the attempt to preserve blood flow to the brain and vital organs.

"Blood pressure 54/27!" The charge nurse called out.

"Suction, please," Alendretti asked as he moved the lung out of the way looking for the source of bleeding.

Christy handed him the suction catheter and he worked it in and around the chest cavity suctioning out blood.

"The pericardium looks okay. I think the bleeding is from one of the pulmonary arteries or veins. If I could just get around the lung to see better..."

Christy looked up at the respiratory therapist. "Can you advance the tube into the right main stem and drop the tidal volume in half please?"

The RT quickly deflated the balloon and advanced the endotracheal tube which naturally followed the tracheal bifurcation to the right thereby only inflating the right lung.

"Good call, Christy, that helped," Alendretti said over his shoulder as he continued to search for the source of bleeding.

"Do you see anything yet?" Christy asked.

"Maybe...Yes! Got it! Hand me some gauze!"

Christy hand a small stack of four-inch square gauze pads to Alendretti's extended hand. He quickly inserted it into the pulmonary tree and clamped down on one of the pulmonary artery branches. He suctioned the area clean and watched for blood. Nothing.

"We got it! Cycle her blood pressure and get Dr. Bynum on speaker please!"

"BP 63/30."

"Keep the blood going wide open. Platelets and FFP too." He ordered before looking at Christy. "You mind throwing in a central line?"

"You got it!"

"I mean, I'd do it, but my hands are tied," he smiled weakly.

"I would say so," Christy answered back.

"Can I have a Cortis kit, please?" Christy asked out loud. "Let's also back the endotracheal tube to its original position and increase the tidal volume."

The tech began to open the central line kit as Christy sterilized Marina's right upper chest. She inserted a small syringe to a large needle and inserted it into Marina's chest, guiding it just under the middle of her collar bone. Dark red blood began to fill the syringe signaling the needle was in the Subclavian vein. She removed the syringe being careful to keep the needle in the vein. Christy grabbed a coiled metal wire from the kit and fed the wire into the needle securing access to the large vein. She then removed the needle keeping the wire in place. She used a scalpel to make a small incision along the wire and then fed a large plastic sheath onto the wire. The sheath was fitted around a hard plastic tube which dilated the tissue as Christy advanced the assembly down the wire and into the vein. Once the sheath was fully inserted, she removed the wire and dilator tube. She screwed an IV cap onto the Cortis sheath and the nurse attached an IV tube connected to a bag of packed red blood cells, which immediately began infusing while Christy anchored the sheath to Marina's chest with a suture.

Dr. Alendretti had been on speaker phone apprising Dr. Bynum of Marina's condition. Bynum told him to pack her up and get her to the OR immediately.

"What can I do for you, Tony?" Christy asked.

"Come with me. If she crashes on the way, I'll need you to help me code her," Alendretti said as he looked around the room. "Are we about ready?"

"Just about," The charge nurse said as the team of nurses and techs were readying the several IV poles and transferring the monitor leads to a portable unit.

Alendretti looked in the direction of the respiratory therapist and spotted Joe for the first time.

"Joe!? What are you doing in here?"

"That's Marina, Tone. I carried her in."

"Holy..." Alendretti caught himself before completing the expletive. "This is Marina? I had no idea! I'm so sorry, Joe! I was so caught up in what I was doing I didn't even recognize her or notice that you were in the room. I'm sorry, man."

"No worries, Tone, just keep her alive for me..." Joe said as voice began to crack.

"We're doing the best we can, Joe, but it's bad. Pray, man," Alendretti said solemnly. "Okay, are we ready to go?"

"Ready," came the reply.

"Alright, let's go then."

Joe followed behind, watching the team wheel Marina out the doors and down the hall. Tony was hunched over Marina, awkwardly walking with the stretcher while his left arm remained in her chest clamping her artery. Christy kept vigil as she walked alongside. Chief Ramsey had been keeping watch outside the trauma bay.

"Rammer, we need to check on Tran. He's at Erie County Medical Center in Buffalo. Go with Eddie and let me know the minute you know something. They're taking Marina up to the OR. We're going up with her."

"Aye, Joe. How is she?"

"I, uh, I don't know, Matt," Joe had trouble speaking the words.

"Roger that, Joe. Go look after your sister. I'll be in touch," Ramsey said, laying a hand on Joe's shoulder before heading for the exit to find Sierra.

The medical team meandered through the halls until going through a set of double doors marking the entrance to surgery. A nurse stopped Joe, telling him he would have to wait down the hall in the waiting room. Joe looked back through the doors and watched the team hurry on down the hall. They turned the corner and his sister disappeared.

Chapter 57

A few minutes later, Christy, devoid of the surgical gown, returned from the surgery suite and located Joe in the waiting room. Being a Saturday morning, Joe was the only one in the deserted area. He sensed Christy's presence and looked up. He jumped to his feet and began to run in her direction. Christy did the same and they met in a tight embrace. The emotions of the past two hours caught up with Christy and she began to sob into Joe's chest as he held her tight. Several minutes passed without a word being spoken.

Dr. Alendretti walked in and quietly knocked on the wall. Joe and Christy both looked in his direction.

"How is she, Tone?"

"She's still alive. Dr. Bynum is working on her right now. She's critical, but in good hands. We'll know more soon when Ray gets finished. Oh, and I've got your dad down in the ER."

"Oh, that's right!" Joe exclaimed. "How is he?"

"He's got a concussion, a fractured clavicle, a couple of rib fractures, and a bruised lung, but he'll be okay. Joe? What in the world is going on?"

"I wish I knew, man. Short version is someone wants me dead and they're going through my family to get to me. Which room is Dad in? I need to go see him."

"He's in the other Trauma Bay. Your mom and Anita Bonetti are with him."

"Do they know about Marina?"

"You know what? I don't think so. I didn't even know that was her until I saw you."

"Okay, Tone. Don't tell them anything. I'll go down and let them know."

"Okay, Joe. Is there anything I can do for you?"

"Not right now, Tone. Thanks."

"Okay, listen, I don't mean to run out on you but I'm the only doctor in the ER until noon and I'm majorly backed up. I've gotta get back down there."

"Sure, Tone. I understand. I'll see you down there," Joe said and then nodded, "Go on."

"Alright man," Alendretti said as he turned and began rapidly walking out, "I'll see you down there.".

"Hey, Tone?"

Alendretti stopped and turned back. "Yes?"

"Thanks, man."

"Of course, Joe," his friend smiled and headed out.

"Do you want to head down and check on your dad?" Christy asked.

"I do, but I'd like to get a sit-rep on Marina first."

"That'll probably be a while yet."

"That's alright," Joe said, as he led Christy to a set of chairs and sat down next to her. "Everything happened so fast, I haven't had time to check on you. Are you okay?"

"Physically, I'm fine. Emotionally? I don't know. I think I'm still in shock."

"Well, for somebody in shock, you sure took charge in the ER downstairs and handled yourself quite well, if you ask me."

"Training took over. Thank God," she added.

"Well, Marina's alive because of you. I can't even begin to tell you how grateful I am that you were there for her."

"Joe!" Christy gasped in astonishment. "Were you the one that shot that man?"

"Yes," Joe nodded solemnly.

"It just hit me!" Christy said as she turned to face Joe directly. "Marina and I would both be dead had you not shown up when you did. He was about to shoot both of us! We would both be dead, right now, if it weren't for you! How did you find us?"

"You don't want to know," Joe said.

"Why wouldn't I want to know?"

"Suffice it to say that I had to do use some methods of questionable ethics and bend a few laws. I could potentially go to jail for this. The less you know the better."

"Jail!?" Christy asked astonished. "Those men tried to kill us! The man you shot had a gun pointed at my head and was pulling the trigger when you shot him. You were defending us. What were you supposed to do?"

"I know what you're saying Christy, but this state has some funny laws and there are no Stand Your Ground laws. It's never cut and dry, even in self-defense."

"Seriously? We could face charges over this?"

"Well, I could," Joe answered. "I don't think you will. That guy you shot had a gun pointed at you and Marina. That's much more defensible."

"Joe, I killed three people," Christy said solemnly.

"Three!?"

"Yes."

"Holy crow! What happened? Wait," Joe said taking a deep breath and calming down. "I want to know everything. Starting with the bike ride."

Christy spent the next several minutes recounting the details from the ambush, their capture and ultimately their escape. Joe listened intently without interrupting. He waited until she was finished retelling the sordid events before he asked questions.

"Unbelievable," he said slowly shaking his head. "How did you disarm that guy?"

"Remember when you encouraged me to take Krav Maga?" Christy asked with an impish smile.

"Are you serious?"

"Yep. You remember my friend Stacy?"

Joe nodded.

"We train three times a week and we go to the indoor range a couple times a month as well."

"Christy, that's so awesome! Look how those skills saved you and Marina this morning."

"I still say God was looking out for us but, yes, having a few skills helped. I was so scared, Joe, but it was like an autopilot kicked in. Is that what it's like for you?"

"In many ways, yes. Fear is a real thing, but it can be used to make one hyper-vigilant and combat ready. Training helps immensely. That's one of the reasons we're always training."

"Alright," Christy said staring Joe in the eyes. "Your turn. How did you know where we were? Just the things you can tell me."

Joe took a deep breath. The reality was he had indeed given into Pandolfino's demand and there was going to be an exchange of Joe for Christy and Marina. Using their inter squad comms, Kowalski and Rammer hatched a plan. Joe was in the dark as Pandolfino had him remove his radio before leaving the house as part of the deal. Sierra and Moreno had recently crossed the bridge and were heading to Niagara Falls to scope out Terry Woods' auto shop for a possible raid. Ramsey instructed them to high tail it to Pandolfino's house on Cayuga Island and pick him up, along with Kowalski and Stinnet. They followed closely behind Joe who was driving in Pandolfino's car. Ostensibly, Sierra and Moreno were going to be the ones the girls were released to while Pandolfino's men freed their boss and took Joe into custody. Ramsey, Kowalski, and Stinnet had gotten out of the truck, unnoticed, and snuck up through the back of the motel to get the drop on Pandolfino's men; however, when they arrived, they found Christy and Marina in a shootout. As Joe was pulling in, he saw Christy peak around the back of the car and fire at one of the men. Joe, still armed, pulled the car in close to the action and hopped out. As soon as he had a shot, he fired and killed the man.

"Let's just say their boss led us to where you were at. We had a plan to get you back, but you and Marina had already done the heavy lifting for us. You really are a warrior, Christy."

"I don't know. I don't feel like one. I was scared, and I'm still quite shaken up."

"That's normal for all of us."

"Maybe, but I'm a physician. I save lives. I don't take them."

"You did save lives today, Christy," Joe said, as he threw his arm around her and pulled her in close. "You saved two of the most important lives in my world."

Christy reached her hands around Joe and pulled herself in close. Her head rested on his chest and the two sat together in silence for a few minutes. She felt safe and natural in his arms. The tension built by the morning's ordeal seemed to melt away. She was in a good place.

The vision returned. She saw herself with Joe and their young children playing in the snow during Christmas and swimming off his parent's dock in the summer. His family, his wonderful family, all around. Hers was there as well. She had never thought like this until she was certain she was about to be killed. Was this her heart deceiving her into an unequally yoked relationship or was God showing her that He had a plan for them? The heart could be deceptive. The scriptures were clear on that. She would continue to pray on it, but she was content and at peace for now. They weren't doing anything wrong and Joe's presence was soothing. *Give it time, Christy.*

Their peaceful silence was interrupted by a knock at the waiting room entrance. They both looked up to see a grim-faced Dr. Bynum.

Chapter 58

*J*oe and Christy stood together and faced Dr. Bynum as he entered the room. He blinked upon recognizing Joe and Christy.

"Joe? Are you here for Marina Schmidt?"

"Yes, sir, she's my sister. How is she?"

"She's critical, but I think she's going to pull through."

"Oh, thank God!" Christy exclaimed as she hugged Joe.

Joe held on tight and breathed a heavy sigh of relief. "Thank you, Dr. Bynum."

"I think your girlfriend here is thanking the right person. Your sister is a miracle. Most people don't even make it to the hospital, let alone survive a gunshot like that. That was God watching over her."

"True, but you still did your part in the OR."

"I simply threw a few stitches into her pulmonary artery. It was Dr. Alendretti who got to her in time enough to locate the bleeding, apply pressure, and get her to me. He's the one you should be thanking. And this young lady," Dr. Bynum said indicating Christy. "You came up with her too, didn't you?"

"Yeah, I came in with her and gave Dr. Alendretti some help," Christy said humbly.

"She kept her alive in the truck, intubated her in the ER, started a central line, and assisted Tony, Doctor Bynum. I'm not letting her sell herself short."

"That's right, you're emergency medicine. Down near Atlanta?"

"Yes, sir. Duluth."

"Were either of you with her when she was shot?" Dr. Bynum asked in his deep baritone voice.

"She was," Joe said.

"And how did you survive?"

"I shot the man who shot her, and Joe took care of the one who was about to shoot me."

"Wait! You shot someone?"

"Yes, sir. I didn't have much choice."

"I see," Dr. Bynum said as he looked up at Joe. "It sounds as though your situation has escalated."

"You could say that, sir." Joe nodded. "They've decided my family is fair game."

"Anything I can do to help?" He asked. "I may be a surgeon but, if you recall, I was a snake eater like you and I still have skills."

"Sir, I'm deeply honored by your offer, but you've done enough. I can't thank you enough, as it is"

"If you change your mind, you know where to find me. Your sister will be in the PACU for another hour and then we will move her up to the Surgical Trauma ICU. I'm going to leave her on the vent overnight just in case she shows evidence of bleeding and needs to return to the OR. If all goes well, I hope to extubate her tomorrow and get her up walking just as soon as possible. She has a chest tube, just like you did, but hopefully I will be able to remove that in a couple of days. Now, what questions do you have for me?"

"How are her vitals?" Christy asked.

"Much better. Blood pressure is in the 90's systolic after releasing the aortic clamp and we are continuing to give her blood. She's not out of the woods yet, but definitely heading in the right direction."

"When can we see her?" Joe asked.

"Once she's up in the STICU, but she will be on the vent and sedated today."

"Yes, I'm aware of that. I just want to see her. My parents will too."

"Wait a minute. Is that your dad down in the ER?"

"Yes, sir."

"I'm admitting him to my service for the night. I was about to go down and see him. Let's head down there together." Bynum said and then started out the door. With a lowered voice, he leaned into Joe and asked, "Same incident?"

"Yes."

"I'm so sorry, Joe. I really hope you get this buttoned up as soon as possible. Where are the police with all of this?"

"The honest ones were apparently warned off the case, sir." Joe said as they entered the stairwell.

"Are you kidding me?" Bynum asked in outrage.

"Negative, sir."

Bynum was quiet until they exited the stairwell on the main floor.

"Warned off the case. Does this have anything to do with a certain organized crime family?"

"Affirmative, sir."

"Good copy. I'll see to it there is a security presence on your sister and your dad's rooms. It's the least I can do. My other offer still stands."

"Thank you, Dr. Bynum."

"Like I said, it's the least I can do. Listen," he said as he stopped in front of the nurses' station, "why don't I give you a few moments with your folks before I come in. I'll hang back here and look at your dad's CT scans and place his admission orders. Will that be alright?'

"Sound's perfect, sir. And thank you. If it weren't for you, this conversation I'm about to have with my parents could have been a lot worse."

"Well, thank God it's not, son," Dr. Bynum said with a solemn nod as he stepped into the nurses' station.

Joe looked at Christy and took a deep breath as they stepped into the trauma bay.

"Joe! Christy!" His dad exclaimed joyfully.

"You found them!" Maria said ecstatically, as she jumped up and greeted her son with a strong hug followed by one for Christy. Stepping back, her smile turned to a look of concern. "Where's Marina?"

"She's upstairs," Joe said being sure to look at both of his parents. "She had to have surgery, but she's out and in recovery."

"What happened, son?" Jack asked.

"She was shot," Joe said pressing his lips together and nodding solemnly.

"Shot? How? What happened?"

"Why don't you let me tell them, Joe? I was with her."

Joe nodded as Maria returned to her seat next to Jack. Christy pulled up an exam stool and took a seat next to Maria.

"Joe, take my seat," Anita offered as she stood.

"No, thanks, Mrs. Bonetti. I'm good."

Christy began to recount all of the events from the moment they were ambushed on the bikes to when Joe and his team arrived. Maria sat stoically as she listened, but Joe could see his father's facial features betray the inner rage that was brewing.

"We heard quite a commotion next door a little while ago," Maria stated. "Was that Marina?"

"Yes, Mom, it was. We had no idea you guys were in here."

"Tony Alendretti took care of your father. Did he take care of Marina too?"

"He and Christy both did," Joe went on to explain what all was done and Christy's involvement.

"They saved her life," Dr. Bynum proclaimed as he entered the room.

"It sure sounds like it to me," Jack answered while Maria grabbed Christy's hand. "Hello again, Dr. Bynum."

"You too, Mr. O'Shanick. I'm sorry we keep meeting under these circumstances. I am happy to report that, thanks to this young lady here," he said indicating Christy, "and Dr. Alendretti, the worst seems to be behind for your daughter, but we are watching her very closely."

"Thank you, Doc," Jack responded. "I'm forever in your debt."

"Nah," Bynum waved dismissively, "that's my job and it's my pleasure when we get a win. We'll take good care of her. Now let's talk about you. Tell me what happened."

"Unfortunately, I don't remember much. The four of us were biking down around the Beaver Island area when somebody hit me and Tran from behind. I woke up a few minutes later, Tran was bloody and not moving, Christy and Marina were gone," Jack said the last while holding back tears.

"And who's Tran?"

"Tran Van Truc," Joe spoke up. "He's one of my men, sir. Came up here the other day to help look after my family after my incident. He's been shot multiple times and was flown out to ECMC."

"Any word on him?"

"Not yet. Two of my men just got there, but they were told they're not family and aren't allowed to see him or get any updates."

"I'll straighten that out, Joe. I trained there. Those are my people. They're just doing their job and following HIPPA rules, but I'll call over there and explain the situation. You guys are his family."

"Hooyah, sir."

"In the meantime, Mr. O'Shanick," Bynum said, turning his attention back to his patient.

"Jack,"

"Thank you. Jack," Bynum said. "I think you are already aware of your injuries. There is nothing life threatening or surgical, but I do think we should keep you overnight for observation. I just want to make sure your bruised lung doesn't give you any breathing trouble."

"I think I'll be fine, but I understand."

"Very well. I just need to examine you myself and then I'll go enter your admission orders. How's your pain, right now?"

"It's not bad as long as I don't move my arm."

"Good. Then don't move your arm," Bynum said with a smile as he donned his stethoscope and leaned in to listen to Jack's lungs.

A few minutes later, Dr. Bynum completed his exam, reassured the O'Shanicks that he would take good care of Marina and left the room. No sooner had he left when another knock came at the door. They looked up and saw Detectives Peretti and O'Keefe in the entrance.

"I'm sorry to bother you folks, but we need to ask some questions."

Chapter 59

Buffalo, New York

Benton "Bubba" Bell took a sip of his coffee as he drove the security golf cart around the grounds of Erie County Medical Center. A retired police officer for the City of Buffalo, Bubba began working security for the hospital to supplement his pension. It also allowed him to afford season tickets for the Buffalo Bills. Working a few days a week was worth it. He was able to enjoy an annual cruise with his wife and take his son and his aging father to Bills games.

The work was usually light. They had younger security guards to handle the violent and crazy patients. Bubba usually patrolled the grounds and helped visitors find where they were going. In the winter, he drove around in a comfortable heated SUV but, on nicer days, he preferred the openness of the golf cart. This morning was turning out to be one of those perfect Western New York mornings when his radio crackled with his call sign.

"MCS 4 to MCS 9."

"MCS 9, go ahead 4," Bubba responded.

"We have a complaint of a suspicious person running around the Grider Street parking lot. Suspect is white male, tall, muscular, wearing military-style tactical clothes. Please investigate."

"MCS 9 responding," Bubba spoke into his radio and replaced it on his belt. He reached down with his right hand and felt his service weapon as he steered towards the Grider Street parking lot. A minute later he entered the lot and began to look around. Sadly, there was a lot of drug abuse in this part of town, not to mention mental health patients. One never knew what to expect. Bubba scanned the expansive parking lot. *There!* Running along Grider Street was a man who fit the description. Bubba sped along the outer section of the parking lot gradually catching up to the man. The man was running at an impressive speed but Bubba eventually caught up with him.

"Excuse me, sir? Sir?"

The man didn't appear to hear him. Bubba saw wireless earbuds in the man's ears. He pulled in front and waved the man down. The man continued to run in place as he came to a stop alongside the golf cart and removed one of his ear buds.

"Yes, officer?"

"Where are you headed in such a hurry?" Bubba asked.

"I'm just getting in a morning run."

"I've got a report of some guy in military clothes running around the parking lot like a madman. Everything okay?"

"Yeah, fine. I'm sorry for the confusion, but I'm really just getting in a jog while I wait on a buddy inside having surgery. I don't want to get too far away so I'm just using this sidewalk as a track."

"A jog? That don't look like no jog to me!" Bubba said with a smile. "How fast you running?"

"I don't know, about a six-minute mile pace."

"In boots and fatigues?" Bubba asked incredulously. "Shoot! I oughtta take you up to the psych ward myself."

Ramsey laughed and gave an innocent shrug.

"Alright, crazy man. Knock yourself out. Just don't run anybody over."

Ramsey waved as the security guard pulled away. He replaced his ear bud and resumed his run. He had lasted ten minutes caged up in the waiting room. He was furious. Furious that one of his men was in critical condition, furious that he and Sierra were not being updated, furious that Joe and his family were repeatedly being attacked by a bunch of mobsters for reasons unknown, furious that the law, in this case, left Joe and the team virtually hamstrung to do anything about it and furious that they had no idea why this was happening. Ramsey needed to blow off some steam and clear his head. A good run always did that for him. He left Sierra in the waiting room with instructions to call him just as soon as he learned anything.

The music had paused when he had taken out one of the ear buds. Upon replacing it in his ear, the music resumed. It was one of his running mixes. Like Joe, Ramsey was a lifelong Rush fan. One of many things they bonded over. The Analog Kid, a personal favorite was a fast-paced song about a boy dreaming of the endless possibilities of his future. His pace sped back up, spurred on by the brilliantly played frenetic Alex Lifeson guitar solo which transitioned into the final chorus.

When I leave I don't know what I'm what I'm hoping to find
And when I leave I don't know what I'm leaving behind

The words had spoken to Ramsey during his youth and they were still relevant all these years later. He was thirty-eight. Having enlisted in the Navy straight out of high school, he would complete his twenty years at the end of the month. He could retire with a full pension and move on to something else. *But what?* In his case, he actually knew what he would be leaving behind and he wasn't ready to give it up. The Teams were his life. The men in his unit were his family, his brothers. The incidents with Joe and now Tran only served to magnify that. He knew the day would come when the Navy told him to stand down, that his operating days were over, but he wasn't about to slack off and give them reason to do so.

It was another reason why he was furious. Inside, he was conflicted. These mobster scumbags had inflicted heavy casualties on Joe's family and now the team. His brothers. Joe was his commander but, in many ways, he was like a little brother to Ramsey. The kind of brother who had the brains and ran things but needed a big brother to have his back. That's how Ramsey saw himself. Ramsey had never married. The team was his family and Joe's family was like a second family to Ramsey. As such, he took all of these attacks personally.

The Catalano organization was waging war on Joe's family and the team. What needed to happen was war needed to be visited on every remaining mobster in that organization, in a swift and sure manner. Until every last one of them was out of the picture, they remained a threat. Doubly so, now that several of their members had been killed or arrested. Ramsey had no doubt he and the team could take them out, but it wouldn't be lawful and he did not think they could evade suspicion; furthermore, they had an honor code to live up to and he could not imagine placing his men in a position to violate the code.

"...I serve with honor on and off the battlefield...Uncompromising integrity is my standard. My character and honor are steadfast..."

Ramsey thought about those words and the rest of the Navy SEAL Creed.

"...My loyalty to Country and Team is beyond reproach. I humbly serve as a guardian to my fellow Americans always ready to defend those who are unable to defend themselves..."

He asked himself if that loyalty to team made him honor bound to defend the team even if it meant running afoul of the law. What about defending those who are unable to defend themselves? There was a band of ruthless criminals who were a threat and, indeed, had harmed his team and a family he loved. To make matters worse, they were being protected, no *enabled,* by a few corrupt police officers and politicians. If he, Joe, and the rest of the team didn't defend them, who would? The ethical dilemma offered bad consequences with whichever choice he made. Dishonorable discharge, loss of pension and potential life in prison on one side; further loss of life to his teammates and people he loved on the other side. However, the creed summed up his training. Actually, it defined who he was. Joe and the rest of the team for that matter. The choice wasn't that difficult after all.

Ramsey's phone began to chime in his earbuds interrupting his thoughts and the cinematic song *Red Barchetta.* He spoke the command to answer the call and heard Sierra's voice on the other end.

"Yeah, Eddie?"

"Tran's out of surgery, Chief. The surgeon will be out to talk to us in a couple of minutes."

"Be right there," Ramsey said as he ended the call and double timed it to the ER entrance.

The final approach to the ER was a drive-up ramp. Ramsey finished his run with a sprint up the two hundred foot incline. He paused his Garmin Tactix watch and checked his run metrics as he walked into the ER waiting room. 3.9 miles. His fitness OCD tempted him to run back down and up the ramp to push it to the four mile mark, but he quickly put that out of his mind. Tran was first and foremost.

Ramsey strode through the waiting room and spotted Sierra standing with a nurse. The nurse led them into a family counseling room and told them the doctor would be with them in a few minutes. They each chose a seat and sat down.

"Any word from Joe, Chief?"

"Yeah, he called a little while ago. His sister survived surgery and will be in the ICU."

"Man! That's good news! She didn't look so good when we picked her up. I thought her ticket was punched."

"Me too, Eddie. That was close."

"Anything from the other guys?"

"KK called. They got what they needed out of Pandolfino."

"What are we gonna do with him?"

"They're turning him over to the FBI. The two girls who were there will testify they were both abducted and forced into prostitution. Stinnet found a pile of drugs and paraphernalia to hand over as well. The girls will testify to the prostitution ring the organization is running. They say there are about eighty of them altogether locked up at that motel. If the police haven't found them yet, the FBI will. Ought to be enough to send several of those guys up the river and help keep Joe out of jail."

"How are they going to explain what they were doing at Pandolfino's in the first place?"

"I told KK to tell them we were looking for Christy and Joe's sister and had a tip that they would be at Pandolfino's. We were outside and saw two women in his bed unconscious and thought it was them. We broke in to rescue them. Wrong girls, but it led us to find the right ones and look what else we found. It's thin, but it should satisfy the Feds who are getting a major bust out of this."

"Works for me," Sierra nodded somberly.

Both men sat a minute in contemplative silence before a knock came from the door. They looked up and saw two doctors dressed in blue scrubs. One wore a doctor's white coat.

"Hello. I'm Dr. Snedeker, one of the trauma surgeons, and this is one of our chief residents, Dr. Young," the older surgeon said, indicating the younger surgeon in the white coat. "Are you here for Tran Van Truc?"

"Yes, sir, we work together," Ramsey answered, not one to talk about what they actually did.

"Does he have any family here?"

"No, sir, he's originally from Seattle. We're it."

"Gotcha," Dr Snedeker answered thoughtfully. "Do you know anything about what happened?"

"A little, sir. We weren't there, but we were told he was hit by a truck while riding a bike and then shot and left for dead."

"That's the report we got too," the surgeon answered with a nod. "Well, here's what we know so far. Mr. Truc suffered a fractured collarbone, a fracture leg, and a couple of rib fractures. That's the good news. None of those are critical. Unfortunately, he was shot in the right shoulder which injured his lung, but the most crucial injury was a gunshot to his neck. It grazed his carotid artery which caused what's known as a dissection. The dissection is a separation of the layers that make up the wall of the artery and it can cause blood flow to be disrupted which, when involving the carotid artery can cause a stroke."

"Is it repairable?" Ramsey asked.

"Yes. In fact, the vascular surgeon just finished up with him. We don't know whether or not he has had any neurological damage, but his initial CT scan showed what we call collateral blood flow which means blood from the other carotid artery was able to supply the entire brain. We will be repeating the scan in a little while along with an MRI/MRA of the brain and hopefully, there won't be any damage, but it's too early to tell; meanwhile, an orthopedic surgeon is in fixing his leg and his collarbone as we speak."

"Anything life threatening at this point?"

"Not that we've found, no."

"Any idea of when we will know how he is functionally?"

"Likely tomorrow. The MRI study will show us if there is any evidence of stroke, but the big test will be when we take him off sedation and see what he does once awake."

"Roger that. What can we do in the meantime?"

"Just hang tight for now. We'll keep you updated as we learn more."

"Thank you, sir."

"You guys military?"

"Navy."

"Say no more. I was a Navy flight surgeon once upon a time. Tactical clothes, physically fit. I think I know what you do and it doesn't involve driving submarines. Is Mr. Truc one of you as well?"

"Yes, sir. One of the best."

"That's high praise. I take it you're his Chief?"

"Correct, sir."

"Let me have your number. I'll keep you updated personally."

"I appreciate that, sir."

"It's the least I can do. We appreciate what you do for us, gentlemen."

"Thank you, sir," Ramsey and Sierra both said, as they stepped out into the hall and went their separate way from the surgeons.

Ramsey and Sierra strode purposefully toward the exit. Neither spoke. Sierra could tell his chief petty officer was brooding and chose not to say anything. Chief Ramsey was the strong silent type. Reserved and good to the men but could become a dangerous machine of war when his switch was flipped. They walked to Sierra's pickup truck where Ramsey opened the tailgate. They both hopped up and took a seat.

Ramsey took a deep breath and let it out slowly. Sierra could hear the air as it flowed through the mustache of Ramsey's goatee. As chief petty officer, Ramsey always looked for opportunities to train and shape the minds of his junior operators.

"What are your thoughts, Petty Officer Sierra?"

"I think we have one teammate clinging to life who may never operate and another teammate who has been attacked several times along with his family. These are our brothers, Chief," he said as he turned and looked Ramsey in the eye. "I think it's time to get our frogman on and get some payback."

"Roger that," Chief Ramsey nodded solemnly.

Chapter 60

Niagara Falls, New York

Detective O'Keefe scribbled furiously in his notebook as he recorded Joe's version of the events at the motel. He and Peretti had already taken Jack and Christy's statements. O'Keefe suppressed a smile. They had them. This was too big to cover up. This was going to put a serious hurt on the Catalano family. Maybe then, they wouldn't be such a big threat and the powers that be could weed out the corrupt cops who were on the take.

"You clearly saw the suspect shoot in Ms. Tabrizi's direction before he moved in closer?" Detective Peretti asked.

"Yes, sir. In fact, he took several shots at Christy *and* my sister."

"And when you saw him move in closer and point his gun at Ms. Tabrizi, that's when you took your shot?"

"Yes, sir."

"And you say you shot him twice?"

"Yes, sir. Double tap to the head."

"Thank you, Mr. O'Shanick," Detective Peretti said as he closed his small notebook. "Ms. Tabrizi, your involvement sounds like straight up self-defense. I don't see any need for charges at this time pending the investigation, but we will need a sworn affidavit recounting your experience."

"I understand, Detective," Christy answered.

"Mr. O'Shanick," Detective Peretti said as he redirected his attention to Joe, "your involvement sounds like you were coming to the aid of Ms. Tabrizi and your sister Ms. Schmidt."

"Yes, sir," Joe said in agreement.

"It seems to me that you saved their lives," Detective Peretti ended the statement with raised eyebrows.

Joe acknowledged him with a subtle nod.

"Therefore, it gives me great pain to inform you that your actions, under New York State law, if not found justifiable by a judge or a jury, would be contained within the definition of second-degree murder."

Joe froze. His parents and Christy looked at Detective Peretti with astonishment.

"I'm afraid I'm going to have to take you into custody, son. I'm sorry. Please stand and face the wall."

Joe stood quietly. Two hours ago, he was prepared to face charges; however, the events, as they transpired, led him to believe they had accomplished their mission in such a manner as to avoid arrest. The realization of what was happening left him speechless.

"What are you doing!?" Jack O'Shanick yelled from his stretcher as he bolted upright ignoring the sharp pain in his ribs.

"My son just saved the lives of two defenseless women! Our daughter and this fine young doctor who, twice herself, saved our daughter's life! He's a hero! Now you're going to cuff him and lock him up like a common criminal? Really?"

"Sir, I agree with you," Peretti said apologetically. "I don't like it any better than you do, but I'm obligated by law and I have to do my job."

"If you guys were doing your job, we wouldn't be in this mess!"

"I understand, sir, and all I can say is I'm sorry. I take no pleasure in this," Peretti responded calmly before turning his attention back to Joe. "Mr. O'Shanick, if you could place your hands on the wall, I need to search you."

Joe complied as his family and Christy looked on in shock.

"Detective O'Keefe, could you please read Mr. O'Shanick his rights."

O'Keefe slowly pulled out his Miranda card and reluctantly began to read Joe his rights. Detective Peretti finished the search, gently brought Joe's hands behind his back and placed him in handcuffs as O'Keefe finished.

"Joe," Jack began in a more subdued manner as Peretti began to lead Joe to the door, "I'm giving Tom Brinkworth a call right now. He's a defense attorney and a trusted friend. We'll get this straightened out. I promise you, son!"

Joe silently nodded a thank you to his father. He looked over at Christy who looked back at him with tear-filled eyes. What was only a couple of seconds seemed a lot longer before Peretti gently took one of Joe's cuffed wrists and led him out of the trauma bay.

As they walked past the nurses' station, a young nurse looked up and saw the procession. She grabbed her phone off the desk and quickly texted off a message.

Chapter 61

" *I* don't care, Lou. O'Shanick is a genuine hero! His family was attacked. He was rescuing his sister and girlfriend who were *abducted* by the mob. You'd have done the same thing! He takes a mobster out and *he* is the one in jail? We should be giving him a medal! He puts his life on the line for our nation for crying out loud!"

"We don't make the laws, Kevin," Peretti said apologetically as he drove. "We just enforce them."

"Well, I feel like a complete schmuck for having to walk him out of that hospital and into the station, cuffs and all, like a common criminal. It was the lowest point of my short, but pathetic, career."

"Take it easy, Kevin. If O'Shanick is clean, he'll walk."

"He *is* clean! You and I both know it, but you said yourself this town is corrupt at high levels. Forgive me if I don't have a lot of confidence in the system working for somebody who just did this community a favor."

"Then let's do our job here and help him beat the charges," Peretti answered as he turned their unmarked car into the motel parking lot.

They pulled up close to the area marked off by yellow police tape and got out of their vehicle. They were met by the sergeant on duty, Sergeant Bryson.

"Everything is sealed off and marked, Detective Peretti. The vics haven't been touched but the medical examiner is ready to take them. After that, I've got something I want to show you."

They stepped under the tape and walked over to the where two men's bodies lay beside the Honda Pilot. Peretti and O'Keefe spent a few minutes inspecting the bodies. The wounds and the positions of the bodies were consistent with the statements they had obtained from O'Shanick and Tabrizi. There were several shell casings marked out where Miss Tabrizi said she and Mrs. Schmidt were hiding. The handguns they used were still there and the shell casings seemed to match. Most notably, there were two shell casings found at the location O'Shanick claimed to have shot the one man who had nearly killed the girls. His driver's license identified him as one Paul Pelliteri, a known member of the Catalano organization. Peretti and O'Keefe recorded every detail in effort to corroborate O'Shanick's testimony.

They moved up to the room where Miss Tabrizi claimed she and Mrs. Schmidt had been held and nearly raped. They found the slain bodies of Terry Wood and Marco Vona just as she had described. The shell casings were a match for the ones they found in the parking lot. Peretti and O'Keefe completed their inspection and exited the room.

"That should do it, Sergeant Bryson. Let the coroner have them."

"Yes, sir. If you'll follow me, sir, I want to show you what else we found."

"Lead the way."

They literally walked to the next room. Sergeant Bryson used the master key to unlock the door and then stood aside as he opened it. Peretti and O'Keefe stepped in to find four young women sound asleep. The room was filled with various articles of clothing and appeared well lived in. Empty food containers and cups cluttered the table and nightstands.

"Is this what I think it is?" O'Keefe asked.

"Yep," Bryson answered. "Every room down to the end, four to a room. A few are stirring, but most are zonked out."

"Poor girls are kept busy all night using coke to stay awake and active for their clients and then sleep like zombies throughout the day. Makes them easy to handle," Peretti commented.

"All these rooms," Bryson began, gesturing with his arm extended down the hallway, "have doors that can only be opened by key from either side. The girls are kept locked up."

"Modern day slavery," Peretti said shaking his head. "God help us, this is going to be a frickin' mess. We have, what? Roughly eighty women, victims of human trafficking, most likely all addicts. They're going to need medical care, addiction treatment, counseling, food, and housing just for starters. You need to get your Lieutenant on this, Sergeant. Tell him to consider this a mass casualty event."

"That's going to take some time to coordinate."

"Well, by the looks of things, Sergeant, they won't be awake for hours. Get a few more units here to keep watch while your team downstairs finishes with the crime scene."

The sound of heavy footsteps resonated from the metal and concrete steps of a nearby stairwell. A stocky white male with a thick beard appeared at the top. He was followed by a younger wiry dark haired man. Both wore khaki pants and navy blue polo shirts with large yellow FBI letters.

"I'm special agent Jennings, FBI," the stocky agent began as he held up his credentials, "and this is special agent Hudgins. Who's in charge here?"

"He is," Detective Peretti and Sergeant Bryson said at the same time as they pointed to each other.

Chapter 62

Hilton Head Island, SC

$\mathcal{H}$e aimed for the light house. His driver slowly arced back before rapidly accelerating forward and emitting a satisfying *tink* when the club head rammed through the teed up ball. It's owner, a fifty-seven-year-old retired Marine still sported a trim athletic build that could generate good club speed. President Jorge "Manny" Galan watched with intensity as his ball soared out over the saltwater marsh. He willed it to stay aloft which it did long enough to clear the marsh and land in the 18th hole fairway of the famed Harbour Town Golf Links. He picked up his tee and watched his ball roll to a stop in the fairway.

"Nice shot, Dad," his son, Tommy, said as he began to tee up his ball.

For the seventeenth time of the round Tommy held honors allowing him to tee off after his father. Tommy stepped up and addressed the ball. He settled his lean wiry frame and, with what sounded like a whip cracking, crushed the ball into a soaring drive that left no doubt of clearing the marsh. The ball landed close to where Manny's ball stopped, but it rolled on for another fifty yards before stopping on the right side of the fairway, leaving a much safer approach to the green on the picturesque finishing hole.

Manny's competitive spirit silently groaned. He wanted to beat his son on just one hole today, but it didn't look like that was going to happen. Not that it came as a surprise. Tommy, a scratch golfer, would soon be starting his freshman year at Georgia Tech on a golf scholarship. The school of legendary Bobby Jones and more recently Stewart Cink, Larry Mize, David Duval and, Manny's favorite, Matt Kuchar, had offered his son, Tommy, a scholarship. Not bad at all.

"Great shot, son!" Manny beamed with pride as they collected their bags and began to walk down the fairway.

He and his wife, Maria, planned this vacation several months ago. Their daughter, Lydia, just completed her sophomore year at Liberty University and would soon be departing to Ecuador for a summer missions project. With Tommy leaving for college in August, this would be their only time together as a family. Their days consisted of golf, endless biking on the many beautiful trails and afternoons on the beach. The beach outings were a challenge for the Secret Service, but Maria and Lydia loved their salt therapy. Manny tried to be as amiable and cooperative as he could with the men and women sworn to protect his family, but he didn't know when they would next be able to vacation as a family. That being the case, he worked out a reasonable solution with his protectors in order to create a memorable vacation for his family. Kids won't remember birthday and Christmas presents, but they will never forget great vacations and experiences.

As he approached the ball, Manny sized up his shot. The direct path was roughly 190 yards over the marsh which guarded the green. *No freaking way.* The safe shot was to aim right for the fairway and hope for a good chip. Manny swung through his ball. It felt good. He tracked it as it approached the apron and watched as it fell short and land in the sand trap. A minute later, he watched as Tommy lofted a high shot that stuck the green about ten feet from the hole.

A few minutes later they putted out. Manny scored a 5 giving him a total of 87, while Tommy birdied the final hole recording a 68 for the day. Any score below 90 was a good outing for Manny but, just once, he would like to break 80. His kid just destroyed him by breaking 70. It was a great day.

As they walked off the hole, Manny spotted his Chief of Staff, Jonathan James Embry rapidly walking in their direction. Manny felt an inner sense of foreboding warn him that something was about to disrupt their, otherwise, perfect day.

"Something up, JJ?" Manny asked.

"Nothing on a national or crisis level, sir. Just some breaking news that I think you would want to know. This way, sir," Embry said as he led them to a nearby path that took them between two condominiums to a waiting dark, heavily armored Chevy Suburban. Two Secret Service members took Manny and Tommy's golf bags as Manny followed Embry into the SUV.

"JJ, is this classified?"

"No, sir, it's on the news."

"Tommy, you can get in as well," Manny said to his son.

They climbed into the back with Embry who handed each a towel and a cold bottle of water. The air conditioning was a welcome respite in the ninety degree heat. As the SUV began to drive them back to the beachfront house where they were staying, Embry brought up a video on his tablet and handed it to his President. A well-known male news anchor appeared on the screen as the news feed began to play.

"In breaking news, a Navy SEAL has been arrested and brought into custody for the murder of a North Tonawanda, New York man. Sources tell us that the arrest came after a shootout which took place at a Niagara Falls motel. The motel is a known place of illegal drug sales and prostitution. The suspect in question is Lieutenant Commander Joseph O'Shanick, whom you may recall was honored by President Galan in a Rose Garden ceremony last October. What is unknown at this time is what O'Shanick was doing at a motel known for drugs and prostitution and why a shootout erupted. We will have more on this story as it develops."

"It's on every major news source, sir," Embry spoke as he turned off the tablet.

"Do we know anything more?"

"Not yet, Mr. President, but I have some people chasing it down as we speak. It goes without saying, sir, that if this guy was involved in something shady, it's going to reflect negatively on you and your campaign."

"I'm aware of that, JJ but I remember O'Shanick well. He struck me as a stand-up guy and an exemplary SEAL officer. We have no reason to believe he was involved in anything shady."

"Nevertheless, sir, the press and your opposition..."

"Which are one and the same," Manny interjected.

"True, sir. The press and the opposition are going to have a field day over this if anything appears out of line. We need to have a statement ready."

"JJ, my statement will be that Lieutenant Commander O'Shanick has been a distinguished leader in the Navy Special Warfare community and that I awarded him The Silver Star for valor in a combat operation. I have no reason to believe that he was involved in anything nefarious and, unless an investigation proves otherwise, I will expect him to be acquitted."

"With all due respect, sir, that's a bit bold and it may come back to bite you if he's found guilty."

"I'm aware of that, JJ, but, I'm not going to hang a decorated Navy SEAL out to dry when I have no reason to do so. O'Shanick has earned my support and admiration and I'm not going to distance myself from him based upon a news report that is devoid of factual information. If the facts prove otherwise, then we will deal with it. Until that time, I want to learn everything we can about what happened."

Chapter 63

Niagara Falls, New York

Joe sat by himself in the overcrowded holding cell. He had yet to hear from his dad's attorney, or anyone for that matter. He knew his dad was working on it, but he had never been on this side of the law before and the unknown made him a bit edgy. Would the charge stick? He ran through the scenario a hundred times and wouldn't have done anything different. Earlier that morning he had made his peace with being arrested and facing prison if that's what it took to free Christy and Marina. The way things went down, he thought he had accomplished the objective without breaking the law. Apparently not. He wasn't having second thoughts. He would do it again. Now he just had to get comfortable with what came next. *No easy day.*

The door at the end of the hall opened up and two officers marched a tall, thin white man into the main room. The man was stone faced as they approached Joe's holding cell.

"Clear the door!" One of the armed officers spoke loudly.

The cell's occupants obediently shuffled away from the door as the officer pulled out a large set of keys and unlocked the door. The man stepped in and waited for the door to close behind him. He calmly backed up to the door, stuck his hands through the slot and waited as the officers removed his handcuffs. This wasn't his first rodeo.

The man looked around the cell. Out of habit, Joe studied the man as he had already done with every other man in the cell. The man had long, dark hair, flecked with gray that was greased straight back revealing a receding hairline. His dark eyes revealed an alertness that could not be concealed by his expressed calmness. Predator, Joe concluded. The man walked over to a cluster of menacing-looking, young black men and spoke to them quietly. There was a familiarity as if they knew each other. A minute later, one of the men began to cuss him out as the rest began to stare him down. He backed away, looked around and appeared to realize that he and Joe were the only white men in the cell. Likely deciding there was strength in numbers, he walked over and sat down with Joe.

"Vinny Scuderi," he said holding out his hand.

"Joe," Joe answered accepting the man's handshake. "If you're looking for backup with your little disagreement over there, you've got the wrong guy," Joe said as he returned to staring straight ahead watching Scuderi out of his peripheral vision.

"Are you kidding me?" Scuderi asked Joe in a low voice. "Those guys don't want any part of me. They know who I am. That was business. You're the one they're interested in, cupcake."

"I can handle myself," Joe answered.

"You can handle four gangbangers? Dream on," Scuderi snickered. "This must be your first time."

Joe didn't answer.

"Yeah, that's what I thought," Scuderi continued. "You're too clean-cut for a con and you've got that deer in the headlights look. Do yourself a favor and stick with me, kid. They love them some virgins."

Joe knew he wasn't exuding fear which made him wonder what Scuderi's angle was. He didn't see the point in arguing so he just remained alert and quiet. Several minutes passed in silence and then Joe noticed the four black men looking in his direction. One of them waved mockingly. Joe ignored them. They began to walk over in a taunting manner.

"You lose your manners, handsome?" The muscular one whom Joe had speculated was the leader asked in an intimidating manner. "I just waved to you and you dissed me, man! What's up with that, Pee Wee?"

"Back off, Pit Bull, he's with me!" Scuderi snarled.

Pit Bull looked at Scuderi in astonishment. "Man, this don't concern you, Scuzz Fairy. You better shut your mouth and move away before I pull what's left of that precious hair of yours out of your greasy Italian head!"

"They're all yours, Joe," Scuderi said as he slid down the bench. "You said you could handle them. Good luck."

"You said what, Pee Wee?" Pit Bull said as he turned his attention back to Joe. "You said you wanted to juke with us? The Power City Playahs?"

Joe saw the four men begin to flex their hands into fists and move, subtly onto the balls of their feet as they began to mentally gear up for a fight. He maintained a relaxed posture, slouched against the wall as he mentally formed a plan.

"Indeed I did, Puss Ball, and you'd be wise to go back over there and keep your distance," Joe said staring the men down.

Two of the men registered looks of concern and took slight steps back but remained bowed up and flexing their fists. That was as good an opening as he would get.

"What'd you just call me you little punk bi..."

In the blink of an eye, Joe used the wall behind him as a base and delivered successive snap kicks to the knees of Pit Bull and the tough standing next to him. Both men dropped to the ground howling in pain and clutching their disabled knees. Joe dropped to the ground and performed a leg sweep on one of the other two, causing him to fall to the ground where Joe quickly delivered a throat punch followed by a palm strike to the nose. He jumped to his feet to address the fourth thug, but he was gone. Joe saw him hiding in the far corner and decided to leave him alone. He grabbed two of the other guys by their collars and dragged them to their end of the cell. He walked back and stood over Pit Bull. The man continued to hold his knee while tears flowed from his eyes.

"Are you crying, Pit Bull? Oh, I'm sorry. Does that hurt? Let me help you."

Joe got down and pinched Pit Bull's trachea shut, cutting off his ability to breathe. Pit Bull stared back wide eyed in fear.

"You sorry street punk! I warned you to stay away from me! I could kill you right now!" Joe seethed through gritted teeth. "Don't you *ever* try me..."

Joe had been so focused on Pit Bull he momentarily lost track of his surroundings. A shoelace had been quickly draped around his neck and cinched tight. Joe quickly reacted, knowing he had mere seconds before he passed out. Already bent over, Joe rolled forward throwing his attacker over the top and onto the hard floor. Joe came down on top of him slamming his elbow into the attacker's solar plexus. He felt the grip loosen slightly and continued with a series of elbow jabs to the man's abdomen and ribs. The man let go of his grip and Joe broke free. He leapt to his feet and turned around delivering a heel strike to the man's ribs. Looking down, he realized his attacker was Scuderi. That was when Joe realized he'd been set up. He delivered another strike to Scuderi's ribs, flipped him onto his stomach and placed a knee in the center of his back. Scuderi let out a blood curdling scream. Joe leaned in and applied a rear choke hold. His head was down close to Scuderi's ear and he began to speak.

"How do you like it, you slimy maggot? I can crush your windpipe and snap your back in one motion. Which is it!?" Joe said giving a strong yank up to emphasize his words.

Scuderi responded with a loud painful front.

"I know this was planned, dipstick," Joe continued. "I know who sent you! I could kill you right now, but I think I'll let you live and see what your bosses do to you since you failed them." Joe threw Scuderi's face back to the floor and stood up. Not wanting to have to go at it with Scuderi a second time, Joe stomped down on the mobster's forearm with the heel of his boot breaking the radius and ulna. That would keep him out of the fight. Joe went back over to Pit Bull and delivered a swift kick to his ribs.

"Both of you go join your friends on that side. Now!" Joe commanded.

The two wounded men crawled over to the other half of the cell.

"Anybody comes over to my side of this cage is going to get the same treatment, so stay over there! Any questions?"

No one answered. They didn't even look in Joe's direction. Joe walked back and sat down on the bench where he could keep his eye on the other half of the cell. Save for some quiet moaning, silence had befallen the cell.

"Dude's crazy," someone quietly muttered from the other side.

Chapter 64

Lewiston, New York

Vincent "The Dazzler" Randazzo drove his Mercedes G Wagon up the drive at a rapid speed and braked to a hard stop in the expansive driveway in front of Bruno Catalano's estate. He quickly got out of the car and stomped up the stairs to the main entrance. Bruno's men knew better than to stop and frisk The Dazzler. There were three men who were never frisked. The other two were inside. As Underboss, Randazzo was afforded certain courtesies.

"Good afternoon Mr. Randazzo. Mr. Catalano and Mr. Rizzo are out back on the grilling porch," one of the inside security men said by way of greeting.

Randazzo grunted in response. He walked out back and found his boss at the table with Sal Rizzo, the organization's consigliere which made him third in charge and chief advisor to Catalano.

"Hey, if it ain't the Dazzler! You're just in time! I just took these off the grill. We got Italian sausage patties with provolone and fresh hard rolls. Get yourself a drink and sit down!" Bruno yelled in greeting to his Underboss.

Randazzo found a Labatt's Blue beer in the mini fridge and sat down. He took a long pull off the bottle and looked at his boss.

"Scuderi screwed up, Bruno," he sighed.

Bruno seemed to ignore what he had just heard. He looked straight ahead as he chewed his lunch. He took a sip of his scotch and then wiped his mouth with a cloth napkin before looking at his underboss.

"What do you mean he screwed up, Vincent? Other than Colucci, he's the best enforcer in the organization. What in God's name happened?" Bruno said his voice rising with the last sentence.

"I'm not sure. He got in on a minor charge, had them place him in the same cell as O'Shanick, even had some gangbangers he knows help him out and O'Shanick still got the best of him. Took em' all out. Busted Scuderi's arm up real good and told him he knows we sent him."

"Took them all out?" Catalano said slowly. "How does that happen? How does one mick take out our best enforcer and a bunch of street thugs? Huh? How does that happen?"

Neither Randazzo or Rizzo answered. They knew when their boss was thinking out loud and didn't want to be interrupted.

"This guy has wiped out half of my organization in the past twenty-four hours! How does that happen? Who is this guy?"

The silence went on indicating Bruno actually wanted an answer to his question.

"The news is sayin' he's one of them Navy SEALs, Bruno," Rizzo spoke up.

"So you're telling me some swabbie in a Cracker Jack suit is tearing up my organization?"

"I think he's had help, boss," Rizzo answered. "There's no way..."

"I don't care if he has the entire Navy and all their Marines with him! He's not taking down my organization! He's one man! You hear me? One man!"

Catalano settled down and took another bite of his Italian sausage burger. He chewed in silence for a minute and then washed it down with another sip of his scotch.

"The two of you are gonna take care of this today. O'Shanick goes into the funeral home and he don't come out. You hear me?"

Both men nodded.

"Good. No more screwups. This ends today."

Chapter 65

Niagara Falls, New York

Tom Brinkworth smiled as he drove past the Hyde Park Ice Pavilion. He had spent many memorable years there playing youth and travel hockey. He had thrived in those leagues, enough to have earned a scholarship to Cornell where his skills and leadership led to his being named captain his senior year. Tom had briefly considered pursuing a run at the pros, but he had gained acceptance to law school and, weighing the odds, determined it was the wiser course. His competitive spirit naturally led him towards litigation and he found his niche as a criminal defense attorney. Tom preferred the term "defender" which suited him well since his hockey position was defense.

He and Jack O'Shanick went way back. They had grown up near each other on Grand Island, played sports together and were both sailing enthusiasts. They still saw each other frequently, even though Tom had moved off the Island. He preferred the lake front condos in downtown Buffalo where he kept his sailboat, aptly named *Defender*. The racing fleets were large on Lake Erie resulting in plentiful racing events and good competition. Jack often crewed for Tom in a weeknight racing series since the only races on the Niagara River were held on weekends. Tom had been out for a pleasure sail with some work colleagues when Jack called. Tom would drop anything for Jack's family. They were good folks, Joe in particular. Unfortunately, he was way over by Point Abino on the Canadian side and miles away from Buffalo when Jack called. It took a long time to get back. Consequently, he had missed Joe's arraignment, but bail had been set and Tom was on his way to spring the young man.

Tom had gotten an all too brief picture of what happened from Jack. According to Jack, Joe had acted in defense of his family; however, the incident was all over the news which was painting a much different picture. Tom wanted to get the details from Joe as quickly as possible before a false narrative was ingrained into the public. Selecting a jury that was already biased by a narrative would be a challenge, to say the least. The sooner they got ahead of this, the better.

A few minutes later, he pulled his SUV into an open space and stepped out. He quickly entered the police department and walked over to a familiar area. An older officer sat at the processing desk. He had a full head of silver hair and a bushy grey mustache. The officer looked up as Tom approached.

"Can I help you, sir?"

"Yes, sir. I'm here to post bail for Joseph O'Shanick."

"Oh yes, him." The clerk smiled grimly. "Are you his attorney?"

"Correct. Tom Brinkworth," he said as he handed over his identification.

"I just need you to fill this out for me, please."

"No problem," Brinkworth said as he took the clipboard and began to fill out the appropriate information.

"If you ask me, that kid's a hero," the duty officer spoke in hushed tones. "Instead of locking him up, they should be giving him a parade."

"Well, I don't put on too many parades, but I'll see to it he's no longer locked up," Brinkworth answered as he handed the clipboard back.

"I hope you do, Mr. Brinkworth," the officer said as he gave the clipboard a quick once over. "Follow me please, sir."

The officer led Brinkworth through a locked door, down a hall and into one of several consultation rooms. He offered some coffee which Brinkworth politely declined. He then left to retrieve O'Shanick.

Footsteps echoed off the walls after the metal door shut. The sound of the hard leather soles on polished concrete grew louder as the silhouetted figure approached.

"O'Shanick!"

Joe stood at the sound of his name.

"Hands through the door. You're coming with me."

Joe walked to the cell door, turned his back and extended his hands through the slot. A pair of handcuffs clicked as a stocky officer with close cropped dark hair secured Joe's wrists. Joe stepped away from and turned to face the door as the officer unlocked it using a large thick key. The officer grunted as he glanced at the other men still seated together at the end far away from Joe. With a hand on his sidearm, the officer opened the door. Joe stepped out as the officer closed the door behind him. Another officer joined them, this one tall and slender with equally short hair and a nose that had obviously been broken before. They silently led Joe down the hall.

"May I ask where you're taking me?"

Joe's inquiry was met with silence from the two officers as they walked toward a door at the far end. Different scenarios ran through his mind. Was he being charged with more crimes? Was this something to do with the dust-up back in the cell? Joe was hoping it was his dad's attorney coming to meet with him or, better yet, bail him out. Arriving at the door, the tall officer pulled out a large ring of keys, selected a key and unlocked the door. He opened it and they led Joe into the hall he had come through hours earlier.

Brinkworth silently flipped through the emails on his phone as he waited for the officer to return with his client. He had checked his email a few hours earlier and there were already fifty new ones, most of them junk. He often went down the list and unsubscribed but, for each source he unsubscribed, it seemed like ten new sources appeared. Technology. The door opened and the same officer appeared. He was alone.

"Where's my client?" Brinkworth said cocking his head to look behind the officer.

"He was transferred."

"Transferred? What are you talking about, transferred?"

"Transferred to another facility."

"When did this occur?"

"Just a few minutes ago. I just found out myself when I went back there. I'm sorry, sir."

"Where is he being transferred?"

"They're taking him to the county lock up out near Lockport."

"Officer..." Brinkworth leaned forward to read the man's name tag, "...Girardi, your short answers are forcing me to ask a lot of questions here and it's going to stop or else I'll have no choice but to suspect you are trying to hide something from me. You should have already told me, but now I have to ask. *Why* was my client transferred?!"

"They told me there was an altercation with some other guys and they transferred O'Shanick for his own safety."

"What kind of altercation?"

"I'm not sure," Girardi said with a shrug.

"Officer Girardi, do you expect me to believe that a red-blooded, Italian male police officer like yourself learned of a jail altercation involving a Navy SEAL and did not care enough to inquire of the details?" Brinkworth finished his question with a piercing stare.

"You're right, sir, I'm sorry. The brass frowns on us giving out information," Girardi said sheepishly.

"I'm Lieutenant Commander O'Shanick's legal counsel, Officer Girardi. Any information involving my client is not only acceptable to share with me, but it's expected. Now let's hear it."

"Apparently, some local gang members tried to intimidate your client and he let them have it. Messed them up real bad."

"And this caused the powers that be to worry for my client's safety? So much so that they proceeded with his transfer even though I was already here to post his bail?"

"Sir, in all honesty, I don't know. The word came down from on high that he was to be transferred and he was transferred. We're just grunts here. We carry out the orders and that's it."

"Call the transporting officers. Have them turn around and bring my client back here. Now."

"Sir, I'm not authorized to give that order. I'm sorry."

"Then get whoever gave that order on the phone and I'll tell him myself."

"I'll try, sir. First, I have to find out who gave the order. One minute," Girardi said as he turned and left the room. Ten minutes later, he returned with a panicked look.

"Sir, I'm sorry, but it turns out the detective on duty called relaying the order from his boss."

"And that would be?" Brinkworth prompted.

"Captain Battaglia, but we tried calling him and no one can reach him."

"So you're telling me that there is no one around who can order the transport to return with me client?"

"That's correct, sir. I'm sorry."

"Something's not right here, Officer Girardi," Brinkworth said standing up. He opened his wallet and removed a business card. "I want Captain Battaglia or whoever gave the order to call me as soon as possible. I'll be on my way to the county holding center. I better hear from them before I get there. Rest assured, this is highly irregular, not to mention inconvenient, and this department has some explaining to do."

Brinkworth handed over his card and stormed out of the room.

Chapter 66

Hilton Head, South Carolina

The receding tide left a wide path of compacted sand that stretched north and south for miles along Hilton Head Island. The late afternoon crowd had thinned considerably, leaving the Secret Service detail a bit less anxious about President Galan enjoying a bike ride along the beach with the First Lady. A former enlisted Marine, President Galan was exceptionally respectful to the job his protective detail had and was usually deferential to their needs in order to make their job easier. He knew a bike ride along the beach was a difficult endeavor for his detail, but this was a favorite activity of First Lady Maria and he worked a compromise with his detail. The truth was there was no good way for the Secret Service to secure the beach and ensure the safety of their protectees. That being the case, they agreed to ride during low crowd times. The protective detail rode in a loose protective ring around the President and First Lady while other agents were strategically placed up and down the beach.

The first half of the ride was intense. Maria was also a retired Marine and the first couple remained fitness enthusiasts. The ride up the beach had been a fast paced ride to keep their heart rates up. The return ride was a leisurely ride to enjoy the beach, the salt air, and the sound of the waves. President Galan was savoring the moment. For the past hour, he was able to forget about being the leader of the free world. He was simply, Manny, husband to the beautiful Maria, father to Tommy and Lydia, enjoying a bike ride on the beach with his treasured wife.

They pulled up in front of the beachfront home a friend had lent them and dismounted their bikes. As they began to walk them up to the house, Manny could smell the appetizing scent of charcoal. He looked and saw smoke emanating from the grill on the back porch.

"Josh?" Manny said turning to Secret Service Agent Josh Peters, "Did somebody fire up the grill?"

"Yes, Mr. President. I asked Agent Comstock to have the charcoal ready for when you returned. I hope that was alright?"

"I would have done it, but you won't hear me complain, Josh; thank you."

"In all honesty, sir, it was done with selfish motives. We remember the steaks you grilled last fall at Camp David, and we didn't want to wait the extra twenty minutes for the charcoal."

"Ah, well played, Josh. Well played," Manny said with a grin.

"That means I need to get right on the salad and the Mexican Street Corn," Maria commented.

"We're way ahead of you, ma'am. Your daughter and Agent Fischer have already shucked the corn and are making the salad."

"Not without me, they're not! I so rarely get to cook anymore," Maria said as she began to trot out in front with her bike.

Manny fondly watched his wife run off ahead. Her silky long dark hair was pulled back into a ponytail which swayed back and forth behind her San Diego Padres cap as she ran. Combined with her trim and toned figure, she could have passed for a woman in her twenties. Her beauty was only magnified by the beautiful soul from within. She was godly woman who loved to serve others and who loved to experience life at her husband's side. *Man, am I blessed!*

The pleasant moment was brought to a halt when Manny saw his Chief of Staff emerge from within the house. His quickened pace and stern look alerted Manny that he was either about to receive bad news or be in for a long night. Likely both.

"JJ, by the look on your face, I'm getting the feeling you're about to pull me from grill duty."

"Nah," Embry said with a dismissive wave. "Even I know better than that. This will only take a few minutes. If you would come with me please, sir?"

Manny leaned his bike against the half wall bordering the patio and followed his Chief of Staff into the house. Embry led him into a well-appointed study that served as Manny's office while on vacation. Even on vacation, he was still the president. On a large flatscreen was the paused image of a large cable news outlet. Embry picked up the remote and pressed play. As it played, a well-known anchorman, feigning great concern, led with an update on Joe O'Shanick's arrest. He repeated the reports from earlier in the day and then the screen opened a remote box in the right upper corner. The familiar and unwelcome face of a well-known senator appeared. The live remote was, as nearly always, being filmed with the Capitol rotunda in the background.

"Here with live commentary on this topic is Arizona Senator and presidential candidate, Senator Robert Fowler. Senator Fowler, it's good to have you on the program once again. Thank you for joining us."

"The pleasure's all mine, Mike. Thank you."

"Senator, have we learned anything new about the arrest of Navy SEAL Joseph O'Shanick?"

"Mike, let me begin by saying that, although we don't yet know all the facts, it's pretty conclusive that this man, a man whom President Galan considered worthy enough to honor with a Rose Garden ceremony at the White House, was heavily involved with a criminal organization. We may not know all of the details of this particular incident, but it appears his family, a wealthy family from a well to do area of New York State, was in on it with him. What exactly their involvement was is anyone's guess at this point, but the family owns a large construction business and the criminal organization in question is known to be heavily involved with drug and human trafficking."

"Senator Fowler, what will this mean for Lieutenant O'Shanick and will this in any way reflect back upon President Galan?"

"That's an excellent question, Mike. As a member of the Senate Armed Forces Committee, I proudly stand with our brave men and woman who put their lives on the line to defend our way of life. I think it's shameful that the nefarious actions of Lieutenant O'Shanick will reflect poorly on the brave men and woman who proudly serve our nation, particularly those who serve in the special forces. It's a national disgrace made even worse by the fact that Galan so willingly gave this man a medal and honored him publicly. It serves to illustrate how, yet again, this president has shown very poor judgement and has a very poor sense of character. The American people deserve better. If I'm elected president, I'll work hard to reimagine our military into an entity that serves the hard working men and women of our nation. An entity of honor and integrity that represents people from all walks of life. Not a military of renegade hoodlums that embarrass us time and time again like we have seen under Galan. Our military will be something that all Americans can, once again, be proud of and black marks like this will be a thing of the past."

"Senator Fowler, as always, your comments are always uplifting and enlightening. Thank you for being with us this evening."

"Thank you, Mike."

Chief of Staff Embry turned the screen off and looked at his President.

"What do you want to do about this, Mr. President?"

"Nothing," Manny stated.

"Nothing? Senator Fowler is rising in the polls and the early favorite to be his party's presidential nominee next year. You just saw Mike *Windbag* totally suck up to him and give him a free spot on national news. Slimy politician or not, Fowler is a political pro and he's going to exploit this O'Shanick incident to make you look bad. My job is to prevent that. I think you need to issue a statement distancing yourself from O'Shanick before this gets any worse."

"Negative."

"Excuse me, sir?" Embry asked astounded.

"Negative," Manny repeated. "I'll do nothing of the sort. I know O'Shanick to be a squared away, highly motivated SEAL officer. I have no reason to believe he has any criminal involvement. When I was in the Corps, my men came first. That's doubly so as Commander in Chief. I will stand behind my men until all the facts are in. I will not abandon them based on the report of a bunch of biased pundits who are seeking to make me a one term President. If the true facts show that Lieutenant Commander O'Shanick is guilty of criminal conduct, then I will rethink my support. Until then, we stand behind him. Is that clear?"

"Yes, Mr. President."

"Good. Now that doesn't mean we shouldn't look into the matter. Keep beating the bushes, JJ, and see what you can learn. I'll do the same on my end."

"Yes, Mr. President."

"Is there anything else, JJ?"

"No, sir. Not at this time."

"Very well. Keep me informed. I'm going to go throw the rib eyes on the grill before the charcoal burns out."

Manny turned and exited the study. He entered the kitchen and found his wife and daughter hard at work preparing the Mexican Street Corn, one of Maria's many specialties and an old family favorite.

"If I didn't know any better, I'd say you two were sisters."

"Dad, you always say that," Lydia rolled her eyes as Maria smiled.

"That's because it's true, Princesa. Oh!" Manny said pointing out the window. "Look how beautiful the sun lights up the ocean right now."

As Lydia and Maria looked out the window, Manny quickly grabbed a spoon and scooped a huge portion of the spicy, buttered corn out of the bowl. Maria tuned back and caught him.

"Jorge Manuel Galan, you put that down right now! You'll wait until dinner like everyone else!"

"Hey! You can't talk to me like that. I'm the president!"

"Not in my kitchen you're not! In here, I outrank you."

"Oh yeah?" Manny asked teasingly.

"Yeah!" Maria teased back. "Now let me try a little."

Manny held the spoon up and Maria tasted some of the corn. She smiled and nodded as she chewed, satisfied with the result. Manny downed the rest with a smile and leaned over the countertop to kiss his wife.

"Eww, stop it, you two! You're gonna make me lose my appetite."

"Lydia's right. Go cook the rib eyes. Everyone is starving," Maria said before smiling slyly at her husband and mouthing the word, *"Later."*

Manny grinned back at his wife with a gentle nod. *Now this is a vacation!* he thought to himself as he picked up the platter of rib eyes and headed out to the grill. The charcoal was just right and Manny immediately began placing the steaks on the grill to sear. Always appreciative of their staff and in-house protective detail, Manny and Maria went out of their way to include them in a nice meal. His rib eyes were always a favorite. Seasoned with Lowry's seasoning and then grilled to perfection over charcoal while splashing them with Worcestershire Sauce.

After two minutes, he flipped all of the steaks to sear the other side. He took a sip of iced tea as his thoughts returned to Lieutenant Commander O'Shanick. It was a potential pitfall politically speaking, but Manny was not a traditional politician. He still thought of himself as the Marine Sergeant Major he once was, only on a much larger battlefield. Senator Fowler was a consummate politician, to be sure, but he was also sneaky and underhanded. Manny had long suspected the man had a closet full of skeletons and they would, one day, be his downfall. At least they should be. In today's culture it seemed as though the rapscallions were now the celebrated while the honest and moral were sneered upon by the press and Hollywood. Manny refused to let that dictate his actions.

The right thing would be to look into O'Shanick's situation, gather the facts and make a sound decision. Embry had some men on it, but it had only been a few hours and his search hadn't turned up much yet. Time to play another card.

"Josh, would you mind doing me a favor?"

"Sure thing, Mr. President," the agent responded.

"Have the signals officer get ahold of Captain James Bennett, United States Navy. He's a Naval Special Warfare Task Group Commander."

"Yes, sir," Agent Peters said as he stepped into the house.

Chapter 67

Lockport, New York

*B*rinkworth purposefully strode up the long sidewalk that led to the Niagara County Jail entrance. Although many people considered it an eyesore, Tom actually enjoyed looking at the concrete and steel diamond shaped holding facility attached to the administrative building. He gave it a quick glance but was too focused to take it in this evening. He entered the building and presented himself to the front desk.

"Attorney Tom Brinkworth here for Joseph O'Shanick."

"Yes, sir. If you could fill this out while I look him up," the heavy-set female officer said as she handed him a clipboard.

"He was just transferred here from the Falls PD," Brinkworth said as he began filling out the government forms.

"Which is probably why I can't locate him in the system," the officer said as she stared at her computer screen. "Hold on, let me make a call."

Brinkworth listened to the officer as she spoke into the phone. By the time she hung up, it was apparent nobody knew anything about O'Shanick's transfer.

"I'm sorry sir, your client isn't here and there is no transfer on our schedule. Are you sure he was coming here?"

"Yes. I just came from the Falls. They told me he was being transferred here and that the van had just left before I got there."

"Are you sure it was this facility?"

"Yes, they told me the Niagara County Jail near Lockport," Brinkworth responded with frustration. "He was just arrested a few hours ago. A decorated war hero who has never been arrested before. I find his being transferred highly irregular to begin with and now he's unaccounted for? Unacceptable. This facility needs to get in touch with NFPD and find my client. Now," he finished glaring at the hirsute officer.

"I understand, sir. Let me see what I can do. You're welcome to have a seat over there," she pointed to a small seating area as she turned her attention to her phone and began dialing.

"I appreciate that," Brinkworth said calmer. "The transfer order came from a Captain Battaglia. You might want to start with him."

The woman nodded as she dialed. Brinkworth remained standing at the desk seemingly looking at his phone while he listened in. She made several calls. Each one seemed to be a dead end. A few minutes later she hung up for the fifth time and sighed.

"I'm terribly sorry, sir. The only person that knows anything is an Officer Girardi who confirmed the transfer was supposed to come here. Nobody else knows anything."

"I see, and what about Captain Battaglia?"

"He's off duty. They got in touch with him on his cell phone and he said he has been salmon fishing out on Lake Ontario all day and has never heard of your client and certainly never administered a transfer order."

A dark sense of foreboding descended on Brinkworth. He pulled out his wallet and retrieved one of his business cards.

"Here is my card. My cell is written on the back. If you learn anything, *anything,* about my client, you call me immediately," he said as he handed her the card and turned to walk out.

He turned back to the desk. "My client is missing. This is on your department and the Falls PD. The Catalano family has been after him for days. It would be in the best interests of this department and Niagara Falls PD to find my client as soon as possible before something unspeakable happens. You'd best be on that phone making that happen! Heads are going to roll for this!"

Brinkworth turned and quickly strode out to his SUV. Upon getting in, he fired up the vehicle and started back out onto the main road.

He activated his Bluetooth and voice activated a call. A groggy voice answered on the other end.

"Jack, it's Tom. We've got a problem..."

Jack pressed the button to end the call. He swallowed hard as he looked around the room. Jacob, Sean and Anna along with Jacob's wife and Sean's fiancé all stared back at him with concern.

"Joe's missing," he spoke quietly.

"He's missing?" Jacob asked. "How can that be?"

"From what Tom told me, Joe got into a fight in the holding cell. Two police officers showed up a little while later saying they had orders to transfer him out to the county jail and took him. Tom went to meet him at county, only Joe never arrived and there was no record of his transfer. Nobody knows where he is."

"You've got to be kidding me!" Sean exclaimed. "Two guys just waltz into the jail claiming some bogus transfer order and make off with Joe? How does that happen?"

"I wish I knew, son."

"We need to go find him," Jacob said as he rose to his feet.

"Freakin-A-right we do!" Sean said as he also stood.

"Hold on, boys," Jack said motioning with his hands to calm down. "Tom said he's lighting a fire under the city police, as well as the sheriffs, to find him. I know how you feel, and I admire it, but you don't have the first clue where to look and I don't need you out there getting in the way of the police. People end up shot that way and we've had enough of that with Marina and Tran. Wait, Tran...," Jack stopped in mid-sentence as he seemed to be lost in thought.

"What is it, Dad?" Jacob asked.

"Joe's team. If anyone can find him, they can!"

"That's right!" Anna exclaimed.

"I need to get ahold of Chief Ramsey, or any of them for that matter! Do any of you have a way to reach them?"

"No, but Christy might!" Anna offered. "She's up in the Trauma ICU with Mom checking up on Marina. I'll go get her!" Anna said as she began to stand.

"Anna, wait," Jack grunted as he sat up. "I want to go with you."

"Dad, you're in no condition to go. I'll do it," Anna politely tried to dissuade her father.

"I'm fine," Jack said, as he unhooked his pulse ox cord and swung his legs off the bed. "I need to personally tell your mom what's happening."

"Well let me at least get you a wheelchair," Anna offered.

"You're not wheeling me up there like some invalid," Jack said as he slid off the bed and stood with a grunt. He took a breath and blinked his eyes. "Okay, let's go."

Ramsey and Sierra sat quietly as they listened to the ventilator and held vigil over their fallen brother. Tran lay motionless in his ICU bed with a seemingly outrageous number of lines and tubes connected to various monitors, equipment and IV pumps. They had each taken turns talking to him. Having had several comrades injured in combat, both men knew that even heavily sedated and injured patients could still hear. Many of their comrades had regained consciousness only to vividly recall words that were said to them and even people praying over them.

"His favorite book is *Atlas Shrugged,*" Sierra said looking over the bed to his Chief Petty Officer. "He's been trying to get me to read it. Gave me his old copy. It's in my duffle bag back at the O'Shanick's. Tomorrow, I'm gonna bring it in here and start reading it to him."

"Sounds like a good idea, Eddie. I like it," Ramsey said as he felt his phone begin to vibrate.

He looked at the screen and saw it was Christy calling.

"Hey Christy, how's Marina?"

"She's stable for now, Matt, but there's another problem."

"Now what?" He sighed.

"I'm going to put Joe's dad on the phone and let him explain."

"Chief, it's Jack O'Shanick."

"Yes, sir," Ramsey said as he abruptly stood. "What's going on?"

"Joe's gone missing..."

"Bring me up to speed, sir."

Jack spent the next several minutes filling Ramsey in on everything from Joe's arrest to the circumstances surrounding his disappearance. Ramsey listened quietly. He occasionally spoke up to clarify a detail or ask a pertinent question.

"We're on it, sir. We'll find him," Ramsey said concluding the call.

"What's up, Chief?" Sierra asked with obvious concern.

"It's Joe. He was arrested for the shootings and now he's missing. C'mon, we've gotta go."

The two started for the door, but Ramsey turned and went back to the bedside.

"Tran," Ramsey said, as he squeezed his teammate's hand and leaned down close to his ear, "Joe's in trouble and we're going to find him. Hang in there, brother. We'll be back soon."

Ramsey and Sierra hastily exited the Trauma ICU and quickly walked down the hallway. People moved out of the way as the two warriors cast a dangerous presence while they purposefully strode through the busy unit. Ramsey felt his phone vibrate again. Retrieving it, he did a double take when he saw the name on the screen.

"Chief Ramsey here," he answered.

"Rammer, Bennett here. Can anyone else hear us?"

Captain James Bennett was the Task Force Commander over several SEAL platoons and support units serving in the campaign against the Central American cartels of which Ramsey's platoon had recently returned after nearly a year of deployment. Bennett was a legendary SEAL and a highly regarded leader. Despite their difference in rank, Bennett and Ramsey were good friends. They had endured BUDs together as part of the same boat crew and served many combat tours together.

"No, sir," Ramsey answered, as he pointed Sierra to the stairwell, thus bypassing the elevator.

"Okay, I'm on my private cell. This is strictly informal. Two friends who went through BUDs together, so please speak freely. Frogman to frogman."

"Roger that, to what do I owe the honor?" Ramsey asked with an inkling of the reason.

"This issue with O'Shanick. It's all over the news. Do you know anything about it?"

"I haven't seen the news, but I'm right here in the middle of it. Eddie Sierra and I are leaving Tran Van Truc's ICU bed right now where he is recovering from multiple gunshot wounds after the mafia ambushed him and some of Joe's family. Joe's now missing. We think the mafia took him. It's a Charlie Foxtrot, sir."

"Whoa. Slow down, Rammer. Start from the beginning and tell me everything."

"Roger that, sir. Did you see the news report, a few days ago, of a guy surviving a plunge over Niagara Falls?"

"I did."

"That was Joe, sir. Drown proof training works."

"Are you kidding me? That was O'Shanick?"

"It was indeed. He is one drown proof, buttoned up, watertight frogman, sir, but there's more to the story. A lot more."

Chapter 68

Lewiston, New York

"It's kinda like the good ol' days, Dazzler. Don't ya think?"

"What are ya talkin' about, Rizzo?" Randazzo asked.

"You know. Whackin' a guy." Rizzo answered as he drove.

"I whacked that Russian mob fella last month," Randazzo countered. "You know, the guy who tried cuttin' in on our arrangement with the PCP's?"

"Who?"

"The Power City Playahs, you chooch. The black gang that distributes for us."

"Oh yeah, those guys. That was you who whacked that guy? What was his name? Vitaly?"

"Somethin' like that," Randazzo answered.

"Yeah, I heard they found him hanging from a hook in the freezer at that restaurant they own over on the Boulevard. Why didn't you just get rid of the body at Bruno's funeral home?"

"I was sending them a message, Rizzo. Sometimes ya gotta send a message," Randazzo said factually as he studied the road up ahead. "That's the spot coming up. Turn here."

They turned off of Lower Mountain Road onto a small gravel road lined on both sides by trees.

"There they are," Rizzo nodded towards the white transport van pulled over on the side of the road.

Rizzo eased his Cadillac over onto the side of the road, stopping just behind the van. The two got out and approached the van. The doors opened and the two officers got out of the van. The four men met at the side of the van and quietly greeted each other without using names. They opened the doors and, while Randazzo trained his gun on Joe, the officers quickly removed the lock that secured him to the van floor.

"You make one wrong move, ya Mick, and I'll paint the inside of this van red. It ain't my van so I really don't care."

Joe nodded his understanding. He knew their endgame. They had already tried to kill him several times. This guy, Randazzo, Joe concluded based on Costello's description, wasn't bluffing. Joe wasn't going to make it easy for them, but he stood no chance against four armed men with his hands and feet cuffed. He would wait for a better opportunity. If he got one. He wasn't kidding himself. He was likely going to die. Soon. That didn't change his resolve. *Never out of the fight.*

They pulled Joe out of the van and frogmarched him back to the car. Rizzo hit his key fob and the trunk popped open. The two officers manhandled Joe into the trunk and slammed it shut. Joe rolled allowing him to face the back of the car and tried to listen in on the conversation. From what Joe picked up, the men agreed that the officers would claim they were hijacked at gunpoint, by a group of men in ski masks, and made to drive to a side road where they were forced to hand over Joe. Soon after, they parted ways and went to their respective vehicles.

As Randazzo and his associate got into the car, Joe began to quickly assess his situation. The good news was they had left his wrists secured to his front. The bad news was his ankles were tightly shackled and his wrists were shackled to his waist giving little room for movement of his extremities. Joe wriggled around and had to arch his back to allow his hands to feel around where the trunk latch was. Since 2001, auto manufacturers have been required to install an emergency release handle allowing people to release themselves from within the trunk. The inside of the trunk was dark, but he eventually located the release handle.

Joe thought through his escape options. A lot depended on how quickly the two men noticed he was missing. Joe figured a two minute head start would leave enough ground for them to cover that he would have a reasonable chance of escape. Being chained up and wearing an orange jump suit, he would look like an orange Tyrannosaurus Rex desperately trying to find a restroom. A stealthy and hasty escape was off the table.

Rolling out of the trunk while stopped on a busy street might be a better option. They would be less likely to shoot him with witnesses around. His chains and jumpsuit would immediately identify him as a prisoner, but at least he would remain alive if returned to jail. The problem was, he had no idea where they were heading. Joe knew he would be able to tell if they were in the city or a busy area, but there was no guarantee they would wind up in such a place. He would have to jump soon. The trees would provide a chance at cover. It was better than nothing. He decided he would wait for the car to slow and make his move. Too fast and he could injure himself. If they were stopped, the mobsters might notice and catch him before he even hit the woods. The sun hadn't set yet, but it had dropped behind the Niagara Escarpment which cast a dark shadow on the area. The tall trees intertwined over the narrow road providing even more shade. Joe hoped the relative darkness might provide enough cover that they wouldn't immediately notice the raised trunk in the rearview mirror. No matter what he chose, his chances would be slim. Regardless, anything was better than remaining in the trunk waiting for the inevitable bullet in the head.

It sounded like the transport van had just performed a three-point turn and passed them the opposite way. Joe felt the car shift into gear and swing left to perform a similar turn. He grasped the release handle and waited for the right moment. Having paid attention during the drive out, he knew Lower Mountain Road was a quarter mile away. They would have to slow to a stop before turning. The car accelerated briefly before it began to coast to a stop. Anything more than twenty miles per hour and he would probably injure himself. That left little room to jump. Being inside the trunk, it would be difficult to accurately estimate their speed. He waited. *Now!*

Joe pulled the release handle. The trunk rose slightly. He lifted a leg over the edge and pushed himself up with his hands. He balanced on the edge. It was now or never. Joe rolled out and tucked into a ball as he fell. He hit the hard ground with a jarring thud and rolled roughly fifteen feet before stopping. His recently fractured ribs screamed in protest, followed closely behind by every appendage, but a quick head to toe survey told him nothing was broken. Joe wasted no time rising to a crouch. The trees lit up red in the glow of the brake lights as he quickly shuffled to the side of the road and dashed into the tree line.

Chapter 69

Hilton Head Island, South Carolina

"*I*'ll get back to you shortly, James. Thank you," President Galan ended the call and handed the secure phone back to the signals officer.

"Stay close, please, Tim. I'll be calling him back in a few minutes."

He had taken the call out on the patio while his family policed the kitchen. Manny walked over to the knee-high stone ledge that bordered the patio. He placed a foot on the ledge and stared out at the Atlantic Ocean lit up orange by the setting sun behind him. Captain Bennett had just called him back with the sitrep on Lieutenant Commander O'Shanick. The news reports were misleading. Nothing new there. O'Shanick was in real danger. The legal charges were the least of his concern. Something had to be done and fast.

Manny crossed his forearms over his knee, took a deep breath and exhaled. What needed to be done was a quick hostage rescue. That posed two problems. No one actually knew where O'Shanick happened to be and, other than a local SWAT team, there was no hostage rescue unit that could be assembled on such short notice. From what little he knew this was a contract hit. Ordered by whom, no one knew, but there would be no negotiation or demand for ransom. For all he knew, O'Shanick might already be dead. The safe political play was to do nothing. It was out of his control and the only actionable option he could think of was flirting with the boundaries of the Constitution. If he wasn't careful, he could jeopardize his career. That establishment hack Fowler was already demagoguing him on national television and for what? For awarding a war hero a medal. A war hero being cast as a shady criminal by a news media that didn't have all the facts. Even if and when all the facts were made public, they may not back off their narrative. His first term honeymoon with the press as the first Latino President had been short lived. His tough stance on crime and immigration made quick work of that.

Screw em'! I came here to do the right thing, not win a popularity contest.

Manny laughed to himself. This was politics. Being elected, heck even getting Congress to act on the president's behalf, was every bit a popularity contest. Doubly so in the age of social media and cable news. It was all speeches, sound bites, and photo ops. The things that really mattered were easily overlooked by a slick marketing and media campaign. Senator Fowler and the media would negatively criticize Manny regardless of how this played out, so he couldn't let that affect his decision. A life was at stake. Perhaps more. There was no time to debate. He had to decide now. Manny thought of King Solomon who, when God offered to grant him anything he asked for, eschewed riches and power, but rather asked for wisdom to lead. *Well played King Solomon. Well played.*

Prompted by this thought, Manny, as he had many times before, prayed for wisdom. As he finished, he felt Maria's warm presence as she stepped up next to him and placed a gentle hand on his back.

"Anything the matter?" She asked.

"Yes, a situation has come up. I can't divulge the details, but lives are at stake and the best solution may not play well with the establishment."

"Since when has that ever stopped you?" Maria said as she leaned in with a knowing smile.

"It usually doesn't, but this one skirts the boundaries of the Constitution and I need to get it right. I could be impeached over this."

"These lives that are at stake. Are they American citizens?"

"Yes."

"So their lives, ergo their rights, are being threatened?"

"Yes."

"Then I would think the Constitution is on your side, Manny; besides, I've never known you to put your career ahead of anyone. You'll make the right decision."

Maria kissed her husband on the cheek and quietly disappeared back into the house.

"Tim," President Galan said looking back at the signals officer, "please get Captain Bennett back on the line for me."

The waterfront beach house at the O'Shanick house was a beehive of activity as the six remaining men quickly donned their gear and loaded equipment into the two pickup trucks. Petty Officer Kowalski brought the team up on all of the intel that had been collected over the past twenty-four hours. Frank Pandolfino eventually broke and had proven to be a treasure trove of intel. Chief Ramsey followed by conducting an op planning session with the entire team. The target was Bruno Catalano's estate. Their objective was to infiltrate the estate, neutralize his security in a non-lethal manner and take the mafia don alive. Catalano would be pressed for intel on Joe's whereabouts and, if need be, used as exchange collateral. Ramsey secretly wanted to personally put a bullet in Catalano's head and every last member of the organization as, only then, could he have confidence that the threat to Joe and his family might be neutralized. He knew they couldn't do that, but he at least hoped they could get Joe back alive while sending a lot of bad guys to prison. Catalano chief among them.

"KK, let's have you and Ricky ride with Eddie. Mule, you're with me and Stinnet. Stinnet, you drive."

"Aye, Chief."

The men piled into the trucks and got on the road. They headed up East River Road toward the North Grand Island Bridge which would cross them over the river into the city of Niagara Falls.

Chief Ramsey keyed the microphone on his inter-squad radio.

"Comms check, sound off."

"KK, Echo Six, checking in."

"This is the Mule, Echo Seven, checking in."

"Sierra, Echo Eight, checking in."

"Moreno, Echo Fifteen, checking in."

"Crazy Cartso, Echo Sixteen, checking in."

"Rammer, Echo Three. Alright boys, you know the plan. Neutralize all targets and take the HVT alive. We need him if we are gonna get Joey O back alive. We're on shaky ground here, so the ROEs are we don't fire unless fired upon. Even then, we likely don't have legal cover; therefore, it would be best to get the HVT without loss of life. We'll get Joe back and deal with the fallout later. Is everyone good?"

His inquiry was answered with a series of affirmatives. They crossed the bridge in silence. To their west the setting sun burned bright orange as it disappeared behind the mist of Niagara Falls. It was a shame they never got the chance to visit the natural wonder. Ramsey felt his phone vibrate. He removed it from his tactical vest and looked at the screen. This was a must take call.

"Chief Ramsey..."

Ramsey listened on for a minute before ending the call. He immediately keyed his comms mike.

"Boys, we've just been granted our hunting license. We are weapons free at the first sign of hostile intent."

Chapter 70

Lewiston, New York

Joe clutched his chains in attempt to quiet them as he slowly worm-crawled through the brush. He couldn't do the same for his leg chains, which caused him to proceed at a snail's pace to minimize the telltale clinking. Keeping some tension on the leg chain by spreading his feet apart helped a little. Up head a few yards, Joe spotted a slight depression holding some standing water. If he could just get there and get muddy, he might be able to camouflage his bright orange jail issue jump suit. Being a SEAL, he was quite adept in the art of concealment, but doing so in a bright orange jumpsuit and loud metal chains was an unwanted challenge.

Randazzo and, by Joe's guess, Rizzo, the consigliere, were haphazardly searching through the brush closer to their car. Every yard Joe put between them was a slight improvement in his chances of escaping. Joe was nearly upon the standing water. He had hoped it would mean some mud in the brush he was currently in, but it was dry ground covered by leaves. He would have to move out from the brush to get muddy, but it was worth the risk. He watched intently for the two men to look the other way. Being so low to the ground, they were difficult to see. If he couldn't see them, odds were they couldn't see him. Ever so cautiously, Joe inched his way toward the water. The ground began to soften as he neared the edge. He belly crawled through the mud and then carefully rolled onto his back. He rubbed mud onto his forearms meticulously trying to avoid making any noise with his chains. The chains restricted his arms to where he couldn't reach his face. Rolling back onto his stomach, Joe took a breath and buried his face in the mud. Satisfied that he had camouflaged himself as well as possible, Joe began to inch back into the brush.

Their voices were getting louder. It couldn't be helped. The short distance Joe could crawl in a couple of minutes could be covered in ten seconds walking. Joe wanted to put more distance between them but, with Randazzo and Rizzo getting closer, movement was becoming too risky. He was going to have to either fight or go for cover. He may have had the element of surprise, but Joe was unlikely to succeed fighting two armed men while restricted by shackles. To his left the woods gave way to what looked like a cattle field with a pond about a hundred yards away. If he could only make it to the pond undetected, he was certain he could hide underneath the murky water with only enough face exposed to allow him to breathe. It was too much ground to cover in the twilight evening where he could still be spotted. The brush appeared a bit thicker up ahead. It wasn't ideal, but it was the best option at the moment. Joe quietly inched his way into the thickest spot and assumed a face down position while trying to pretend he was a rotting log.

The voices of Randazzo and Rizzo grew louder. Joe slowed his breathing to minimized and movement. He heard their footsteps as they walked by him just a few feet from his position. By their conversation, Joe could tell they were beginning to doubt his whereabouts.

"I dunno, Vince, he could be anywhere by now."

"Are you freakin' kidding me, Rizzo? In that get up? No freakin' way. He's around here somewheres."

"Well, it's gettin' dark. How are we ever going to find him? These cell phone lights ain't enough."

"Shut up and keep lookin', Rizzo. If we show up empty handed, Bruno will be shovin' us into the crematory. We gotta find him."

Their voices faded slightly as they walked past Joe. He decided to stay put for the time being as he didn't know how much farther they would go before turning back. He didn't have to wait long. The two men reversed course and came back down the road in Joe's direction. He buried his head once again. He would have liked to have spread some leaves over himself, but his restricted arms were nearly useless on his belly. The two men came so close that Joe could feel the ground vibrate as they slowly walked past.

"It's no use, Vince. We ain't never gonna find him now."

"Will you shut up and keep lookin'!"

"Are we on the reservation?"

"We're close, Rizzo. Why?"

"Cuz we should get a couple of Tuscarora out here. They'd find him in no time."

"You know any Tuscarora?" Randazzo asked sarcastically.

"No. Not really."

"Then shut your pie hole and keep looking."

Joe remained motionless until the sound of their voices had decreased enough to where he felt it was safe to move. He looked longingly at the pond and weighed his odds. They had walked by him twice, nearly stepping on him and failed to notice him right under their noses. He thought he had been lucky. The concealment wasn't nearly as good as he would have liked. He'd be much better off at the pond. It was dark enough now that, if he remained silent and started now, he felt reasonably certain he could make it to the pond. From there he could monitor and wait his two pursuers out until they gave up and moved on. Joe glanced over his shoulder and saw they were nearly back to the corner. He wouldn't get a better chance to move.

Joe began a slow belly crawl through the brush toward the open field. He maintained tension on his chains to keep them from rattling, thus drawing attention. He reached the edge of the brush and ran into a barbed wire fence. He silently winced in pain from the unexpected sting of the barbed wire on his forehead. A few inches lower and he might now be blind. Even with his now well acclimated night vision, Joe couldn't make out the barbed wire in the darkness. He used his hands to feel the ground in front of him but could not feel another wire. Since the problem wire was at forehead level, he decided to crawl under it. Due to the handcuffs, Joe was unable to raise his hands while prone. He slowly rolled onto his back keeping care to not make any noise. He could now use his hands to lift the wire ever so slightly while he slithered underneath.

Once clear of the wire, Joe rolled back over and began to move with earnest toward the pond. Movement was much easier over the clear ground. The occasional cow patties left a little to be desired, but he had crawled through worse in training. The safe haven of the pond loomed up ahead.

Beyond the pond, the land rose several hundred yards up to a modest house with an adjacent barn which was barely discernible in the dull glow of a solitary light. The house had several interior lights on. Joe figured he could walk up to the house when the coast was clear. His appearance would certainly cause an alarm, but all he needed was for the house owners to call the Niagara County Sheriffs while he sat on the ground like a good boy. Once in the Sheriffs' custody, he would be safer than he was now. A lousy plan, but the best he could come up with.

Joe inched closer to the pond. Randazzo and Rizzo could still be heard, but less so now that he had put some distance between them. He was beginning to think he had a chance.

Suddenly, the angry bark of two large dogs began to emanate from up by the house. Joe hoped beyond hope they were either indoors or caged up. No such luck. By the rapidly increasing volume of the barking, Joe could tell they were heading straight for him. Joe's old nemesis, Mr. Murphy of Murphy's Law had just made his usual timely appearance.

Chapter 71

Ricky Moreno silently worked his way through the woods. Kowalski and Sierra followed closely behind. They had parked on the other side of the woods and were quietly approaching the side of Catalano's estate. The three men moved like ghosts, slowly and methodically stepping over and around anything that could create even the slightest sound. The absent moon resulted in an eerie darkness that was slightly improved by their night vision goggles. As Moreno approached the edge of the woods, the well-lit Catalano house created a bright glare in his goggles forcing him to turn them off. He slowly raised the goggles before he peered around a tree to examine the side of the house.

He stared at the back wall of a large four-car garage. A six-foot-high wrought iron fence began at the front corner of the garage and extended across the well-manicured front lawn. From there, it cut through a thick patch of woods to the road and then continued adjacent to the road until it formed the front gate. Moreno looked for security cameras and saw two. One at the front corner of the garage looking over the front lawn and one on the back corner of the house looking over the expansive back yard. He would be unseen between the two. Moreno quickly crossed the open ground to the garage wall. Kowalski and Sierra covered him as he slowly moved along the wall toward the fence. He listened for the two dogs Pandolfino had told them patrolled the grounds. He didn't hear them but suspected they were about as promised. He reached into a cargo pocket and retrieved a Ziplock bag containing several small balls of ground beef that were mixed with liquid Lorazepam. Moreno tossed the balls over and through the fence and then rejoined his teammates in the woods. They retreated back into the woods where Moreno and Sierra began to imitate the guttural sounds of two cats squaring up for a fight. A pair of Doberman Pinschers materialized almost immediately. Moreno and Sierra ceased with their noises and watched the stately canines as they stared into the woods with curiosity. Their keen noses picked up the scent of the ground beef and they quickly found the balls and devoured them. Anytime the dogs appeared to be ready to head off, Sierra would quietly make a brief cat call to hold their interest. Approximately fifteen minutes passed and one of the Doberman's laid down followed a minute later by the other one.

Kowalski keyed his mike, "Zeus and Apollo neutralized. Second element moving to recon point."

Ramsey responded with two clicks of his mike. He smiled at the Magnum PI reference.

The trio worked their way toward the back of the house while remaining concealed in the woods. They inched close to the clearing and surveyed the area. Two men sat on the porch smoking cigars. Sierra studied them through the scope on his Remington R25 7mm-08 rifle. A very large man in a poorly fitting suit sat next to Bruno Catalano. Both were engaged in conversation as they puffed on their cigars. There were no other men in sight.

Sierra whispered into his microphone, "Echo Three, this is Echo Eight. I've got eyes on the HVT. He is seated on porch accompanied by one tango."

"Roger that Echo Eight, you have eyes on plus one. We have two tangos on front porch. Unknown inside. First element to neutralize the tangos in front. Move into position and stand by."

Kowalski answered Ramsey with two clicks on his radio. He and Moreno then moved back through the woods while Sierra covered them and monitored the porch. They moved until were even with the back of the house and then crossed the open ground. A covered grilling porch sat about six feet above the ground. The security camera was located on the vary back corner of the porch, thus unable to see Kowalski and Moreno. Kowalski leaned his back against the brick wall below the porch and squatted down. Moreno deftly stepped up

Kowalski's thighs and shoulders to reach the porch in seconds. He took Kowalski's rifle and then reached down with a hand to help his teammate scale the wall. Kowalski effortlessly climbed up without a sound. The two took positions behind a tiled countertop/bar giving them good position on Catalano who sat sixty feet away with his large friend.

"Echo Three, this is Echo Six, second element is in position," Kowalski quietly spoke into his mike.

"Roger that, Three, stand by."

Kowalski peered around the side of the bar and studied the large man. The man had a look that said personal security. His size was meant to be a deterrent. Many such men had brute strength, but lacked speed and agility, leaving them vulnerable in hand to hand combat. Kowalski knew better than to presume this, but he hoped it was true.

"Echo Six, this is Echo Three. Both tangos neutralized out front. Stand by to execute."

Kowalski answered with two clicks.

"All units execute in three...two...one. Execute, execute, execute!"

"Don't move!" Kowalski yelled as he and Moreno popped up from behind the counter with their rifles trained on the men. The large man jumped up and spun towards the two SEALs extending his right arm. He quickly fired in their direction getting two errant shots off before Kowalski returned fire. His shots found their mark and the man's lifeless body collapsed to the floor.

"Shots fired! Weapons free! One tango down!" Sierra yelled into his mike as he searched for other hostiles.

"Clear on the back porch!" Kowalski spoke as he moved in on Catalano.

"First element through the door and clear. Commencing house search."

"Hands up, Catalano!" Kowalski yelled as he approached the mafia boss.

Catalano sat in his outdoor lounge and casually took another puff of his cigar. He looked at Kowalski in a manner as if sizing him up and said nothing. His head suddenly jolted forward when Moreno struck him in the back of the head with his rifle stack.

"He said hands up, pendejo!"

Catalano reflexively grabbed the back of his head with his left hand. Moreno, waiting for this, grabbed Catalano's wrist and twisted his arm down behind his back. Kowalski grabbed the other wrist and did the same. Catalano dropped his cigar in the process. Moreno placed a zip tie and then pulled the mobster upright by the back of his hair. Kowalski got in his face.

"Where's O'Shanick?"

"Who?" Catalano asked.

"You know who I'm talking about. Where's O'Shanick?"

"O'Shanick?" He said shaking his head. "I don't know no O'Shanick."

Kowalski unsheathed his knife, jammed Catalano back into the chair with a forearm and held the knife up against his throat.

"Does this jog your memory?" He asked menacingly.

"Nope. Put your toy away, frog boy. I know you won't kill me."

"What makes you so sure?" Kowalski said through gritted teeth, as he held the knife up so close to the skin a bead of blood began to form.

"Because I'd already be dead right now. Just like Tino right there. You need me alive, don't you?" He smirked.

"This is Echo Three, house is secure, I'm coming out to the back porch," Chief Ramsey announced over the radio as he emerged from the house.

Kowalski looked up.

"Find anything out yet, KK?"

"We're working on it, but he doesn't think he needs to talk."

"Oh? Is that so?" Ramsey asked as if surprised.

"Yeah, caglione, that's so," Catalano replied smugly. "I know who you chumps are. You can't do nothing to me. As a matter of fact, when my lawyer hears of this, every one of you's is gonna be lickin' the boots of every wise guy in the clink. You have no idea who you're messin' with!"

Ramsey lashed out with a quick jab which connected with Catalano's nose with a sickening crunch. The mobster's eyes were shut tight in reaction to the excruciating pain. Ramsey then grabbed Catalano by the lapels, pulled him up onto his feet, and slung him up over his shoulder. He walked down a wide set of steps to the large swimming pool which was lit up in a brilliant blue. He then flung the mob boss into the deep end.

"Let's see what he thinks of drown proof training," Ramsey said as he unslung his rifle and removed his tactical vest.

With his arms zip tied behind his back, Catalano floundered about desperately trying to get his head above water. Ramsey watched for another half a minute and then jumped into the water. He swam under Catalano and vaulted him to the surface. Ramsey worked up into a rescue swim and pulled the man into shallower water. Catalano spent a minute coughing and choking on water while his nose bled steadily. Ramsey spun him around and got right up in the mobster's face.

"I know exactly who I'm dealing with, you low life," Ramsey said through clenched teeth. "*You* don't know who *you're* dealing with! That's our brother you've tried to kill. He has put his life on the line many times over for each and every one of us and we *will not hesitate* to do the same for him! So if you think you can scare us with a prison sentence, you are sadly mistaken!"

Ramsey emphasized the last part by head butting Catalano on his broken nose. The man responded with a blood curdling scream followed by more choking. Ramsey immediately hurled him back into the deep end. He let Catalano struggle under the water for about half a minute and then pulled him back to the shallow end. Catalano emerged from the water in a raging coughing spurt, followed by a minute of retching.

"Ready to talk, *caglione?*" Ramsey asked menacingly.

Catalano weakly nodded as he struggled to overcome his uncontrolled coughing.

"That's more like it," Ramsey said in a more even voice. "So tell me, Bruno. Where is Joe O'Shanick?"

Chapter 72

"You've got to be kidding me!" Joe quietly hissed out loud as he got to his feet and shuffled as fast as he could in the gait restricting chains. The pond was only fifty yards away. The dogs might swim after him, but he stood a better chance in the water. The barking got louder. Joe winced at the telltale sound of his rattling chains, but it couldn't be helped; besides, the dogs had basically outed him with their barking. He could see them now. Silhouetted by the dim light up by the barn, two large dark shapes charging quickly around the pond. Joe knew it would be close. He felt like he was in a three-legged race lashed to a drunk partner. The barking morphed into a guttural growl as the dogs came ever closer. Not good. Fifteen yards. The pond was right there. The safety of the water, a SEAL's refuge, just yards away, but there were two canines close and closing quickly. Joe loved dogs but, right now, his two pursuers looked like demonic creatures in the dark. Five yards away. *Almost there...*

With a savage growl the first dog leaped through the air and collided with Joe, knocking him over just a foot from the water's edge. Joe swung his shackled arms to sweep the angry dog away from his neck. It was a large black dog, but that was all Joe could make out in the dark. Joe then curled into a tight ball, doing the best he could to tuck his head into his arms to protect his face and neck. The large dog bit his leg but came up with a mouth full of pants leg. He maintained his grip and shook with all he had, while the other dog loudly barked and watched the alpha dog work Joe over. Joe kicked and tried to roll his way into the water. The large dog, possessing amazing strength, pulled and tugged while threshing Joe's leg about. For every inch Joe won, the dog seemed to take it right back.

In desperation, Joe rolled onto his back, planted both of his feet and lunged head first for the pond. His head and shoulders cleared the small sloping bank, but the large dog refused to let go. As a result, Joe was upside down on the bank, on his back with his head in the muddy water. Joe performed a sit-up to breathe while he continued to kick at his attacker in effort to break free. He had little mechanical advantage and quickly found himself under the water with his right leg being violently shaken.

A loud gunshot rang out and Joe found his leg suddenly free. Joe wasted no time flinging his legs up so as to summersault backwards into the safety of the water. Something caught his leg chain. His head still under water, Joe violently tried to kick himself free, but whatever had him wouldn't let go. Suddenly he felt himself being pulled back up on the bank. As Joe's face emerged from the water, he saw he was being dragged by Randazzo and Rizzo. He suddenly missed the dogs who were now nowhere to be seen.

Randazzo held his gun pointed at Joe and walked backwards while using his left hand to drag him by the leg shackles. Rizzo grunted as he bore the brunt of the work dragging Joe with his left arm. Joe kicked and thrashed wildly while yelling for help. Anything to draw attention.

"Ow! Mother..." Rizzo started into a tirade of profanity after Joe torqued his wrist. "Shut him up, Vince!"

"I hear ya," Randazzo said.

The two let go their grip on Joe's leg chains. Knowing their plan was to kill him, Joe decided the fight was going to be on right then and there. He had nothing to lose. Randazzo wound up and kicked Joe in his side, striking his already broken ribs which caused a sharp jolt of searing pain. Joe did his best to ignore it and swung his legs into the side of Randazzo's left knee. The kick stunned him but was not hard enough to knock him to the ground. Rizzo began kicking Joe from the other side. His Bruno Magli shoes were soft around the toes causing Rizzo to wince in pain. He switched to the sharp heel and began stomping on Joe's torso while Joe focused on Randazzo. Joe tried to follow up his first strike with a heel strike to Randazzo's knee while both men continued to kick him. His heels connected and Randazzo fell to the ground. Joe rolled to his right and shifted his attention to Rizzo, who was still stomping viciously. He momentarily stunned Joe when his heel connected with Joe's left temple. Joe shook it off and tried to time a leg sweep, which failed. Amidst a flurry of kicks, Joe tried again. And again. And again. His strength was waning as he continued to fight. The chains restricted his ability to do so and the repeated kicks he was receiving were taking a toll. Joe wondered why they didn't just shoot him and be done with it but, for some reason, they hadn't and he was still in the fight. The Navy SEAL Creed, years ago burned into his mind, began to run through his thoughts as he continued to fight off his attackers. A specific section kept repeating:

I will never quit. I persevere and thrive on adversity. My Nation expects me to be physically harder and mentally stronger than my enemies. If knocked down, I will get back up, every time. I will draw on every remaining ounce of strength to protect my teammates and to accomplish our mission. I am never out of the fight.

Joe kicked and kicked again. He finally caught Rizzo off balance and swept him off his feet. Rizzo's head landed down by Joe's feet. Joe lashed out with a heel strike to the face and then slipped the chain around the front of Rizzo's neck. He crossed his feet behind Rizzo's head and used a scissors hold to tighten the chain around his neck. Rizzo's eyes began to bulge and he desperately clawed at the chain with his hands. Joe tightened the pressure. It was kill or be killed. A sharp blow struck Joe in his left temple and everything went black.

Chapter 73

"Stinnet! Sierra! Get the trucks up front post haste!"

"Aye, Chief!" Both men said as they leapt over the porch railing and took off through the woods.

Ramsey turned his attention back to Catalano whom he held up in the shallow end.

"You've got one shot at this, Bruno. If we don't get our man back alive, I'm holding you responsible. You gave the order. This is on you! Now, are you sure there is no way to call your boys off?"

"I told you. I don't have a phone. They're too easy to trace. Tino makes all my calls for me."

"And you have no idea what his code is?"

"No! I swear on my mother's grave, I don't!"

The dead guard's cell phone took a fingerprint to open. Kowalski pressed every one of the guard's fingers to the sensor, but it wouldn't unlock.

"Then you better hope we get there in time or I'm personally launching you off the Grand Island Bridge! We'll see how well *you* can handle Niagara Falls!" Ramsey said as he began to drag the mob boss out of his pool.

Ramsey slammed Catalano down into a chair and proceeded to put his gear back on. He shook his head in disgust as he strapped his tactical vest on.

"I've fought in Iraq, Afghanistan, and just recently in Central America, not to mention about another dozen corrupt third world nations. I've seen unimaginable evil everywhere I've been and you're just as depraved as anything I've ever seen. How does a sick bucket of slime like you sleep at night? Belay that. I don't think I can stomach the answer," Ramsey said as he fit his earpiece back into his ear.

"Echo Seven, you got the house secured?" Ramsey spoke into his mike.

"Affirmative, Echo Three. We found two house staffers here. Both look like underage illegals. You might want to have a look."

"Negative, Echo Seven. Secure the tangos for the feds to pick up. We'll bring the illegals with us. Be out front in two mikes."

"Two mikes, aye."

Ramsey finished donning his gear. He grabbed Catalano by the arm and forcefully yanked him to his feet. They quickly walked through the house and out the front. Kowalski and Moreno were finishing securing the two remaining guards to a large tree. Ramsey stared in disbelief at the sight of the two guards seated, facing opposite sides of the tree, bound to each other by their wrists and ankles around the tree like two oversized environmentalists refusing to let the tree be cut down.

"Whiskey Tango Foxtrot, KK?" Ramsey chuckled while shaking his head.

"I don't know, Chief. I kinda like it."

"Lord have mercy, KK. Did you open the gate for Carter and Sierra?"

"Yep. Done."

Ramsey spotted the trucks racing up the driveway.

"Here they come now. Let's mount up."

The trucks screeched to a halt and the men tossed a few bags and some odds and ends in the beds. Moreno and Kowalski escorted the two young girls into the truck with Sierra. Mueller helped Ramsey hoist Catalano into the back seat of their truck. Mueller got in with him. They took off down the driveway and out onto the main road. Ramsey removed his helmet and ran his fingers through his hair. He took out his phone and began to dial 911 and then stopped. The police could get to the funeral home much earlier than the team, but they were the ones who took Joe out of the jail and got him into this mess in the first place. Ramsey was sure they weren't all corrupt. It was more likely just a few, but he couldn't risk it. If the wrong ones showed up, Joe was dead for sure. With a sigh, he put his phone back and turned to face Catalano in the back seat.

"I've got a few more questions for you, Bruno."

Chapter 74

Niagara Falls, New York

*J*oe rolled into the forward part of the trunk when the car came to a halt. After a brief pause, Rizzo stomped on the gas and Joe rolled into the back of the trunk. He had regained consciousness a few minutes earlier when he was dropped into the trunk. He quickly realized that his arms had been duct taped to his torso. Similarly, his legs had been wrapped in duct tape rendering him an immobilized mummy.

The last thing he remembered was strangling Rizzo with his legs. Based on the pounding headache at his temples, Joe guessed Randazzo must have clubbed him with the butt of his handgun. He could feel several scratches on his arms and back. They must have dragged him across the barbed wire fence and through the woods. The scratches itched as much as they burned and Joe was unable to do anything about it. Potentially worse, Joe hated the feeling of having his arms immobilized to his sides. He wasn't claustrophobic, per se, but being in a narrow tunnel or a torpedo tube where he couldn't freely move his arms always made him extremely uncomfortable. So long as he could focus on the mission, he was able to put the thoughts out of his mind. This was worse. Way worse. Through the back seat, Joe could hear Randazzo and Rizzo talking and he rolled in closer to listen.

"I wish we coulda just shot him and left him, Vince."

"I hear ya, Riz but you heard the boss. He says we gotta whack him at the funeral home, cremate him into ashes, and film the whole thing."

"Why do we gotta film it, Vince? I don't like that. What if someone sees it and we get busted? There ain't no defending us with a video like that! We'll be hung for sure!"

"Relax, Riz. Bruno needs proof that we whacked this guy. That's all. He ain't gonna use it against us."

"Are you kiddin' me, Vince? With something incriminating like that? He'll own us!"

"Like he already doesn't? We work for him, Riz. Remember? We're part of his family. La Cosa Nostra. There ain't no leavin' unless it's in a casket. You know that."

"Yeah, I know. I just don't like the thought of someone filming a video of us doin' the job is all."

"Riz! What are you doin'?! You just went through a red light, you halfwit! Oh, man! There's a friggin' cop right there! Yep! He just hit his lights, you frigging moron!"

"Vince! I didn't see it! I swear! I was all distracted by you cuz you wouldn't shut up! Oh, man! We're busted for sure!"

"Calm down, would ya, Riz! Get yourself together and play it cool. Maybe it's one of our boys. Just pull over and let me do the talkin'. Capeesh?"

"Yeah, yeah, I got it, Vince. Smooth."

Joe listened as the next several minutes were silent. Rizzo and Vince whispered inaudibly until Joe heard the officer's footsteps as he approached the car. He immediately began to thrash about and make as much commotion as he could. Unfortunately, his motion was severely limited by the duct tape. He grunted as loudly as he could through the duct tape over his mouth, desperately trying to grab the officer's attention.

"Is there a problem, officer?" Rizzo asked.

"License and registration please."

"Sure, officer. Here you go."

"Can I see your license, too, please, sir?" The officer spoke looking at Randazzo.

"Absolutely, officer," Randazzo replied as he handed over his license along with a hundred-dollar bill and a courtesy card from Captain Battaglia.

"Oh, I see. You know Captain Battaglia?" The officer asked, quickly handing the license back.

"Yes, sir. We go way back."

Joe continued to thrash about as the two mobsters made small talk with the officer. He was finally able to generate some noise by slamming his heels down on the trunk floor.

"Well, I pulled you over because you ran a red light back there."

Joe kicked harder.

"Yeah, I got distracted by this mug yellin' at me," Rizzo said raising his voice to drown out Joe's commotion. "Guy keeps naggin' me like he's my wife or somethin'. You know?"

"Yes, sir. I understand," the officer said while he handed the drivers licenses back. "I aced the driving test at the academy. but my wife still tells me how to drive. She says..."

The officer stopped in mid-sentence and looked back toward the trunk. He stood erect, placing his hand on his holstered sidearm.

"Can you open your trunk for me, please?"

"What? My trunk?" Rizzo asked.

"Yes, sir. Now please."

"Yeah, sure officer. Let me hit the latch here."

Rizzo leaned forward as if to release the trunk latch. He suddenly sat upright, trained his gun on the officer and fired two shots into the officer's chest. He put the car in gear and sped off.

"You stupid mutt!" Randazzo shouted from the passenger seat. "What are you doing?"

"I had no choice! He was gonna check the trunk! What was I supposed to do?"

"You was supposed to kill him if you was gonna shoot him! You shot him in the chest!"

"Yeah? So?"

"So he's wearing a vest, you moron!"

"Oh, man! Oh, we are hosed, Vince! Now what?"

"Now he's calling every cop in the area and they're gonna be looking for us! Turn left up there on Pine and get us to the funeral home! We can hide the car in the garage."

Rizzo turned left and raced up Pine Avenue. He mumbled curse words to himself the entire way. A few blocks later they turned left onto the side street where the funeral home was located just behind the stores on Pine. Randazzo jumped out and punched the code into the garage to open the door. Rizzo pulled in and they immediately closed the door. Randazzo set up one of the funeral home's stretchers and wheeled it over to the trunk. He and Rizzo wrestled O'Shanick out of the trunk. Joe tried to resist, but he was wrapped so heavily in duct tape that he could barely move. They dropped him onto the stretcher and secured him with the restraints. They wheeled Joe into an elevator that was used for transporting bodies to the basement where the embalming and cremation took place.

Once in the basement, Joe took quick stock of the surroundings and was immediately alarmed at the realization of where he was. He struggled against the duct tape and chains with everything he had, but nothing would budge. As a Navy SEAL who had seen quite his share of combat, he had long accepted that he could die. That didn't mean he had to accept it when it came. He may only have a few minutes, but he would use every second to fight with everything he had.

"Set him up by that table, Riz and we'll put him in that cardboard coffin."

Joe continued to struggle.

"Yeah, did ya hear that, ya mick?" Randazzo said looking down at Joe. "You know what's comin', don't ya? Not so tough now, are ya?"

Joe thought he could feel the tape loosen just slightly. It might just be wishful thinking, but he pressed on. The two men grabbed him at each end and slid him onto a sheet of cardboard. They then folded the cardboard up around him, securing the tabs, but leaving the top open and then rolled the table into place. Joe looked down toward his feet and saw a stainless steel door open revealing a dark chamber. His cardboard coffin didn't allow him to see the chamber completely, but he knew what it was. Joe kept trying to break free. Was it his imagination or was the tape really beginning to loosen?

"How do you wanna do this, Vince? You want me to film you shooting him?"

Randazzo looked down on Joe in thought. A decorated Navy SEAL. He had put up a good fight but, even with help, he had been no match for organization. Sure, they had taken out a lot of their soldiers, most of them in fact, but when the old guard stepped in, it was game over. The Dazzler took pride in that fact, but the thought of losing so many of their soldiers today cast a dark cloud of anger. And for what? Who put out the hit? Bruno gave the order but Randazzo knew Bruno had no personal involvement with this guy. It certainly was no favor. Bruno was so committed that he was willing to sacrifice the entire organization to carry out this hit. Bruno was under orders. That's why he wanted this recorded on video. He needed proof that he had carried out the order. He was scared. Who carried that kind of weight to make Bruno dance like that?

Better yet, when did Bruno go soft? That wasn't good for the organization. Weak leadership trickled down and made for a weak organization. As underboss, Randazzo wasn't going to let that happen. He loved Bruno like a brother, but he couldn't excuse weakness. It might be time to make a move. He would have to beat an accessory to attempted murder charge, thanks to Rizzo, but he would deal with that later. Right now, it was time to make a statement. His face broke into a sadistic smile.

"No, Riz. I'll handle this."

Randazzo pulled out his cell phone and opened the camera app. He selected the video option, held it in front of O'Shanick and pressed the button to record.

"Before me is Navy SEAL Joseph O'Shanick," Randazzo began with a purposeful gravelly sound to disguise his voice. "Mr. O'Shanick was condemned to death for crimes and indiscretions worthy of death. Since then, Mr. O'Shanick chose to resist his sentence and has piled up several sins against the Catalano organization. Anyone who chooses to sin against or oppose the Catalano organization, commits a sin so egregious as to forego any degree of mercy in their inevitable sentence. Let this execution serve as a warning to anyone who would dare attempt to cross our organization."

Randazzo panned out from Joe's face and filmed him from head to toe pausing on the gaping door of the cremation chamber.

"Joseph O'Shanick, for your sins against our family, you will leave this world in the flaming reality of the afterlife you are about to enter."

With his left hand, Randazzo pushed Joe's cardboard coffin along the rollers and into the chamber, while he filmed Joe futilely attempting to resist his fate. From off camera, Rizzo rolled the table out of the way while Randazzo slammed the chamber door shut. The loud metallic thud echoed off the concrete walls and faded into a deathly silence.

Chapter 75

Christy pushed a cucumber slice around a Styrofoam plate with a plastic fork. She hadn't eaten all day. None of them had until Tom Brinkworth returned an hour earlier with a large antipasto salad and a lasagna from a local Italian restaurant. Joe's brothers, Tommy Marina's husband, and Jack had eaten, but neither Marie nor Anna nor Christy had the appetite. Brinkworth had been in and out of the room on his phone, hounding his contacts with the sheriffs for updates on Joe's whereabouts, but had gained very little information.

It was past visitor's hours and an older and rather crotchety charge nurse had reminded the O'Shanick family of this twice until Brinkworth reminded her of the family's situation in a stern fashion. The charge nurse had not been seen since. The O'Shanick family remained gathered in Jack's room intermittently praying as they held vigil for Tran, Marina, and Joe. The petite Anna lay in bed next to her father, while Marie dozed off in a chair next to Jack's bed, Her reading glasses perched on her small nose while her arms clutched her open Bible against her chest. Jacob, Tommy and Sean sat stoically watching the Blue Jays - Orioles game. Jacob's wife, Barb, left to help Abby at the restaurant allowing Sean to be with his family. She had offered to drive Christy back to the Island but, to Marie and Anna's relief, Christy wanted to stay. She wouldn't want to be anywhere else under the circumstances.

It was beyond comforting to be with Joe's family, but her mounting concern for Joe had left her without an appetite. She had been pushing her salad around for nearly an hour. Her parents had called earlier, shocked at the news report and even more shocked when she explained her involvement. They weren't angry with her, but their concern was certainly palpable. Her mother and Maria spoke for a while as well. Two kindred spirits who had struck up a friendship after having met at the White House last fall. It seemed to have calmed Christy's mother. The family dynamic and their spiritual unity was a major reason they weren't more distraught than they already were.

Christy finally stabbed the cucumber with her fork, but then set her plate down and closed her eyes. The day's events replayed in her mind. Everything from the biking incident to the events at the motel seemed to play in fast forward until right before Marina was shot. Christy vividly recalled the vision she had of her and Joe with children. It couldn't have been for more than a second, but it played out like a short movie. Then her would-be shooter was taken out by Joe. The events sped back up; the ride in the truck, working on Marina in the ER with Dr. Alendretti, all the way to Joe being taken away in hand-cuffs. Was that it? Would that be her last memory of Joe? Had his mob captors already killed him? *No!* Christy sat upright. No, that would not be the end! That vision was nothing she had ever even thought about before. She could vividly see their two children, a young boy and girl, both with dark hair laughing as they jumped off the dock at Joe's parents' house. Laughing as they landed in Joe's protective arms. A warrior, a protector and a comforter. Joe had run from God. He had wrestled with God, but God was not done with him yet. There was a plan! Joe was still in danger, but he would get through it. *That verse!*

"Christy? Is everything alright?" Jack asked from his bed as Maria began to stir.

Christy looked over at Jack. "It's Joe. There's a plan for him. He has to be okay."

"What? Have you heard from him?" Jack asked confused.

"No. I'll explain later. He's in danger right now, but I think he's going to make it through. But we need to pray right now!" Christy said as she stood up and walked over to Jack and Maria. "Maria, there's a Psalm about protecting us from our enemies. Psalm 59. Do you know the one I'm referring to?"

Maria gasped. She pulled her bible off her chest and turned it around to show Christy. It was open to that very Psalm.

"It was the last thing I read and prayed on before I dozed off."

"That can't be a coincidence!"

"Could you please read it out loud, Maria," Jack asked, wincing as he and Anna sat up.

Maria sat and rearranged her reading glasses. Christy and the rest of the room leaned in as Maria began to read.

"Deliver me from my enemies, O God; protect me from those who rise up against me. Deliver me from evildoers and save me from bloodthirsty men. See how they lie in wait for me! Fierce men conspire against me for no offense or sin of mine, O LORD. I have done no wrong, yet they are ready to attack me. Arise to help me; look on my plight!"

Chapter 76

"Are you serious, Vince? You're really gonna cremate him alive?"

"Yeah, Riz! What's it to ya?"

"I dunno, it just seems kinda wrong. Don't ya think?"

"Are you frigging kidding me? After what he's done to us?" Randazzo pointed at the chamber door. "You forgettin' how many of our guys he and his buddies killed in the past twenty-four hours? We should be doin' this to all of them! In fact, that's what I'm gonna do! Nobody messes with our family and gets away with it! What's wrong with you, Riz? You goin' soft on me?"

"No, Vince, geez," Rizzo spoke nervously, "it's just, I dunno, we used to have a code. Ya know? An honor code."

"Yeah? Well, to me, that code says anyone who kills one of us is gonna die a painful death. This cockroach is gettin' what he deserves. I got no remorse. You got a problem with that?"

"No, Vince, I'm good."

"Good. Then let's light him up," Randazzo said as he walked over to the control panel.

"You know how to work this thing, Vince?"

"Yeah," Randazzo responded confidently. "Who do you think used to do this for Bruno when he first bought the place?"

"How long does it take?"

"About three hours," Randazzo said as he turned on the control panel and began to program the settings.

"Three hours? We gonna just sit down here that whole time?"

"You can if you want to, Riz, but I say we head through the tunnel over to the club and drink to the honor of those we lost today. We'll come back later, get rid of the ashes and shut the place down."

"Just like that?"

"Yeah, just like that."

"Are you forgetting that every cop in the city is looking for us right now?"

"I'm aware of that. They won't come look for us at the club. They know it's off limits. We'll get one of the guys to drive us home and we'll have one of the new guys get your car to the chop shop."

"They still know we shot that cop. They'll be lookin' for us, Vince!"

"You mean *you* shot the cop. I just happened to be in the car."

"What are you saying, Vince?"

"I'm saying you might have to serve some time but, since you didn't kill the guy, if Rosati gets the right judge, he'll cop you to a lesser charge. It shouldn't be that bad. That's if they don't pin O'Shanick on us," Randazzo said pointing to the cremation chamber. "So we play this cool, we clean up our mess, ditch your car, and they can't pin nothing else on us. No body, no crime. Now shut up and let me start this thing," Randazzo said as he checked the settings and pressed the ignite button.

Chapter 77

The deep black darkness of the chamber was nearly suffocating. Joe could barely hear the muffled voices of Randazzo and Rizzo through the insulated heavy chamber door. The fire-resistant bricks of the chamber deadened all remaining sound. Resigned to his fate, Joe had given up trying to break free of his restraints and duct tape; instead, he tried to mentally prepare himself for what was about to happen.

But how exactly does one prepare for this? In a minute or two, the chamber would be filled with flames. He could accept dying, but in such a manner? It would be unimaginable pain, but how long would it take? Joe tried to focus on something else. Anything. He thought of his family, his teammates, Christy, all that might have been.

Christy. How did she become such a central figure in his life? They met during a botched rescue mission. She had many alluring qualities but, Joe had been a skeptic, if not an atheist, and her religion overshadowed the good. Yet here she was, not even a year later and her influence on his life could not be overlooked. She had befriended him and patiently walked him through...what? A truth quest? Was that it? Yes, he believed it was. She never once preached at him. It was more like she led him to ask the right questions. The important questions. The answers had been there all along. Joe had to admit he just didn't want to look for them. It was easier not knowing. At least he had thought so. But now what? Did he actually believe in God like Christy does? Like his family does? Joe had fought it for years, but here and now, yes, he actually did believe.

Joe wondered if that meant he was about to pass from one existence to another? To eternity? Who would he meet? Would it be Jesus like his mother and Christy believed? How could they be so certain? Would He even accept Joe or would he pass from one flaming reality to another? What if it was Buddha or Allah? Joe had killed a lot of mujahideen over the years in combat. Had he been on the wrong side of that equation? Joe didn't think so, but he honestly didn't know. *Why didn't I ask Christy when I had the chance?*

Would it matter? Even if he knew it was Jesus and he asked for forgiveness, could he be forgiven at the last minute? That just didn't make sense. Another question he wished he could ask Christy. What was it she had said? *Seek the Lord while He may be found. Call on Him while He is near.* He recalled his mother saying that to him as well. His dad, too for that matter. Was it too late? Could he be found here in this death chamber?

Joe was startled by the sound of a clicking noise followed by the loud hiss of gas. A second later, the chamber erupted in a bluish-white glow of flames. His time was up.

Chapter 78

S ierra quietly inserted the key and unlocked the deadbolt of the main entrance to the funeral home. He held the door open as Ramsey and the rest of the team stealthily made their entrance. The main floor was quiet and unlit. Using their night vision goggles, the team quickly cleared the rooms as they made their way to the stairs leading down to the basement.

During the drive over, Chief Ramsey pumped Catalano for the layout of the funeral home. In an effort to appease Ramsey, Catalano told them they were likely too late, but he would help them anyway. His life as a free man stood a better chance in a courtroom if he was found to be helpful in the end. He didn't think the SEAL questioning him would actually toss him off the Grand Island Bridge, but there was a fierce darkness to the man and Catalano decided not to take any chances. He had already provided him with the funeral home keys before they left his house, he may as well see it through and take his chances in front of a jury. Who knows? It could be a hung jury or a mistrial. Stranger things had happened, often by design.

As prearranged, Moreno broke from the team and went to a utility room where the electrical panel was located. Ramsey, Sierra, Kowalski, and Mueller located the basement stairs and silently made their way down. A light glowed from somewhere below. Ramsey could hear two men talking. He desperately hoped they were still in time. Catalano said they were supposed to shoot Joe on camera and then cremate his body. There wasn't a second to spare.

With practiced familiarity, Ramsey and the team stacked up at the bottom of the stairs. The landing made a sharp right turn into the room. This kept the team concealed, but it also didn't allow the team to see into the room. Nothing they weren't used to. Standard door breaching and room clearing techniques gave them the advantage.

From the back of the stack, Mueller briefly placed his left hand on Sierra's shoulder, who in turn placed his on Kowalski's, who did the same to Chief Ramsey. The ready signal received, Ramsey clicked his microphone key twice signaling for Moreno to cut the power. The lights went out, and with a practiced choreography, Ramsey led his team into the cremation room.

"Don't move! Put your hands where I can see em'! Now!" Ramsey shouted as he brought his rifle to bear on one of the two men he saw through his night vision goggles. Both men were startled and instantly froze. *Where is Joe?*

"Clear!" Came the call from Sierra and Mueller as they finished their sweep of the room.

"Clear! Just these two, Chief," Kowalski finished.

"Restrain them!" Ramsey said as he flipped up his goggles and snapped on the flashlight mounted to his helmet. The other men did the same. Sierra and Mueller moved in to restrain the men while Ramsey and Kowalski covered them with their rifles,

"Where's O'Shanick?" Ramsey demanded.

A look of panic came over Randazzo and Rizzo. Neither man said a word as their arms were being restrained behind them.

Ramsey cuffed Rizzo's ear with an open palm slap.

"I said, where's O'Shanick?!"

Rizzo closed his eyes and sighed in defeat.

"He's in there," he said inclining his head toward the cremator door. "What's left of him."

Chapter 79

The night lighting cast a soft amber glow along the quiet hallway. Christie and Maria quietly talked and prayed as they walked along at a moderate pace. The hospital floor's layout provided a fairly large rectangular track which, according to Christie's Garmin watch, was approximately a tenth of a mile per lap. Both had grown restless in Jack's room. They found their laps around the medical-surgical floor were therapeutic.

Dr. Alendretti had dropped by earlier to check on Jack. He reported that he paid a visit to the STICU and learned Marina was waking up, taking her own breaths, and following some basic commands while sedated on the vent. Very promising news. He had not been aware of Joe's disappearance and became quite alarmed upon his learning of what happened. Wanting to help, he asked if there was anything he could do, but he knew full well it was out of their hands. Seeing that Christy was still in her biking clothes, he made a trip to the doctor's lounge and brought her back a set of navy blue surgical scrubs. Having another shift in the morning, he sadly made his exit, but he promised to return before his shift began.

Christy walked the floor wearing just her socks and borrowed scrubs. Her bike shoes were still back at the motel. Even without shoes, her tall slender frame seemed to tower over the petite Maria. They talked quietly as they walked, causing Christy to subconsciously lean in slightly. They prayed intermittently for Marina, Jack, Tran, and Joe. Just the night before, they had been laughing, having a great time playing Euchre and not twenty-four hours later, their world had come crashing down and no one really knew why. Why were these men after Joe and why were they willing to kill anyone around Joe just to get to him?

As the hours passed, they still hadn't heard from Chief Ramsey or anyone else from Joe's team. Christy and Marina openly shared their concerns that the longer they didn't hear anything, the worse it could be. The not knowing was the worst part. Nevertheless, they both continued to pray and believe that Joe was going to be alright. Was it wishful thinking or was it faith? How would he survive if he had been captured by a ruthless band of criminals who had already tried to kill him several times? Christy didn't want to give up hope, but the realist in her was beginning to prepare for the worst. She thought about Maria. This dear sweet woman walking next to her. She appeared young enough to be Christy's age, yet possessed a motherly quality and a spiritual wisdom true to her actual age. Qualities that drew Christy to her and provided great comfort during a time of great distress.

Facing the very real possibility of Joe's fate, Christy knew she would be deeply saddened. She had really begun to think of a future with him, a thought further fueled by that vision she had seconds before she thought she was about to die. Sad wasn't the word. Hurt. Broken. Yes, Christy admitted to herself, there was a level of attachment that had developed despite their differences in faith. How much more painful would it be for Maria and the rest of the O'Shanick family? Christy tried not to think of it. She wanted to be hopeful. Maria was trying to be hopeful, but it seemed that, as time went on, the stress and reality was beginning to wear on them. They continued to walk.

Christy shared some of the things she experienced with Joe when they had been captured by the cartel. Maria never knew that Joe had freed himself from handcuffs and killed two men, preventing Christy from being raped. Her initial reaction of horror was soon replaced with a contented smile as she thought of her son in a heroic manner. She smiled even more when Christy revealed how Joe had cooked them meals, with spartan supplies, onboard a sailboat being tossed in a violent storm. Christy continued. The stories were helping her as much as they were Maria.

A few minutes later, Christy felt her phone vibrate. She pulled it out of her back pocket and looked at the screen. Anna had texted:

Chief Ramsey is back.

Christy's heart sank. There was no mention of Joe. Not good.

"Maria, Anna just texted and said that Chief Ramsey is back."

Maria stopped and looked at Christy. "But not Joe?"

"I don't know," Christy paused as her eyes began to water. "She just said Chief Ramsey is back,"

Christy barely got the words out before she and Maria both broke down in sobbing tears. Maria reached out for Christy and they pulled into a tight hug as they cried over the reality they were about to confront.

"Joe's a good man!" Maria said as she cried into Christy's chest. "He's a good man. And you're a good woman! You've been so good for my Joe. I saw you two together one day! I saw this!" Maria continued to sob into Christy's chest.

"I saw this." Her crying softened as she looked up at Christy. "And you have been like a daughter to me. A friend and a daughter."

Christy nodded through tear filled eyes as she looked down at Maria.

"I don't want to lose that, Christy."

Christy gently shook her head in agreement.

"No matter what happens, you're one of mine, Christy. From now on, please call me Ina."

"Yes," Christy nodded through tears, "Ina."

"Thank you," Maria smiled as she turned while leaving one arm wrapped around Christy. "We will go face this together."

Christy and Maria somberly walked arm in arm back to Jack's room. They paused to gather themselves before stepping into the room. With a deep breath, they both entered.

"Well, if you two aren't the best thing my eyes have seen all day!"

Christy and Maria gasped in unison. There before them, scratched up but smiling and none the worse for wear stood Joe.

Chapter 80

"But how?" Christy asked after she and Maria had finally disengaged from their long tearfully joyful embrace with Joe. "We thought...I mean...What happened?"

"Are you guys really sure you want to know?" Joe asked.

"Yes!" Came the reply from everyone in the room.

"Joe O'Shanick!" Maria began, "After what we have all experienced today, we need to know. You tell us right now."

"You better listen to your mom, son," Jack said with mock sternness, causing everyone to laugh.

"Yes, sir," Joe replied. "Rammer, I'll need you to help fill in some of the gaps because I have some questions of my own."

"Roger that, Joe," Ramsey said as he leaned against the wall with a grin, happy to see his close friend back among the living.

Joe spent the next twenty minutes chronicling his ordeal since his arrest. Ramsey added the parts involving the team's search for Joe. As it turned out, Randazzo's diabolical decision to cremate Joe alive may have been the turning point that kept Joe alive. Had he shot and killed Joe before he placed him in the cremator, the team may have been too late and Joe wouldn't be telling his family what all had happened. Between Joe and Ramsey, they were able to piece together how Joe had survived the execution. Joe recalled the moment the flames ignited. Seconds later, they flamed out. He and Ramsey determined this was the moment Moreno had cut the power in preparation for the team's assault on the cremation room. By cutting the power, the computerized cremator shut down. This must have triggered a default response which automatically closed the gas valves. Ramsey and the team, upon learning that Joe was in the cremator, immediately opened the door. The cardboard containing Joe had still caught fire but the team was able to pull Joe out and extinguish the flames. Joe suffered first degree burns on his exposed arms and ankles, but nothing else.

Ramsey was so enraged that he and Mueller nearly threw Randazzo and Rizzo into the cremator, but Joe talked them down.

Stinnet had been holding Catalano out in the truck. Ramsey had him bring the mob boss into the funeral home and then called Special Agent Jennings, who was only too glad to come by and arrest the leadership of the Catalano organization. Jennings assured Joe and Ramsey that he had plenty of charges and evidence to use against the mobsters in court.

Detective O'Keefe showed up with arrest warrants for Randazzo and Rizzo as well. He and Jennings worked out a plan that was amiable for both of them. He then apologized to Joe for what had happened and encouraged Joe to contact Tom Brinkworth who made quick work of getting Joe released from jail. Joe would still have to return to court. He still had a murder charge on him, but Brinkworth was confident the charge would be dropped. There were no charges on any of Joe's teammates. Investigations of the day's affairs would be conducted, but Special Agent Jennings wasn't too keen on taking down anyone who had just heroically rescued Marina and Christy, Joe, and dozens of young female human trafficking victims, all while taking down a resurgent organized crime family. Neither Special Agent Jennings nor Joe or anyone in his team knew that, should any of them face charges, a full presidential pardon would be made.

O'Keefe released Joe from his cuffs and drove him back to the jail where he was quickly processed out with all of his belongings. Ramsey was waiting for him and they drove directly to the hospital while the rest of the team headed back to the O'Shanick house in Sierra's truck.

"Joe, are you telling me that had your team been just a few seconds later or had they not cut off the power, that you would have been burned alive?" Jack asked.

"Yeah, Dad. I can't see it any other way."

"That is nothing short of a miracle, son," Jack said in astonishment. "Chief Ramsey, my family and I owe you and the team a debt of eternal gratitude, sir. Because of you, our family is whole today."

"It goes both ways, sir. Your son has led this team through more close calls down range than any of us can count. We owe our lives to him as well, sir."

"You're a good man, Chief. As fine as any chief I ever served with in God's blue Navy. I'm glad you're with Joe. If you ever retire from the Navy and want to give construction a try, come look us up."

"Thank you, sir," Ramsey said with a nod.

Jack looked over at Joe and shook his head in amazement. "Your mom and Christy never gave up. They were sure you would be alright. When I learned what happened, I thought for sure I had lost my son today. I prayed asking for a miracle. Now I'm looking at that miracle."

"Many miracles, Jack," Maria said in acknowledgement. "From the moment that boat ran over Joe, to his surviving a trip over Niagara Falls, Marina surviving," Maria said with a smile directed toward Christy, "Tran surviving, and Joe surviving. There are so many miracles, we cannot count."

"She's right Joe," Jack spoke. "You're still with us because God has been watching over you. He has a plan for you, son."

"They're right, Joe," Jacob added while Sean and Tommy nodded along.

"You're right, Dad. Mom. Everybody," Joe said nodding as he looked around the room. "For years, I refused to believe. I looked for every reason not to believe. He may have had to throw me down and step on my head to get my attention, but He's got my full attention now."

Christy wrapped her arm around Joe's arm, gave a strong squeeze and leaned in against him. Christy and Maria made eye contact and shared a contented smile.

Chapter 81

Upper Niagara River, Grand Island, New York

The late afternoon sun lit up the river in a dazzling orange as it descended toward the mist of Niagara Falls. Joe eased the main out to catch every bit of the gentle west wind. There was enough of a breeze to gently push his father's sailboat, a sleek Cal-33 sloop named *O'Shan's Seven* upriver at a comfortable speed. The water surface was calm and made a gentle lapping sound against the hull as they sailed on.

Christy finished trimming the genoa foresail and moved over to the starboard side for an unobstructed view of the river ahead. She wore black capri leggings, biking sunglasses, and an athletic gray University of Tennessee Volleyball t-shirt. *Biking spandex, the Mexican skirt this morning at church, scrubs, workout clothes. Was there anything she didn't look good in?* Yes, Joe admitted, he was really beginning to think of her in such a manner. He still thought she was out of his league, but here she was, sitting by his side on an evening sail.

Christy was supposed to have flown home, but she had called her director and explained how she was in the middle of the story making headlines in the national news and her director rearranged her schedule, flipping her shifts for next weekend. She would be staying through Wednesday, much to Joe's delight and that of his family. They really had taken to her, and she to them. Joe liked how that was working out.

Marina was awake and doing well. She had been taken off mechanical ventilation earlier today. When Joe and the family came by to visit her this afternoon, they found her sitting up in bed talking. Dr. Bynum planned to have her walking in the morning and, if all went well, to move her out of the ICU.

Tran too was showing improvement. He was following commands on the vent and the trauma surgeon at ECMC was optimistic that Tran would be able to come off the vent in a day or two and should make a complete recovery.

Jack came home earlier this afternoon. He was sore and wearing sling, but insisted he would be able to work tomorrow. Maria wanted him to take the week off to recover, but she knew her husband would prove to be the stubborn Irishman he was and work anyway. He was home tonight resting, kind of. The Minnesota Twins were in Toronto for a four game series. Jack, a Blue Jays fan, and Ramsey, a big Twins fan, were settled in to watch the game and making plans to drive up to Toronto this week to take in a game in person. Suddenly, the two were best buds.

Lieutenant Commander Harrison had directed Ramsey and Mueller to remain with Joe for the week to help look after Tran. Joe was confident the mafia threat had been neutralized, but he suspected that Harrison also wanted a little security around Joe and his family for a few days, all things considered. Ramsey's water born interrogation of Bruno Catalano had revealed that the organization was indeed carrying out the hit on Joe as a "favor" to *Los Fantasma Guerreros,* the cartel Joe's platoon had nearly decimated over the past year. Joe had personally accounted for the deaths of several of the cartel's leaders and the arrest of the cartel head, Hector Cruz, who currently sat in prison awaiting trial. According to Catalano, a man named Fernando Escobar, formerly the cartel's chief attorney and, like all of the cartel members, former Mexican special forces, had assumed the position as head of the cartel after the vacuum created by Cruz's arrest. In an effort to rebuild the cartel and to regain respect, Escobar had leaned on several stateside crime organizations to put the hit on Joe in exchange for a reduction in drug prices; therefore, the threat was still real but, due to the virtual elimination of the Catalano organization, he was likely safe for the time being. However, Lieutenant Commander Harrison assured Joe that Escobar and the cartel would soon be dealt with.

Joe certainly didn't mind that Ramsey and Mueller were still around. Neither did his sister Anna, so it seemed. Joe and Christy had invited Mueller and Anna along for the sail, but Anna grabbed Mule by the arm and took him kayaking. *Where did that come from?*

The rest of the team packed up in Sierra's truck and headed back to Virginia Beach after the big lunch Maria prepared for them after church. Maria had been abeam with pride having been accompanied to church by Joe, Christy, and a squad of Navy SEALs. It was only overshadowed by the joy of Marina's improvement and Joe's rescue. Oh, and the fact that, for the first time, Joe actually wanted to be in church.

"So what do you think? A little nicer than last time?" Joe asked looking over at Christy.

"Oh, I don't know," Christy said with a teasing grin. "Last time we were on a beautiful sailboat in the middle of the Caribbean. That's pretty tough to beat."

"Yeah, while being chased by a cartel through a tropical storm," Joe responded. "That is pretty tough to beat."

"Don't forget the Ramen noodles topped with seawater, Joe. You can't get that at just any resort."

"No," Joe said with a laugh, "I guess you can't.

Joe glanced up to check their heading and made a slight correction on the steering wheel.

"How're you holding up?" Christy asked, her head tilted slightly with a look of concern.

"I think I should be asking *you* that question. You had quite the close call yesterday with Marina."

"I'm still a bit shaken up, truth be told, but what I went through seems trivial to what Tran and Marina are experiencing, not to mention all that happened to you."

"Christy, there is nothing trivial about your ordeal yesterday. You could have just as easily been seriously injured or worse. The fact that you weren't? Well, I'm extremely...we're all extremely grateful you're okay."

"Thank you."

Joe didn't want to leave it at that. There was more to be said. Much more. He didn't know where he and Christy stood. He could now admit to himself that he was interested. Very interested. Was she? Joe still couldn't fathom that a refined woman such as Christy, a physician no less, would be interested in a simple door kicker like himself. She probably earned ten times the income Joe earned and that was unlikely to change unless he was to resign his commission and land a rare, but well paying, security or consulting job in the private sector. Did that matter to her? For some reason he didn't think it did, but he still couldn't ignore it.

"Well, you're very much loved here. By everyone," Joe added.

"Well, that feeling goes both ways, Joe, and *you* are very much loved here too. You should have seen the vigil your family had going for you last night. It really began to look hopeless, but nobody was ready to give up, especially your mother and me. We wore a track into that hall walking laps as we prayed for you."

"Well, I definitely needed it. Thank you."

"Can I ask you a difficult question?" Christy asked as she removed her sunglasses.

"Of course."

"Did you think you were going to die?"

Joe sat down, leaving his left hand on the wheel. He raised his sunglasses as well and propped them atop his head.

"Yes, but in a different way. Every time we go outside the wire the reality of dying is there. We're aware of it, but don't really *think* about it, at least not to the point where it's something you dwell on or feel is imminent. Even yesterday, the reality was there but, the moment they put me in the cremation chamber? That was a whole different level of reality. At that point, I *knew* my ticket was about to be punched. Much more so than when I went over the falls. I was too busy trying to make it to shore to dwell on it at the time. And then when I actually went over the Falls? It was so fast and surreal that it never really registered. Does that make sense?"

"Yes. In fact, that's what it was like for me yesterday. Marina and I were so occupied with trying to escape, that, even though I thought for sure we would be killed, I didn't have time to dwell on it. Then after that, I was immediately occupied with saving your sister. Not long after that, you disappeared. This is actually the first I've even thought or talked about it."

"And you're okay?" Joe asked.

"Yes, better than I thought I would be, but maybe that's because I'm not afraid to die."

"You're not?"

"No. I know where I'm going," Christy said with a confident look.

"You really believe that, don't you?" Joe asked.

"Yes," Christy nodded.

"But don't you want to live?" Joe asked. "Don't you want to get married someday? Have children? Travel? Experience life?"

"Of course. I want to do all those things as long as I'm here, but none of us are guaranteed our next breath. I could have died yesterday. I could die in a plane crash on Thursday. If that were to happen, I will be in the presence of God, the Creator of the universe. Nothing is this world can compare with that. No experience or accomplishment can measure up to that. Look around you, Joe! Look at that beautiful sunset behind us. Look at this amazing river we are sailing on. Or how about the majestic waterfall just a few miles downstream? One of the seven natural wonders of the world. They're all beautiful and magnificent. but they're all *creations*. Things God created. No creation is greater than its creator. Don't get me wrong. I don't have a death wish. I intend to live life to the fullest and experience everything I can but, once I'm in the presence of God, in His kingdom, this will all pale in comparison and I will not wish to return. Nobody will."

Joe sat silently looking at Christy, processing what she had just said.

"I'm sorry, Joe. I didn't mean to get preachy. I know you don't like that."

Joe's mind flashed back to his urgent thoughts while he was waiting to die.

"Actually, Christy, this is the exact conversation I have been wanting to have with you."

"It is?" She asked surprised.

"Yes, it is. You asked me about whether or not I thought I was going to die. The answer was, yes, I absolutely thought I was going to die and I spent several minutes immobilized by duct tape in that dark chamber thinking about it. Those were the most terrifying moments of my life. Worse than any combat, worse than when my primary chute failed during a night HALO, and worse than going over the Falls. And do you know why?"

"I can't imagine, Joe. Why?"

"Because for the first time in my life, I knew God is real and that I was about to face him. Only I had no idea what I was about to face or who for that matter. I felt totally unprepared."

"Yes, that would be terrifying."

"It is, but you're not terrified. My mom isn't. No one in my family is. You all believe in Jesus and the God of the Bible and His salvation, but how can you be sure?"

"Because that's where the evidence leads, Joe."

"Evidence? I thought Christianity was all about faith?"

"To a certain degree, yes, but that faith is based on evidence. Or, better said, my faith is trusting in the One to whom the evidence has led me to believe."

"Which begs the question; what evidence?" Joe asked as he continued to steer them upriver.

"Well, you have already admitted that you now believe in God when just a few months ago you told me you were agnostic. Isn't that right?"

"Yes. I was definitely agnostic, if not an atheist."

"But not anymore?"

"No. I do believe in a creator and intelligent design. You have convinced me of that."

"Okay, Joe. *How* did I convince you? By simply saying God exists?"

"No. You gave many plausible reasons; the creation of the universe, the fine tuning, life, DNA, to name a few. It makes too much sense."

"So what you're saying is I helped you come to that conclusion based on logic, reason, and scientific evidence. We didn't even talk faith or crack open a Bible, did we?"

"No, we didn't. Okay, I get your point, but that just tells me *a* god exists, but not which god."

"You're right, Joe. It doesn't," Christy said smiling.

"What are you smiling about?"

"Because I've been wanting to have this conversation with you for a long time."

"Really?"

"Yes!"

"Then why didn't you?"

"Because it wasn't the right time. You didn't want to know. I've been waiting for you to want to know."

"Well, I guess that moment arrived last night at Catalano's funeral home. Do you realize how close we came to never having this conversation?"

"Yes, I do and I would have severely regretted that," Christy said reflectively. She then sat up and smiled, "But we're here now. You and me, in our happy place on a sailboat, where we have had many such conversations in the past. So, what do you say?"

"I say bring it on. It's time I figure this whole thing out."

"Great!" Christy said as she put her long legs down and sprang to her feet. "But first, I need a Diet Coke. You want one?"

"Sure, please."

Joe looked on admiringly as Christy glided her toned, but lithe, frame gracefully down the ladder into the salon like a seasoned sailor. She emerged a minute later with two cans of Diet Coke and a gift-wrapped box.

"What's this?" He asked as Christy placed the cans in the cup holders and handed him the box.

"A little something I picked up for you today at the church's bookstore."

"Ah, let me guess. It's the sequel to the book you gave me last year, *I Don't Have Enough Faith to be an Atheist*?"

"No," Christy said with a laugh, "not quite. Different author. Did you like that one though?"

"Yes, I actually did. In fact, we probably wouldn't be having this conversation had I not. Between that book and our talks I've come this far, haven't I?"

"Well, a lot of what you're questioning me about was covered in that book."

"You're right and the authors make a convincing argument about Christianity, but I guess the skeptic in me wasn't ready to buy in completely."

"Then you may relate to this book. It was written by a journalist who was an atheist and set out to prove, through scholarly evidence, that there was no evidence of Christ's resurrection."

"And I take it he failed?"

"I wouldn't say he failed. Let's say he discovered something life changing. But I'm mad at you," Christy said pretending to pout. "*I Don't Have Enough Faith to be an Atheist* is my favorite book and I happen to think Geisler and Turek make a brilliant argument. Did you know Frank Turek was a Navy man like you?'

"No, I didn't."

"Yep," Christy nodded. "Naval aviator and he speaks very reverentially of you SEALs. I attended a presentation of his two years ago and he led off with a story about a Navy SEAL named Michael Monsoor. Are you familiar with him?"

"He served before my time, but every SEAL knows of Michael Monsoor. He was in Team 3. Dove on a grenade in Iraq to save his teammates. He was posthumously awarded the Congressional Medal of Honor. There's now a ship named in his honor."

"Greater love has no man than this, that he lay his life down for another," Christy quoted somberly. "Well, I think you should give that book another read, but after you read this one," Christy pointed to the box in Joe's hand.

"I'll need both hands," Joe said looking over the box. "Would you mind taking over the helm for a while?"

"I would love that," Christy smiled as she sat down next to Joe and took control of the wheel.

Joe removed the gift wrapping and opened the box. He removed the book entitled *The Case for Christ,* by Lee Strobel. He immediately opened it and leafed through the pages until he came to the introduction and began to read.

Christy reveled in the moment. A moment that, barring a miracle, never would have happened. The serenity of the sailboat gently pushing upstream, the setting sun in a warm breeze and Joe's presence. His presence was peaceful and calming despite his warrior profession.

Christy looked up and admired his ruggedly handsome face. Irish features like his dad, green eyes that turned a fearsome dark when the warrior was awakened, but lit up and dazzled when he laughed around the table with his family. Dark hair and tan skin like his mother. Bulging muscles that stretched his Navy t-shirt. Of all his desirable physical attributes, not one of them could measure up to the man on the inside. The man she knew him to be. There were two kinds of warriors: wolves and sheepdogs. Wolves attack the flock whereas sheepdogs protect. Joe was a sheepdog, a protector, and the flock was safe with him. It made her think of the Good Shepherd. She was going to introduce him to the Good Shepherd tonight. Joe will like the Good Shepherd.

Chapter 82

Playa de Mujeres, Mexico
Six weeks later

" TOC, this is Echo One, passing Shula."

"Good copy, Echo One, we read you passing Shula. Be advised, ISR showing four tangos in the arena."

"Copy that, TOC, four tangos."

Joe communicated the information across the intersquad comms and gave the command for his men to move into their respective assault positions. Fernando Escobar, the new head of the *Los Fantasma Guerreros* cartel, had recently returned to beachside vacation home after a night in his nightclub. Two days ago the Task Force Group's Intelligence received a tip, from an informant, that Escobar had recently arrived with three of his top lieutenants. Escobar kept many residences and was never known to stay in any one place for long. Foxtrot Platoon missed him twice over the last month, most recently by just a day last week at his Nuevo Laredo residence.

Although technically in a training cycle, Echo platoon was spun up for this mission. Joe was due to leave for DEVGRU's Green Team in a month but was still the commanding officer of Echo platoon for the time being. All currently deployed platoons in theatre were occupied with a major interdiction effort further south. Echo platoon flew into Naval Special Warfare Unit 8 headquarters in Panama last night and spent the day in preparation for this op. They parachuted into the Caribbean with two RHIBs (Rigid Hull Inflatable Boat) after dark and made their way to shore. Escobar's estate was a walled in mansion tucked in amongst several seaside resorts, just north of Cancun.

During the boat ride in, Joe wondered if it was pure circumstance or divine appointment that allowed his platoon the chance to bag Escobar. The new cartel head had ordered Joe's assassination. Revenge was the only reason Joe could figure. Likely a favor to the imprisoned Hector Cruz, the former cartel head. Initially, Joe couldn't believe the Catalano organization would go to the lengths they did to carry out an execution order for a Central American cartel; however, over the past several weeks, Joe learned that the cartels wield extensive influence over organized crime and prison gangs throughout the United States. By controlling the bulk of the drug supply that enters the United States, they controlled the principle means by which these criminal organizations generate their wealth; furthermore, their vast wealth and power has given the cartels great influence among key government officials and organizations. President Galan was inflicting significant damage on the cartels through his war against them, but their reach and resources were expansive and there remained much to be done. Joe and his platoon were here to capture Escobar, but also to show that it was inherently dangerous to be at war with the United States. For Joe and Echo Platoon, it was much more personal.

Their orders were to take Escobar and his lieutenants alive, if possible, and collect all valuable intel. Joe, personally, wanted to put a bullet in the man's head, but he knew Escobar was a treasure trove of intel, thus the reason Captain Bennett wanted him alive. Nevertheless, the man's execution order had nearly killed Tran and Marina. Christy for that matter as well.

Marina was fully recovered and back working for their parents. Tran was also recovering nicely and was back in Little Creek. His gunshots were all healed but his lower leg fractures had required surgery. Tran was awaiting the removal of his leg cast and the green light to begin running.

The Internal Affairs department of the Niagara Falls Police Department, with the help of Detectives Peretti and O'Keefe arrested Captain Battaglia and three others within the police department on various corruption charges. Two of whom were the officers who had transferred Joe into the hands of Randazzo and Rizzo. O'Keefe used Terry Wood's cell phone to discover Trina Borelli was the nurse who had attempted to kill Joe by placing the potassium chloride in his IV. A search of her phone revealed she had texted Captain Battaglia regarding Joe's arrest, something he had tried to deny. Both were in jail awaiting trial. Detective Peretti had subsequently been promoted to replace Battaglia as Chief of Detectives.

FBI Special Agent Jennings and his office had solid indictments on Bruno Catalano and what was left of Pandolfino's crew. Confessions by Catalano and his men led to further investigations and arrests resulting in the near complete dismantling of the organization in general. Joe was happy to have played a role in that but the cost to his family and Tran made it bittersweet at best.

"Echo One, this is Echo Eight. Overwatch in position. I have eyes on two tangos," came Eddie Sierra's call.

"Roger that, Eight. Stand by," Joe quietly spoke.

"Echo One, this is Echo Six, in position on the beach gate. I have eyes on the other two tangos," Kowalski added.

"Roger that, Six. All units stand by to execute wall breach."

Joe switched to call in an update to the Tactical Operations Center known as TOC which sounded like "tock" on the radio.

"TOC, this is Echo one, passing Levy."

"Good copy, Echo One, passing Levy."

Joe toggled his inter squad comms mike, "All units, execute in three...two...one. Execute!"

Sierra, concealed in the vegetation on a hill between the main road and the estate, fired his sniper rifle at the first sentry, re-centered his aim on the second sentry and fired again. Two metallic clacks sounded as the silenced rounds found their marks, dropping both sentries. Simultaneously, Kowalski dropped the two sentries who were guarding the beachside approach to the estate.

Joe and his men were split into two separate three man firing elements. They silently vaulted the six foot wall surrounding the estate and made for their respective breach points. Joe's team approached the rear of the house which was made mostly of tempered hurricane proof large windows. Mueller peaked around the corner and, satisfied he would not be seen, dashed around and placed a breaching charge around a set of French doors. He ducked back around the corner and gave Joe a thumbs up.

"Echo One this is Three, ready on your command," came Ramsey's voice announcing their breaching charge was set out front.

"All units, stand by to execute," Joe called out over the comms. "Three...Two...One. Execute!"

Mueller and Moreno simultaneously triggered their charges resulting in controlled explosions at both entrances. Joe held his rifle at close ready while one of their new replacements, Petty Officer Third Class Lewis, tossed two flash-bang grenades through the freshly blasted hole and ducked back around the corner. After the ensuing explosions, Joe cleared the entry followed by Mueller and Lewis. He immediately buttonhooked right and visually dissected his section. Joe saw movement and immediately trained his M-4 on the target as his mind quickly processed the target. A dark clad man held a rifle while he grimaced in effort to clear his head of the bright lights and deafening sound of the flash-bang. He was not one of the high value targets better known as HVT's. Joe squeezed his trigger and put two rounds into the man's chest. Joe quickly checked the rest of his area of responsibility and, seeing it was clear, fired a finishing round into the man's forehead.

"Clear!" Joe yelled as he heard the metallic sound of a silenced rifle firing to his left.

"Clear!" Mueller sounded off.

"Clear!" Lewis answered.

Joe began to lead his fire team through a systematic room sweep of the lower floor while Chief Ramsey's team swept the upper level. They stepped up from the sunken living room into a dining area connected to a large kitchen through a butler's pantry. Mueller tossed a flash-bang through the narrow pantry. Lewis entered first followed by Joe and Mueller. The kitchen appeared empty. Joe signaled for Mueller to open the pantry. Mueller did so as Joe kept his rifle trained on the target. A shirtless man was crouching inside. Using his Spanish, Joe commanded the man to hit the floor. Mueller promptly restrained the man with zip-ties while Lewis kept watch. They moved on through another eating area, a well-appointed billiards/gaming room and found their way to the front entrance with a sweeping staircase on the right and closed doors to a study on the left. Mueller kicked open the double doors while Lewis tossed in a flash-bang. Two loud gunshots erupted before the flash-bang went off. Joe entered first followed by Mueller and Lewis. They arrived just in time to see a man jump out the open window.

"Squirter! Squirter just jumped out a lower floor window on the south side," Joe yelled into his comms mike.

"Got him, Boss!" Sierra replied.

They finished sweeping the room and found it otherwise unoccupied. Joe began to hear gunfire upstairs. It was not silenced. Somebody was shooting back.

"Echo Three, this in Echo One. Ground floor is clear. You got a sit-rep?" Joe asked over the comms.

"Two tangos down, stacking up for master bedroom now, but there is an active shooter inside."

"Roger that, Three. I'm on my way."

Joe instructed Mueller and Lewis to recheck the ground floor while he went upstairs.

"Echo Six, squirter heading your way!" Sierra's call came over the comms.

"I'm on it!" Kowalski responded.

Joe took the stairs two at a time. A large hallway led down the center of the house ending at an alcove with a set of closed double doors at the far end. Ramsey stood on one side while Moreno and Stinnet took up positions on the other. Sporadic gunfire came through the closed doors. Joe crept low and against the wall until he arrived next to Ramsey.

"Stinnet just prepared a charge. Next time this cockroach reloads, Stinnet is placing the charge on the doors," Ramsey quickly updated his commanding officer.

"Flash-bangs and go?" Joe asked.

"Affirmative. Unless you give me the go ahead for a home-wrecker?" Chief Ramsey said referring to a the more lethal grenade. Flash-bangs were meant to neutralize enemy combatants in an enclosed room by temporarily stunning them through the blinding light and deafening noise when they detonated. They were not lethal and thus useful for clearing a room that may contain hostile combatants along with innocents and hostages. Conversely, "home-wreckers" were lethal by means of a strong thermobaric explosion.

"I wish, but we need him alive, Chief"

The gunfire paused. Stinnet kept low as he dashed to the door and stuck a small charge over the knobs. He dashed back into position.

"Flash-bangs ready!" Ramsey yelled as he and Moreno each held up a grenade.

Ramsey signaled the go ahead and all four men turned away from the door. Stinnet thumbed the igniter switch and the doors blew inward in a loud explosion. Ramsey and Moreno tossed their flash-bangs into the room and all four men turned away with their hands over their ears and eyes shut to avoid any effect of the explosions. The grenades went off and the men immediately filed into the room using standard entry technique. Joe, being the last in the room, had the center area and saw the open French doors leading out to a balcony. A sinking feeling set in as the other men announced their areas were clear. Stinnet and Moreno rushed into the cavernous bathroom and found a terror-stricken young woman, with bleach blond hair, hiding in a bath tub the size of a small swimming pool. Joe and Ramsey rushed to the balcony doors and carefully looked out. With years of training and familiarity, they conducted a silent count with their rifles and hooked out to secure the balcony. It was empty.

Joe instantly turned his attention to the ground below and saw their man swimming toward the edge of the pool that stretched out below them. The man glanced back, and Joe instantly recognized the face.

"Echo Six, HVT is squirting out the back!"

"Echo Six is engaged with the other squirter, sir!" Sierra spoke over the comms.

"Figures," Joe said as he slung his M-4 and hurled himself over the rail into the pool fifteen feet below.

Joe popped up, made for the closest edge and lifted himself up onto the decorative concrete deck. He could hear Ramsey yelling in

Spanish telling Escobar to stop. Joe wasted no time sprinting around the deck as Escobar, clad only in boxer shorts, ran for the beach. Joe pursued in full sprint hoping to catch Escobar before he reached the gate. Behind him he heard another splash.

Escobar showed signs of having once been fit, but who had begun to lose the battle at the waistline. Despite his tactical gear and rifle, Joe was able to gain ground. Escobar reached the gate and, rather than unlock and open it, hurled himself up and over the white stucco wall with relative ease. Joe quickly dismissed the brief surprise. After all, Escobar *had* been Mexican Special Forces in the not too distant past, just like all the other members of *Los Fantasma Guerreros.*

Joe made easy work of the wall and doubled his efforts as Escobar made straight for the surf.

Mistake, Joe thought. The water is SEAL domain.

Escobar reached the packed sand of the surf zone and turned for the resort just down the beach. Joe took a page from his football days, picked an angle of pursuit and ran through the soft sand to cut him off. He quickly closed the angle and leapt through the air making a diving tackle. Joe and Escobar crashed onto the hard sand, Joe taking the brunt of the impact on his left shoulder. Sharp pain instantly shot through the top of his shoulder making it difficult to hold onto the struggling cartel chief. Joe quickly wrapped his legs around Escobar's torso and clamped down with his arms in a rear chokehold. Escobar countered with repeated elbow jabs to Joe's ribs. Joe ignored the searing pain in his shoulder and the jabs to his ribs as he clamped down harder. He thought of his dad, Tran, Christy, and Marina. This man put into motion the events that nearly killed and severely injured some of the people closest to Joe's. Joe gritted his teeth as he clamped down harder. The elbow jabs began to weaken. How many thousands of lives had ended at the hands of this man's cartel? How many woman had they enslaved through human trafficking? How many millions of people's lives have they destroyed through the drugs they traffic? The families? The cost to society? A primitive growl surged through Joe's clenched teeth as the rage inside emerged. Escobar went limp. Joe was so enraged, he no longer cared. He ignored his better judgement to stick to the mission and bring this scumbag back alive to face justice.

Joe continued to apply the pressure. He was going to end it, right here, right now. For Tran, for Marina, for Christy...

Let him go, Joe.

The voice was quiet but authoritative. Joe eased up slightly as he tried to discern what he had just heard. It must have been his imagination but he could also easily believe Tran, his father or Christy could have said that is if they were standing right next to him. Was it his conscience? Joe took a deep breath and relaxed his grip. Escobar rolled off to Joe's side. Joe laid on his back, trying to catch his breath as Chief Ramsey came running up.

"Joe? Are you alright?"

"Yeah, Chief. I'm good. Help me up. Would you?" Joe said as he extended his hand to his friend.

"What about him?" Ramsey asked as he pulled Joe to his feet.

"I think he's still alive," Joe said looking down at Escobar. "Was that you telling me to let him go?"

"I didn't say anything," Ramsey said as he knelt down to check Escobar's pulse. "Why? Did you hear something?"

"Probably just my imagination. Does he have a pulse?"

Ramsey nodded.

"Lucky for him. I came within seconds of choking the life out of him."

"The thought crossed my mind too, Joe. Let's get him in the boat before one of us decides to act on it."

Joe keyed his mike, "All units, gather up any intel and prepare for extract in five mikes."

He switched and radioed the ops center.

"TOC this is Echo One. Lombardi. I say again, Lombardi. Requesting extract."

"Good copy, Echo One."

"That's it, Joe. We got em'. All of them," Chief Ramsey said as he reached out with his hand.

Joe shook Ramsey's hand and was immediately pulled into a brotherly hug.

"It's done, Joe."

Epilogue

Little Creek, Virginia

The squad bay was quiet. The rest of the platoon was out on a training evolution. Joe was sidelined with a shoulder injury. His dust up with Escobar had resulted in a shoulder separation and a torn labrum. The Orthopaedic Surgeon at the Naval Hospital thought Joe would likely need surgery but was willing to try six weeks of physical therapy first. Joe wasn't surprised. Ramsey has SO3C Lewis check Joe after the op. Lewis was a trained corpsman and had evaluated Joe's shoulder on the flight back to Panama. He suspected what the orthopaedic surgeon and yesterday's MRI confirmed. Either way, Joe would not be operating anytime soon. He was immediately taken out of the rotation with Echo Platoon but it also meant he was medically disqualified from DEVGRU's Green Team. The news was like a gut punch to Joe. They had just returned from their mission in Cancun four days ago on a collective high note and now this. The reality of that very possibly having been his last mission as an operator was beginning to set in.

Joe stripped out of his tactical uniform and packed it along with his other clothing and belongings into a large duffel bag. He donned a pair of cargo shorts and a gray athletic t-shirt along with his Hoka One running shoes. Everything packed, Joe zipped up the duffel bag and used his healthy right arm to hoist the straps up onto his shoulder. Joe took one last look at the squad bay and stepped out. The door shut loudly behind him as he started down the hall. Joe was without a team and he suddenly felt so alone.

Ramsey had caught up with Joe shortly after Joe had returned from his orthopaedic visit. They both knew this would take Joe out of Echo, effective immediately, which was confirmed shortly after by Lieutenant Commander Harrison. Ramsey told Joe he would call him after their training op and they would meet up with some of the guys at their favorite watering hole. That would help. Joe needed something. His brothers in the team would be a plus. Christy had just finished a stretch of nights this morning. She usually got up around 5pm so he would give her a call before heading out with the guys.

He and Christy had not seen each other since June up at his parent's house when everything went down. The remainder of the week with her had been extremely pleasant and relaxing. Since then, they talked by phone, texted, and FaceTimed nearly every day. There was definitely something there. It was palpable to Joe, but he couldn't define it. They had certainly become close friends. Their conversations had moved way beyond those of Christy simply mentoring Joe as he stumbled through his new discovery of faith. They shared intimate and personal details with one another and talked often of seeing one another again. He needed to talk to her and see how she felt. She seemed interested but Joe really didn't know. He hesitated to raise the subject for fear of scaring her off. On the other hand, he couldn't stand being in limbo. They had plans to meet back up at Joe's parents' house the last week of August before Joe started Green Team. That was a good sign to Joe and he hoped they could pin down where they stood and what each other was looking for. At least that had been his plan. Now with this injury and a shakeup in his plans, that was probably shot.

His meeting with Lieutenant Commander Harrison had been even more sobering than his meeting with the orthopaedic surgeon. LCDR Harrison was a good commanding officer and. In many ways a friend. He discussed Joe's options at length with full understanding of Joe's desire to resume operating. They both knew the odds were slim at best. Joe was an officer, a newly promoted Lieutenant Commander and there just weren't many operating billets for officers who had already completed two deployments in command.

Joe's stomach began to growl as he stepped outside. It was only 11:00 but he hadn't had breakfast. He decided he would drop his gear off at his apartment and treat himself to some Pho at his favorite Vietnamese restaurant. He slipped his sunglasses down over his eyes and walked through the parking lot with his head down to avoid the sun as it beamed down on him.

As he neared his truck, a slender pair of long athletically toned legs came into view. They were connected to an equally toned upper body topped with long dark hair pulled back to reveal an exquisite face with high cheekbones and eyes that lit up as Christy ran to embrace Joe.

Joe dropped his bag and pulled her in with his good arm.

"Wow! You just made my day!" Joe exclaimed. "I can't believe you're here! Didn't you just finish a shift a few hours ago?"

"Yes, I did but I just felt like I had to be here for you. I hopped on the first plane out of Atlanta after my shift. I hope you don't mind."

"Mind? Are you kidding me? I just had one of the worst days of my life. Your showing up like this is exactly what I needed. How long can you stay?"

"I'm off for the next six days," Christy answered, "But what happened? How bad is your shoulder?"

"Bad enough to keep me out of DEVGRU. At least for now but it could be permanent."

"Oh, Joe! I'm so sorry to hear that. When Matt told me you were likely going to be medically relieved of your command today, I had no idea it would include your shot at DEVGRU."

"Wait. Matt?" Joe asked acting confused. "As in Matt Ramsey?"

Christy nodded.

"When did he talk to you and what did he tell you?"

"He told me your shoulder was badly injured and that you were going to have to step down today. He's afraid that's going to devastate you, Joe. He's very upset over this. Your whole team is. They know how much this means to you. So do I. I hope you're not mad that he called me."

"I'm not mad at all," Joe smiled shaking his head. "That's one chief who knows how to look after his officer. You're exactly what I needed."

"Oh, good," Christy said relieved. "I was a little nervous showing up on you unannounced like this. So what's your schedule like the next few days?"

"Actually, it's wide open," Joe said as he picked up his duffel bag and tossed into the back of his truck. "Lieutenant Commander Harrison just gave me a week's leave to consider my options."

"Your options?" Christy asked as she opened the passenger side door. "What does that mean?'

"I can step up into an operations officer billet here while I rehab my shoulder," Joe said as he climbed into the driver's seat. "If I don't get another shot at DEVGRU, I can continue on here and one day command several platoons like he does. I could also move out to Coronado and fill a training officer's billet at BUDs or I can do something else in the Navy. Outside of the teams."

"Is that it?"

"I can also hang up my Trident, resign my commission, and do something in the real world."

"Oh no, Joe! Are you actually thinking about that? This is your life! It's who you are!"

"Christy, the reality is my time as an operator is probably up. I'm losing my Green Team slot and I have a very slim chance at ever operating again. If I can't operate, I don't know if I want to stay in. Maybe I will but I just don't know yet."

"What will you do if you get out?"

"I don't know. There are plenty of possibilities, but I don't have a plan yet since I don't know what my status will be with the teams."

"Well there's a first," Christy commented as she looked over from the passenger seat.

"What do you mean by that?" Joe asked.

"From the moment we first met, Joe O'Shanick, every time I have ever asked you what's your plan you have always answered me with 'I'm working on it.'"

"You're right. I should be working on it," Joe said thoughtfully. "Okay, first thing, I'll get to work on this shoulder with PT and maybe even get a second opinion. Once we know where that stands, then I can consider what my real options are."

"Are you really off for the next several days?" Christy asked.

"Yes, why?"

"Then I can help you with your shoulder. Let's drive over to the Naval Hospital and get a copy of your MRI."

"What are we going to do with that? You know somebody around here that can give me a second opinion?"

"Nope. Not here. Nashville. My brother Jason is one of the best sports medicine orthopaedic surgeons in Tennessee. I trust him completely. If anybody can get you operational, he can; besides, I think it's time you and my family got to know each other."

Joe looked over at Christy in shock.

"Really?"

"Yes!"

"Okay," he said with awkward shyness.

"Okay, then," Christy said with a laugh.

"So we're driving to Nashville? Today?"

"No, silly. We're flying. It's on me and you're not going to argue. You've saved my life twice now and it's the least I can do especially if it saves your career."

"But..."

"Shhh! No buts!" Christy ordered with a big smile. "This is what you get for not having a plan."

They drove on in a pleasant silence for a few minutes. Joe steered with his left hand resting on the bottom of the steering wheel while his right hand rested on the shifter between the two front seats. Joe noticed the contented grin on Christy as they drove on. She really was one of a kind. He finally broke the silence.

"Thank you, Christy."

"No thanks necessary, Joe. You're invaluable to me."

"Can you help me with one other thing, then?"

"Of course, Joe. What is it?"

"If this plan doesn't work, will you help me figure out the next plan?"

"Absolutely, I will," Christy said as she reached over and grabbed Joe's hand.

"I hope you're a big part of that plan, Christy," Joe said turning his hand over and grabbing her hand.

Christy looked at Joe and smiled, "I'm working on it."

The End

About the Author

*J*ohn Galt Robinson is a practicing emergency medicine physician. He weaves his experiences from the exciting, tragic, and sometimes humorous world of emergency medicine into a much larger story with intriguing characters who tackle relevant social issues in a fast-paced adventure. John grew up just upriver from Niagara Falls on Grand Island, New York. He earned his medical degree at East Tennessee State University after a previous career as a Certified Athletic Trainer. He lives in South Carolina with his wife and family where he is an active sailor and triathlete.

His first book, *Forces of Redemption*, has been well received.

Author's Note

Dear Reader,

My first novel, *Forces of Redemption*, was intended to give the reader a glimpse into the horrors of human trafficking. Although this story followed a different path, it does touch on the domestic side of human trafficking. In reality, the horrors are far worse and far more widespread than can be explained in the context of a novel. This problem is just as much domestic as it is foreign. Human trafficking is an enemy that must be fought on a grand and individual scale. Nations and states must rise in defense of those who cannot defend themselves but we, as individuals, can contribute as well. Neighborhood awareness, serving in a ministry or shelter and community involvement are a great place to start. Donating time or resources to a ministry or charity that fights these battles is another great option. While conducting research in preparation for this novel, I learned of a ministry, made up of volunteers who locate and rescue victims of human trafficking. They are retired Navy SEALs, private investigators, law enforcement investigators, and other servants. Their organization is named Saved In America. If you would like to learn more about them or financially support them, please visit their website www.savedinamerica.org.

In this novel, I featured a ministry named Adult and Teen Challenge that really exists and has scores of treatment centers nationwide which serve to rehabilitate and train people who have walked the path of addiction or a troubled lifestyle. Adult and Teen Challenge houses and trains people to leave their troubled past behind them for good.

Please strongly consider financially supporting this vital ministry. For more information, please visit their website www.teenchallengeusa.org.

One final note, I hope you have enjoyed reading this novel as much as I have writing it. As I write this, I am hard at work with the next novel in this series. Joe and Christy will be back in a new and different adventure along with some familiar friends and some new villains. As Christy learned, what she does matters. May this be said of each of you.

Thank you,

John Galt Robinson

Forces of Redemption

During a hectic Emergency Department shift, Dr. Christine "Christy" Tabrizi rescues a young Honduran girl from the gang that has been prostituting her and discovers the horrors of human trafficking tracing all the way back to the cartels in Central America. Christy volunteers for a mission in Honduras, to help rescue as many young girls as possible from the Cartels that control them. Joe O'Shanick is part of a Navy SEAL platoon deployed in Central America and finds himself in the midst of hostile territory when the President of the United States, a man of Mexican-American heritage who sympathizes with the human condition in Central America, declares war on the Cartels. In the middle of a tense hostage scenario, Christy and Joe's paths collide, and they must rely on each other and their respective skills to escape with their lives.